"THEY'RE GODDAMN PHANTOMS!" HAWK HUNTER YELLED.

The two unmistakable shapes — turned-up wings, reverse-V tail section — appeared over the horizon and streaked toward the Kingfisher. Hawk put the World War II-vintage floatplane into a dive and within seconds was cruising 50 feet above the jungle's tree tops, throttle opened all the way.

"We're in for a fight, Brother David," Hawk shouted. "You got a handle on that gun back there?"

"I have," came the reply.

Within seconds the two F-4s had pulled up a quarter mile behind the Kingfisher.

"When I give the word, open up on the nose of the nearest plane," Hawk said. "Don't let up until you have to, okay?"

"Okay," came the stoic reply.

"Hang on!" Hawk shouted. Then he reached over and cut his engine . . .

TOP-FLIGHT AERIAL ADVENTURE
FROM ZEBRA BOOKS!

WINGMAN (2015, $3.95)

by Mack Maloney

From the radioactive ruins of a nuclear-devastated U.S. emerges a hero for the ages. A brilliant ace fighter pilot, he takes to the skies to help free his once-great homeland from the brutal heel of the evil Soviet warlords. He is the last hope of a ravaged land. He is Hawk Hunter . . . Wingman!

WINGMAN #2: THE CIRCLE WAR (2120, $3.95)

by Mack Maloney

A second explosive showdown with the Russian overlords and their armies of destruction is in the wind. Only the deadly aerial ace Hawk Hunter can rally the forces of freedom and strike one last blow for a forgotten dream called "America"!

WINGMAN #3: THE LUCIFER CRUSADE (2232, $3.95)

by Mack Maloney

Viktor, the depraved international terrorist who orchestrated the bloody war for America's West, has escaped. Ace pilot Hawk Hunter takes off for a deadly confrontation in the skies above the Middle East, determined to bring the maniac to justice or die in the attempt!

GHOST PILOT (2207, $3.95)

by Anton Emmerton

Flyer Ian Lamont is driven by bizarre unseen forces to relive the last days in the life of his late father, an RAF pilot killed during World War II. But history is about to repeat itself as a sinister secret from beyond the grave transforms Lamont's worst nightmares of fiery aerial death into terrifying reality!

ROLLING THUNDER (2235, $3.95)

by John Smith

Was the mysterious crash of NATO's awesome computerized attack aircraft BLACKHAWK ONE the result of pilot error or Soviet treachery? The deadly search for the truth traps RAF flight lieutenant Erica Macken in a sinister international power-play that will be determined in the merciless skies — where only the most skilled can survive!

Available wherever paperbacks are sold, or order direct from the Publisher. Send cover price plus 50¢ per copy for mailing and handling to Zebra Books, Dept. 2553, 475 Park Avenue South, New York, N.Y. 10016. Residents of New York, New Jersey and Pennsylvania must include sales tax. DO NOT SEND CASH.

WINGMAN

—THE TWISTED CROSS—
Mack Maloney

ZEBRA BOOKS
KENSINGTON PUBLISHING CORP.

ZEBRA BOOKS

are published by

Kensington Publishing Corp.
475 Park Avenue South
New York, NY 10016

Fourth printing: August, 1991

Printed in the United States of America

The way to Hell is paved with gold . . . .

—K. H. Darling

Prologue

It has been almost four years since America lost World War III . . .

Four long years since the bloodiest deception in history— when the American president, his forces victorious against the Soviets in Europe, was assassinated by his traitorous vice president. Then, playing out the long-range communist plan, the vice president allowed the country's defenses to be relaxed long enough to permit a flood of Soviet nuclear missiles to obliterate the American ICBM force while they stood in their silos.

The sneak attack left the country's heartland dead from the Dakotas down to Oklahoma. Now a nightmare of neutron radiation, the region is known to all of The Badlands.

Under the harsh provisions of the New Order, as the Soviet-imposed "peace" treaty came to be known, the United States was united no more. Instead, the American continent became fractionalized—split up into a scattering of small countries, kingdoms and anarchic free territories. Under this imposed rule, to carry the American flag or to even speak of the United States was illegal and punishable by death.

But peace did not come with the installation of the New Order. To the contrary, the American continent had been aflame with war ever since. Major battles on the east coast marked the first anniversaries of the Soviet-inspired rule.

Later, the criminal armies of The Family, operating out of New Chicago, moved against the free enterprise gambling state of Football City, formerly St. Louis. However, in each case, the Free Democratic forces were led to victory by the famous jet fighter ace, Hawk Hunter, the Wingman.

These first victories of the forces of freedom proved to be short-lived, however. Even before the smoke had cleared from the Battle for Football City, the Soviets were secretly infiltrating thousands of troops and tons of equipment into the eastern half of America. These forces, under the control of a ruthless Soviet KGB agent named Viktor Robotov, attempted to take over the western half of the continent, but were defeated by Hunter and his allies in a devastating series of battles known as The Circle War.

Later, in the guise of his Mediterranean alias "Lucifer," Viktor was confronted once again by the Wingman, this time allied with a British-led mercenary fleet centered around the salvaged nuclear-powered aircraft carrier, the *USS Saratoga*. "The Lucifer Crusade," as the Mideast battle came to be called, ended with Hunter and his allies preempting Viktor's conquest of Europe by bottling up his enemy fleet in the Suez Canal. A Nazi-garbed gunman stole Hunter's revenge by killing the evil Viktor at the conclusion of the battle.

Back in America, the stage was now set once and for all for a major confrontation between the democratic forces of the West and the Soviet-backed armies who controlled the lands east of the Mississippi. Under the threat of a huge, Soviet-financed mercenary army sailing to invade the American east coast, Hunter and the new United American Army won a stunning string of victories to gain control of several major cities in the East—a campaign which culminated in a major confrontation in the country's former capital, Washington, DC. It was here that the remnants of the hated Circle Army, reenforced by troops of the elite Soviet *Spetsnaz*, planned a ceremony of iconoclasm—the destruction of "everything American."

The battle that followed, won by sheer determination by the United American Army, not only destroyed what was

8

left of The Circle, but also forced the Soviet mercenary fleet to return to Europe without firing a shot.

Thus America was united again.

But soon afterward, there were rumblings of a new threat on the country's southern borders . . .

Chapter 1

The three F-4 Phantom jet fighters attacked the unarmed airliner without warning.

"Take evasive action!" the pilot of the Boeing 727 yelled to his crew even as the first of the green-camouflaged attackers laid a burst of cannon fire across the bigger airplane's starboard wing.

"*Jesus!* Where did they come from?" the airliner's navigator cried, trying to get an exact fix on their position.

No one answered him. The 727 pilot was too busy putting the big plane into an evasive dive; the co-pilot was punching buttons on his radio.

"Mayday! *Mayday!*" the second-in-command screamed into his mike. "This is civilian charter Flight 889 . . . We are under attack by three fighters . . . approximate position, fifteen nautical miles south of Memphis . . . at fifteen thousand feet . . ."

Suddenly the air was filled with the horrible sounds of screaming jet engines and cannon fire. The second F-4 roared in on the airliner head-on, its nose gun blazing wildly. The 727 pilot yanked the big airplane to the right, limiting the Phantom's hits, but still sustaining damage to the airliner's portside engine cowling.

All the while the copilot continued to put out his distress call. "Mayday! Mayday!" he yelled with no small amount of panic in his voice. "*Any* friendly aircraft in the area . . . We are being attacked by three fighters . . . identity unknown . . . Any friendly aircraft in the area, please assist us!"

The pilot put the 727 into yet another gut-wrenching maneuver in an effort to avoid the third Phantom now peeling off to begin its strafing run. The copilot never stopped broadcasting his frantic SOS calls. But the navigator knew it was hopeless. A quick check of his radar screen told him that besides the three attackers and themselves, there were no other aircraft — friendly or otherwise — within twenty miles of them.

"Call back to the passengers," the pilot yelled over to the copilot while pulling the 727 out of a steep bank. "Tell them to prepare for a crash . . ."

The copilot immediately switched his radio to internal and quickly relayed the pilot's message back to the airliner's 86 terrified passengers.

Just then the third F-4 found the 727's cockpit in its sights and unleashed a long barrage of cannon fire.

The shells ripped into the airliner's flight deck, puncturing the copilot's left shoulder, smashing the navigator's legs and knocking both men unconscious. At the same time, the pilot was hit in the face with a shower of broken glass from the instrument panel shattered by the cannonfire.

Suddenly the cockpit was awash in oil, hydraulic fluid and blood. Through stinging, blurry eyes, the pilot could see the three F-4s regrouping off to his left.

"One more pass and we're going down . . ." he whispered grimly to himself. Already the 727 was dangerously losing altitude. The Phantoms had succeeded in blasting away the airliner's port wing stablilizers and damaging its centerline tail engine. It was all the pilot could do to keep the big airplane from flipping over.

He looked over at his bleeding crewmen and thought "Only a miracle can save us now . . ."

The pilot managed to plunge the 727 into a large cloud bank, all the while knowing it would not be enough to shake his attackers. The airliner was trailing a long line of black smoke that any pilot with two eyes could follow. As soon as he emerged from the cumulus, he saw one of the F-4s had streaked up and over the cloud bank and was now bearing down on him at 10 o'clock. Already he could see the nose of the Phantom light up with the telltale signs of the cannon's muzzle fire.

"This is it . . ." he said, resigned to his fate.

Suddenly, the onrushing F-4 exploded . . .

The 727 pilot shook his head once, just to make sure he wasn't already dead and dreaming. In the next instant, he had to jar the airliner hard to port to avoid colliding with the high-speed flaming debris that seconds before was an intact enemy Phantom.

"What the hell is going on here?" he yelled looking back at the hurtling wreckage, the slightest hint of hope running through him.

He managed to pull it out of its hard bank and level out at 5000 feet. His aircraft was still smoking heavily and his muscles were snapping from the strain of holding it right side up.

But he was still airborne . . .

Just then he saw one of the two remaining Phantoms streak underneath him and pull up on his left, nose gun blazing. The 727 pilot's heart sank, realizing his death sentence had merely been postponed.

But then, just as his life began to flash before his eyes for the second time in less than a minute, this F-4 also exploded into a ball of yellow-blue flame. Once more he had to put the 727 into a steep dive to avoid smashing into the flaming wreck of the second Phantom.

Having dodged the bullet twice, the pilot was now determined to at least make a controlled crash landing. He reached over and tried to shake his copilot out of his unconscious state. But it was no use — the man's shoulder was practically shot off and he was bleeding heavily. And if anything, his navigator was in worse shape.

Just then, the third F-4 appeared directly overhead. As the 727 pilot struggled with his controls, he watched in horror as the Phantom peeled off sharply and dove right for him.

"This guy ain't going to miss . . ." the airline jockey

thought.

Already the F-4 was firing—the muzzle flashes from its nose seemed to take on an angry look, vengeance for his two downed comrades. The first few cannon shells began peppering the windshield of the airliner, sending another spray of broken glass and hydraulic fluid into the pilot's face.

Now nearly blind, the 727 pilot was suddenly aware of another airplane, this one off to his right. In an instant he knew it was not an F-4. It was smaller, delta-winged and painted in a distinct red-white-and-blue color scheme.

Just on the verge of passing out himself, the 727 pilot saw this new airplane streak right across his flight path and turn in a screaming climb to meet the oncoming F-4. Now it was this mystery airplane's nose cannons that lit up—and with six times the intensity of the F-4.

The Phantom tried to pull out of its strafing dive, but in doing so, exposed its unprotected underside to the awesome cannon barrage from the other jet fighter.

It was over in a matter of seconds . . .

This time there was no flaming wreckage to avoid. The Phantom was simply obliterated.

Still unaware who the life-saving Good Samaritan was, the pilot once again tried to rouse his copilot. This time the man responded, though groggily.

"Can you get hold of the controls, even with one hand?" the pilot asked him. "We're only twenty minutes out from New Orleans."

The copilot did as he was told, trying not to look at his wounded shoulder.

"What happened?" he asked, his face a mask of shock and puzzlement.

"I'm not sure," the pilot said as he grabbed the radio mike and started broadcasting to New Orleans tower. "But someone up here likes us . . ."

The 727 came in for a smoky, but successful wheels-up landing at the New Orleans' International Airport. Emergency crews surrounded the airplane immediately, washing it down with foam as its passengers leaped, walked or crawled out of the wreckage.

Despite the hundreds of cuts on and about his face, the pilot helped the rescue crews extricate his copilot and navigator before accepting any medical attention himself. He was sitting on the back bumper of an emergency van, talking to the base doctor when he finally took stock of what had just happened.

"We were jumped by three fighters . . ." he told the doctor. "They had us dead to rights. Then suddenly, the first two just blew up—*boom! boom!. . .*"

"Blew up or were shot down?" the doctor asked him as he cleaned out the pilot's nastiest cuts.

"Well, that's just it," the 727 pilot said, just now enjoying the indescribable rush of realization that he was still alive. "There *was* another airplane out there. The guy got the third Phantom with a shot that I didn't think was possible. He put his jet into a screamer of a climb. It must have had six Goddamn cannons in its nose. All of them firing. Smoke. Fire. Jesus, it was unbelievable!"

A military officer from the airport's security forces had joined them by this time and had heard the pilot's story.

"What did this other airplane look like?" the officer asked. "What color was it?"

The 727 pilot, still jittery from the ordeal, had to stop and think a moment.

"It was all painted up . . . it was red, white and blue," he said finally. "It looked like a delta-type wing. But I've never seen an airplane like it. Ever . . ."

The doctor wrapped a bandage around the pilot's head, covering his left eye and ear.

"Red, white and blue, you say?" the military man asked. "You sure?"

The pilot nodded, gingerly feeling the wounds under his bandage.

"And it was a flashy, souped-up kind of delta-wing?"

Again, the pilot nodded.

The officer looked at the doctor and shrugged. "Could it

be?" he asked the physician.

The doctor shook his head. "If you mean who I think you mean . . ."

The pilot looked up at the two men. "Who are you talking about?" he asked.

Just then, as if to answer his question, all three of them heard a high whining sound, the unmistakable call of a jet fighter. Shielding their eyes against the hot Louisiana sun, they saw a jet fighter streak over the base and turn for a landing. The airplane was a delta-wing design and was painted in red, white and blue.

"Well, I'll be damned . . ." the military man said. "We're finally going to get to meet him in person . . ."

"Meet *who?*" the pilot said, his voice tinged with exasperation.

"Meet your guardian angel," the doctor told him. "You guys just got your asses saved by the guy they call Wingman . . ."

Chapter 2

The military commander in charge of security of New Orleans International Airport was a Cajun named Hugo St. Germain. A former officer of the Texas Republican Army, The Saint served as governor, protector, confessor and all-around fix-it man for the parishes surrounding the city they still called the The Big Easy.

Huey was also a friend of General Dave Jones, the commander of the United American Army, whose forces had two months before finally destroyed the hated Circle Army and its Soviet backers in a series of climactic battles that stretched from the Mississippi River to Washington, DC. The Saint was the only person at the New Orleans airport who knew that Jones's right hand man, Major Hawk Hunter—the famous Wingman himself—was flying in. He was not surprised when he learned that Hunter had saved the 727 airliner from the bushwhacking F-4s.

Now Hunter sat before him in Huey's executive airport offices, diving into a big bowl of gumbo.

"Who were they, Hawk?" Huey asked, digging into his own bowl of gumbo. "Organized air pirates? Or just free-lance troublemakers?"

Hunter wiped his mouth with a large cloth napkin and took a swig of his beer.

"Hard to say," he answered, his mouth still half full. "There was something strange about them. You don't see many pirate gangs flying something as sophisticated as Phantoms. Yet, these days, who knows?"

17

He took another mouthful of the stew and added: "Also there were actually four of them."

"Four?" Huey asked. "Really?"

Hunter nodded. "One of them stayed way out of the fight, twenty-five miles away," he said. "I'm sure he was off the airliner's radar screen. After I took care of first three, I lit out after him, but he was gone in a shot. A good flyer, too. He went down to the hard deck, real quick—treetop level. Then, by the time I picked him up on my long-range APG radar, he was climbing at a 45-degree clip, heading south.

"I was low on gas and figured I'd best keep that airliner in front of me, just in case . . ."

"Well, we sure appreciate the help," Huey said. "We're lucky you came along when you did. Any idea who was riding in that 727?"

Hunter shook his head between swigs of beer. He hadn't thought about it before. He had just assumed the airliner was on a routine civilian hop.

"It was our Goddamn football squad," Huey said, his voice a mixture of anxiety and relief. "They were coming back from a try-out at Football City. Christ, if they had gone down, this city would have been throwing funerals for a month . . ."

Another wipe of his mouth and Hunter asked: "What were they doing flying without an escort?"

Huey shook his head. "Beats me," he said. "We sponsored the team's flight up there and back. And I personally gave the pilot enough cash to buy protection round-trip . . ."

Hunter shrugged. "He probably lost it all in the casinos," he said. "Or at the cathouses . . ."

Football City, formerly St. Louis, was now the continent's gambling mecca. It got its name from the fact that just after World War III, an enterprising Texan named Louie St. Louie, had an enormous 500,000 seat stadium built and instituted a 24-hour-a-day, 365-day-a-year football match to be played between two 500-member, free-substituting teams. Bets could be made on any increment of the game—from the quarters up to the entire year's match—and the resulting revenues proved incredible.

Trouble was, many of the criminal elements around the continent — all of them Soviet-backed — became envious of the good thing St. Louie had going. Thus Football City had already been the scene of several full-scale battles and one authentic war, all in its short four-year history. But now with the United Americans in control, however tenuous, of both the eastern and western portions of the continent, things were beginning to return to normal in Football City.

"The good news is that the team did really well up there," Huey said, scooping up the last few spoonfuls of his stew. "Played their asses off . . ."

Hunter drained his beer. "I heard they were going to start exhibition games up there," he said. "Glad to hear your boys did well."

Just then a thought came to The Saint. "Hey, Hawk," he said cautiously. "You don't think those F-4s were sent after my guys as part of some, you know, gambling scam, do you?"

"You mean, eliminate your opponent *off the field?*" the pilot asked.

"Yeah, something like that," Huey replied, his round face sagging in worry.

Hunter dismissed the notion immediately. "No, I doubt that was the case," he said, reassuring the stout little man. "First of all, the Football City Secret Service is the best on the continent. If someone was planning to carry a football grudge that far — as in trying to shoot down the other team — those guys would uncover it quicker than you could say 'Hike!' Then, knowing St. Louie like I do, he'd launch an air strike on that team's training base that would blast them back to playing tiddlywinks."

"I'm glad to hear that," Huey said. "Hate to think someone wanted to ice our boys. Maybe you don't know it, but they also double as our Rapid Deployment Force. You know, like a SWAT team to handle snipers, bomb threats, hostage crises, things like that. They're good. *Damn* good. Especially in skyscraper work. For some reason, these guys just love to work in tall buildings. And the way things are in town these days, I'd hate to lose a gang like that."

He poured himself another beer from the pitcher on the

table and refilled Hunter's glass as well.

"I'm certain those Phantom-jocks out there today were just looking for trouble," Hunter said. "I could tell by the way they were acting. They certainly didn't hit your airliner when it was totally to their advantage. It was almost as if your guy just happened to come along . . ."

"Then they *were* air pirates?" Huey asked, another look of worry coming over him. They hadn't had any major air pirate activity in his neck of the woods in more than a year.

"Again, I doubt it," Hunter said. "These guys were more organized than a pirate crew. That's what was so weird about it. Besides having this fourth airplane watching over them, they were really right on the beam. They went for individual attacks. One at a time. Not the swarm tactics that pirates use.

"And these guys were shooting to kill. Not like pirates, who just want to disable you first, force you to their airbase so they can rob you."

The Saint wiped his brow with authentic relief. "As far as I know, the 727 crew didn't get any warnings over the radio from the attackers."

"See?" Hunter asked. "These guys weren't your usual air thieves. They wanted something else."

"Such as?" Huey asked.

"Maybe to send a message," Hunter said with a shrug. "Though just what message that may be, I don't know."

Hugo lit his pipe and changed the subject. "Can I ask just what it is you are down here for?"

Hunter nodded. "It's not really top secret or anything," he said. "I know Jones called and told you I'd be coming."

"He did," Huey said between puffs. "But that's all he told me."

Hunter ran his fingers through his long dark blond hair.

"Jonesie just wants me to talk to an old pal of his down here," he said cautiously. "He had a message from the guy last week. That's really all I know. Jones would have come himself, but he's still busy, trying to get things straight and running back in DC."

Huey blew out a long plume of pipe smoke. "You boys

certainly kicked ass on The Circle," he said with a grin. "Believe me, there's a lot of people in this country who are very, *very* grateful . . ."

"It's not over yet," Hunter said, just a little wearily. "Sure, we're in control of the major cities. But there's a lot of territory in between them that we don't have a handle on. At night, the highways and backroads are just as dangerous, just as unlawful as before. The air routes are no better. We still have a lot of air pirates roaming around, especially up north and out west. In fact one of our big convoys was attacked three days ago just outside the Badlands.

"And there are still many small outlaw armies on the loose, especially down here in your neighborhood."

"Yeah, tell me about it," Huey said, refilling his pipe.

Bourbon Street was absolutely mobbed when Hunter arrived downtown.

It was still early — only about 9 PM. Yet the famous street was crowded with all kinds of people — soldiers, merchants, hookers and assorted shady characters. The vast majority of them were carrying some kind of weapon, so Hunter didn't look out of place at all, wearing his brown camouflage flight suit, his helmet bouncing from his belt, his well-worn M-16 slung over his shoulder. Everywhere he looked there were people. The bistros, cafes, barrooms and brothels were overflowing. The night air was thick with jazz and the sweet, peppery smell of New Orleans cuisine. If Hunter hadn't known better, he would have sworn it was Mardi Gras already . . .

But the pilot knew he'd have to forego the many temptations of Bourbon Street and its back alleys. His mission here was much more serious than he had let on to The Saint. Only for that reason had Jones been able to talk him into making the trip.

The memory of the past few weeks was as painful as it was fresh . . .

After the last war, Hunter headed north — up to Free Canada, to where his long-time girlfriend, the beautiful Dominique, lived. Just before the climactic battles at Syracuse and Washington, DC, Hunter and Dominique had had a sobering rendezvous at a small airfield on the Free Canadian border. At that time she made it all too clear that she was tired of waiting for him to fight this war and that war. It was time for her to go on with her own life, she had decided, as complicated as that may be.

So after The Circle had been defeated, Hunter went up to Free Canada, specifically to Montreal, and tried to find Dominique. He was crushed when he learned that she had gone west with a group of friends — Free Canadian government officials mostly — and an entourage of security people. Apparently they were all living in the Canadian Rockies at a far-flung retreat and wouldn't be back in Montreal for some time. It was even hard for him to get a precise location of this secluded resort in the northern mountains. All that he was sure of was the place was practically inaccessible by air.

Disappointed, he hung around Montreal for a few days, trying to meet people who would know more about Dominique. A million questions burned in his mind, the biggest one being: Did Dominique go west with a new lover?

He did meet several friends of Dominique's but he was reluctant to put the question to them directly. Instead, he wrote a long letter to her and left it in care of the security people who protected her trendy Montreal townhouse. Then he headed back down to DC, still wondering if he had blown the one and only true romance of his life . . .

He had intended to make his visit to DC brief — just long enough to tell Jones that he was considering retirement from the fighter pilot/hero business. What better time? The continent was back in one piece again and the Circle Armies all but decimated. The threat of invasion — whether by the Soviets directly or by their proxies — was at its lowest likelihood since the end of World War III. If there was to be a time for him to hang up the old crash helmet, now was it.

However, it took Jones only about ten minutes to talk him out of it . . .

America was hardly out of trouble. While the industrial and manufacturing base on the West Coast of the continent had survived the devastating effects of both the most recent battles and the earlier Circle War, the eastern half of the country was in shambles. As before, the major vehicle of trade between the two coasts was still the air convoy. Parades of 30 to 40 cargo airliners, watched over by escorting fighters, flew back and forth between the coasts on a daily basis. However, the expense involved in moving the much-needed material to the east was always growing, as was the cost of hiring on the protecting escort fighters.

After the campaign to reconquer the eastern part of the American continent was executed by the United Americans and their allies, one suddenly crucial post-war initiative involved determining the status of the Panama Canal. The reason was simple: If the East Coast was to survive, it would need all the help the West Coast could send it. This would be much more than could be moved by the air convoys, no matter how big they might be. The bulk of the material would have to be moved by ship, so the use of the sealanes became critical. Yet hauling everything around the tip of South America would be almost as costly and time-consuming as flying it across North America in convoys. This problem focused attention on the Panamanian waterway.

The trouble was, no one in the United American Army or its allies knew just what the situation was in the Canal Zone. With the seemingly endless series of wars that had recently wracked the North American continent, no organized recon expedition had ever been assembled to go down to the zone and thoroughly check it out. Manpower was at a premium as were reliable recon aircraft and the situation in North America took precedence over sparing valuable men and equipment for a dubious adventure way south of the border. Besides, before the second war with The Circle, most just assumed the intricate canal locks were either destroyed or had fallen into disrepair and thus the waterway was closed. This is what ship captains on both coasts believed—they avoided even going near the Canal Zone or the Panama isthmus itself. Bizarre rumors persisted that the Pacific side of the impassable waterway was inhabited by heavily-armed Satanic cultists, who shot first and didn't bother to ask ques-

23

tions afterward. Another story had it that the Ku Klux Klan had claimed the entire country as its own, and that any stranger with so much as a slight tan was suspect and summarily shot. Some old salts even claimed that cannibals now ran wild in Panama, eating anybody and everybody who dared set foot in their territory.

No small wonder then that as far as anyone knew, no ship captain had attempted a shortcut voyage through the Canal since the Big War and lived to tell about it. The rare ship that *did* sail from the West Coast to the East or vice versa these days went by way of the tip of South America.

But as puzzling as the situation seemed, there was now a new, more frightening report on conditions down in the Canal Zone. And investigating this latest rumor was the reason Hunter was in New Orleans in the first place.

Hunter walked halfway down Bourbon then took a right onto Orleans Avenue. If anything, this street was even more crowded. The cast of characters was the same — soldiers in as many different uniforms representing various armed groups or militias, gun salesmen, gold exchangers, moonshiners, sleazy insurance hawkers, hookers of every age and proclivity and the usual gaggle of black market traders. The only thing *not* for sale — in the open anyway — were drugs, which under the new United American Government were strictly *verboten*.

The Wingman made his way through the crowd until he finally reached his destination: A place called 33 Thunder Alley. "Alley" was a good word for it. Two blocks down off Orleans Avenue, it was so narrow, it seemed a motorbike would have had a hard time navigating its way through, never mind an auto or a truck. The alley was a confusion of overhead wires, fire escapes and clotheslines. At ground level, his eyes went blurry from the combination of multicolored neon lights advertising tiny taverns, cathouses, pawn shops and money changers that lined the skinny passageway. This electric rainbow was offset by old gas-powered street lamps, which despite the competition, still managed to give the cluttered buildings a strange, bluish-green glow.

Hunter walked down the alley until he reached a battered red door that had "33" carved into its frame, courtesy of a stiletto jackknife, no doubt. He opened this door to find a cramped hallway and another, even more garishly-painted crimson door.

There was no bell or buzzer, so he rapped on the door three times.

"Who the hell is there?" he heard a gruff voice shout from the other side. At the same time he also detected the unmistakable click of a round being loaded into a rifle chamber.

"I'm Major Hawk Hunter of the United American Air Force," Hunter yelled out, seeing no reason to mince words. "I'm a friend of Dave Jones and I'm looking for a guy named Captain Pegg . . ."

All the while, Hunter was silently slipping his M-16 off his shoulder and into firing position.

"Maybe Pegg ain't here!" came the reply. Jones had told him that this man, Pegg, was an old duffer—mean and ornery. The voice behind the door was harsh and well-worn. It seemed to match.

"And maybe I flew all the way down here for nothing!" Hunter counterpunched. "And maybe Pegg is a crazy old man who's eaten too many clams . . ."

The door swung open before he finished the sentence. Suddenly he was staring down the barrel of no less than a German-made Heckler & Koch G3 SG/1 sniping rifle. Behind the rifle was a typically-grizzled old timer, complete with worn-out boat captain's cap and corncob pipe.

"That's some heavy artillery you got there, Pops," Hunter said, bringing his own M-16 barrel up to bear.

"And I'd aim to use it too!" the man growled, adding a nervous chuckle as he took stock of the business end of Hunter's M-16.

"Well, you don't have to use it on me," Hunter said, slowly lowering his rifle. "Are you Captain Pegg?"

"I am!" the man said defiantly, not moving his rifle an iota.

"Well, I'm a friend of Dave Jones," Hunter told him. "And I hear he's a friend of yours. He said you'd be expecting me . . ."

The old man lowered his gun only a notch. "*You're* this 'Wingman' guy?" he asked in his gnarled tone of voice. "Cripes, from what I heard about you, I expected you'd have sprouted a pair of wings . . ."

Hunter had to smile. With his battered cap, pipe, unshaved face and heavily-muscled forearms, the old guy was right out of a Popeye cartoon.

The man lowered his powerful rifle and managed a gap-toothed smile. "Okay," he said. "You look like a flyboy. C'mon in."

Hunter stepped inside the small flat and it too looked as authentic as Captain Pegg. It was a clutter of sea paintings and photos, fishing lines, hats, parts of lobster traps and shrimp kettles, plus a couple dozen empty liquor boxes. A small lamp on the room's table competed with the neon barrage coming from outside the flat's single window.

"Nice place . . ." Hunter said.

"It's comfortable for someone like me," Pegg said, dropping into a large overstuffed chair. "Besides, I ain't here much. Spend most of my time out on the open sea."

Hunter drew up a wooden chair and sat down. Pegg reached into a cabinet beside his seat and came up with a bottle and two glasses.

"Hong Kong brandy," he said, opening the bottle and giving it a sniff.

He poured out two stiff belts and handed one to Hunter. The pilot took a sip and was genuinely surprised. The stuff was actually good. Most booze running around the continent these days was nothing more than glorified rot-gut.

"Aye, I surprised you!" Pegg said, his eyes gleaming. "Bet that's the best hootch you've tasted in a while . . ."

"That it is," Hunter said, suddenly finding himself talking like Pegg.

"How is my old friend, David?" Pegg asked Hunter through a sip of the brandy. "I haven't seen him since the Big War started. We grew up in the same neighborhood, you know. He, his twin brother Seth and me. They went into airplanes and I took to the sea."

"The general is well," Hunter answered. "Of course, he's

26

up to his ears in work, trying to coordinate repair of all the war damage, as well as getting the Reconstruction Government running smoothly . . ."

"My hat's off to you guys," Pegg said, actually tipping his cap. "You ran those Circle bastards and their commie friends right out of the country. Lot of us are proud of you all . . ."

Hunter took a good swig of the liquor. "Thanks, Captain," he said. "But, believe me, the hard part is just beginning."

"You'll do fine," Pegg said.

Then suddenly the old man became very serious.

"Did David tell you why I contacted him after all these years?" he asked Hunter.

The pilot shook his head. "No, not really," he replied. "Just that you had some very critical information on the Canal . . ."

"Not just information," the old man said, his face creasing with worry. "A dire warning, my boy. There's trouble brewing down there that will make your latest brawl with The Circle look like a finger fight . . ."

"Tell me about it," Hunter said, leaning forward a little.

Pegg relit his pipe and through a swirl of smoke, began his strange story.

Chapter 3

Earlier that year, Pegg had been hired to pilot a medium-sized coastal freighter out of New Orleans down to the Amazon. Inside its hold were three tons of frozen shrimp—a birthday present, he had heard, for the Queen of Brasilia (the current name of Brazil) from her husband. While no self-respecting seaman like himself would ever be caught actually eating frozen shrimp, Pegg took on the job because it promised good pay for little work.

The first leg of the trip went well. The shrimp was delivered and payment received from the King of Brasilia himself. But then the monarch had a proposition for Pegg and his crew: Would they carry another load of cargo down to Buenos Aires? Being an old merchantman, Pegg knew that this was how the hauling business usually worked: one job frequently led to another. In fact, he had anticipated such a thing and thereby had leased the trawler for three months.

Pegg and his crew took on the King's cargo—heavily-sealed containers with invulnerable laser combination locks—at the Brasilia port of Macapa on the mouth of the Amazon and made Buenos Aires six days later.

"Now Buenos Aires is a very strange place these days," Pegg said to Hunter, pouring out another couple of drinks for them. "Everybody—men, women, kids and grandmothers—wears a uniform. Everybody is in the army."

The Brasilian king's cargo was off-loaded and again, Pegg was asked to take on another assignment. This one was to bring more sealed cargo to Lima, Peru. Pegg said he took three full days to think the job over as it entailed sailing around the southern tip of South America through the treacherous waters off Cape Horn.

"I'd done it once before," Pegg said. "Vowed then I'd never do it again . . ."

But the lock-step military government of Buenos Aires promised a fortune (in gold, no less) for Pegg if he agreed to make the voyage. For despite their obvious military might, the Argentines no longer had sailable ships, much less anyone who had the skills to navigate the typhoon-like passage at the southern tip of the world.

Pegg put it to a vote to his crew. Seven men agreed to go, four chose to jump ship in Buenos Aires. Pegg collected a third of his payment in advance and set out, his crew supplemented by a half dozen Argentinian marines, none of whom could speak English.

The passage around the cape was predictably nightmarish, Pegg claimed. One crewman and a marine were washed overboard as the freighter was battered by hurricane-like winds and 25-foot waves. The sky was as dark as midnight even in the middle of the day. The waters were so churned up that Pegg claimed he and his crew saw all kinds of strange creatures — giant eels, serpents and squid — riding on the surface. Sharks were jumping out of the water like flying fish. Seagulls and albatross continually smashed into the hull of the freighter, content, according to Pegg, to commit suicide rather than to drown in the hellish sea. For three straight days, Pegg and his crew did nothing but bail water, both by hand and diesel-driven pumps. Two men dropped dead of exhaustion. Another went insane and jumped overboard — Pegg said they inexplicably heard his screams for more than an hour . . .

Finally they made it to the southwestern-most islands at the tip of Chile where they docked and recovered for two days. Then they set out northward on the more placid waters of the Pacific.

"That's when the voyage started getting very strange," Pegg told Hunter.

The captain was asleep in his berth one night just as the

29

ship was halfway to Lima when he was awakened by an ear-splitting crash. Quickly out of bed and into his boots, Pegg ran to the bridge to find that his ship was now dead in the water. Right off its bow was no less than a battle cruiser.

"Looking back on it, if I had to guess, I would say it was of Italian design," Pegg recounted. "It might have been a *Veneto*-class warship. Very sleek-looking. Very modern. It looked like it was very fast for a ship of its size."

But the cruiser's crew was anything but a gang of friendly Italians. They had rammed Pegg's ship on purpose, and before Pegg had a chance to tie his boot lacings, a 50-man heavily-armed boarding party was crossing over to his small ship.

"Everyone of them looked alike," Pegg swore to Hunter. "Tall, blond, all the same age and weight. It was the strangest thing, as if they were all first cousins or something . . ."

No one in the boarding party said a word. They simply took up positions at various points on the freighter's deck after having shot the two Argentine marines who had dared to raise their guns to them. After that Pegg wisely ordered his crew not to resist.

On a given signal, the strangers commenced searching the ship. Under the light of the cruiser's powerful search-lights, they quickly hauled up the 12 sealed containers that Pegg had taken on in Buenos Aires and one man, an officer in charge of the raiding party, was able to disarm the sup-posedly foolproof laser locks.

To the surprise of Pegg and his crew, the 10 foot-by-10-foot boxes were filled to the brim with gold.

"Not gold bars, either," Pegg told Hunter. "Gold objects. Plates. Goblets. Crucifixes. Chains and necklaces. Rings. And coins. Thousands of gold coins . . ."

"The Argentines put all that gold . . . on a freighter?" Hunter asked. "Why?"

"Good question, Major," Pegg told him. "And I believe the answer is this: It was all part of their plan. The gold, in fact, was a payment to these men on the cruiser, or more accurately, their superiors. Blood money. Protection money. Call it what you like. It was never intended to make it to

Peru at all.

"And neither were we . . ."

Once the raiders took all the gold onto the cruiser, the boarding party shot one more of the marines, then returned to their warship.

"We breathed a sigh of relief when that ship turned away from us and started heading north," Pegg said. "But what fools we were!"

The cruiser sailed away about ten miles, then, without warning, launched a Swedish-built RBS-15 anti-ship missile at Pegg's freighter.

"I saw it coming," Pegg said. "I had just enough time to shout a warning to my crew. About half of us made it over the side before the missile hit . . ."

The powerful RBS-15 hit the freighter just above the waterline and instantly obliterated the vessel. Pegg and another crewman—a man they all called "Goldie" because of his mouthful of gold teeth—were blown out of the water and landed in a sea of burning oil and debris.

"We caught hold of a big chunk of wood that went floating by," Pegg said. "Then we kicked our feet as fast as we could, just to get away from the burning wreckage."

Although they heard the cries from some of the other crewmen, they weren't able to find any of them in the smoke and darkness and confusion. They paddled around until dawn and finding no other signs of life, set out for the coast of Chile, luckily just three miles to the east.

The two men made landfall after 10 hours of grueling paddling, all the while, Pegg said, fighting off man-eating sharks with their bare fists. Once ashore they sought refuge in a nearby woods and soon met some villagers who gave them food and warm clothing.

"We were near a town called Tongo, Chile, which is about seven hundred miles south of the border with Peru," Pegg said. "The place was all but abandoned. Only old people and young women lived there. We asked them: 'Where is everybody?' But they couldn't answer us very well because we didn't speak their language and they couldn't speak ours. We got the impression that all of the other villagers had been taken away. Maybe by slavers, I remember thinking at the time."

The small harbor at Tongo was filled with fishing boats and Pegg and Goldie offered to somehow buy one of the vessels. Instead the villagers told them they could have one for free, if they agreed to take part in a strange ritual.

"They wanted us to make love to all of the young women in the village," Pegg claimed. "Their men were long gone and the young females were getting themselves damp . . ."

It took three weeks for Pegg and Goldie to fulfill their agreement. Once done, the villagers indicated that the seamen should take the best vessel in harbor as none of the boats would ever be used again anyway. Pegg selected the largest one in the small fleet—a 30-foot tuna boat—and set out.

"We decided to go north," Pegg said. "Even though that was the direction that the cruiser took, we knew it was better than going back down around the cape."

Staying as close to the shore as possible, they sailed the tuna boat up the South American west coast, catching fish along the way to sustain them. Using their engines only when necessary, the favorable currents took them up past Peru and Ecuador.

"We were going to sail it right up to California," Pegg said. "But off the coast of Colombia our engine started acting up. Then it died completely. At the same time the currents reversed and started to drag us due west, out to the open sea."

They drifted for another two weeks, Pegg said, their only nourishment coming from eating the huge sea turtles Pegg said he caught off the top of the waves with his bare hands.

Still, they had no water left and soon both men were near death.

"Two angels floated down and landed right on our stern," Pegg said. "Both Goldie and I were lying on the deck, too weak to move, just waiting for our Maker. I saw Goldie's spirit lift right out of his body, I did. But then I pleaded with seraphs to send him back. And they did . . .

"A day later we were picked up by a tramp steamer carrying a Japanese captain and a huge Filipino crew. They were carrying rubber — for tires — from Manila all the way over to Morocco. The captain told us he could make ten thousand bags of gold if he made the trip in two months. So he was shooting for passage through the Canal. The Canal! We thought he was crazy, especially with all the horror stories we had heard. But he knew we were both experienced sailors, so he kept us on."

According to Pegg, the Japanese captain thought he had it all figured out. He was confident he could handle any situation in the canal zone. And with seemingly good reason — the Filipino crewmen doubled as soldiers and there were no less than 150 of them. And the steamer itself was bristling with 3-inch and 5-inch deck guns, as well as a dozen heavy machine guns. It also carried a number of fast attack boats that could quickly be lowered over the side.

"They were well-armed," Pegg reported. "And the soldiers drilled and practiced on deck four hours a day and another two hours at night. They were a crack outfit by the time we made it to the islands that guard the entrance of the Canal."

The captain sent two squads of his soldiers ahead in two attack boats. The plan was for the craft to scout ahead of the steamer, checking for any hostile forces on either side of the waterway. The bonus was that the attack craft crews were also knowledgable in the kind of water locks used in the Canal.

"A lot of people don't realize that more than half the length of the Canal is actually a lake and a river," Pegg said. "You enter a set of locks from the one side. They gradually raise you up about eighty-five feet until you are at the right level. Then you sail for about twenty-five miles until you reach the other set of locks and they lower you back down and out you go.

"The locks themselves are fairly elaborate, but the Japanese captain knew they required hardly any machinery or pumps. It's all done with gravity. He didn't believe the hoodoo stories and figured that there was an even chance the locks were still working, or at least could be made to work by his attack craft guys . . ."

The scout boats made it to the first lock, and to their surprise, found it to be in working condition, manned by no more that a half dozen sleeping guards of undetermined but apparently non-cannibalistic origin. The scouts reported back to the steamer to proceed, and within hours, the ship was through the first locks and sailing on.

"Everything was going smoothly," Pegg said. "*Too* smoothly. Oh, we took a few sniper rounds along the way, but the steamer gunners would just open up with those five-inch guns and that would be the end of that!

"The Japanese captain thought for sure he had out-smarted everyone, that he was making history! That is, until we were about halfway through the channel . . ."

As Pegg told it, he had just finished eating breakfast when they heard the lookout give a yell. By the time Pegg made it to the bridge, he and the others saw that one of the attack craft had just blown up.

"It was about a half mile ahead of us," Pegg said. "And the bastard just blew apart. At first the captain thought it was a mine. Then the other boat got it, and after that, we knew it wasn't no mine."

Pegg claimed that the second attack craft was shot at by hundreds of weapons, firing from both sides of the Canal.

"It was unbelievable!" the sea captain said. "They hit that boat with rockets, surface-to-surface guided missiles, big guns, little guns, heavy machine guns. Everything but the kitchen sink. Whoever was doing the shooting was definitely trying to send a message . . ."

That message was that the steamer was going no further. Soon after the attack craft were sunk, a small fleet of gun-boats surrounded the steamer, and soon she was being boarded.

"They were just like the guys that had blown us up off Chile after taking the gold," Pegg said. "Same uniforms, same strange look on their faces. Tall, blond and no expres-sions. Like a bunch of first cousins."

Just like before, the boarding party shot anyone on the ship who looked like a soldier, as opposed to a sailor. In the case of the steamer, this was more than one hundred men.

"Just lined them up on the bow and shot 'em all," Pegg said. "One at a time . . . but not before they looked into each guy's mouth. In fact, they yanked out a few teeth from a couple guys right then and there. Then they shot 'em."

The mysterious raiders then ordered the captain to move the steamer to a dockworks that had been built on the far edge of the waterway. Pegg said there were at least a dozen other ships there—all sizes, under different flags.

"It was a floating graveyard; they had all fallen for the same ruse." Pegg said. "Like a spider sucking a fly into its web, we sailed right into their trap."

Once docked, the steamer was searched thoroughly no less than five times.

"They didn't care about the rubber," Pegg reported. "They were looking for only one thing . . . *gold*.

"They didn't find any, although they were convinced we had some on us. They tortured the captain until he finally died. Then they gathered up what was left of us—about fifteen in all—and started prowling around in our mouths, just like they did to the Filipinos they shot. It wasn't until they came to me that I realized what they were doing. If you can believe it, they were looking for gold fillings!

"When they got to poor Goldie, they yanked his mouth empty. Then they just threw him overboard, shot him and watched him die."

Why Pegg wasn't shot then and there, he never found out. Instead the strange troops locked him and a few of the surviving steamer mates in a makeshift jailshack.

"We was there for two days and nights," the captain said. "No food. No water. Nothing. Like they had just abandoned us.

"Then, on the third night, we heard a bunch of explosions. Suddenly there's a hell of a gunfight going on right outside our shack. It went on for more than an hour. We heard mortars, big fifties, rocket-propelled grenades. Choppers flying overhead. People yelling over loudspeakers. Strange music blaring until it split your eardrums. It was incredible!

"Then, something—I think it was an RPG—hit our

building. Blew the side right off it. Killed three Filipino fellows, the poor bastards. Me and the others didn't hang around to cry. We just lit out into the jungle.

"I'm an old man and still I've never run that fast in my life . . ."

Chapter 4

The bottle of Hong Kong brandy was gone by the time Pegg had nearly finished his tale.

Jones had told Hunter that Pegg, being an old salt and all, might be prone to exaggeration. Yet the pilot knew that despite the story's fantastic flourishes, there had to be a kernel of truth underneath.

"I haven't got to the good part yet!" Pegg said, relighting his pipe for the umpteenth time.

Hunter shifted around in his chair and said: "So tell me. What happened next?"

Pegg gave out a hoot, then a long, raspy cough. "I crawled through that jungle all night," he said. "I saw lots of soldiers running around. These guys in black, plus other guys in green jungle camouflage outfits. Choppers everywhere. They were shooting at each other and here I am, a man my age, clambering around in the bushes in the middle of them.

"Morning came and I had made my way a good piece down the side of the waterway. I could see the east side locks and of course, they had these blond-haired goons crawling all over them.

"I spent the whole day just watching them. They had a bunch of skindivers working for them and it seemed like they were planting things in the middle of the channel . . ."

"Things?" Hunter asked. "What kind of things?"

Pegg shrugged. "Long silver tubes," he said, closing his eyes in an effort to remember. "Flashing lights on them.

37

You should have seen the contraption they was carrying them in. It looked like a big gray box on a piece of toast. They had it fitted out like an egg crate. And they handled each one of those tubes just like it was eggs. Real careful like . . ."

Hunter ran his hand through his hair, trying to make some sense of the story. "So how'd you finally get back, Captain?"

Pegg began to say something, when suddenly a shot rang out . . .

Hunter was down on the floor in less than a second, dragging the old man down off his chair with him. The shot had come through the flat's single window, smashing the thick glass and catching Pegg square in the jaw.

Hunter raised his M-16 and shot out the room's only light. Then he lifted Pegg up on his knee.

"Goddamn it . . . the dirty bastards must have finally caught up with me . . ." the old man managed to say, despite his wound.

Just then another shot came through the window. Then another. And another.

Hunter dragged Pegg's limp body into a far corner, then he quickly crawled over to the broken window. Through the haze of neon lights and fog, he saw two figures moving in the shadows across the alley.

Not wanting to shoot any innocents, Hunter nevertheless unleashed a long burst from his M-16 on to the wall directly across from the window and just above the two skulking figures. As always, his trademark tracer rounds produced a frightening iridescent stream of fire and lead. Instantly, the two shadows started to run.

Hunter moved back to Pegg and quickly checked his pulse. Finding one, though weak, he burst out of the flat and lit out after the two fleeing figures.

The snipers had made two mistakes: First they had assumed that Pegg was alone when they took a shot at him through the window. Second, they had chosen to run down further into Thunder Alley instead of retreating back out to Orleans Avenue.

What they didn't know was the alley was a dead end.

Hunter was no sooner past the place from where the gunmen had fired when he picked out the two figures running away at top speed. He followed them, running as fast as he could, his flight boots striking the grimy wet alley pavement with a succession of sharp cracks. The chase went on for only 20 seconds or so, when the gunmen turned a slight bend in the road and found themselves facing a brick wall.

Hunter skidded to a stop just as the two men wheeled and fired at him. He was able to dodge their combined barrages, and a split-second later, he cut them both down at the legs with an economical burst of M-16 tracer fire.

Unlike most other New Order cities, the gunfire actually *attracted* a crowd—this one from the small alley bistros and cathouses.

Two regional militia men were soon on the scene, and after Hunter quickly identified himself, they joined the pilot in walking over to the two wounded men.

"This guy is dead . . ." one of the militiamen said, reaching one of the snipers first.

"Dead?" Hunter asked, legitimately surprised. "I aimed for his legs. I want these guys alive . . ."

He was bent over the body by this time and quickly saw that it wasn't his bullets that had ended the man's life. There was a long stream of black fluid running out of the man's mouth, and his ears were bleeding.

"Poison . . ." Hunter said, quickly reaching down and closing the man's eyelids. "Capsule under his tongue. He bit it when I cornered him."

Hunter quickly moved over to the other man who lay crumpled in the far corner of the blind alley. He at least was stirring, although he had taken at least four bullets in both legs. Oddly, this man's head, like his companion's, was shaved clean.

Hunter reached down and grabbed the man by his collar. *"Who are you?"* the pilot asked him harshly.

The man managed to open his eyes and look straight at Hunter. Then, of all things, he coughed out a laugh . . .

"Fuck you," the wounded man said in a voice just tinged

39

with some kind of accent. Then he dramatically made a quick chomping motion with his jaws, and a second later, a long stream of inky black came spilling out of his mouth, too.

"Jesus, he killed himself, too . . ." one of the militiamen said in disbelief.

"Who are these guys anyway?" the other soldier asked.

Hunter stood up and shook his head. "I'm not sure," he said, turning quickly and heading back for Pegg's flat. "But I've got to find out . . ."

The old sea captain was barely conscious when Hunter returned.

He bent over the old man, making him as comfortable as possible. Off in the distance he heard the wail of a siren approaching. He was sure it was the New Orleans military police. They would be able to get Pegg to the hospital.

"Who were they?" Hunter asked the old man, somewhat stemming the flow of blood from his jaw with his jacket. "Who knew you were here besides Jones?"

Pegg opened his eyes slightly. The gleam was still there. "*They* knew!" he growled. "They . . . they must have tracked me down . . . The bastards wouldn't even let me finish my story . . . I never . . . even got to . . . the best part . . ."

"Who *were* they, dammit?" Hunter said with exasperation. It seemed like Pegg was more upset over having not finished his yarn than by being shot in the jaw.

"The first cousins . . ." Pegg managed to say, before he slipped into unconsciousness. "The bastards that are running the Canal . . ."

Hunter rode in the back of the police van as it whisked Pegg off to the hospital.

The old man was slipping in and out of consciousness, but Hunter knew it was best that he didn't press him for details of the would-be assassins. The fact that both men had chosen suicide over capture was chilling enough.

40

Four hours later, Pegg was patched up — his fractured jaw was wired and he was stitched from his ear to his chin. The military doctors assured Hunter that the old buck would probably make it, though the recovery process would be a lengthy one, due to Pegg's age. Hunter told the medics to spare no expense in treating Pegg, then the pilot visited the man's room.

Pegg couldn't speak, but he weakly gave Hunter a thumb's up sign.

Leaning over the man's bed, Hunter told him: "We'll get the people responsible for this . . ."

Pegg's eyes started to water as he clasped Hunter in a handshake. Just then, a gorgeous middle-aged nurse walked in and announced that it was time for Pegg to get some rest. Pegg took one look at the nurse, then managed a slight smile through the tangle of wires around his mouth.

Hunter gave him a wink and whispered to him in a mock scolding voice: "Behave yourself . . ."

Chapter 5

The sun was just starting to come up when Hunter left the hospital.

It had been dark and somewhat confusing when he rode into the place hours before in the back of the police van, so the pilot was somewhat surprised to find the hospital was so close to the city's docks. Now, as he walked out near the Toulouse Street Wharf, he could smell the tantalizing aroma of New Orleans waking up. There was no shortage of eateries in the area, and the air was a mixture of flapjacks, eggs on a grill, coffee and biscuits.

He knew he had to report to Jones as quickly as possible. But, judging by the hectic night he'd just put in, he decided to allow himself some chow before heading back to the New Orleans airport to retrieve his F-16.

But as with so many of the things in his life, it was if he was guided by some invisible hand to the cafe he chose to breakfast in. It was a small joint that hung out over the water, attached to the edge of an active pier. Inside there were only a half dozen window-side tables and a counter with ten or so stools. Hunter walked in and took a small window table within leaping distance of the door, hanging up his hat and M-16 in the process.

A pretty black waitress appeared, took his order for coffee and a plate of flapjacks and home fries, tnen disappeared back into the small kitchen. Hunter quickly surveyed the other clientele—two hookers drinking tea at the far end of the counter, three sailors sobering up at the far table, plus a couple of militiamen nearby—and decided everyone was generally harmless.

His meal arrived quickly and he immediately dug in. But three mouthfuls later, he found his attention drawn away from the stack of jacks and glued onto a large ship that was just entering the harbor.

"What the hell is this?" he thought to himself through a gulp of coffee.

It was a luxury liner. Big, sleek and all white, it appeared to be flying a hundred different flags. For the next ten minutes he watched in suspicious fascination as the ship was nudged into a nearby pier by a squad of tugboats. Once it was close enough, he noted the ship's decks were lined with a couple hundred passengers. They all seemed animated enough, as if they had actually just returned from a pleasure cruise. He wouldn't have been surprised if he'd seen them all start throwing confetti and streamers.

His waitress returned to fill his coffee cup and he took the opportunity to point out the newly-arrived ship.

"What's with 'The Love Boat?'" he asked her.

She took a quick look at the white ship, now almost completely settled into a berth close by and laughed.

"Why that's the *Big Easy Princess*," she said, matter-of-factly. "Coming back from another 'Cruise to Nowhere,' I suspect."

"It docks here regularly?" Hunter asked.

"Sure does," she said. "Been doing so for about the past six months. It goes out for about two weeks at a time. Comes in, stays a few days, then heads back out again."

Hunter reached inside his shirt and came up with two bags of real silver.

"Where's it go?" he asked her, pressing the money into her hand. The savvy waitress immediately knew that he had just paid about ten times too much for the meal.

"From what I hear, it travels all over," she said, still clutching the bags of silver. "Sometimes Barbados, or Saint

Thomas or Saint Croix. Sometimes all the way down to Colombia."

A bell went off in Hunter's head.

"Any place special in Colombia?" he asked.

Now she eyed him suspiciously. "Are you a cop?" she asked.

"No," he said, deftly producing another bag of silver. "Are you?"

She shook her head and smiled. "Can I sit for a minute?" she asked.

He reached over and pulled out the small table's other chair. "Be my guest," he said.

A half hour later, Hunter was pushing a baggage cart down the pier where the luxury liner had docked.

He was dressed in a nondescript pair of denim coveralls and a woolen cap—both articles of clothing courtesy of the diner waitress. He took his place in amongst the small army of baggage handlers loitering around the ship's gangway and pretended to smoke a cigar. All the while he was taking in every detail possible about the *Big Easy Princess*.

This was no ordinary cruise liner. True, while its decks were lined with what looked to be fairly ordinary passengers and some soldiers, its fore and aft sections boasted at least a dozen gun mounts. Also its mast was bristling with a forest of sophisticated radar hardware and, easily spotted by his well-trained eye, a number of missile guidance and tracking systems. He even noted unmistakable scrape marks along the port side of the ship which indicated that small boat launches—probably attack craft—were lowered and raised regularly.

He was sure there could be much more evidence found inside the hull of the boat, but Hunter had no plans to steal aboard to find it. He didn't have to. He knew a drug-running ship when he saw one . . .

Drugs were a nasty fact of life in New Order America.

Just because the United American Army had defeated The Circle didn't mean that criminality had suddenly come to a screeching halt across the continent. The skies were just as dangerous to fly in and the roads just as treacherous to move on as before the final defeat of The Circle. And the fractured nation's seemingly endless cycle of drugs and money kept spinning along.

When Jones and the United Americans set up their Reconstruction Government in Washington following the war, not one of the top command men was laboring under any illusions. The continent was still a scattering of ever-changing independent countries, kingdoms, cantons, shires, free states and territories. All the new government in Washington could hope to do is solidify the continental defenses to keep out foreign interference and to restore some semblance of order to the larger cities east of the Mississippi. These two tasks alone were next to impossible. So the leaders in Washington knew that things like drug-running, gun-running, air piracy, slavery, forced prostitution and so on would stay on the national landscape for some time to come.

Hunter realized this too, and it was not so much that the ship before him was most likely loaded to the gills with drugs that had caused him to take to the disguise and get a closer look. No—it was the route the boat had taken to *get* those drugs that interested him.

The waitress had told him she'd met an unsavory character who had booked passage on the *Big Easy Princess* just a month before. The man had swaggered into the diner just after disembarking and bragged that he had enough cocaine to keep a small city high for a year. He claimed that he had scored the stuff in Colombia, specifically in the port of Buenaventura, which was close enough to Medellin, still the recognized coke capital of the world.

What had Hunter's brain buzzing in all this was the fact that the man hadn't bragged about picking up his illegal "booga-sugar" in the Colombian harbors of Cartagena, or Santa Maria, or Riohacha. These port cities were located on the Caribbean coast of the South American country.

Buenaventura, on the other hand, was located on the

Pacific side.

What Hunter wanted to know was, assuming Pegg's somewhat fantastic tale of entrapment and horror on the Canal was true, how the hell was the coke boat able to make the passage through Panama without so much as a scratch?

Chapter 6

It was dark and drizzling by the time Hunter made it to the prearranged rendezvous spot.

He had postponed his plans to return to Washington. A quick radio call to Jones that morning had them in agreement that there was still some more information to be had in New Orleans. Now the sun had just set, and Hunter found himself shivering slightly, out on the isolated swampy bayou in the chilly mist. He faced the north and waited.

Ten minutes went by. Then he felt a familiar vibration start at the back of his neck and run down his spine. His brain got the message on the instantaneous richochet.

Off in the distance. Getting closer. Two aircraft . . .

He had never been able to come up with a better item for this sensation other than simply calling it *the feeling.* It was many things and it was a solitary thing. It was ESP. It was *déjà vu.* It was synchronicity — that state of affairs described as "meaningful coincidences." He simply knew things that he had no logical reason for knowing. It was that feeling he got whenever he climbed into his airplane and not so much *flew* it as became a *part* of it. It was also the feeling he got when he knew that aircraft were approaching even before they showed up on any radar set. *The feeling . . .* It had saved his life more times than he could count. No one else had it — just him. And not a day had gone by when he didn't wonder why.

Closer now. About two clicks away . . .

He pushed up his coat collar again, and tried to wipe the

dampness from the bill of his baseball cap. He was glad he had taken the precaution of wrapping the M-16 in plastic before setting out for this place. The moisture would have done a job on his tracer ammunition.

They're here . . .

He strained both his eyes and ears and concentrated on the darkened skies to the north. He heard them before he saw them. The unmistakable whirring sound of a chopper engine; the clean powerful whistling sound made only by the Cobra . . .

The Cobra attack helicopter was a frightening piece of machinery.

Forty-eight feet long, fourteen feet high, the insect-like chopper could haul ass at 175 mph. It carried a three-barreled 20-mm M197 cannon in its nose turret, and a variety of gun pods, rocket pods, missile launchers and even flame-throwing equipment on its two side pylons. Yet even with all this firepower, the Cobra could maneuver like a hummingbird. Up, down, sideways, backwards. All very quickly, and, fairly quietly.

Its very name did it justice: long and thin with a lethal snout. From Viet Nam to World War III to the post-war American battles, the Cobra had served well. Just *thinking* about the chopper and what destruction it was capable of delivering — against ground troops, tanks, gun emplacements, ships — caused many an enemy of America fits, if not nightmares.

And no one flew Cobras with more skill and daring than the famous Cobra Brothers . . .

A few seconds later he saw them.

Still two blinking red lights way off in the distance, but undoubtedly the people he'd been waiting for. He hunched up his coat again and retrieved a small flare from one of its many pockets. A quick strike on the fuse and the flare came alive with a brilliant red glow.

Two minutes later, the pair of two-seat helicopter gunships came in for a perfect landing on the soft, marshy field. Another two minutes went by until both chopper rotors wound down. Then three men — a pair from Cobra Two and a single from Cobra One — emerged from their cockpits and walked over to Hunter, who was waiting at the edge of the clearing.

"Hey Hawk, Baxter's all upset that he couldn't come along." The man doing the talking was Captain Jesse Tyler, the commanding officer of the four-man non-related Cobra Brothers. His partner, the pilot of Cobra Two, was Captain Bobby Crockett. He and Tyler had been friends and allies of Hunter ever since before the first Battle of Football City. Both Texans, when Hunter first met the Cobras, they had been supporting themselves as free-lance gunship jockeys. But since those first continental battles, the Cobras had been in the employ of the democratic forces exclusively. Tyler and Crockett were joined on this trip by Crockett's gunner, Lieutenant John "John-Boy" Hobbs.

"How was it that Bax stayed behind?" Hunter asked as he shook hands with all three men.

"He pulled the low card," Crockett said. "Says you owe him a bottle of good stuff when you get back . . ."

Hunter laughed and said: "If we do the trick down here, and find out what we need to know, I'll gladly give him a jug."

Hobbs produced a thermos and soon all four of them were drinking thick black coffee.

"So what's the situation, Hawk?" Tyler asked. "We had to leave pretty quick in order to make our refueling connections and get down here in reasonable time. So Jones really didn't have much time to fill us in . . ."

Hunter shook his head. "As usual, it's complicated," he said. Then he quickly told them an abbreviated version of Pegg's saga, adding in the assassination attempt and his own investigation of the cruise liner. It was this last part that found the Cobra team most surprised.

"You mean we've been fighting our asses off up north and the folks down here have been taking vacation cruises?"

Tyler said. Goddamn, we're in the wrong line of work . . ."

"They've been taking cruises all right," Hunter said. "But not ordinary, down-home folks. From what I can see, the passengers on that boat are almost all drug dealers. And I'm not talking about the kind of guys who stand on street corners and begin every conversation with: 'Psst, hey buddy . . .' "

"So we're talking about big-timers," Tyler confirmed. "People with millions who want *more* millions . . ."

"That's the animal," Hunter confirmed. "The passenger list is very exclusive, and, I'm sure, a ticket to Cokeville, Colombia doesn't come cheap."

Each man took a long swig of coffee.

"But how in hell do they make the trip?" Crockett asked. "Either they're going around South America the long way or your old captain's been at sea too long . . ."

"Or they've been able to make a deal with the weirdos running the Canal," Hunter said, stating a third option. "And that's why I asked you boys to come down here tonight. I've scoped out a guy who can tell us everything we want to know. It's just a question 'convincing' him to do it . . ."

Tyler drained his coffee and poured himself another cup. "Well, we're all ears, Hawk," he said.

The plantation was located right on the edge of the Segnette Bayou, about 15 miles south of the port of New Orleans.

Earlier in the day, while he was still disguised as a baggage handler, Hunter had instinctively picked out one particular cruise liner passenger. For soon-to-be-obvious reasons, the man would have been hard to miss. When he required no less than six taxis to transport him and his rather large retinue of bodyguards away from the docks, Hunter tagged him as being one of the biggest rollers to get off the ship. Quickly flagging down a taxi, the pilot followed the suspect's convoy of cabs out of the city and into the Segnette Bayou. After a 30-minute ride, the half dozen taxis turned into the front gates of an enormous plantation. The place was complete with an authentic-looking antebellum mansion, various farm buildings, many acres of land and the mandatory scattering of honeysuckle bushes and weeping willow trees.

Hunter told his driver to keep right on going past the front gate of the plantation. Eventually, they made a U-turn and headed back to New Orleans. A few bags of silver unloosened the lips of the driver on the return trip, giving Hunter enough information to identify the bigshot passenger as one Jean LaFeet, a wealthy gambler/smuggler/criminal, who was well-known in New Orleans.

A trip to the headquarters of the newly installed military governor for downtown New Orleans told Hunter that LaFeet was suspected of everything from mass murder to kidnapping and selling young girls. It was rumored that the man kept as much as a quarter *ton* of cocaine on his own premises, just for personal use, while dealing many more thousands of pounds of the stuff on a weekly basis. He was also widely known as a Circle collaborator, and it was said that more than a few Soviet and Cuban officers had passed through the gates of his mansion before the last war.

The military governor told Hunter that it was just a matter of time before he and his militia moved in on LaFeet, but there were other more pressing concerns within his jurisdiction at the moment. Hunter told him he understood and, at that point, put in the call for the Cobra Brothers.

The Wingman had continued his research by spending the afternoon drinking in some dockside bars and carefully asking the right questions of the right people for the right amount of silver. It never ceased to amaze him how a glass of whiskey and a few silver coins would get people talking and the phenomenon was especially true in New Orleans. He thought maybe that was one of the reasons they called it the Big Easy.

Through several bottles of booze and a couple dozen games of pool, he learned that not only was LaFeet a ruthless murderer, drug dealer and sexual deviate, he also surrounded himself with a small army of criminals and wackos who shared his penchant for brutality, narcotics and under-age sex objects.

With a track record like that, Hunter felt no compunc-tion about taking on LaFeet and his minions.

It was just a few minutes before midnight when the two Cobras began a high and wide circling pattern over the plantation.

Hunter was in the gunner's seat of Cobra One, the seat left vacated by Baxter when he drew the low card. The fighter pilot was familiar with the two main pieces of hard-ware crammed into the cockpit. One was the Cobra's per-sonally designed early warning threat radar system. One punch of the button and Hunter knew that there were no anti-aircraft radar systems keying in on the two circling attack choppers. The second piece of equipment consisted of two triggers. One could unleash any one of the six TOW missiles locked under the Cobra's pylons; the other operated the fearsome M197 cannon protruding from the Cobra's chin.

Also jammed inside the cramped cockpit with him was a half-gallon jar of honey which he had bought in town and a fine-strand, but sturdy fisherman's net . . .

The plan was simple. Cobra Two would make some noise to attract LaFeet's henchmen while Hunter and Tyler in Cobra One did the heavy lifting.

At the stroke of midnight, Cobra Two went into its act. While the pilot Crockett brought the gunship in low over the plantation's mansion, Hobbs activated the chopper's awesome flamethrower. The long stream of kerosene-fueled fire lit up the dark surroundings like it was daylight. Hobbs's target was a hay barn about 50 yards from the main house. Two passes and the wooden structure was en-gulfed in flames.

As predicted, the surprise attack brought LaFeet's men running. To the man they were amazed to see a Cobra gunship wheeling out over the swamps and turning back toward them. Armed with rifles, shotguns and only a few

52

dated Thompson machineguns, the 20 or so bodyguards squeezed off a few token rounds apiece and then sought the nearest hiding place as the chopper roared overhead.

Hobbs unleashed a TOW missile on the next pass, guiding it by way of his NightScope glasses to a priceless 1932 Rolls Royce touring sedan that was parked outside the mansion's elegant front entrance. The missile impacted just behind the driver's seat, blowing the expensive vehicle 15 feet into the air. It came down in a shower of fiery pieces of metal.

Only a handful of LaFeet's men dared to crawl out of their holes and take a few shots at the Cobra as it roared over again, its powerful cannon blazing away at nothing in particular. Inside the mansion, several sirens were going off, and LaFeet's collection of guard dogs — Dobermans and pit bull terriers mostly — were barking up a storm. Both Crockett and Hobbs noticed that lights were going on and off inside the huge house in crazy, panicky patterns.

While Cobra Two continued its 130-decibel attack, Cobra One was being relatively quiet in setting down on the mansion's roof. A flat deck, used no doubt by LaFeet and his friends to sunbathe and God knows what else, served as a convenient landing pad for the gunship. No sooner had Tyler put the copter down when Hunter popped his canopy and crawled out of the cockpit, his flight helmet secured on his head, his trusty, tracer-filled M-16 rifle up and ready.

Like Hunter, Tyler was a man of gadgets. A lot of the functions on Cobra One were automatic, controlled by a powerul minicomputer in the pilot's control panel. But a number of them, such as the engine starter, the oil and fuel pumps and, most importantly, the nose cannon, could also be operated by remote control. So before Tyler climbed out with his own M-16 in hand, he punched a pre-programmed set of instructions into the ship's computer. Then he strapped on a small control box to his belt and raised its long thin antenna. Only then did he join Hunter on the roof.

They had to shout to one another, so loud was the racket Cobra Two was making with its once-every-ten-seconds strafing passes.

"How do you know that we'll be able to find this guy so easy?" Tyler yelled to Hunter.

"Don't worry," the fighter pilot hollered back. "I guarantee he'll be the only one still left inside the house."

Tyler shrugged and nodded. He was a good friend of Hunter and trusted him to no end. They had been on many missions together, some quite similar to this one. He never once doubted The Wingman's instinct, intuition, smarts, and just plain guts and he wasn't going to start now.

They picked the lock that bolted the door to the deck and quietly crept inside and down a set of stairs. This brought them to a third floor set of bedrooms, all of which were deserted. They moved down an ornate, curved staircase to the second floor, their ears starting to hurt from the obnoxiously loud, never-ending siren blasts.

Suddenly, from down the hall, Hunter heard a very nasty sound. Both he and Tyler whirled around to see three attack dogs—a Doberman and two pit bulls—heading straight for them.

"Jesus Christ!" Tyler yelled out, at the same time squeezing off two long bursts from his M-16 at the dogs. He caught the Doberman in mid-leap, the force of the bullets slamming the mutt against the wall. The two pit bulls got it from ground level, though it took about a dozen bullets each to knock them down.

"Damn!" Tyler cursed. "I hate killing animals . . ."

Hunter looked at the three bleeding carcasses and nodded. "Yeah, me too," he said.

They continued the search down the long hallway. At the end of the corridor they saw a room with two large wooden doors, one of which was partially open. A stream of light was coming from the room.

"I've got a feeling . . ." Hunter whispered to Tyler.

The chopper pilot nodded and together they inched their way toward the doorway. All the while, the noise outside from Cobra Two's repeated attacks had gotten even louder.

Hunter was first to reach the open door and he carefully peeked through the crack. Then he turned to Tyler and said one word: "Bingo . . ."

One more look, and then Hunter stepped back and suddenly kicked the door in. Tyler was at first surprised at Hunter's quick action. But once he got inside the door, he instantly understood.

The room was a large "playpen." From its ceiling hung a variety of leather straps and chrome chains, most of which ended in handcuffs of some kind. The walls, too, were decorated with holding devices and manacles, all used, no doubt, in connection with weird sexual practices.

There was also a scattering of liquor bottles and drug paraphernalia lying about, as well as several tables of uneaten or picked-over food. The floor was covered with women's — or more accurately — girls' underwear. Overall it looked as though the place hadn't been cleaned in weeks.

But it was in the center of the room, lying propped up on a massive bed that Tyler got his biggest surprise.

There was a man on the bed, his face wearing a ghost-white mask of terror. But he was no ordinary man. Tyler estimated that he weighed at least 550 pounds.

"Jesus, is *that* him?" Tyler asked Hunter.

"It's him," Hunter said, walking over to the man and sticking his M-16 right up to his nose. "Be hard to mistake this cupcake . . ."

Instantly, Tyler knew why Hunter had brought the fisherman's net along.

"Who . . . who are you?" LaFeet asked, trying to control his bladder as he sat paralyzed at the sight of the two armed men.

"None of your business, Tiny," Hunter told him harshly. "Now get up. You're coming with us . . ."

"Where?" LaFeet asked, his voice barely above a terrorized whisper.

"We're going for a ride," Hunter said, jabbing the man's chubby cheek with his M-16 barrel. "Now, get the hell on your feet . . ."

With great effort, LaFeet managed to roll over and off the bed. He was dressed in what could only be described as a mu-mu, the front of which was covered with stains from

55

dropped food and drink and who-knows-what else.

"You got any women locked up around here?" Hunter asked him sharply. "Anyone you're holding against their will?"

LaFeet was taken back by the question. "No . . ." he said. "I just got back today . . ."

"In other words, you haven't had time to round up—or should I say, *kidnap*—anyone," Hunter growled at him.

The man's face turned beet red. "Who *are* you people?" he whined, raising his voice to be heard over the continuous racket outside.

"I said that was none of your business," Hunter shot back at him. "Now start walking . . ."

The man took a deep breath and looked as if he were about to cry. Just then two of his bodyguards appeared at the door.

"Boss!" one of them cried out, letting loose a wild barrage from his semi-automatic rifle before Tyler put a burst into the man's shoulder, knocking him out. His companion immediately dropped his own gun, ducked out of the doorway and was heard quickly retreating down the hall.

"Let's get the show on the road, Hawk," Tyler said. "Crockett and Hobbs can't keep these clowns occupied forever."

Hunter shoved LaFeet hard on the shoulder and the big man reluctantly started walking. Out of the room, down the hallway and up to the stairs to the third floor, it was slow going because LaFeet was forced to stop every few steps and take a few gulps of air. Meanwhile, Tyler had turned a switch on his remote-control box which sent a radio signal to the Cobra One's computer, ordering it to start the chopper's engines.

"If everything's working right, we can take off in less than a minute and half," Tyler said checking his watch.

Once on the third floor, both Hunter and Tyler had to literally push the man's substantial backside up the narrow staircase leading to the sun deck. It was the hardest either of them had worked in months.

"Jesus, I can see being overweight," Tyler drawled. "But

56

this guy is ridiculous . . ."

They finally made it to the roof, LaFeet exhaustedly dropping to his knees and rolling over involuntarily. As promised, the rotor blades on Cobra One were turning, its engine warming up.

"Come on," Hunter said to Tyler, wiping his brow. "Let's get him into the net . . ."

Now LaFeet felt *real* terror strike his heart.

"You're not going to *carry* me with that thing, are you?" he screamed.

"You guessed it," Hunter said, retrieving the net and beginning to wrap it around the huge man.

"No! I won't let you!" LaFeet screamed. Then he started calling out the names of his bodyguards, adding: *"Help! Save me!"*

Hunter reached inside his pocket and came up with a squirtgun. Without hesitation, he squeezed one long stream into LaFeet's face. The man went out like a light.

"Chloroform," Hunter said to Tyler as they finally managed to wrap the net around LaFeet's ample frame. Then the pilot added: "What's the lift capacity of your bird?"

Tyler had to think a moment; it was a rare occasion for him to lift anything.

"I'm not sure," he finally had to say.

"Enough to lift lard-ass here?"

Tyler looked at his chopper then back at the prisoner. "Well, I guess we're going to find out," he said.

Chapter 7

It had stopped drizzling and the bayou air was heavy with swamp flies when the two Cobra gunships returned to their original meeting place.

Cobra Two set down first, Crockett and Hobbs quickly leaping out of their cockpits to help secure the human bundle swinging from the bottom of Cobra One. Once the fisherman's net was unhitched from the hovering chopper, Tyler landed the lead ship and he and Hunter climbed out.

LaFeet was conscious, having come out of his chloroform nap about halfway through the 30-minute flight. He was shaking with fear while the airmen unwrapped him, certain that he was the target of a rather unorthodox underworld rubout.

Actually, all Hunter wanted was information.

"Okay, we can make this simple or we can make it complicated," Hunter said to the man. "But either way, you're going to tell us what we want to know."

They had secured the fat man to the ground spread eagle, using utility cords and part of the fisherman's net. His face was red and puffy, aftereffects for the chloroform shower Hunter had given him. His bizarre evening gown-like outfit was now further soiled with grease and oil and swamp mud. Yet he was studying the face of each of them, a very odd look in his eye.

"I won't tell you anything," he said suddenly, his voice shaky. "Why should I?"

Hunter shook his head in disgust. "*Now* he decides to be a

hero," he said to the others.

LaFeet suddenly became enboldened. "Heroism has nothing to do with it, Mr. Hunter," he said in his odd, squeaky voice.

"*Damn,* he knows who you are . . ." Tyler said.

"I know who *all* of you are," the fat man said. "It took me a while, but now I'm sure. I finally get to meet Hawk Hunter. And the famous Cobra Brothers. Your faces gave you away, gentlemen. And your flag-waving, idealistic, law-abiding reputations precede you. And I know there isn't a chance in a million that you would kill me. It's just not your style, as they say."

"I don't believe this," Crockett said. "This big slob is giving *us* a hard time . . ."

LaFeet laughed. "Do you really keep forgetting you're such well-known heroes?" the rotund criminal asked mockingly . "I'm surprised at you. Torture? A burning stake perhaps? Ha! I know the worst you will do is turn me over to the proper authorities, and believe me, I'll buy my way out of that before you can bat an eye."

"Maybe we can starve him," Hobbs offered.

"That would take too long," Crockett replied, swatting away a swamp fly. "Let's face it: He knows we're the good guys and that we won't grease him under these circumstances."

Tyler looked at Hunter. "It seems like this poor excuse for a human being has us over a barrel."

Hunter, who had been quiet all during LaFeet's bragging, now stepped forward again. In his hands was the half gallon jug of honey.

"Maybe," he said. "Maybe not . . ."

He unscrewed the honey jar lid and stuck his finger inside.

"Good batch," he said, licking off a portion of the sticky sweet stuff. "And I have a feeling that our pal here isn't the only one hungry out in this swamp . . ."

To make his point, Hunter held up his honey-dipped finger and within seconds it was covered with dozens of the pesky swamp flies.

LaFeet was the first one to make the connection. Suddenly his swagger vanished and was replaced with his old friends, fear and groveling.

"You wouldn't . . ." he whined.

Hunter just nodded and poured out a heaping, dripping portion of the honey on to the jar lid. He stepped closer and stood directly over the big man.

"Tell us about your little cruise to Colombia," Hunter snarled at him.

"No . . ." LaFeet said. "No way . . . I can't . . . They'll kill me if I tell you how I got the . . . the stuff . . ."

"We don't give a *damn* about your nose candy," Hunter shot back. "How did you get through *the Canal?*"

LaFeet was momentarily taken back by Hunter's question. But he quickly began shaking his head.

"They'll kill me if I tell you *that,* too," he said.

Hunter didn't want to beat around the bush any longer. It was hot and sticky and very uncomfortable out in the swamp, and the honey on his hand and in the jar lid had attracted a swarm of the pain-in-the-ass "miggee" flies.

So he took the honey lid and poured out a long stream of the sticky goo over LaFeet's head. The big man had rather long hair and the honey quickly matted it down.

"Jesus Christ! No!" he yelled. But it was too late. Within seconds, his face was a mass of honey and swarming flies.

"How did you get through the Canal?" Hunter asked again, even more harshly.

"I *can't* tell you . . ." LaFeet screamed. "They'll hunt me down. They hunt *everyone* down . . ."

Hunter applied some more honey to the man's face and shoulders. Another few thousand flies immediately showed up.

"Who's running the Canal these days?" Hunter pressed. "How come that cruise liner got through?"

"God, man, this is inhuman!" LaFeet screamed as he involuntarily sucked the bug-drenched honey into his nose and mouth. The man's face was now actually hard to see with so many swamp flies and other assorted insects flying around his head.

"So is murder and selling under-age girls . . ." Hunter said as he dumped another load of honey down the front of LaFeet's mu-mu. He and the other three airmen then walked a few yards away and sat down to wait, playing their utility flashlights on the tortured 550-pound man.

"Look! Ants!" Hobbs called out, being the first to spot the dual stream of red insects now crawling up LaFeet's legs and torso to catch the lower drippings of honey.

"Talk, big boy!" Hunter yelled out, swatting a few ants away from himself.

"No! I can't!" LaFeet screeched, spitting out globs of honey and insect-laced saliva.

"You will . . ." Hunter countered.

Ten minutes passed and it appeared as if every representative of the insect kingdom was now either crawling on or orbiting around LaFeet's massive frame. The man continued to yell and squeal like a pig. He repeatedly tried to break free of his restraints, but to no avail. Another ten minutes went by, Hunter and the others calmly drinking more coffee as armies of flying and crawling things flocked to the honey-drenched big man.

Still, it wasn't until two large, nasty-looking swamp snakes showed up, the fat man finally broke down . . .

"Jesus Christ! All right! *I'll talk!*" he screamed. "Just get rid of those fucking snakes! *I hate snakes!*"

Hobbs accommodated his request, picking off both snakes with two well-placed shots from his Colt .45 automatic sidearm.

Hunter got to his feet, brushed himself off and walked over to the bound man. The honey jar was still open and ready.

"How did that cruise liner pass through the Canal?" he asked LaFeet. "I hear the guys running things down there shoot first and ask questions later . . ."

"Not if you pay 'em, stupid!" LaFeet screamed.

"Pay?" Hunter said. "You mean you *can* deal with them?"

"Not just anyone, flyboy," LaFeet answered, his mouth still sputtering bugs and honey. "Arrangements are made ahead of time. They're businessmen. If they want to deal with you, you pay them a toll. If they don't want to deal with you, or if you just bust in there half-assed, you're grease."

"How many of them are there?" Tyler asked, coming up to stand beside Hunter.

"How the *fuck* would I know?" LaFeet shot back. "I didn't take a head count for Christ's sake!"

Just because LaFeet decided to talk didn't mean the insects had given up getting dibs on the honey. If anything, more bugs were swarming around him. He looked so uncomfortable it gave Hunter a slight case of the willies.

"Who are these guys down in the Canal?" Hunter asked him. "They're not your blow buddies from The Circle . . ."

"No way," LaFeet answered. "These days The Circle couldn't run a swimming pool, never mind the fucking Panama Canal."

"So, who are they?" Hunter asked him again. "Locals? Mexicans? Mid-Aks?"

LaFeet even managed a sinister laugh at that one. "Yeah, right, Mid-Aks," he said. "I don't know who the hell they are . . . But they sure ain't Mid-Aks . . ."

"I think he's bullshitting us," Crockett said.

"I do, too," Hunter said, adding with feigned nonchalance: "Lieutenant Hobbs, could you please go round up a snake?"

Hobbs, a country boy who knew his way around a swamp, immediately jumped to his feet and started looking in the underbrush.

"Jesus! No!" LaFeet hollered. "I hate fucking snakes!"

"Then you better start making some sense," Hunter told him.

"What's the toll?" Tyler asked the man. "Guns? A slice of your drug haul? Girls?"

LaFeet made a great effort to shake his head. "No, no . . . These guys really don't give a damn about that kind of stuff. All they want is one thing: gold."

Hunter was not totally surprised to hear that. Another piece of the puzzle had just fallen into place.

The fighter pilot pressed in on LaFeet, standing over

him, his boot on the man's ample neck. "I'll ask you for the last time: Who's in charge down there?"

"I don't *fucking* know!" the fat man yelled, his eyelids now partially clogged with a glob consisting of more bugs than honey. "The officers are foreigners . . ."

"Foreigners?" Hunter said. "You mean Russians?"

"No, not Russians," LaFeet said, letting out a long, slow, exhausted breath. He was caving in. "I'm not sure, but I think they might be Germans . . ."

Chapter 8

Hunter was back in DC less than two days later.

Before he left New Orleans, he arranged to have LaFeet turned over to the military governor. Then he paid a visit to the hospital to see Captain Pegg. Hunter was heartened to learn from the man's doctors that, although the old buck was still in rough shape, he was getting better.

Now, Hunter was in Jones' temporary Washington headquarters, which was located in the now mostly-deserted Pentagon building.

"Damn, this is all we need," Jones said disgustedly as he listened to Hunter's report on the situation in the Canal and who was running things down there.

Tyler, Crockett and Hobbs were also in attendance, as was the usual group of the United Americans' top echelon: former Thunderbird pilots, J. T. "Socket" Toomey, the hipster of the bunch; Ben Wa, the Oriental fighter ace and Mike Fitzgerald, the fighter pilot/soldier turned millionaire-entrepreneur. Also there was Captain "Crunch" O'Malley and Captain Elvis Q of the Ace Wrecking Company; Major Frost of the Free Canadian Air Force; Major Douglas Shane of the elite Football City Special Forces and Colonel Ken Stagg of the New York Hercules Heavy Air Lift Corporation — "New York Hercs" for short. Each man had played a crucial part in the liberation of the eastern half of the country from the Soviet-backed Circle forces, and especially during the climactic battle for Washington, DC.

Still as Hunter looked around the room at his friends and

allies, he couldn't help but feel a certain presence was missing: Captain John "Bull" Dozer, the valiant leader of the famous US Marine "7th Cavalry," was no longer with them. The man had died bravely during a major battle between the United Americans and The Circle at the Washington Monument. In his stead was Dozer's longtime second-in-command, Captain Lamont Johnson. Known as "Catfish" to his friends, Johnson was a mean-looking six-foot-seven black man who once played defensive end for the San Diego Chargers of the old NFL.

"So what are our options?" Jones asked, throwing out the question for discussion. "I mean, the good news is that the Canal is in working order. The bad news is there's a bunch of hobnails running it."

"I don't think we have more than one or two choices," Ben Wa said. "We certainly can't do business with these Canal guys, not with the information we have on them now."

"Stomp 'em," J.T. kicked in, adjusting his ever-present sunglasses. "Lay an air strike on the bastards . . ."

"We've got to know a lot more about them before we do that," Jones said, slightly scolding the somewhat impulsive fighter pilot.

"Sure do," Frost said. "An air strike might knock out their operations for a while, but that doesn't mean they're going to turn tail and run and never come back."

"Also an air strike might damage the locks or the Canal itself," Stagg added. "Then we'd be kicking our own ass."

"It seems to me that any airstrike would have to be followed up by some kind of ground operation," Catfish said. "I mean, not only do we have to grease these guys, we also got to get control of the Canal."

"And learn how to work it," Frost said.

"Okay," Jones said, tapping his pen on the meeting table. "We're already talking about a major operation here. Air strikes, a ground invasion, then occupying *and* operating the Canal ourselves. Those are all tall orders . . ."

"But they have to be done, General," Tyler said, speaking for the first time. "We can fly all the air convoys we want from the West Coast to the East, but they'll never be able to move enough supplies for us to even consider a realistic reconstruction program. We need an open water route."

"What we need first is *intelligence*," Hunter said. "What is their strength? In men? In equipment? Do they have SAMs? Do they have aircraft?"

Crunch spoke up. "That's our department," he said, nodding to his partner, Elvis. "You all know one of our Phantoms is now in a recon mode. It's high time we flew down there anyhow. We can take more pictures of that place in one day than anyone has taken in a hundred years."

"That's true," Jones said. "But these guys don't strike me as our usual ass-backwards type of opponent. They sound slick. Organized . . ."

"*Committed* . . ." Hunter added. "Committed to a cause of some sort. They're heavy into gold, but I also get the feeling that it's just the fuel for some kind of fire. Like a weird political type of thing."

"You mean like left-wingers? Or right-wingers?" Tyler asked.

"I mean like *fanatics*," Hunter answered. "It's just a hunch. But I saw those guys who shot at Pegg crunch those cyanide capsules. Well, let's face it, that's fanatical behavior."

Everyone around the table nodded almost at once.

Hunter continued. "So, if we go flying around down there, believe me, these cats will catch on very quickly that something is up. And, I'm sure, just like those guys greased themselves, the people in charge will do something drastic."

"Well, dammit, we're back at square one," JT snarled.

"Which is where we should be," Jones said authoritatively. "Our successes in the past haven't come because of any advantages in manpower or equipment. They've come because we use our heads and think things out. No sense in changing that now . . ."

Everyone took a swig of whatever they were drinking and stole a deep breath.

"Phase one is always gathering intelligence," Jones began again. "And in this case, I agree, that recon overflights would be premature at this point. We've got to get a man in on the ground down there and get the big picture."

"I'm going," Hunter said immediately.

There was no need for discussion, no reason for argument. It was a foregone conclusion; everyone in the room knew that the dangerous job would fall to The Wingman.

The only question Jones had was: "How?"

Hunter shrugged. "If the Hercs can drop me in," he said, making it up as he went along. "I'll snoop around. When I've seen enough, I'll call and someone gets me out."

"Feel like lugging a mini-cam with you?" Crunch asked. "It's a small one—hold it in one hand. Lightweight. Good on batteries."

"That's a good idea," Jones said, making a few notes. "I think if you could, getting good video would help us on this one . . ."

"Sure, why not?" Hunter said. He planned on traveling light anyway. Carrying a small camera would be no big deal.

Jones closed his notebook, an indication that the meeting was over. "Work up your plan, Hawk," he said. "Get together with your support guys. You and I will talk it over one more time and then I suggest you jump off as soon as possible."

Chapter 9

Eighteen hours later, Hunter was strapped into one of the jump seats in the back of a New York Herc C-130 cargo plane.

"About another hour, Major," one of the crewmen called back to him from the cockpit. "Holler if you need help suiting up."

Hunter stood up and began the long process of getting ready to jump out of a moving airplane. First he fastened on his main and auxiliary parachutes. Then he checked his front and rear knapsacks—they contained everything from water purification tablets to a small, hand-held SAM pistol of his own design. Next came his utility belt and holster, his NightScope goggles, his M-16 and finally, his flight helmet.

"Forty-five minutes . . ." came a call from the cockpit.

Hunter routinely rechecked his map, lining up the topography on the paper with the terrain outside the C-130's small window. He was heartened to see that they were right on course, a credit to the '130 pilot. The New York Hercs were a great team—the best in cargo lift he'd ever seen. And they were, to a man, just as committed to the causes of freedom and the reunification of America as Hunter or any of the other United Americans. In other words, they were his kind of people.

The trip down to Central America had been eventless. The Herc took off from DC at sunrise the morning after the planning session. Fighter escort was provided by two Football City F-20 Tigersharks, hot-shit aircraft that were legitimately the best in the world next to Hunter's own F-16XL. The small convoy stopped for refueling in Football City itself, then again in Dallas. In addition, they all took on additional gas during a mid-air refueling session over the Caribbean about an hour ago, courtesy of the Texas Air Force.

So now it was dark and they had just passed over the eastern coastline of what used to be Costa Rica, but was now known simply as Big Banana. Now for the first time he could see Panama. His designated drop zone was just over the edge of the Mosquito Gulf, about 10 miles from the "eastern" Atlantic-side entrance to the Canal. More accurately, it was the *northern* entrance as the Canal, as Panama itself, actually ran more north to south than east to west. Further complicating things was that due to Panama's crooked elbow shape, the Pacific entrance was actually more to the east than the Atlantic side.

But geography aside, Hunter planned to set down as close to the shoreline as possible, then hoof it to the Canal.

Time passed. Hunter felt the C-130 start to descend slowly.

"Twenty minutes, Major," the Herc crewman called back.

Hunter took a succession of deep breaths and rechecked his two parachute harnesses. He decided to review his plan once again, but found his thoughts drifting back to the night before, when he and most of the United American allies attended a football match at RFK Stadium between a Football City All-Star team and a pro team from San Antonio, Republic of Texas. It was one of the first of many exhibition games that had been scheduled around the continent as another means of solidifying and unifying the United American cause.

The game was a good one—the Texans won in OT, 48-46. Hunter and his friends had had great seats, near the fifty yard line. But still, the pilot's mind hadn't been on the game for all four quarters.

He had sat beside Major Frost and after a few beers, the conversation came around to Dominique.

Hunter told the Canadian the latest on his beautiful girlfriend, how she had somehow hooked on with a group of prominent Canadians and was now on an isolated retreat in the Canadian Rockies. Although Frost wasn't familiar with the particular people Dominique had fallen in with, he was aware of similar "human encounter" groups that were springing up in Free Canada.

"Some of them are quite innocent," the Canadian had told him. "They are little more than social clubs. But others are quickly attaining cult status. Not quite along the line of America's cults of the sixties and seventies, but not that far away either . . ."

"I've never really known Dominique to be a 'joiner,' " Hunter had told Frost.

He remembered the worried look that came over the Canadian at that moment. "These groups apparently are especially attractive to people *just* like that," he had explained. "People who are isolated. People who are having problems adjusting to this crazy world . . ."

Hunter then posed a question he wished he hadn't. "Just what do these people do on retreat?" he asked.

Again, Frost admitted he knew little about it all, but because Hunter was his friend and he believed in telling it like it is, he told the fighter pilot that some of the groups practiced "open living."

"Fairly open sex, is a better term for it," Frost explained. "All very safe, of course. But it's an encouragement to share everything—apparently including your bed—anytime, with anyone you want . . ."

It was those last three words that had stuck in Hunter's mind. *"Anyone you want . . ."*

Hunter and Frost had finished the conversation with a handshake and a promise from the Canadian to look into the particular group Dominique had joined.

"Five minutes, Major Hunter," came the call, effectively breaking into Hunter's daydream.

He took a deep breath and rechecked all his equipment one more time, thankful that he had something else to dwell on. He reached up to his left chest pocket and felt the folds of the small U.S. flag he always kept there. Wrapped inside the Stars and Strips was a picture of Dominique. He patted the bulge three times; whenever he was about to embark on a dangerous or critical mission, he always took the time to concentrate on what the two items in his pocket meant to him. They represented the two most important loves in his life: his country and his woman. Many times he had vowed to fight — to the death if necessary — to protect either one, or both.

It was a vow he made once again . . .

"One minute, Major!" came the cry from the crewman. The Herc crewman walked back and helped Hunter hook up and move to the jump door, checking his equipment one last time.

"Thirty seconds . . ." called a voice over the nearby intercom.

"All set, sir?" the crewman asked him.

Hunter nodded. "Ready as I'll ever be," he said.

The intercom crackled again: "Ten . . . nine . . . eight . . ."

"Good luck, sir," the crewman told him.

They shook hands, Hunter tapped his pocket once more for luck, and on the count of "three . . . two . . . one!" he stepped out of the C-130's door and into the deep black sky.

The air was hot and dry, but Hunter found the breeze at 6500 feet somewhat refreshing. His descent was intentionally leisurely — the more time with which he could scope out any and all possible landing sites. He retrieved his map and using a penlight, checked it once again. It told him that a small clearing about a half mile from a cove looked to be an ideal landing spot. Flipping down his NightScope glasses, he spotted the small field without too much trouble. He instantly calculated his altitude and descent speed against the speed of the wind then pulled and tugged on his chute lines a half dozen times, getting himself into the proper alignment to spiral down to his designated bull's-eye.

Planning, planning and more planning . . .

That's what made operations like this one work, Hunter thought as he slowly drifted down past 5000 feet. Cover all the bases, check and recheck your initial information, determine your alternatives, compute the risks and then, go to it . . .

As Jones had said, that's what had made the United Americans so successful in the past. No sense in changing it now.

As he passed 2500 feet, Hunter couldn't help but feel a rush of pride run through him. There was no sense in denying that his input and actions were responsible for a good part of the success of the American democratic forces. He knew when things got rough, people just naturally looked to him for the solutions. And why not? Just as the big fat slob LaFeet had said, Hunter was famous — a well-known personality in the post-World War III landscape. His face was as recognizable overseas as in America and the stories of his exploits — most of them true, a few of them exaggerated — were recounted all over the world. He was as close to being a comic book super-hero as humanly possible — and he knew that in times of crisis, people seek heroes.

And now here he was, dropping in on a pitch black jungle forest to scope out yet another enemy that threatened the stability of the still-fragile American continental unity. He already knew the script: he would land safely, walk to the Canal, get some valuable video pictures, return to Washington and plan the operation which would punch out the clowns who were running things in the Canal Zone these days. Then the critical water route would be open, the East Coast would get its much needed supplies and the long-awaited American Reconstruction could begin.

72

He hit the ground running several minutes later, circling down onto the clearing with natural aerial aplomb. He took a too-quick scan around and started to gather up his chute.

Just another day at the office, he thought.

That's when he looked up and saw no less than a dozen M-16 barrels staring him right in the face . . .

Chapter 10

Colonel Hanz Frankel took a handful of cool water and splashed it into his face.

It was hot. *Damn* hot. Already 87 degrees and the sun had only been up for two hours.

"God, how I hate this weather," Frankel said to his aide-de-camp. "Give me the coolness of the *Swabian Jura* any day."

His aide, a captain named Rolfe, nodded as he too dipped his hands into the bucket of ice water the two men were sharing. They were sitting on the porch of a rundown villa, looking out on the tiny harbor which made up one side of the small island called Las Perlas. To their backs, four miles away, was the Pacific entrance to the Panama Canal. In front of them, anchored about a half mile offshore, were two ships: a small freighter flying North Korean colors and an ocean ferry sailing from what used to be Timor, now known as the Sunset Islands. As many as a dozen smaller attack craft were buzzing around the two ships. All the while, a large, Italian-built attack cruiser of the *Veneto*-class was slowly moving back and forth near the entrance to the harbor, keeping a suspicious eye on both vessels.

It was only recently that Frankel's commanders had decided for him to set up shop on the island, having outgrown their old "trap them in the Canal" strategy. Now it was up to Frankel and his small army of soldiers and sailors to act as sentinels for the Canal entrance. He was the High Command's gatekeeper, so to speak,—the one who decided what ships could pass and what ships could not. And no matter what his decision, he was backed up by the large battle cruiser prowling the sea lanes close to the island, as well as the thousands of troops occupying the Canal itself.

Frankel and Rolfe watched as one of their attack craft sped to shore and tied up at a nearby dock. An officer jumped out of the boat and double-timed it up to the villa. Out of breath and sweating, the officer handed two documents to Rolfe, saluted and ran back to to his craft.

"The Koreans claim they are carrying three tons of uncut poppy paste from Burma," Rolfe said, reading the first document. "They've been out two weeks and say they are heading for a processing plant in Cuba."

Frankel rubbed his eyes and splashed more water on his face. His heavy, bulky uniform was causing him to chafe around the neck and shoulders.

"Is their vessel armed?" he asked, dabbing his brow with a damp cloth.

Rolfe flipped over two pages in the document, which was actually a collection of notes made by his men while interrogating the freighter's captain just minutes before.

"Yes," Rolfe answered. "Two 20-millimeter anti-aircraft guns fore and aft. Two Chinese anti-shipping missile launchers amidships."

"And they are carrying gold?" Frankel asked.

"Our men saw at least three hundred and fifty bags in the captain's safe, sir," Rolfe replied.

Frankel pulled on his scruffy beard in thought.

"All right," he said finally. "Confiscate one of the missile launchers and collect all the gold. Then let them pass. Next . . ."

Rolfe turned to the other report. "Free-lancers out of the Sunset Islands," he said. "Claim they are on their way to San Juan to exchange female slaves for a load of cocaine and milk sugar . . ."

"And there are women on board?" Frankel asked, raising his binoculars to get a closer look at the ocean ferry.

"Our men saw at least a hundred," Rolfe replied. "Mostly Oriental, but some whites."

"How old?"

Rolfe flipped another page of the report. "Teenagers, young twenties, our men estimate," he said.

Frankel shook off a thrill that involuntarily ran through him. It was only recently that he had partaken in the sex-with-teenage-girls fad that seemed to be sweeping the globe.

"It's a dangerous journey from the Sunsets to San Juan," he observed, still watching the flat, squat ferry. "What are they carrying for arms?"

Rolfe quick-studied each page of the report. "Our men didn't find any large weapons," he concluded. "Just a couple fifty-caliber heavies, and a few RPGs."

Frankel snorted a sinister laugh. "Sailing across the Pacific without deck weapons?" he said. "And heading for San Juan? I must assume these men are fools."

"They are not carrying any gold either, my colonel," Rolfe added, he, too, fighting down a jolt of excitement.

Frankel lowered his spyglasses and mopped his brow again. "Then they *are* fools," he declared. "Or liars. Such people must be made an example of . . ."

Rolfe waited a few moments, then asked: "Your orders, Colonel?"

Frankel closed his eyes in thought, then said: "Confiscate the females and check the crew for gold fillings. Then you know what to do from there."

Rolfe couldn't suppress giving his superior a salute. "*Yes*, my colonel," he cried out, bursting with enthusiasm. His day was made. "And, do you wish to . . . review the females personally?"

Frankel leaned back in his chair, placing his high leather boots up on the villa's railing and putting a damp cloth across his forehead. He closed his eyes and wished for just the slightest of breezes.

"Of course, I do," he said nonchalantly.

Thirty minutes later, the North Korean freighter raised its anchor and sailed toward the entrance to the canal, less one missile launcher and 350 bags of gold. After another half hour, the ocean ferry was also permitted to sail out of the small harbor—but only as far as the deep water.

"Are you in position?" Rolfe asked into the radio microphone, watching as the ferry made for the open sea.

"We are," came the reply from the second-in-command of the Italian attack cruiser, which was now also turning slowly out of the harbor entrance.

"Then do it," Rolfe said, his voice almost giddy.

No sooner had he spoken when the cruiser opened up with its two large foredeck guns. Two huge shells came crashing down close by the ferry's midsection, near-misses but devastating nevertheless.

"Fire again!" Rolfe ordered into the radio.

"Yes, sir," came the reply.

Three seconds later the big guns opened up again. This time the shells ran true. One smashed right into the fleeing vessel's wheelhouse, another caught its bow.

"Once again!" Rolfe called out.

For a third time the big guns spoke, delivering two direct hits on the ferry's midships. The vessel immediately capsized, its decks awash in fire and smoke.

"Good work!" Rolfe called into the radio, his excitement so acute he felt a stream of warm body fluid run down his leg. "If you wish, you may close in on the wreckage and shoot any survivors . . ."

Chapter 11

"No way is this guy Hawk Hunter . . ." the soldier in the green camouflage poncho said. "I have it on good authority that Hunter was killed over in Saudi Arabia last year."

The man he was talking to, a jungle fighter named Dantini, shrugged.

"Hey, I heard the same stories," Dantini said, working his way through the noontime meal of corn mush and tomatoes. "But why would some guy come floating down on our turf and claim he was Hunter? He'd have to be a complete idiot to think he'd get away with it."

The man in the poncho, a lieutenant named Burke, threw the remnants of his lunch back into the campfire and wiped his mouth with his sleeve.

"Well, how about those crazy bullshit stories he's been telling us, Major?" Burke said.

"Like what?" Dantini asked, washing down his meal with a swig from his canteen.

"Like the British actually stopped Lucifer's fleet at Suez? With just *one* aircraft carrier?" Burke said in a sarcastic tone.

Dantini stretched out and undid the laces on his jungle boots. "He didn't say they *stopped* the fleet with one aircraft carrier," he told Burke. "He said they fought a delaying action in Suez until help arrived . . ."

Burke laughed. "Yeah, right," he said. "And if you believe that one, you must believe that he and his boys kicked ass on The Circle, too."

Dantini reluctantly nodded. "Well, that one *is* a little hard to swallow," he said. "But, look at it this way: How would we know either way? We've been down in this Goddamn jungle for almost two years straight. For all we know, *anything* could have happened up there . . ."

Burke shook his head in frustration. About a dozen other soldiers in the 100-man helicopter assault company had finished their meal and had gathered around to listen in on the discussion.

"Look, Major," Burke said, leaning forward to make his point. "First, the guy claims he's the famous Hawk Hunter. Then he tells us that the Russians hauled all these SAMs into the Badlands, but that he and his merry band beat them anyway. *Then,* he says he and these Brits tow — *tow!* — a motherfucking aircraft carrier across the Med and used it to beat Lucifer, who only raised the largest Goddamn army on the globe.

"And then, he says he flew back, and he and his gang not only knock off The Circle, and The Family, but they recapture all the territory east of the Mississippi, too?

"I mean, you've got to admit sir, that's really stretching it . . ."

Dantini was almost too tired to play devil's advocate. He and the company had been on the move for two days straight and he was beat. He didn't want to get involved in a prolonged discussion with Burke, who, besides being an exceptional fighter, was also an expert debater.

But they *did* have a prisoner on their hands and he *was* claiming to be the famous Hawk Hunter. The man seemed to be a straight shooter and didn't hesitate a micro-second in telling them about the supposed string of victories he and his allies had pulled off against Lucifer, the Soviets and The Circle. Still, Dantini was skeptical, as would anyone who had been out of touch with North America since right after the original Battle for Football City.

"Okay," he said to Burke. "Let's go at it from another angle. Do you know what Hawk Hunter actually *looks* like?"

Burke had to think for a moment. "Just from photographs," he said finally. "Newspaper pictures and so on."

Dantini turned around to the 25 or so troopers who were listening in. "Anyone here ever see Hawk Hunter in the flesh?"

To a man, the troopers shook their heads.

"Well, I don't know what he looks like either," Dantini said. "Yet, that guy was almost certain that we'd recognize him. I mean, if he's lying, he's *damn* good at it."

"But, sir," Burke said, taking a different tack. "If those creeps down in the Canal Zone wanted to keep tabs on us, say as part of some really way-out plan, do you think it's beyond their abilities to plant someone here who could claim he was the famous Hawk Hunter? I mean, just in the time we've been fighting them, look at the resources they've come up with. They're experts in psych-war — as good as the Russians or even better."

Dantini removed his jungle hat and took another swig from his canteen. "But turn that argument around," he countered. "Why would they go through all the trouble of dropping someone in here who just *claimed* to be Hawk Hunter? They must know that we'd be, at least, suspicious, right? Do you think that *they* think we're so dumb as to greet with open arms someone *impersonating* Hawk Hunter?"

Burke had to shrug. "Well, that's a good point," he conceded. He thought a minute, then added: "So what you're saying, sir, is that the guy locked in that tent over there is *actually* Hawk Hunter?"

Dantini shook his head slowly and looked over at the sealed-up tent. "I just don't know . . ." he said finally.

Chapter 12

One thousand miles to the north, in the midst of the Mexican Yucatan peninsula, another noon meal was ending.

But far from corn mush and sun-dried tomatoes, the revelers were eating steak and drinking exquisite Bulgarian wine. They sat at a finely set table, complete with linen cloth and napkins, finger bowls, silver utensils and goblets. Three large candelabras adorned the table for 20, although the sharp Yucatan breeze made it impossible for their wicks to stay lit.

This was not a typical setting for the men working nearby. The elaborate arrangements were set in place to honor a visit from an emissary of the High Commander. Work at the remote Yucatan site — a collection of ancient Mayan ruins called Chichen Itza — had been proceeding ahead of schedule and reaping benefits beyond anyone's expectations. Thus the visit from one of the High Commander's men.

"It gets this hot everyday?" the emissary, Adoph Udet, asked, downing a mouthful of steak with a half a glass of wine.

"Yes, my general," the newly-appointed man in charge of the site work, a colonel named Krupp, responded. "Our heat peaks around mid-afternoon. The nights are pleasantly cool, though I can assure you . . ."

Udet wiped his mouth and pushed his empty plate away from him. "Well, I'll take your word for it, Colonel," he said, barely suppressing a burp. "I must leave well before sundown."

Krupp wasn't surprised to hear that; this area of the Yucatan peninsula simply wasn't safe after sundown. Krupp looked down the length of the table at his staff—captains and majors, young men all. And a glance around the clearing, which sat in the shadow of Chichen Itza's largest excavated pyramid, reassured him that more than 100 of his best troopers were on guard duty at the moment. What bothered him was that he had to double that number when night fell . . .

"A fine feed," Udet said, lighting his pipe, "in a very adventurous setting."

He turned and checked to see that his own entourage of guards—three squads of black-shirted special forces troops—was still close by. Only that the mysterious High Commander, a man Udet had never actually met, ordered him had he dared to chopper into this remote hell hole to recognize the work of a low-level officer such as Krupp.

But even a callous officer such as Udet had to admit that Krupp had taken over this command under very difficult and mysterious circumstances. One month before, the original commander of this co-called "recovery" mission, a veteran lieutenant general named Heinke, had simply disappeared—vanished at dusk one night while walking his perimeter. His aide-de-camp and several other officers swear that the man was there one moment and gone the next. Intensive searches found nothing. By design Krupp, who was Heinke's second-in-command, was well schooled in Mayan archaeology. He was named commander of the mission three days later.

But there was a limit to everything including the heaping of praise. Udet nodded to one of his aides, who in turn ran back and spoke to the pilots of the three Hind helicopters that were waiting nearby. Seconds later, the whine of the chopper's electro-static starters began to permeate the air. Krupp had been congratulated enough. The visit was rapidly drawing to a close.

"Our leader is well pleased with you and your men's work," Udet said, reciting the words from a small card provided to him by yet another aide. "Your discoveries here were well beyond what was expected of you, especially under your somewhat unusual circumstances. Through your efforts, our cause will be much enriched."

Krupp bowed his head gracefully. He knew the short speech was prepared well in advance and most of it given to any number of successful commanders out in the field such as he. Still, it never hurt to receive accolades — stale as they may be — from a man so close to the High Commander.

"I thank you and my men thank you," Krupp said, reciting a short speech of his own. "Even in these less-than-ideal conditions, our efforts and work bring us great pleasure, as we know the High Commander and our people will benefit. As always, you honor us with your presence."

On cue, the officers seated at the table broke into a brief round of applause.

The meeting over, Udet stood and gave a wooden wave to the officers. As one, Krupp's staff stood and snapped to attention. One long salute from Udet and then the man turned on his hob-nailed heel and made for his Hind helicopter, his small army of bodyguards surrounding him in a human phalanx.

As he watched the chopper's blades start to whirl and half of Udet's special forces troops squeeze into the big Soviet-built chopper, Krupp felt a tug on his elbow. It was one of Udet's entourage, a man named Strauberg.

"You have the summary list?" he asked sternly.

At that moment, Udet's helicopter lifted off and headed south back towards Panama. From then on, Krupp knew the formalities of the visit had ended.

"Yes, I do," he answered.

"And the shipment? It is ready?" Strauberg asked impatiently.

"Again, yes," Krupp said. "Do you plan to take it with you now?"

Strauberg, a small unpleasant man, screwed up his face

until it was rat-like. "Of course!" he hissed. "After all, that was the purpose of our trip here."

Krupp knew that Strauberg had intentionally launched the verbal jab at him The little man had "the fever" — military protocol meant nothing to him.

Thirty minutes later, Krupp's men completed loading a half dozen wooden crates onto one of the two remaining Hinds. Inside the hold of the copter, Strauberg was taking a frenzied inventory.

"Eighteen bars, four chalices, four plates and a necklace measuring two feet in length," he said, ticking off the items before him and checking them against Krupp's summary list. "Three hundred and fifty coins and one statuette. It is all here . . ."

Standing beside the ratty little man of undetermined rank, Krupp breathed a sigh of relief. He couldn't imagine what would happen to him should any of the pieces be missing.

"That's nearly a month's work," he told Strauberg. "I hope it is handled with care."

Strauberg's little face turned red with anger. "Are you suggesting that I would actually mistreat this shipment?" he asked defiantly.

"Not at all," Krupp said quickly. "I beg your pardon if you misunderstood me . . ."

Strauberg looked at Krupp with a murderous gleam in his eye. "Is the woman still reluctant in cooperating?" he asked Krupp, changing the subject somewhat.

"Yes, she is," Krupp answered. "And she is increasingly growing weak from the repeated injections."

"Just keep her breathing," Strauberg said. "We have only a few more sites to go. Then, she can be disposed of."

Now it was Krupp's eyes that grew narrow with anger. He believed that little more than a piece of cheese and a strong metal spring would be needed to dispose of the disgusting little man before him.

Strauberg folded the summary list and tucked it inside

his shirt, then signaled the Hind's pilot to start his engines. Krupp could tell that Strauberg hadn't bathed in a long time, a situation excusable if the man were actually out in the field like Krupp and his troops. But Strauberg's downright smelly demeanor was a disgrace especially because the man was assigned to comfortable and clean lodging back in Panama City.

It was another symptom of the fever, Krupp thought. Strauberg had forsaken a bar of soap for a bar of gold . . .

Chapter 13

Hunter carefully removed the splinter from the back of his hand and wished his stomach would stop growling.

He was mad at himself for being so foolish, so cocky. The smugness that he treated himself to during his parachute descent was quickly cured when he dropped right into the hands of the helicopter troops. But when his recounting of the recent events in continental North America was met with only blank stares and even a few derisive laughs, he knew it was Fate punishing him for letting his ego inflate so — albeit for a short time.

Now he was sitting on the thick branch of a huge, rickety jungle tree of some kind, picking splinters out of his hands and elbows and keeping an eye on the chopper force's campground at the same time. Escaping from the sealed-off tent had been easy. Climbing the tall tree nearby had been more difficult. It was dried out and dying and some of its branches tended to disintegrate under his weight as he scampered up. But it gave him a great vantage point of his would-be captors, people he didn't exactly consider his enemies.

What fascinated him most about the chopper troops was their equipment.

From his perch, Hunter counted nine large helicopters in the clearing, with several more, smaller rotary aircraft in a gulley about a quarter mile beyond. Of the nine big ones near him, five were CH-47 Chinooks, venerable choppers that had been around since the 1950s. Sometimes described as a "flying sausage," the Chinook employed two large front and rear rotors and in some later models, turbo-jet engines, to lift its long, tube-like frame. The Chinook had many uses: it could carry up to 44 troops and therefore could be employed as an assault aircraft. It could carry more than 10 tons of equipment, due to its powerful engines, and so had a history as a resupply aircraft. And it was a rugged bird, able to take a lot of abuse from weather, wind and salt water spray, so it had been employed for years by the US Marines aboard their amphibious assault ships.

But this was the first time Hunter had ever seen Chinooks outfitted as gunships.

He did a double take when he first noticed the gun muzzles protruding from both sides of the Chinooks. Yet close inspection confirmed that the chopper troops had outrigged both sides of their CH-47s with heavy guns — everything from .50-caliber machine guns to what looked to Hunter to be small howitzers. They had also installed guns in the nose, belly and rear of the Chinooks.

"Mini-Flying Fortresses," was the term first came to Hunter's mind, thinking back to the famous, gun-studded B-17 bombers of World War II.

But if some ingenuity had been used in outfitting the Chinooks, then a touch of mad scientist had been applied to the two CH-54 Skycranes in the chopper team's possession.

The Skycrane was aptly nicknamed. When unloaded, the bird looked like a large chopper that had somehow lost its mid-section. In reality, the aircraft was simply an engine and tail rotor connected to a cockpit. With this "skeletal form" and its four, wide-out wheel assemblies, the chopper had a definite giant bug-like appearance. The beauty of the Skycrane was that it could lift just about anything — 20 tons worth — that fit inside or underneath its "missing space." Cargo containers, fuel bladders, trucks, jeeps, even other helicopters, the Skycrane could pick them up and set them down better than anything flying in the Free World.

It also came equipped with a "purpose-designed container," a box about the size of a small railroad car that could fit snugly into the 'Crane's lift and carry area. From his vantage point, Hunter could see that the chopper team had lined up six of these PDCs alongside their landing area. It appeared as if each one had a separate purpose. One was cut through with gun ports, another appeared to be a missile launching platform. Still another looked like it was used for carrying troops, and a fourth was outfitted with various radar, infrared and, so it appeared, AM/FM radio broadcasting antennas. The two remaining PDCs were heavily camouflaged and fairly hidden away, so he couldn't determine their specifics. But his intuition told him they leaned to the more outrageous duties.

Rounding out the team of nine big choppers were two, French-built *Aerospatiale* Super Frelon naval helicopters. About the same size and shape as a CH-53 Sea Stallion, the Super Frelons had been used by the French Navy for years as antisubmarine aircraft. In addition to its long range and record of durability, the Super Frelons also carried a nasty sting: many were able to carry and launch the much-dreaded Exocet antishipping missile. And sure enough, Hunter could see two Exocets hanging underneath both of the Frelons in front of him.

It took him a few minutes to process all this information. He couldn't help thinking just what the Cobra Brothers would have thought about all this chopper madness. Still he had come to a reasonable conclusion: Despite his rude greeting and capture, he had to admit that he liked the chopper troops' style. They had obviously come upon the mostly cargo-carrying fleet of helicopters and had adapted them nicely for attack duties. This showed Hunter a great amount of initiative, a talent not usually found among the scumbucket armies of the crazy New Order world.

But just how the chopper team used all their firepower was another question entirely. And Hunter's gut reaction told him that he'd better find out.

Lieutenant Burke led the six-man search team back into camp, hot, sweaty and exhausted.

Burke told his troops to stand down and get something to

ea:. It would be dark soon and he was sure Major Dantini would want to dispatch yet another search party to look for the escaped prisoner.

Burke unstrapped his pack and rifle and went to Dantini's command tent, where he found the officer poring over maps of the Canal Zone as usual.

"Any sign of him?" Dantini asked his junior officer. The dejected look on Burke's face already provided the answer.

"Nothing," Burke confirmed. "It's like the guy just disappeared . . ."

Dantini shook his head and took a sip from the glass of tequila in front of him.

"Jesus, the guy somehow gets out of a sealed-up tent in record time, then melts into the jungle like he was The Phantom or someone," he said, feeling the welcome sting of the hard liquor going down his throat. "Maybe he *was* Hawk Hunter . . ."

Burke sat down on the tent's cot and rubbed his tired eyes. "I'll organize a night patrol," he said wearily. "We'll sweep the ridges up north again, then double back along the beach."

"That won't be necessary," a third voice said suddenly.

Burke looked up to see a man standing behind Dantini, pointing a gun in the general direction of the major's head.

It was the escaped prisoner.

"How . . . how the hell did you get in here?" Burke blurted out. It was as if the man had simply materialized out of thin air.

"Trick of the trade," Hunter said, lowering the gun slightly, causing Dantini to breathe a sigh of relief.

For an instant, Burke wished he had carried his own gun into the tent with him. But in his next thought, he doubted whether he would have actually used it on the prisoner.

"What do you want?" Dantini asked, still not daring to turn around.

"I want to get down to the facts," Hunter answered quickly. "I don't believe we're enemies. So, I suggest we just call a two-minute truce here and talk. Okay?"

Dantini thought it over and eyed Burke. They both nodded in agreement. With that, Hunter walked out from behind Dantini and stood between them.

"What will it take for me to convince you guys that I am who I say I am?" he asked them, a slight hint of exasperation in his voice. "I mean, I *really* am Major Hawk Hunter, formerly of the US Air Force; formerly of the Thunderbirds. More recently I've flown for the Pacific American Air Corps and now the United American Air Force . . ."

Dantini managed to take another gulp of his tequila. "Okay, let's say you *are* Hawk Hunter," he said. "What are you doing here, dropping in on a bunch of chopper dinks like us?"

"I had no idea you guys were down here?" Hunter said in all honesty, again feeling the pang of his own misjudgment in selecting a landing zone. "I was dropping in to do some recon on the people who are now running the Canal."

Dantini's left eyebrow immediately went up in a sign of interest.

"You're here to spy on The Cross?" he asked.

"Cross?" Hunter asked. "Is that the name of the gang occupying the canal?"

Dantini grew suspicious once again. "Yeah, 'The Twisted Cross,' to be exact," he said, his eyes narrowing. "It would seem that someone like Hawk Hunter would know that . . ."

Hunter had to agree. "You got me there," he said, managing a grin. "But believe me, just like you guys ain't exactly up on what's going on in North America, we're in the dark as to what the hell is going on down here. It isn't as if you can just pick up a newspaper these days."

"And they sent you down here to find out?" Burke asked skeptically. "Seems like a lousy job for a big shot like yourself . . ."

Hunter grew a bit angry at the man. "Well, now I see you guys *are* out of touch," he said. "In my organization — the United American Army — there are no 'big shots.' Everyone pitches in. Everyone has input, whether he's a rifleman or a general or the guy who cleans the pots. Sure, there are officers and there are enlisted men. But rank isn't an excuse to turn down a mission.

"I was chosen for this recon because I'm pretty good at sneaking in and out. Simple as that . . ."

Dantini laughed. "Well, judging by the way you dropped in on us, I think you should do a little more work on the 'sneaking in' part."

"Okay," Hunter said smartly. "And someday, I'll tell you how I got into your tent . . ."

The comment zapped both men. It still appeared to both of them that Hunter used other-worldly means to appear in the tent.

"Besides," he continued, "I'd like to think that my dropping in on you was actually a good omen. A meaningful coincidence . . ."

"How so?" Dantini asked.

Hunter shrugged. "I think we can work together," he answered. "It doesn't take a genius to figure out you guys are going up against this Twisted Cross gang. Well, so am I. And, if the info I bring back with me warrants it, and I'm sure it will, the entire resources of the United American Army will be up against them too."

"Now this is sounding serious," Dantini said.

"It *is* serious," Hunter replied. He then took the next five minutes telling the two men about his encounter with Captain Pegg, the assassination attempt on the old man and their interrogation of Jean LaFeet, the world's biggest slimeball.

"You guys are obviously North Americans," Hunter concluded. "You've got to appreciate the fact that the Canal has to be in friendly hands for us to keep the continent together, and keep the frigging Sovs and their shithead allies out . . ."

Dantini rubbed his three-day growth of beard.

"Well, our goals aren't as lofty," he said. "I mean, we're just hired help down here."

"Hired by whom?" Hunter asked.

"A bunch of local landowners and business men, both here in Panama and in Big Banana," Dantini said, pouring out another glass of tequila for himself. "Let me start at the beginning. Most of us are ex-US military — some of us are Army, some Marines. We were doing duty in the Canal

Zone when the Big War broke out. Like a lot people, we were stranded for a while, then, when the New Order went down, we just didn't feel right, returning to America.

"We had three choppers, so we started hiring out as a land convoy protection service. Down here the birds come in handy when the guys driving the convoy trucks have no idea what's around the next bend. We made some money, bought new equipment, bought more choppers and expanded the business.

"Then about two years ago, the Cross started showing up around the Canal Zone. They hired some Colombian gangs, outfitted them as military units and kicked ass on the various local armies that were based along the Canal . . ."

"So The Twisted Cross didn't do much of the fighting themselves?" Hunter asked.

"That's right," Burke answered him. "They had the Colombians do their dirty work for them. But, get this: as soon as the Canal was in their hands, they turned around and massacred their hired hands. Killed about twenty five hundred Colombian mercs, just like that . . ."

"These guys play rough," Hunter said in classic understatement.

"So did the Colombians, up to that point anyway," Dantini said. "But after they greased those mercs, no one, anywhere in the area, wanted to fuck around with The Cross."

Hunter nodded. He had heard it all before. "They were sending a message," he said.

Both Dantini and Burke agreed. "And it was received down here, loud and clear," Dantini said.

Hunter took a few moments to let it all sink in. The stories of brutality of The Cross by Pegg and now by the chopper team matched up.

"But you guys have gone up against The Cross, right?" Hunter asked.

"Yeah, that's what the locals hired us to do," Dantini confirmed. "But we're just in the beginning stages of something that will take a few years at least. Frankly, we're just harassing them now. Hit and run stuff. We hit them, then we move. They look for us and we hide from them. When the smoke clears, we establish a new base and hit them again."

"It's a vicious cycle," Burke laughed.

"And only sporadically effective," Dantini added.

Hunter was just about to say something when he felt a tingling sensation run down his spine.

"Damn," he whispered. "And you guys don't have any SAMs, do you?"

Both Dantini and Burke were mystified. "What the hell are you talking about?" Dantini asked him.

But Hunter didn't hear him. His equipment, captured when he blundered down into the chopper team's territory, was stacked near the entrance to Dantini's tent. He quickly scooped up one of his knapsacks and was already out of the tent and in the center of the chopper team's campground. Dantini and Burke quickly ran up behind him.

"Aircraft coming!" Hunter said, facing the south. "Four of them . . . Get your people into shelters, now! We've got about five minutes . . ."

Dantini scanned the sky in every direction. "I don't see or hear anything," he said cautiously.

"Trust me," Hunter yelled over his shoulder as he sprinted over to one of the team's choppers.

Chapter 14

Major Jann Hoxter, flight leader for the four F-4 Phantoms, put his airplane into a screaming dive.

Directly ahead of him was the clearing near the beach where a TV-camera equipped recon drone had spotted suspected enemy activity earlier in the day. Careful analysis of the drone's information confirmed that the area was being used by the band of helicopter mercenaries that had been harassing The Twisted Cross for some time.

Finding the enemy chopper unit had been nearly impossible — until now. The exorbitant price paid to a South African arms dealer for the ultra-high tech video drone was now looking like a very good deal indeed. Apparently it had been able to accomplish in two days what the Cross's own intelligence operatives had been trying to do for nearly 18 months . . .

No sooner had the information from the drone been processed when Hoxter's superiors ordered an immediate air strike on the enemy camp. Military sensibilities would have called for dropping anti-personnel bombs on the chopper base, followed up by barrages of air-to-surface missiles. But in this case, the sensibilities were overridden from above. A message had to be sent. Therefore, the cannisters slung under the wings of Hoxter's flight were filled with hundreds of gallons of napalm, the jellied gasoline cocktail that was a favorite signature of the High Command of The Twisted Cross.

While his three charges circled above, Hoxter rolled in on

the suspected target, intending to make one, fast sweep of the area. His prestrike orders were to absolutely confirm enemy troops and equipment in the target zone before bombing—napalm didn't come easy or cheap these days and there was no sense wasting it if the enemy troops were no longer around.

Hoxter's hopes rose when he spotted a line of tents at the edge of the clearing, and next to them, two large Chinook helicopters. Oddly, the place looked deserted—almost as if the enemy troops knew the air strike was coming. This bothered Hoxter as he yanked back on his control stick and gained some altitude. His preflight briefing officers had assured him that the enemy didn't have any kind of early warning radar system. Nor did they have any SAMs.

Rejoining the three other F-4s, they immediately circled the target once more, then split into pairs. Hoxter and his wingman, Frugal, would go in first . . .

"Hang on, Lieutenant," Hoxter called back to his rear-seat weapons officer, a man named Minz, as he again put the green-camouflaged F-4 into a dive. He lined up the crosshairs of his jet's Head's Up Display with the row of tents in the clearing, intent on dropping the first of his two napalm cannisters onto the bivouac.

"Steady," he whispered to himself, his finger twitching on the weapons release button. Already he could envision the line of tents being washed over by a tidal wave of sticky blue flame so intense, it would instantly incinerate anyone hiding inside. The immolation would be the first giant step in eliminating the pesty helicopter troops . . .

Lower and lower he went, the F-4 bucking like a bronco in the murky air just above the dense jungle. "Steady," he whispered once again. In his mind's eye he could already see the flames leaping up from the target, the choking black smoke, the victims engulfed in the napalm running in panic seconds before they died.

"All for the cause," he thought. "All for our glorious leader . . ."

He reached his release altitude, took a deep breath and started to squeeze the trigger.

But suddenly he heard a loud *crash!* directly behind him. At the same instant, his rear seat officer cried out in pain.

Hoxter immediately pulled up and out of the dive, twisting in his seat to look back at Minz. He was stunned to see that the rear part of the two-piece canopy had been blown away and that Minz was practically headless.

"What is this!" he cried out as his section of the cockpit rapidly decompressed. Incredibly, it appeared as if someone had hit them with a small, but extremely accurate, SAM.

It was too late for Hoxter to call off his wingman Frugal from his attack run. The pilot watched as the second-in-line F-4 came in low and slow over the target area. Suddenly Hoxter detected a flash coming from behind a line of trees. An instant later, Frugal's F-4 went up in a ball of fire. It hit the ground sideways, the flaming wreckage cartwheeling through the clearing and out onto the beach. It had happened so incredibly fast! Another small antiaircraft missile had made a direct hit on Frugal's doomed Phantom.

Hoxter was confused and on the verge of panic. The last thing he had expected from the bombing mission was accurate and *effective* groundfire. Someone had screwed up badly; someone in the High Command would be punished. But the flight leader faced more immediate problems. The damage to his own jet was already affecting his flight controls. He knew he had to get back to his base — and fast. Still, he twisted his jet up and over the line of trees where the flash had come from and was astonished to see a Chinook helicopter hovering not more than 20 feet off the ground. He knew in an instant the small SAMs had been fired from the Chinook.

Meanwhile the lead ship pilot of the second pair of F-4s had witnessed what had happened and had also spotted the Chinook.

"How can someone shoot so well?" this pilot radioed over to Hoxter.

But the flight leader had no answer. He briefly considered rolling in on the Chinook, but quickly decided against it. The suddenly death of WSO Minz and the downing of Frugal's F-4 had spooked him.

"Shall we go after the helicopter?" the other F-4 pilot asked him over the radio.

"No . . ." Hoxter answered quickly, trying not to let the panic come through in his voice. "Abort the mission. Return to base immediately . . ."

"Good God, how did you learn to shoot like that?"

Dantini and Burke were simply amazed. They had joined Hunter in the Chinook seconds after he had correctly predicted that an air strike was on the way. The fighter pilot had started the engines himself, gunning their throttles in such a way that the chopper was ready to take off in two minutes, about one-tenth the amount of time it normally needed for lift-off.

Once airborne, Burke had taken over the controls while Hunter and Dantini cranked one of the copter's .50 machine guns out of its port window.

While Burke kept the Chinook steady and hiding behind the line of trees, Hunter retrieved the small SAM pistol from his knapsack. The gun was only about the size of a flare pistol. Its projectiles just five inches long. But packed into their tiny warheads was a mini-ultrasonic detecting device complete with an electronic ear he designed to home in on the high-range frequency sounds put out by the whine of a jet engine's turbine blades. When the pistol was fired, the projectile, which was made of depleted uranium, would seek out the nearest source of the particular high frequency and impact near it. Because of the incendiary properties of the depleted uranium shell, the immediate result of a hit was an instantaneous flash fire, meaning direct hits weren't always necessary. Should the small missile hit the airplane's engine, it would more than likely mortally disable it, but the aircraft could stay airborne at least for a while if a good pilot was behind the controls. However, should the projectile hit something flammable such as a fuel tank — or a cannister of napalm — it would cause it to instantly explode on impact.

As Hunter had only two projectiles with him, he knew

both shots had to count. So the computer in his head started reeling off figures for such things as velocity of the small SAM, the rate of its flight path decay divided by the height of the hovering Chinook, the rate of speed of the F-4s and, most important, the distance between him and the target. When the first jet came in, Hunter had Dantini call off its approach profile, then at precisely the right moment, the Wingman squeezed off one shot. It wobbled a little, but nevertheless smashed through the F-4's canopy.

Just a few scant seconds later, Hunter had reloaded and fired off his other missile at the second attacking airplane. It ran truer, finding the volatile napalm cannister attached to the airplane's portside wing weapons station. A microsecond after striking it, the cannister exploded and obliterated the Phantom.

"How *did* you do that?" Burke asked again, once they had set the Chinook back down. "Those were two, one-in-a-million bullseyes!"

Hunter shrugged. "I majored in Advanced Velocity Physics at college," he said.

Dantini looked at him, then at the burning wreckage of the downed Phantom, then back at Hunter.

"Well, I'm convinced," he said, his hand outstretched. "It's an honor to finally meet the famous Hawk Hunter . . ."

Chapter 15

There was no light at all in this part of the cave.

In the complete darkness, the eyes become useless, subservient to the other senses. The far-off scurrying of some cave rodent is picked up by the ears right away. Same for the flapping wings of a distant bat, returning from a nocturnal search for food.

The tongue tastes the damp moisture of the cavern as if it were strong liquor. The nose detects the odor of smoke, even though the nearest fire is a half mile away and out of the cave.

The tips of the fingers yearn to reach out and touch warm flesh . . .

She had lost track as to just how many days she'd been held prisoner in the cave. With no visual confirmation of the changing of day from sunup to sundown and back again, her existence simply became one long night. There was no need for blindfolds down here. And the single thick strand of rope was enough to keep her in one place. Food was eaten unseen and she couldn't remember what color clothes she was wearing. Deprived of what was once taken for granted, her life had been pared down to the very basics.

She was sure now that Hell was little more than a dark cave . . .

Chapter 16

Colonel Krupp topped off his morning meal of eggs and left-over steak with a large cup of thick, black coffee.

The day had dawned in overcast — at least there'd be no sun beating down on them mercilessly as they broke camp and moved out, the officer thought. He stepped down off the back of his command truck, stretched and took a quick look around the camp.

As usual, the tops of the nearby surrounding hills were being patrolled by the camp guards. Even the pyramid itself had a squad of lookouts perched on top, their half-dozen long-range binoculars continually scanning the nearby countryside. And Krupp knew that in the dense jungle behind the pyramid and beyond the hills, no less than four squads — more than forty of his soldiers — walked patrol. Though not a shot had been fired at them during their five-week encampment at the pyramid, Krupp still found it impossible to convince himself that the jungle and the mountains beyond weren't teeming with mysterious dangers of all kinds.

After all, somewhere out there was the missing officer, Heinke . . .

He walked over to their single helicopter, a refurbished Soviet-built Mil Mi-26 "Hook." The copter was a giant. More than 135 feet long, in its service with the Red Army, it could carry up to 70 men. But this aircraft wasn't designated as a troop carrier. In its hold sat something the High Command considered more precious than the relatively puny lives of its footsoldiers.

Inside its hold sat a fortune in gold . . .

The engines for the gigantic helicopter were always just one click away from starting. At least one pilot was always strapped into one of its seats, ready to fire its turbos and lift-off. Whenever a gold object was retrieved from a deep cave, it was immediately carried to the aircraft. These instructions had come directly from the High Command. Should Krupp's encampment be attacked, they wanted to make sure that the so-called "blitz" helicopter—and its precious cargo of bullion—be off and away in the shortest amount of time.

Krupp threw away the rest of his coffee and climbed inside the Hook's expansive cargo hold. It contained ten crates now—four were filled with gold coins, the others were packed with artifacts such as gold plates, goblets and necklaces. This was the final booty from this particular site—the eighteenth shipment of plunder from the secret cave the woman had indicated beneath the Chichen Itza pyramid. Within the hour, the Hook would lift off and meet the two escorting jet fighters that would shepherd it back to Panama.

"Shall we feed the prisoner, my colonel?" Krupp heard a voice behind him say.

He turned to see one of his sergeants holding a small pot containing a disgusting, undercooked egg and beef fat remnants.

"This is all there is to feed her?" he asked the sergeant.

The man shrugged. "She's always given the leftovers," he said. "And our remaining food is packed away."

He dismissed the man with the wave of his hand. He wasn't about to worry what the woman was being fed. More important things were pressing on him, like preparing to get to the next site, some 60 miles away.

To this end, he walked back to the command truck and sent his personal guard to round up his staff officers.

"Who's there?" the woman cried out.

Her ears had detected the soft footsteps coming from the

forward part of the cave. She also heard her voice echo between the walls of the pitch-black chamber.

"Is someone out there?" she called, her voice shaking.

"It's your food," came the gruff reply.

She could sense a faint light working its way down toward her. The shadows it cast frightened her. They always seemed to take on the shapes of large, terrible monsters. Quickly, she wrapped a soiled rag around her eyes, knowing that even a pinprick of direct light from a flashlight beam could damage her already frail, light-deprived retinas.

"I don't want any food," she called out wearily.

"But you must eat," came a snickered reply. "You are our guide. Without you, our work here would be meaningless."

The soldier carrying the small tin of food laughed, his sadistic tone echoing perversely around the cavern. She batted away the hand he put on her breast, but felt her own wrist squeezed hard as he forced her hand between his legs.

"I know you want to eat," he said, holding her hand tight against the fly of his uniform pants. "Now give Hans a rub and he'll leave your food."

"I don't want any food!" she screamed, struggling and momentarily succeeding in pulling her hand back from him.

He laughed again, roughly grabbed her breasts and then put his mouth to her neck.

"Eat now," he said in a heavy voice. "We move soon and you will not get fed until we get to the next camp, many miles away."

She felt tears coming on, and try as she might, she couldn't hold them in.

"Give it to me," she said, reaching out for the tin.

The soldier obliged her, then ran his hands all over her shapely young body while she forced down the runny yolk and small bits of fat.

"You get smarter every day," he said to her, finishing his liberties and taking the tin from her. "Just be sure you do not tell them of our little arrangement. If you do, I will be forced to slit your pretty throat . . ."

Tears were running down her face now, moistening the

dirty rag she used to protect her eyes and causing it to smell awful.

"Please . . ." she sobbed, feeling dizzy and insane again. "Please tell me what color my hair is . . ."

Chapter 17

The clouds had also covered the sunrise down in Panama, something Hunter took to be a lucky sign.

He was lying flat out in a clump of bushes no more than 25 feet from a control house for the "eastern" side locks of the Panama Canal. His face was covered with green paint and several different kinds of twigs and bushes were tied to his back, arms and legs. Even his M-16 was draped in green vines and twigs.

In his hands was the mini-video camera—a device that worked best when there was no direct sunshine. The cloud cover above the waterway allowed him to take long slow sweeps of the canal and the lockworks without worrying about the sun's glare screwing up the camera's cathode ray tube and possibly washing out an important shot.

He'd been at it for nearly an hour, recording the routine comings and goings of the military men running the locks, as well as their many small attack craft cruising the waterway. The camera's short, but nevertheless effective, zoom lens allowed him to key in on a number of defensive positions on both sides of the Canal. He was especially interested in the numerous SAM batteries—mounted Blowpipes and Rolands—in evidence on both shorelines and atop many of the lock's administration buildings. In addition to the SAMs, there were also many large gun emplacements. Some featured South African Armscor G5 155-mm howitzers; others had rare Soviet-built S-23 180-mm guns. Dozens of smaller gun sites also dotted the landscape.

All of it defense in depth against an airborne attack.

Everywhere he looked there were soldiers—all dressed in either the drab khaki uniforms or the smart, intense all-black outfit. To a man they were well-armed with either M-16s or AK-47s, plus more than a few guns Hunter recognized as Mausers and Enfields. Several soldiers drifted by carrying RPG launchers and even TOW anti-tank weapons.

He counted a half dozen different helicopters buzzing about—Soviet Mi-24 Hinds mostly, but he had also spotted a few ancient Soviet-built Mi-4 Hounds. And higher up, he had tracked the vapor trails of twelve F-4 Phantoms, the venerable fighter-bomber that seemed to be the jet aircraft of choice for The Twisted Cross.

Phantoms had carried out the aborted attack on the chopper team's encampment and now the skies above the Canal were positively lousy with them. But what bothered Hunter most was the fact that he had tangled with Phantoms on his trip to New Orleans. Could the fighters that attacked the airliner over Louisiana have been flown by pilots of The Twisted Cross?

It was just one of many questions running through his mind.

The official name of the chopper team was the Central American Tactical Service—CATS for short. Hunter and Dantini, the overall commander of CATS as well as its corporation's president, had stayed up all night, discussing the movement which would bring them here to the very edge of the Canal.

It had been a simple plan that nevertheless required a lot of coordination. Although they staved off the air strike, the CATS were forced to abandon their convenient, seaside encampment and look for a new, more secure forward base. Being experts at relocation, the entire chopper force was packed and gone within 45 minutes of the F-4s' attempted napalm attack.

Eight of the big helicopters, as well as the rest of the

smaller ones, immediately moved to a new base on one of the northernmost islands in the Mosquito Gulf, a spit of land called Bocas del Toro. Meanwhile, Hunter, Dantini, Burke and ten of Dantini's best troops took one of the Chinooks on a long, arcing journey out over the Caribbean and back into the more eastern part of Panama. Landing on yet another island, one of a chain called San Blas, they were ferried to the Panamanian mainland on rubber rafts. Then they walked, reaching the Canal just at dawn. Hunter had been shooting footage with his small video camera ever since.

"The guys in the black uniforms are members of what they call The Party," Dantini, who was one bush over from Hunter, explained to him in a voice barely above a whisper. "It's almost like an organization within an organization. Their guys call all the shots within The Twisted Cross. What they say, goes."

"Almost like an elite officer corps," Hunter said, training the camera on two black-uniformed officers who were standing just outside one of the canal locks station. "Or should I say, more like Hitler's SS."

"Now you're getting the picture," Dantini replied.

Hunter knew what the man meant. It had been unspoken even before he arrived in Panama. And the word never left the lips of Dantini or Burke or any of the soldiers in CATS. It was as if the word was too horrible, too repugnant even to speak. But there was no denying just what The Twisted Cross stood for, both in symbolism and in action. The uniforms the Cross soldiers wore, the way they marched, even the helmets on their heads were all flashbacks to another sinister time earlier in the century when men of their ilk tried to take over the world and destroy it at the same time.

It only took a few seconds, but Hunter closed his eyes and relived one of the most mystifying events of his life.

He was back in the Arabian desert. His arch-foe Viktor stood before him, Hunter having shot down the fiend's helicopter just before his own airplane crashed. Now they stood in contrast: Hunter, holding his M-16 on Viktor, trying with all his might to fight off the temptation of pulling the trigger and ridding the world of one of its

106

worst scourges; Victor mocking him, telling him that democracy and freedom were out-moded in the New Order world.

Suddenly, a shot rang out. Viktor's throat exploded in a burst of blood and bones. Then another shot hit him, right in the center of the back, exiting through his breastbone. He fell face down in the sand at Hunter's feet — dead before he hit the ground . . .

Hunter spotted two uniformed men about a half mile away, holding a rifle with a telescopic sight. They quickly retreated in a desert vehicle. Retrieving his binoculars, he was able to catch a glimpse of the armbands both men wore . . .

Those armbands and the symbol pressed upon them — a red circle with a black twisted design inside — were identical to ones worn by the soldiers now guarding the canal locks.

It made Hunter's stomach turn just thinking about it, but he knew that certain facts had to be faced. Whether they called themselves The Twisted Cross or The Party or nothing at all, the hideous swastika design that each man wore told it all: the people in control of the Panama Canal were Nazis . . .

Hunter and the members of the CATS spent the next three hours moving up and down the bank of the waterway, avoiding Cross patrols and videotaping anything and everything.

The farther they went down the waterway, the more apparent it became that the Cross had lined both sides of the Canal with a startling array of weapons. It seemed as if there was either an anti-aircraft emplacement — whether it be a SAM site or a radar-guided gun — every 50 yards. And the space in the middle was taken up by a grabbag of weapons ranging from the ever-plentiful .50-caliber machine gun nests to the large, long-range howitzers.

"And I thought The Circle was heavy in equipment," Hunter said to Dantini at one point. "These guys seem to have more guns than they do people to operate them."

Dantini agreed. "We've heard that the members of The Party originally started out as arms dealers," he told Hunter.

"They apparently have a ton of money as well as access to a lot of weapons, both new and reconditioned."

"It's that 'ton of money' that worries me," Hunter said. "There are plenty of crackpots around who would love to rule the world but the only thing holding them back is lack of funds. But these guys seem to have a bottomless barrel of cash."

As illustration, he pointed out several gun emplacements that were just now nearing construction. Also, the Cross had heavy earth-moving equipment operating on both sides of the waterway, building roads, docking facilities, fuel stations and even more gun and missile emplacements.

"This is a work in progress," Hunter said to Dantini, capturing it all on video. "These guys are planning to stay awhile . . ."

"Well, we know the Cross has a thing about gold," Dantini whispered to him. "We've both heard stories about their demanding gold for passage through the Canal, even taking gold fillings from people."

Hunter nodded and zoomed in on work being done on a new SAM site about 100 yards from their position.

"Yes, that's true," he said. "But it sure takes more than a bag full of gold fillings to pay for all this stuff. And I can't believe it's all coming from just the gold they extract from ships passing through. They have to be getting it from some other source."

They were about to move further down the waterway when a small boat caught Hunter's attention. There was no lack of Twisted Cross attack craft zipping up and down the Canal, but this particular vessel — a tugboat painted all white — looked unusual. First of all, it wasn't armed to the teeth as was every other attack craft on the water. Secondly, just about everyone on board appeared to be wearing bulky white suits, almost of the style a beekeeper would wear. And those not dressed up in the bulky clothes were wearing even bulkier deep sea diving gear.

They watched as the white tugboat cast off from a dock near the lockworks and cruised to a point almost directly in front of them. The crew dropped anchor and soon there was a lot of activity at the rear of the boat. Five minutes passed and then two men in the old-style deep sea diving gear — complete with large globe helmets — were lowered over the side, several of the crewmen carefully playing out the air lines for the divers.

Another five minutes passed. Then the tug crew was seen lowering two long silver tubes into the water. All the work being done on the tug was slow and deliberate, especially the handling of the silver tubes. Meanwhile, every other craft on the waterway gave the tugboat the widest possible berth.

"They're certainly going through a lot of trouble for whatever the hell they are doing," Dantini observed. "Those suits they're wearing almost look like they're protective in nature, don't you think?"

Hunter was way ahead of him. He knew the deck crew's suits might be anti-radiation suits, the same kind worn by workers in nuclear power plants. And if this were true, it was a good bet the diver's suits were at least partially protective as well. But what was going on? Pegg had told him that he had observed a similar operation — silver tubes being lowered into the water — though he put the location as closer to the lockworks.

Hunter didn't want to jump to conclusions. But something inside him was saying that the biggest threat the Canal Nazis posed was not their overabundance of weaponry along the banks of the waterway, or their apparent overflowing gold coffers, *or* their well-stocked F-4 Phantom air force. Something told him that the real threat lay inside those long silver tubes.

And it was up to him to find out just what they were . .

Chapter 18

"Here it comes!" one of the CATS lookouts yelled excitedly.

Within moments, Hunter, Dantini and Burke joined the other soldiers out on the beach of the small island. It was the middle of the night, two days after their daring reconnaissance mission to the canal. Soon after they had returned to the island, Hunter put in a coded call to a receiving station in Texas, using his miniature radio set. The Texans relayed the message up to General Jones in Washington. It had said, in effect, that Hunter needed some "special equipment."

Hunter would learn later on that it was his old friend Mike Fitzgerald who had come up with the equipment he needed. Fitzie was a businessman first, a fighter pilot second. He was one of those guys who seemed to be able to put his hands on anything at anytime, no matter how rare or obscure it might be.

In this case, Hunter had radioed Jones that he needed a lead-lined diver's suit. Somehow Fitz was able to produce one inside of three hours.

Now as Hunter and the others watched from the beach, one of the New York Hercs C-130s appeared out of the darkness from the north. The big cargo plane was flying very low and without the usual navigation lights. With its heavy green camouflage scheme, it was barely discernible against the dark ocean.

It made one pass, and picking up on the coded flashlight

110

signal from Hunter on the beach, turned around and came in low again, not more than 25 feet off the surface of the water. Suddenly they could see a small package drop out of the side cargo door and hit the water with a splash. Within seconds, a team of CATS soldiers were madly paddling toward the floating package.

The big C-130 turned out to sea, did a wide arc and came back across the shoreline once more. By this time, the CATS soldiers had retrieved the package and had indicated it was still intact. Hunter flashed another coded light signal to the C-130 as it roared past, this one telling them the drop had been successful. The message received, the cargo plane wagged its wings twice then disappeared into the night.

"This is the craziest idea I've ever heard of," Dantini was saying as he and Hunter unpacked the bundle the CATS soldiers had hauled in. "How can you expect to just dive down there right under their noses?"

"Sometimes you've got to take chances," Hunter told him as he concentrated on cutting the many holding lines around the package. "Also, I was hoping you guys could provide a little diversion for me should I get in trouble. Just a bunch of noise would do . . ."

"Damn, you know you can count on us, Hawk," Dantini told him. "We'll blow their fucking eardrums out if we have to. It's just that you don't know exactly what's down there and neither do I. No one does, probably except the high mucky-mucks of the Cross. For all you know, they could have boobytrapped those damn things . . ."

"I hear what you're saying," Hunter told him, finally breaking through the last seal holding the package together. "But I'm down here on a recon mission. My job is to gather as much intelligence as possible. Somehow we've got to find out what the hell they are putting down there and I can't think of any other way to do it."

At that moment he had stripped away the top layer of the bundle's waterproof packing. He reached inside and with some effort, hauled out the large, rather outlandish diving suit.

"Jesus . . ." Hunter murmured, somewhat astonished at

111

the size and bulk of the one-piece outfit.

"It looks like a costume from a bad science fiction movie," Burke said, helping Hunter lay out the beast on the sand. "A *very* bad science fiction movie."

Hunter had to agree with him. The suit looked like a cross between the outfits worn by the Apollo Moon astronauts and a beekeeper's nightmare. It was heavy, due to its lead lining and the two enormous air tanks attached to its back. Its front plate was covered with dials and switches, none of which he had any idea how to operate. The attached boots alone looked like they could fit a size 20 foot.

Hunter could only shake his head. "Where the hell did Fitz get this?" he wondered out loud.

Chapter 19

Colonel Krupp took another look at his map, then motioned for his driver to stop.

The 27-vehicle, heavily-armed convoy screeched to a halt behind his lead truck. It was the fourth time they had stopped in the past hour and each time the blazing sun and the oppressive humidity took its toll on the soldiers as well as their vehicles' radiators.

The convoy had left Chichen Itza more than five hours before, Krupp sending out one last token search party to look for the long-missing Heinke. Since then it had been winding its way south, rumbling over cratered jungle roads and speeding up whenever it reached a rare open stretch of highway.

Still, the pace was too slow for the colonel. He had drawn up a precise schedule for the move, estimating the convoy could make at least thirty miles an hour. But by checking the terrain against his map, it appeared they had yet to travel even sixty miles.

Either that, or they were lost . . .

"Call back and tell them to bring the woman up here immediately," he said to his driver.

The man quickly got on his radio and did as ordered. Soon two more soldiers appeared, leading the hooded woman between them.

"Pass the word down that this is *not* a rest stop," Krupp

ordered the two soldiers. "We'll be moving in less than five minutes . . ."

The two soldiers saluted and quickly ran back to relay Krupp's orders. Meanwhile the colonel lifted the woman up and into the back of his command truck. Only when the rear curtains were drawn and tight did he remove the black hood from her head. A tiny battery-operated lamp was the compartment's only illumination.

She instinctively shielded her eyes with her manacled hands, wincing against the dim light.

"Look at this map," he said to her authoritatively, while still letting his eyes wander over her breasts. She was wearing a multi-pocket field blouse, a short khaki skirt and once-white tennis sneakers, the same clothes she was wearing when they first came into possession of her. But even though her blouse was tattered, her skirt soiled and her hair a bush of dark brunette tresses, she was still beautiful.

"*Look* at this map," Krupp said again, nudging her into the small chair that was pulled up against his planning board. She was groggy, the result of both the many injections of sodium pentathol they had given her over the past few weeks and her nearly constant confinement. Still, she was the only one in the convoy who really knew the territory.

"I need water," she said wearily, moving her wrists in her handcuffs. "I need to go home . . ."

"You're not going home," Krupp told her matter-of-factly, surprising himself by stating the apparent death sentence. "Now just look at the map and tell me if we are on the right track."

"Not unless I get some water," she said quietly but defiantly.

Krupp hastily ripped the canteen from his utility belt and shoved it in front of her. She grasped it between her bound hands and drank a few sips.

"How can you people be so inhuman?" she asked him, still shielding her eyes away from the weak light. "Have you no conscience? No dignity?"

He grabbed her shoulder roughly.

"Read the map!" he hissed at her between clenched teeth. "Tell me if we are going in the right direction."

"How . . . how can I?" she asked in a voice barely above a whisper. "I don't even know where I am. Or even *who* I am . . ."

"You will be on your way to a firing squad if you don't cooperate," Krupp snapped back at her. Every minute this went on was another minute off his schedule. In his mind it was imperative that they reach the next site before darkness fell and the countryside came alive with God-knows-what.

He nudged her again, holding her face just inches from the map. "I think we are following this road," he said, indicating a point on the map just south of Chichen Itza. "But according to the map, we should be seeing mountains off to our west and a river to our east. I have seen neither."

She studied the map as best she could, taking greedy sips of the water as she did so.

"The river is deep in the forest," she said finally. "You cannot see it from the road . . ."

"And these mountains?" Krupp asked. "They, too, have disappeared?"

She wiped her eyes and said: "They aren't mountains. They are merely hills, no more than two hundred feet high. You probably won't be able to distinguish them anyway."

"So you are saying that we continue on this road?" Krupp asked.

"Yes . . ." she said with a heavy, congested sigh, adding defiantly: "Follow it all the way to Hell for all I care . . ."

Chapter 20

Hunter couldn't remember a time when he had felt more uncomfortable.

His face, neck and upper back were covered with scrapes and bruises. Both his shoulders ached, his hip muscles were strained and the blisters on his feet ran from heel to toe. His nose was runny from the dirty oxygen and it was all he could do to suppress sneezing inside the restrictive helmet.

Still, he had to admit, being at the bottom of the Panama waterway was a unique experience . . .

He had been at it for two hours now, having gone into the waterway just south of the point where they'd seen the Cross divers working. He wasn't swimming—the suit was much too heavy for that. It was more like what he imagined walking on the moon would be like.

When he first tested the diving suit in a small lake near the CATS temporary camp, he found it was so bulky and weighty he was afraid that should he fall over, he might not be able to get back up. For this reason he had brought along a sturdy metal rod to use as a staff. It would help him keep his balance and should he topple over, he could use it to right himself again.

About a foot of silt covered the waterway's bottom in some parts, but there were surprisingly few plants and even fewer fish. Instead the floor was covered with all kinds of unimaginable litter. Small sunken boats, pieces of metal construction, a hundred different things made of wood. There were cargo crates, some smashed open, others still airtight. Incredibly long lengths of chain and rope and rubber hose. Automobile tires. Tractor wheels. Car batteries. Shattered windshields. There was even the remnants of some long ago crashed airplane—it looked like a Lear jet with its side blown out, possibly downed sometime during the Big War. And everywhere, hundreds of barrels. It was like some vast underwater junkyard—some of it rotting away, some of it brand new. There was so much of the stuff, Hunter wondered how anything of any size floating through the Canal could miss hitting some of it.

It was amongst all this waterlogged debris that he had to search for the silver tubes.

He had found a short note from Fitz inside the suit after unpacking it—a brief explanation on how the thing worked, what the air limit was and so on. Despite the feeling that he was walking around in a pair of concrete longjohns, he could also appreciate the fact that Fitz couldn't have done any better getting him the exact piece of equipment he needed.

The suit was designed to be used by US Navy submariners, specifically those on nuclear boats. As part of routine maintenance, divers would don the suits and check the underside of the nuke's hull for any radiation leakage. Thus, the suit was not only lead-lined for safety, it also came with a built-in radiation detector (an advanced Geiger counter), a searchlight, a radio intercom and even a stethoscope-type device which would allow divers to listen for any telltale sign of rad leakage. The suit also carried a small, still camera in the visor of the helmet which Fitz had smartly loaded up with film before shipping. All these devices were regulated by the dials and buttons on the breast plate of the suit, controls that Hunter had schooled himself in during his test dives in the small lake.

It was only after three hours of laborious walking—and infernal chafing—did he spot his first silver tube. He was still more than 50 yards away from the mysterious cylinder when his radiation detector started beeping, slowly at first. But the closer he got to the tube, the more rapid the pulse of the warning device. By the time he was within ten feet of the cylinder, the warning beep had changed to one long buzz.

He started snapping photos of the tube from 15 feet out. Now that he was close enough to touch the thing, he made sure to check his radiation level indicator every few seconds. The needle, which moved in relation to the amount of radiation coming from an object, was almost in the green zone of the dial—still far enough away from the red zone which would indicate that he was receiving too much of a rad dose.

He slowly danced around the tube, snapping pictures and memorizing its shape. It was anchored to the cluttered canal floor by way of a concrete block and chain. Its form was smooth and seamless except for the small panel of three lights that was located at its mid-section. Of the three lights—green, orange and red—only the green one was illuminated. Hunter was sure to get as many photos as possible of the panel display.

Then he put the stethoscope on the cylinder and listened for five minutes to the ominous sound of microcircuits whirring, humming and buzzing. Something electronic was alive inside the tube. And that was bad news . . .

He spent a few more minutes at the first tube, then coasted over to a second one that was anchored just 20 feet away. It was identical in every way, including its burning green light. He took a slew of photos of this cylinder too. Then he began the long, slow walk back to the point in the waterway where he could safely emerge.

The journey back was not enjoyable. Hunter's mind was too busy, reeling with facts, figures, theories and probables, all of them bad. Before he dove down to find out, his best hope was that the Canal Nazis were simply storing radioactive fuel—fissionable materials to be used later in weapons — at the bottom of the waterway. But now Hunter knew that was just folly and that the worst case scenario was most likely the actual one. In fact, all the evidence pointed to just one, dire conclusion.

He was not looking forward to telling Jones and the others that the Panama Canal was sown with nuclear-tipped underwater mines . . .

Chapter 21

Frankel wished he had never left Las Perlas island.

He had enjoyed his duty there too much. Intercepting ships seeking passage through the canal, having his troops scour each vessel for any gold — no matter how minute an amount, deciding which ships could pass and which ones would be sunk. It had provided him with much discretionary power, not to mention the pick of the lot of any female slaves "liberated" from the ships.

But he had done his job *too* well . . .

One day he was sitting on the small island villa's porch, dousing himself with ice water and turning thumbs up or thumbs down on those vessels trying to make passage. The next day he was put in charge of a "gold reclamation project" along the waterway itself.

True, he now had an entire 2000-man regiment at his beck and call and his new headquarters sat halfway up a tall hill where the cooling Pacific breezes took the edge off the usually murderous heat. There was no shortage of young wenches for him to use and discard at will, and he actually had access to a rather large wine stock liberated from The Twisted Cross command center in what was formerly known as Panama City.

But the work he commanded was, to his mind, almost counter-productive. An officer of undetermined rank — Strauberg was his name — was in charge of gold acquisition for the Cross. He was a repulsive, dirty little man who wielded great power not only within The Twisted Cross command structure, but also within The Party, the elite overclass. Frankel knew that Strauberg had control of the far-flung gold expeditions up north in Mexico. It was Strauberg who did the final count on any and all gold taken as toll from the passing ships. It was Strauberg who decided how much gold the rulers of such pathetic kingdoms like Brasilia and Argentina would have to pay in tribute to The Cross. And it was even up to Strauberg to count out and weigh the gold fillings taken from doomed sailors on those ships The Twisted Cross decided to sink rather than let pass through the Canal.

But now Frankel, himself a Nazi zealot to the highest degree, believed that Strauberg had gone too far . . .

As he looked out from his headquarters on the side of the hill down onto the mid-way point of the waterway, he once again had to laugh at the folly of Strauberg's latest scheme. Lined up along both sides of the Canal under the watchful eye of his heavily-armed troops were thousands of slaves — natives, Indians, captured seamen — wading in the shallows of the waterway, panning for gold.

Chapter 22

The room deep inside the Pentagon was absolutely quiet save for the soft whirring of the video playback machine.

In stunned silence, the members of the United American Command Staff watched as scene after scene of Hunter's Panama Canal videotape played before the eyes. No one in DC had even dreamed of the extent of control the mysterious soldiers now had in Panama. The frightening display of conventional weaponry deployed along the Canal sobered even the more *gung-ho* members of the staff. And Hunter's evidence, suggested by both the measurement devices and photos he'd taken underwater, that the Canal was now rife with nuclear-tipped mines seemed like a nightmare come true.

But worst of all were the armbands . . .

"Jesus, how could a Nazi organization of this size and power just spring up like this?" JT Toomey asked once the videotape had ended. "Practically right under our noses?"

"Were we so naive?" Ben Wa followed up. "We were spending too much time concentrating on The Circle and the Soviets and ignoring the other threats around us?"

"No . . ." General Jones said in an affirmative voice that cut through the brief soul-searching. "Had we not concentrated on the immediate threats on this continent, we wouldn't be here today, trying to figure out what to do about these guys in Panama."

"But JT makes a good point," the Canadian, Major Frost, said. "How could this fascist gang just suddenly appear? I mean, I hadn't heard the word 'Nazi' uttered in years until Hawk told us about who shot Viktor in the desert . . ."

Hunter spoke up at this point. "My guess is that these guys just didn't suddenly appear," he said. "I'd bet they've been planning this for a while. Gathering their resources, biding their time while we and the Soviets battled it out up here . . ."

"Could be," Major Shane of the Football City Special Forces said. "But where could they have been doing all this planning? And getting the money they would need to buy all that firepower?"

Hunter shrugged. "They could have been hatching this plot from just about anywhere," he said. "I mean, my money says they've been lying low down in South America. We'll all agree that our intelligence-gathering down there is practically nil. For all we know, this Twisted Cross organization might go all the way back to right after World War II. A lot of 'Ratzis' got out of Europe before the end. And a hell of a lot of them went right to South America. They have families, they teach their kids to goosestep. Boom! a whole new generation of the Master Race is born . . ."

"The Rise of the *Fourth* Reich . . ." Frost said ruefully.

"Exactly . . ." Hunter said. "Now, it's just a theory, but try on this scenario: The Big War breaks out and South America comes through without a scratch. Then the New Order is established. Yeah, the governments down there change around, and countries become kingdoms and so on. But that kind of stuff was always going down in SA.

"Now in the past few years, we all know that it's easier in some places to buy an eighty-millimeter anti-aircraft gun than it is to buy a loaf of bread. These Nazis, who have been probably waiting for just such opportunity, sit back and watch us kill each other off. Meanwhile they're gathering money and military equipment on the side. Hell, the guys in CATS are certain that these guys in The Party were arms dealers themselves! They never came to us with their catalogs, but I'll bet a bag of gold they went calling on The Circle . . ."

"Or the Mid-Aks," Ben Wa said. "Or the Family . . ."

"Right," Hunter confirmed. "All our enemies. By selling stuff to them, they were simply throwing more gasoline onto the fire and turning a profit to boot.

"Thus they get the money, they get the weapons and they virtually ensure themselves that between the Soviets and the criminal elements here on the continent, we'll kill each other off in a matter of a few years."

"But what is their point?" Toomey asked. "Sure, controlling the Canal is a big deal. I mean, they've got us by the croggies right now and they just can't seem to get enough gold. But is it an end in itself, or simply one means to an end?"

"I'm sure it's just a small part of the puzzle," Hunter replied. "That's how the Nazis work. Historically, they're the *ultimate* opportunists. Back in Germany before World War Two, they'd try to take over one little beer hall here, a neighborhood there. They use terror. They use psych-ops. It builds and builds, until it seems they're suddenly in total control. Overnight sensations. But really, they've been at the drawing board for a long time."

"Your reasoning makes sense," Jones spoke up. "But then why would they have killed Viktor? Obviously they were tracking him out in that desert . . ."

Hunter nodded. "Again, they simply took advantage of the situation," he said. "I would say they killed Viktor simply because at that time, he was the biggest threat to their plans.

"Viktor had a massive army and was about to relight World War Three. If he had succeeded in invading and conquering the whole Mediterranean, then the Nazis would have had to crawl back into their holes and wait for many years for their next opportunity. So they efficiently nipped

124

the problem in the bud. I just happened to be there at the time . . ."

Another silence descended on the room.

It was Toomey who finally broke it. "So you think their ultimate goal is to . . . well, take over the world?" he asked.

"When hasn't it been?" Hunter answered. "From the day they dropped little baby Adolph on his head, world domination has been their thing.

"The trouble is, this time, they have a shot at actually making it . . ."

Mike Fitzgerald didn't attend the Canal Zone videotape meeting. He didn't have to—he had already seen the videotape many times over.

When Hunter reached Washington with the tape—following a harrowing "parachute in reverse" aerial pick-up by one of the New York Hercs off the Mosquito coast—Fitz was the one on hand to meet him at the airport. Together they immediately split a much-needed bottle of scotch and previewed the startling footage over and over, taking notes of every last detail. Hunter's underwater still shots were to be given the same scrutiny—both men realizing it was in these photographs that the most potentially devastating threat lay.

So 12 hours later, while the Command Staff was meeting, Fitz was still analyzing the underwater pictures. Once the staff meeting broke up, Hunter immediately hoofed it over to the Irishman's intelligence section office which was located halfway around the other side of the enormous, reclaimed Pentagon building.

"No doubt about it," Fitz said, greeting Hunter with the depressing news. "My guys say those tubes are definitely underwater nuclear mines. They estimate each one packs about one-point-two kilotons of explosive power."

"Jesus," Hunter whistled. "That means just one or two of them could destroy the canal. Three at the most."

"Three would be more than sufficient," Fitzgerald said

dryly.

"But I saw two of them no more than twenty feet from each other," Hunter told him. "And we saw them planting a bunch near the locks. And Pegg said he saw them laying them when *he* went through and that was some time ago."

Fitz could only shrug. "It's incredible overkill, I agree," he said. "They may have as many as fifty or even more bobbing around down there."

"Damn . . ." Hunter said in a whisper. "They're able to cut the whole Goddamn country of Panama in two . . ."

Fitz nodded his head in agreement. "If they wanted to, yes," he said. "But there may be a more practical reason for them putting so many mines in the canal. First, you have to consider that your problems in storing any kind of radioactive material are made a lot easier if you do it underwater."

"That's true," Hunter agreed. "Those bastards could lift one or two or a dozen of those firecrackers up at any time and lay them somewhere else."

Fitz lit up one of his trademark torpedo cigars. "Possible," he said. "But not quite that easy . . ."

By this time, Hunter had located a bottle from Fitz's private stock and was pouring out two stiff belts of whiskey.

"Can you explain that?" he asked the Irishman, grimacing as the first swig of whiskey went down.

"Well, it has to do with the design of the mines themselves," Fitz began. "After putting your photos through every analyzing machine we have here, my boys concluded that these cylinders are not your usual contact-detonation mine—thank God! Instead they appear to be on some kind of sequential timing system."

"You mean someone flips a switch and they all go off?" Hunter asked.

"That's possible," Fitz said. "But not all at once. More probably one at a time, depending on the sequence. But it seems like the Nazis have been forced to use a very impractical method to set them up. If some are so close together, one has to figure that when Mine 'A' detonates, it's going to

126

destroy its nearby neighbor, Mine 'B', and so on. The effect will be same. The whole Goddamn Canal will be blown up—along with half the country. But, in a nutshell, it's not the correct way to deploy such as system."

Hunter took another gulp of whiskey and turned this latest information over in his mind.

"So are you suggesting we might have a clue here?" he asked.

Fitz nodded. "Maybe," he replied. "Let's consider a few things. I think it's safe to say that this system is not of the Nazis' own design. I'd say it was given to them—or more likely, they stole it—and they have deployed it in the only way they know how. I mean, there are probably enough mines in the system to blockade the entire coastline of a major country. Christ, fifty remote control nuclear mines, dropped at the right places, could seal off the east coast of America with no problem . . ."

"The same goes for the Baltic coastline of the Soviet Union," Hunter added, stating the flip side of the equation.

Fitz managed a laugh. "I think you may be close to the original purpose of these weapons," he said, taking a long drag on his stogie and an even longer swig of his drink. "I'm betting that if we opened up one of those cans, we'd find a little metal plate that said: 'Made in the USA.' "

Another light went off inside Hunter's mind. They *were* zooming in on something.

"Okay, let's take it a step further," he said. "Let's say the system *was* made here. A top secret project, before the Big War. How many people in this country—be they a scientist or an engineer or whatever—could put together such a system? I'd think it would be a relatively difficult thing to do, no matter what defense contractor you were working for . . ."

"I agree," Fitz said. "And the more difficult the system, the more likely that only a few people—maybe even just one or two—would know just exactly how every single component ticks."

Hunter pounded his fist on the desk for emphasis. "We've got to track down this project in its pre-war life," he said. "It's got to be a Navy system. I'll bet it just wasn't ready when the balloon went up in Europe."

"But somehow, it got into the grubby little hands of the Canal Nazis . . ." Fitz said.

Hunter drained his glass. "Exactly," he said, getting up to go. "And that's why we've got to find out who invented this system in the first place."

Chapter 23

Krupp was the first one to spot the smoke.

"Look!" he had to yell to his driver over his truck's noisy engine. "Over there, to the southwest. See it?"

The driver strained his eyes against the sun's glare on the windshield. It took a few moments, but then he too saw the column of black smoke rising between two mountains.

"I see it, my colonel," he said excitedly. "This means we have found it?"

Krupp had his map out and was checking the nearby terrain with lightning speed. "It just may be, sergeant," he said. "We are behind schedule by a day, true. But we can make that all up now. Quickly, speed up."

The sergeant obliged by flooring the gas pedal on the two-and-a-half ton command truck, waving his left arm out the window at the same time to signal the vehicles behind him that they too should increase their speed.

The convoy wound its way down a mountain pass and up another. All the while, Krupp kept his eyes on the rising plume of smoke up ahead. For the first time in weeks, he felt a burst of pride run through him. This feat he had accomplished had been not easy. Moving the convoy through uncharted territory on long-forgotten roads, with the threat of danger ever-present. It was a triumph of military planning. Such victories reinforced his belief that his cause — and the cause of The Twisted Cross — was correct and destined.

An hour went by during which Krupp heard a chorus of

whoops and hollers coming from his troops behind him — thankful sounds that they had reached their next objective alive and well. They were the sounds of loyalty, Krupp told himself. A song of adventure, of pride, of near-invincibility.

Suddenly he thought of the beautiful woman, tied up in a truck in the middle of the convoy, her head covered with a hood.

Maybe tonight he would have her . . .

Forty-five minutes later the convoy stood at a strange crossroads.

Reaching a straightaway that ran between two mountains, they came upon the source of the smoke. It was a corridor, literally burned through the dense forest. This was Krupp's passageway into the hidden valley known as *Uxmaluna*. Twelve kilometers blasted away by a squadron of F-4 Phantoms of The Twisted Cross.

"They have done a magnificent job!" one of his officers exclaimed as they stood at the entrance to the smoldering path. "Our pilots are very talented . . ."

"It was their bombs that get the credit," Krupp said. He was an infantry officer by trade and therefore distrusted anyone who fought in an airplane.

He walked about 25 yards up the roadway, grudgingly admiring how expertly their passage had been cleared. He reached over and picked up several pieces of still-warm metal.

"See?" he said to the officer trailing close behind. "They used what the Americans called 'blockbuster' bombs. They are like little A-bombs. They carry tens of thousands of these sharp pellets inside their shell. When they explode, it creates a hurricane of shrapnel, but in a very defined area. You will notice that few things measuring more than a half inch square has survived. Everything — trees, branches, leaves, vines, even rocks have been cleared away for us. Only the twigs remain . . ."

"We will ride a road of twigs to our next triumph," the officer said in a tone obviously intended to curry favor with

Krupp.

"Very poetic, Captain," Krupp said icily. "Now go get the woman. Bring her up here."

The man saluted and quickly left Krupp alone. The officer scanned the pathway ahead of him with his powerful binoculars. He could see at least four miles of the blasted-out jungle corridor ahead before it dipped and went around the mountain and down into the valley itself.

"Amazing," he whispered to himself. "What devious ingenuity . . ."

The woman was brought up to him, still bound in handcuffs, her head still covered with the dark hood.

"You're dismissed," Krupp told the officer. "Go back and tell the others to prepare themselves . . ."

The officer duly scurried off, leaving Krupp and the woman alone.

"We are close to our next objective," he told her, untying the rope that held the hood together. "I want you to get a good look at what we can do when we put our minds to it."

He removed her hood, feeling a jolt of excitement as he saw her lovely features once again.

She had her eyes shut tight, knowing by now that she must open them gradually so as not to damage them with a sudden barrage of light.

But this time her head overruled her captive sensibilities. She blinked her eyes barely a dozen times before they went wide with amazement, then absolute horror.

"My dear God, *what have you done here?*" she cried out. She couldn't believe what her eyes were telling her. It looked as if someone had driven a gigantic lawnmower right through the heart of the forest.

"This is the road we follow to Uxmaluna," he said proudly.

Her jaw was wide open in amazement and she found it impossible to close. *"You've destroyed this forest!"* she cried out, not quite believing the extent of the devastation.

"We have dug a path to glory," he corrected her. "Do you think mere forests can stop us on our mission?"

She looked him directly in the eyes. "I can't believe the

131

inhumanity of this . . ." she said, her voice trembling in anger. "Do you have any idea what kind of damage this will do? Everything in these forests is interdependent on each other. Trees shade other trees. They provide oxygen—they actually *clean* the air. They provide food and homes for animals. They keep the water from running off. They keep the soil intact and prevent erosion. Do you know how important that is in a rain forest such as this?"

"These things are of no concern of mine or my superiors," he declared, peeved that the woman would dare lecture him. "Our mission is of the utmost importance. We have just simplified our means of access to the Uxmaluna site . . ."

"What you've done is rip the heart out of this place!" she screamed. "You are animals. No, worse . . . even the animals have an instinct not to ruin their environment . . ."

"Silence!" he screamed at her, raising his arm as if to strike her. "Do you really believe that we care about something so petty as your precious 'environment?' The future of the world is at stake!"

Chapter 24

Hunter's cockpit radio suddenly crackled to life.

"I'm figuring we're about fifteen minutes away, Hawker," he heard Fitz's voice say. "Twenty at the most . . ."

Hunter checked his position against the map taped to his knee and confirmed Fitzie's estimation.

"You called it," he radioed the Irishman. "I'm going to start getting ready now . . . I suggest we descend to twelve hundred and, once we're close, look for someplace flat . . ."

"Roger," came the reply.

With that, both he and Fitz put their AV-8B Harrier jumpjets into a shallow dive. Up ahead, Hunter could see the deserted city of El Paso.

It had been one hectic 36 hours. Between lengthy discussions on what to do about the situation in the Canal and tracking down the origin of the nuclear mine program, he had slept maybe a total of two hours. It didn't bother him though. In times like these, he didn't need sleep.

The United American Command Staff had come to the conclusion that the canal had to be taken away from the Nazis — by force. But they also agreed that to do so would take a major effort — in time, resources, logistics and ultimately in the lives of their soldiers. Contingency planning had commenced immediately. The early thinking was that a combined air, sea and ground attack would be needed — no small undertaking for the still fledgling United American Army.

But before any attack could take place, a solution to the

problem of the nuclear mines had to be found. The United Americans couldn't very well strike at the Canal Nazis only to have the whole waterway, and a good size chunk of Central America, reduced to nothing more than a pile of radioactive mud and ash.

So even though Hunter had gone without much shuteye, he hardly noticed it. The gallons of adrenaline pumping through his body kept him up and alert with energy to spare. Besides, he and Fitz had had a lot of detective work to do. That their sleuthing had been ultimately successful was a reward in itself and brought him more peace than a few hours catching *zzzs* could ever do.

It was after endless hours of probing a mainframe computer once used by the US National Security Agency that they came across an intriguing piece of evidence: it was a memo, stored in the computer, addressed from one Pentagon paperpusher to another and sent just two months before World War III broke out. It was a complaint actually, one guy beefing to the other that the Navy was spending too much time and money on "Project Chesapeake Bay." Specifically, the complainer noted the "huge amounts" of diesel fuel being burned by the half dozen minesweepers being used in the top secret project.

Both Hunter and Fitz knew immediately that they were on to something: the US Navy had very few minesweepers at the outbreak of the Big War. The ones they did have were old and creaky, their engines ancient. In truth, they were probably the most unseaworthy ships in the entire US fleet. So why would anyone use them in a top secret project?

With this clue, they accessed other computer files. Soon he and Fitz were under a mountain of top secret documents dealing with "Project Chesapeake Bay." Sure enough, it involved initial testing of nuclear-tipped underwater mines. Where the Chesapeake Bay connection came in, they never found out. According to the documents, the testing of the first-design dummy warheads had taken place somewhere off the southern coast of Florida. The minesweepers, naturals for this kind of assignment, had been sailing out every day from facilities at the Key West Naval Air Station. And it was there—in underground lead-lined bunkers—that the live nuclear warheads had been stored.

Further investigation led them through a family tree of defense contractors who had been secretly manufacturing components for the nuclear mines, which were code named "Washbuckets." This was where the hard work came in. They sifted through just about every letter written between the Navy and the various companies, looking for one single pattern. Then, late one night, after much cross-referencing and many hours of following false leads, they found the missing link: The majority of the secret-pouch letters concerning "Washbuckets" and "Project Chesapeake Bay" were either written to, about, or at the request of, one Doctor Troy Sandlake, a man who went by the nickname of Ken.

Still more electronic gumshoeing led them to a biography on Sandlake. A top engineer for an obscure but prestigious defense think-tank named the Erica Corporation, Sandlake did everything but make the coffee for Project Chesapeake Bay. He designed the "washbuckets," and their complicated mini-nuke warheads. He single-handedly built the first twenty models, and even went down with the diving teams on the initial trials.

Then the war broke out . . .

It took Hunter and Fitz working on the FBI's central computer to track down three locations where Sandlake might be, if indeed he was still alive. One was his birthplace near Albany, in the Free Territory of New York. Fitzie's crack intelligence agents took only a few hours to confirm that Sandlake was not in the area. The second possibility was Boston, where Sandlake had worked for a time. But that part of the country was now uninhabited, the lasting results of the wars with the Middle Atlantic Conference States that occurred right after the New Order was clamped down.

The third possibility was a small town outside of El Paso where his daughter once lived. A quick check with the Republic of Texas Intelligence Agency confirmed that a man bearing Sandlake's general description had been known to be living in the area.

The Texans even narrowed down the man's whereabouts to an isolated ranch about 30 miles southeast of El Paso, near a town called Clint. But they also reported that the last time anyone had come close to the ranch house — in this case a drifter looking for a handout — they were fired upon by no less than an M60 machine gun. The RTIA had thereafter labeled the man "unsociable."

With this in mind, Hunter and Fitz first located the ranch house from the air, then landed their jumpjets about a quarter mile away. Both men secured the VTOL airplanes, and carrying standard issue M-16s, cautiously set out toward the dwelling.

It was just dusk when they reached the ranch's outer post fence. Using NightScope binoculars, Hunter could see only a single light burning in the sprawling, somewhat dilapidated ranch house. There was no evidence of heavy weapons anywhere outside the house, although he could see several spools of electrical wire scattered about the property.

"It doesn't look like he's expecting company," Hunter said, taking note of the desolate location. "Of course, who the hell else would be way out here in Nowheresville?"

Fitz was about to say something when suddenly a burst of gunfire whizzed over their heads.

"*Jesus Christ!*" Fitz yelled out as they both dove into a nearby ditch. "He *is* unsociable!"

But Hunter knew immediately that the shots hadn't come from the house.

"That was too close to come from his place," he said, gingerly scanning all around them with the NightScope. "Someone's out here with us . . ."

As if to emphasize the point, another burst of gunfire kicked up a small storm of sand and rocks no more than six feet from their position.

"At least two of them," Hunter said, his ultra-sensitive ears keying in on the difference in sounds between the two bursts. "Came from over that-a-way . . ."

Just as he indicated a point north of them with the snout

136

of his M-l6, a third burst of gunfire went right over their heads, this one longer and more sustained.

"They must have NightScopes, too," Hunter said, feeling somewhat miffed at himself for dropping in on his second "hot" landing zone in as many weeks. It was a habit he wished he could break.

"Well, they're getting damn close," Fitz said, checking the magazine in his gun. He was reassured to find it full.

"I know," Hunter said, checking his own clip. "But who the hell are they?"

Fitz shook his head and added: "More important, Hawker, do they know who *we* are?"

"Only one way to find out," Hunter said, tying his kerchief onto the muzzle of his M-l6.

"Be careful," Fitz warned him as he started waving the makeshift flag.

"*We're Americans!*" Hunter shouted out in the loudest voice possible. "We 've got no beef with you! We're from the United American Army and . . ."

His next words were cut off by a long stream of bullets streaking overhead. He was back down in the ditch in a micro-second.

"I don't think they like us," he said with understatement.

"You certainly gave them a chance," Fitz said, who like Hunter was certain that the people doing the shooting would kill them if given the chance. "Now how the hell do we get out of this one?"

"Okay," Hunter said, improvising a bit. "How about you stay here and I'll circle around them?"

"Don't joke at a time like this, Hawker!" Fitz growled at him through clenched teeth.

"Okay, then, how about we split up, and hit them from two sides?" he asked.

"*Yer* going daft . . ." Fitz said anxiously reverting back to his thick brogue.

"Well, that doesn't leave us with many other options," Hunter said. "Except of course, the 'big' option . . ."

"Yeah, well let's give *that* one a try, if you don't mind?" Fitz said.

Once again his words were nearly split in two with another barrage of gunfire. This was immediately followed by three mortar rounds landing in quick succession about 25 feet away.

"These guys are getting on my nerves," Hunter said as he pulled an old silver quarter out of his pocket and gave it a flip.

"Heads!" he called just as he slapped the coin down on the back of his hand.

"Tails it is!" Fitz cried, seeing he had won.

"Jesus Christ, do you *ever* lose?" Hunter asked Fitz as the Irishman strapped his M-16 back on and prepared to move out of the ditch.

"You know better than to ask that," he told Hunter. "Now how shall we work this?"

Hunter thought for a moment, then said: "Wait for the lightshow, I guess . . ." Once again he checked the clip in his M-16; as always it was filled with tracer rounds. "If they shoot back at you or me, then let 'em have it . . ."

"Okay," Fitz said, taking a deep breath. "Be back in a snap . . ."

With that, Fitzgerald scrambled out of the ditch and started making his way back to their airplanes.

Twenty minutes passed. . . .

The last rays of the vivid southwestern sunset were just fading when Fitzie's Harrier appeared high overhead, slowly circling the ranch. Hunter, still scrunched up in the ditch, had been ducking only occasional bursts of gunfire since Fitz had left, and these had been way off the mark. This told him that whoever was firing on him wasn't exactly sure where he was.

But that was about to change . . .

Sensing that Fitz was ready, Hunter dramatically stood up and fired off a long burst of tracers in the general direction of the enemy fire. The early evening darkness was suddenly lit up with ghostly streaks of yellow-red as his phosphorus rounds bounced and ricocheted around the desert scrub brush and rocks.

A split second later Hunter was back in the ditch, hands over his head as the mysterious enemy again opened up on his position.

One stream of gunfire zipped by to his right.

"Now that sounds like an M60," he thought, tuning his ears into the gun's distinctive "budda-budda" reverberation.

Two more barrages came from a slightly different direction.

"Are those Mausers?" he wondered, keying in on the automatic fire's zinging sound.

Then, as if on cue, two mortar rounds came crashing down about 50 feet away.

"Light stuff," he thought. "Probably fifty-one millimeters . . ."

He counted to ten, then he heard another, more deafening *crash!*

"Finally, here come the real fireworks . . ." he thought as he hunkered down further in the ditch. No more than 20 feet above him, Fitz's Harrier streaked overhead, its two 30-mm Aden cannons blazing. He heard two anti-personnel bombs explode during the jumpjet's next pass, followed only by some feeble return fire. Three more subsequent passes were devoted to the powerful Aden cannons.

It was all over in under five minutes. Their plan for Hunter to draw fire had worked beautifully. Crawling up out of the duct, Hunter could see four separate fires burning about a quarter mile from his location. He unleashed another long stream of tracer bullets in the same general direction. But no one shot back this time. Either Fitz had got them all or they had run away.

It took another ten minutes for Hunter to find a suitable landing spot for Fitz's Harrier.

Using his powerful utility lamp, he directed the jumpjet down onto a concrete slab that had once served as a silo foundation. The AV-8B just fit on the improvised hardstand and only Fitz's adeptness at flying the unusual Harrier prevented a mishap.

"Everything quiet?" the Irishman asked his friend as he climbed down from the jet. "I spotted four separate targets out there and I believe I got at least three of them dead-on . . ."

"You done good, Mike," Hunter said. "Haven't heard a peep from them."

The two pilots set out toward the nearest fire, their M-16's up and ready. Reaching it they found three bodies and a destroyed mortar set-up.

Gingerly feeling inside the pockets of one of the stiffs, Hunter came up with a single piece of paper. On it was drawn a small but detailed map of the ranch and the surrounding area. Clearly marked with large black Xs were the four gun positions, all of which were now burning.

"Looks like they were staking out this place," Hunter said. "I think we just dropped in on a party that hadn't really started yet."

"What a coincidence," Fitz said, looking over the remains of the mortar. "That should mean the good doctor will greet us with open arms."

They quickly checked two other targets and found six more bodies. Like the first three, they were clad in nondescript drab green fatigues with no identifying patches or badges.

But it was at the fourth and final location that Hunter found a piece of very disturbing evidence. Four men lay dead at this site, the bodies scattered around a M60 machinegun. But as both pilots could see, the nest itself hadn't been hit by any of Fitzie's cannon fire or antipersonnel bombs.

"This is the one I missed," Fitz said, observing a large crater about 30 feet away made by one of his antipersonnel bombs. "Yet these guys have all been greased . . ."

Hunter played his flashlight beam on each of the bodies. Each one had a pistol in hand and a single shot in the head.

"*Suicides?*" Fitz asked incredulously.

Hunter nodded slowly in agreement. "They iced themselves," he said grimly noting the dead men had shaved heads. "Just like those two triggermen that plugged old Captain Pegg. They even have the same haircuts . . ."

"Do you think, Hawker . . ." Fitz said, trying to find the correct words. "Do you think these guys are Canal Nazis, too?"

"Either that or they all got *real* depressed at the same moment," Hunter answered.

Hunter felt a chill run through him. Both he and Fitz had seen war — too often for his tastes. It was hardly the glamorous adventure that the prewar movies and TV and books would have had people believe. People didn't just fall over and look like they'd gone to sleep after being hit with a bullet or a shell fragment. Bodies — skulls, stomachs, spines — tended to explode when hit by a projectile. And what came out was hardly pretty or glamorous. In reality, it was sickening.

But long ago Hunter had somehow steeled himself against the horrible sights of war. He loathed killing, as did everyone he knew from the United American Army Command Staff on down. But the survival of his country was of the utmost importance to him, and anyone who dared threaten it with arms and killing of their own had to be taken on. That was war.

But taking one's own life was a different story. That passed from an act of war to an act of fanaticism. And frankly, it gave him the creeps . . .

"It takes a lot to put a gun to one's own head, Hawker," Fitz said, mirroring his own feelings.

Hunter nodded glumly. "Yeah, in a situation like this, it's called 'brainwashing' . . ."

He turned toward the ranch house and added: "Let's go see what the doctor has to say about all this."

Chapter 25

The two pilots approached the ranch house from two sides, each one using his NightScope goggles.

When they met on the porch, both Hunter and Fitz shrugged at the lack of incident in walking up to the house. The place itself was a solid, stone structure with a massive oak door that looked thick enough to be bulletproof. In its day the ranch house must have been a sight to see. Now it was more than a little seedy looking.

Inside there was still a single light burning.

"Maybe after all this we'll find out no one's at home," Fitz whispered to Hunter.

"Well, that would be a kick in the ass," Hunter said as he silently lifted the latch on the front door of the rundown structure. It was locked.

"Too simple just to bust it in," Fitz cautioned.

Hunter nodded and backed away from the door. "Okay, give him a yell . . ." he said.

Fitz put one hand up to his mouth and took a deep breath. *"Sandlake!"* he hollered. "We're friends! Don't shoot!"

Silence . . .

"Hey, Sandlake!" Fitz began again. "You owe us a favor man! We just saved yer ass . . ."

Again, nothing.

"Well, if he's in there he's an ungrateful bastard," Hunter said.

"Hawker, why don't you give it a try?" Fitz suggested. "Tell him who yer are."

At that point Hunter was willing to try anything.

"Sandlake!" he called out. "This is Major Hawk Hunter of the United American Army. We're here to . . ."

Suddenly they heard a rustling inside. Then a voice, somewhat weak, somewhat mechanical spoke four words:

"Hawk Hunter is dead."

Hunter shook his head in frustration. "This is getting ridiculous," he said. He was getting sick and tired of everyone from here to Central America and back thinking he was six feet under.

"I assure you he is very much alive and well, Doctor!" Fitz called in. "Open the door and find out."

"You must think I'm as crazy as the others do . . ." came the reply. "It will take a lot more to get me to open this door than a promise to see the famous Wingman."

Hunter immediately resented the man's mocking tone.

"Okay, Sandlake," he yelled back. "Let me say one word to you: *Washbuckets* . . ."

There was another long silence.

"How about three more words?" Fitz yelled out. "Project Chesapeake Bay."

Just then they heard someone fiddling with the lock on the big door.

Both Hunter and Fitz had their M-16s up and ready as the huge oak door squeaked open.

The first thing Hunter saw was another M-16 pointing right at him. The second thing he saw was a tight T-shirt and a lovely pair of breasts.

"What in heaven . . ." Fitz started to say.

Hunter was almost too dumbfounded for words. Standing before them, holding a M-16, was an incredibly beautiful woman.

"Lower your guns gentlemen, and you can come in," the woman said.

Although it might not have been the sensible thing to do, Hunter and Fitz lowered their guns as requested. The woman then lowered hers.

"Is . . . is there someone named Dr. Sandlake here?" Hunter asked, not knowing what else to say.

"Yes . . ." the woman answered "Of course, there is."

She turned and opened the big door wide enough for them to enter. Both Hunter and Fitz's eyes immediately zoomed in on her perfect *derriere*.

"Strange things happen when I'm with you, Hawker," Fitz said to him in a nervously cracking brogue.

"I was about to say the same thing to you, Fitz," Hunter replied.

They both stepped inside and took a quick look at the surroundings. The interior of the ranch house was even more rundown than the outside. Everywhere furniture lay uncleaned, ripped and falling apart. The walls were covered with a thick coat of dust and not one picture was hanging evenly. The floor was covered with an endless carpet of glass and plaster.

Added to all this were numerous bullet holes everywhere.

Hunter turned his attention back to the woman. She was blond, *very* pretty and probably in her mid-twenties. Her figure was picture perfect, the result, Hunter could tell, of much care and exercise.

"We are here to talk to the doctor," he said. "I assume that was he talking to us through the door?"

The woman nodded, an action that served to jiggle her breasts ever so slightly.

"Yes, that was him," she said. "Through his security intercom."

"Are you his daughter?" Hunter asked, thinking another piece of the puzzle was about to fall into place.

But the woman suddenly looked down, a pained expression coming across her. "No . . ." she said, sadly.

Hunter and Fitz looked at each other. It was obvious Hunter had touched a sensitive nerve.

"Just follow me," the woman said. "And be careful of the broken glass."

With that she expertly walked through the rubble on the floor and toward a lighted doorway that obviously led to a cellar.

They followed her down a long set of stairs which led to another huge door, this one made of reenforced steel. With

144

no small effort, the blond beauty yanked the door back just far enough for them to squeeze in.

As opposed to the dingy setting upstairs, the chamber on the other side of the doorway was well lit. The bunker-like room was filled with hundreds of electronic devices, none of which Hunter could identify at first glance. Everywhere there were lights flashing, buzzers buzzing, computer screens displaying row after row of numbers and letters, computer printers working non-stop, spitting out reams of data. Working feverishly over it all were three more beautiful women, attractively dressed in tight jeans and T-shirts, M-16s slung over their shoulders.

"So this is the famous Hawk Hunter, you say?" a voice from the far end of the chamber asked.

Hunter and Fitz turned to see a middle aged man hunched over a work bench that was overflowing with electronic parts, wires and tools. He was wearing large tortoise shell glasses and a typically stained lab coat.

Hunter stepped forward. "I'm Hawk Hunter," he said matter-of-factly. "In the flesh . . ."

"I recognize you from the newspapers," the man replied. "Glad to see you're not dead."

"Me, too," Hunter said. "You're Dr. Sandlake?"

The man was in his late 40s, still somewhat handsome with a healthy shock of graying hair. It appeared as if he shared his female companion's penchant for fitness; Hunter thought the guy might have been a bodybuilder at some point.

"I'm Sandlake," he answered. "Sorry for the rather rude greeting before . . ." he motioned to a intercom-type microphone near his work bench. "Got to be careful in this neighborhood these days."

"So we found out," Fitz said. "Did you realize there were more than a dozen men out there—heavily armed, too?"

"Of course, we did," Sandlake said. "They've been out there for a week now. Or maybe it's only been a couple days. I'm not too sure. But, in any case, did you chase them away?"

"You might say that," Hunter replied. "They *were* enemies

of yours, right?"

"Absolutely!" Sandlake said, thrusting a one finger in the air like a revved-up college professor. "They were trying to starve us out of here, the bastards."

"Starve you out?" Fitz asked. "They had enough fire power to level this place — or at least the top part of the house. Maybe even this bunker, too."

"Ah, yes," Sandlake said. "But you see, that would have meant killing us — or more specifically, killing *me*. And I'm afraid to say those chaps wanted me quite alive."

The man stopped for a quick breath of air, then went on: "I think they were jealous," he said. "You may have noticed, my assistants are quite pulchritudinous."

"If that means 'foxy,' you're right," Fitz said.

Both Sandlake and Fitz laughed at the joke, but Hunter could feel the gratuitous conversation was heading out into the ozone somewhere. And the strangest thing was that while he was talking, Sandlake continued to tinker with some do-dad on his work bench. The man seemed to be working the absent-minded professor routine a little too much. It was as if the two pilots had just dropped in for nothing more than a friendly chat and now were no more than a distraction.

It was time to cut to the quick . . .

"Like we said, we're here to talk to you about Project Chesapeake Bay," Hunter said firmly. "Specifically, underwater nuclear mines . . ."

Sandlake gave out a somewhat nutty laugh. "Well, that *is* funny," he said. "Because that's exactly what those guys outside wanted to talk to me about also . . ."

"You can be sure we are here for a different motive," Hunter said. Then, for the next ten minutes, he patiently explained to the man the situation in Panama and what the United American Army Command Staff felt had to be done about it.

"We have to launch a massive attack on The Twisted Cross," Hunter told Sandlake. "But before we do that, we have to find some way to disarm those nuclear mines."

"We understand you're the expert behind their creation,

is that right?" Fitz asked.

"Yes, quite right," Sandlake said, for the first time turning away from his tinkering. Suddenly he became very serious. "And I am quite aware of the nuclear mine system in the Canal. In fact, gentlemen, I not only created the monster—I'm the one who gave it all to the Twisted Cross."

Hunter almost asked the man to repeat himself.

"You did?" Fitz cried out. "In Heaven's name man, why?"

Sandlake took off his glasses and rubbed his tired eyes. In the course of three seconds it appeared as if he was a completely different person. Gone was the jovial/bothersome professorial *schtick*. It was replaced with the worn-down look of a very troubled individual.

"Come with me, gentlemen," he said, rising from his seat at the end of the work bench. "It's a long, sad story . . ."

Two hours and one bottle of Scotch later, both Hunter and Fitz were shaking their heads in amazement.

Sandlake had led them into a smaller room off his fortified bunker. Mixing coffee with the bitter Scotch, the man talked and they listened.

After the Big War, Sandlake, who had been stranded in the Rockies on a Christmas ski weekend, tried to get transportation back to his office in Washington, thinking that would be the professional and patriotic thing to do. But with the chaos and anarchy that ensued across the country following the Soviet's sneak attack on America's ICBM silos, he finally realized that there wasn't much for him to return to in the nation's former capital. He decided that getting here—his daughter's house near El Paso—was his next best bet.

Traveling by any means he could, including horseback, the doctor made the sometimes torturous 500-mile plus journey in two months. He arrived to find his daughter relatively safe, though grief-stricken that her oil executive husband of just three months had been killed in Saudi Arabia during the first day of the war.

Together, Sandlake, who was a widower, and his daughter

147

struggled to eke out an existence in the isolated ranchhouse. El Paso was nearly deserted and tales of looters and drug-crazed bandits roaming the empty streets were enough to keep civilized people away from the city. Instead, the father and daughter grew their own food and raised some cattle for beef. A small but effective bartering agreement with some nearby survivors filled in the gaps, the Sandlakes usually trading either steaks or one of the doctor's many gadgets in return for clothing and firewood.

Sandlake said it was as close to a comfortable existence as one could expect in post-war, New Order America. Several years went by. News about the outside world was scarce. He and his daughter had heard rumors of great battles being fought up in the center of the continent, and on one occasion, they hid from a band of Circle Army deserters, who ransacked their storage bin. After that, Sandlake built the underground bunker and spent much of his free time manufacturing his electronic do-whats — security devices, mostly — for barter.

This relatively peaceful life came to a crashing halt very early one morning when his home was invaded by no less than one hundred armed men, brought in by a dozen Soviet-made assault helicopters. They were called The Party, and at first, claimed to be arms dealers. However, after a short talk with the leader of the group, a man named Frankel, Sandlake realized that the invaders knew many of the details about Project Chesapeake Bay and the underwater nuclear mines. What they wanted was the location of the actual hardware, which, they made quite clear to him, they wanted to use to solidify their takeover of the Panama Canal.

Sandlake refused to tell them. Two days of beatings and torture followed. It was during this time that the Party members learned that his daughter was actually a doctor too — she held a degree in a particularly strict discipline of archaeology.

Once the intruders learned this, they radioed their headquarters (which Sandlake believed was in Mexico City at the time) and soon some even higher officials of The Party arrived at the ranch. They then turned their torture tactics on his daughter, demanding she tell them everything she knew about ancient Mayan sites in Central America as well as Inca sites in South America. She resisted at first — so much so that a helicopter was dispatched to collect some sodium pentathol — better known as truth serum.

After two days of constant injections, Sandlake's daughter finally broke. Her interrogators knew very well that her branch of archaeology — called "dark zone" archaeology — was the study of the deepest inner areas of ancient sites. Two years before the war broke out, startling discoveries had been made at certain Mayan and Inca sites previously thought to have been researched to the full. "Dark Zone" archaeologists had found a number of man-made caves, walkways and tunnels underneath several Central and South American sites, often accessible only through narrow wet clay passages. These secret chambers had laid undiscovered for years by general school archaeologists as well as looters. The researchers theorized the Mayans and the Incas had used these Dark Zones for religious rituals or as hiding places.

But for what ever reason, in every case, the Dark Zoners found these strange places filled with gold . . .

The Party members were quick to realize they had come upon an incredible coincidence: Not only did they have the man who invented the small, nuclear-tipped underwater mines they sought for the Panama Canal, they also had someone who was an expert in locating long lost treasures of Mayan and Inca gold.

Once again the invaders started beating and torturing the doctor, demanding that he reveal the location of the nuclear mines. Finally, on the climactic 13th day of the nightmare, the Party members stripped his daughter naked in front of him and threatened to rape and then kill her if he didn't give them the information. Sandlake felt he had no choice but to tell, a decision aided by the fact that he too was injected several times with truth serum.

Two helicopters left the ranch and returned four days later to report that they had found the nuclear mines right where Sandlake said they'd be—in the lead-lined underground storage center at the Key West Naval Air Station. Once they had what they wanted, the Party members bundled up his daughter and took her away. Then they took him out to the back of his house, shot him twice in the head and left him for dead.

Now it was Sandlake's time to get lucky. Shortly after the Party members departed, a bartering group happened by the ranch. They found Sandlake barely alive but still breathing and they took him with them. By some kind of miracle, he survived his severe head wounds, though he admitted that his mental capacities were only about 70 to 80-percent of what they once were.

"I was never absent-minded before all this," he told the pilots sadly. "But I came back from the dead. Saw my own body, lying there on the ground, blood everywhere. My blood! Believe me, that can't help but affect you. Now, sometimes I lose track of time, dates, my own past . . ."

Once he recovered, Sandlake returned to the ranch and the underground bunker and immediately began work on a disarming device for the nukes. The "Deactivator" he called it. His short-circuited reasoning had him figuring he could hire some mercenaries to travel to the Canal and put the mines out of action. But his diminished capacity, along with a general lack of equipment, made the project slow going. Even when he recruited the four young women—no dummies, they were all graduate students in engineering from Texas A&M before the war—the work on the deactivator device dragged on. He made a mistake of trying to barter for some much needed equipment via an arms dealer working on the outskirts of El Paso. He thought that through this individual, word got back to The Twisted Cross that he was still alive.

The smaller group of Canal Nazis *had* landed just two days before. Surprised at the defensive firepower mounted by the doctor and his lovely assistants, they decided to play it safe and lay siege to the ranch, hoping to starve them out and retrieve whatever parts of the deactivator they had completed. Sandlake spent those past 48 hours intentionally entering misleading data into computers, so as to confuse the Nazis should they succeed in getting into his bunker.

"An incredible story," Hunter told the man.

"You should get all this down in writing," Fitz told him. "Should they ever start printing books again, this one will be a bestseller . . ."

"But the final chapters aren't written as yet," Sandlake said glumly. "At least I hope they haven't . . ."

"They haven't," Hunter told him. "First of all, we'll have a chopper here in the morning. You and your assistants are coming back to DC with us. You can work on the deactivator there. You'll have a lot more resources and more people to help."

"But what about my daughter?" the man asked, close to tears. "She's been missing for so long . . ."

"Don't worry about it," Hunter said decisively. "I'll get your daughter back for you . . ."

Chapter 26

More than 1200 miles to the south as the crow flies, Colonel Krupp was sitting in the back of his command truck, drinking heavily.

His convoy was now halfway to the Uxmaluna site, the bombed-out, burned-away road provided for them proving to be very slow going. Two hours before, he had called a halt to work for the day, his troops mistakenly praising him for stopping a full four hours early. But he hadn't done it for their sakes. He would have worked them 24 hours straight if he thought he could get away with it.

His reasons for knocking off early were totally selfish and devious. That was why he had spent the last hour fortifying himself with a jug of bad banana brandy. He was an awful drinker. Having no experience with it, he tended to overindulge at all the wrong times. This occasion would be no exception.

Before him, tied to his fold-down bed, was the woman. She was stripped naked, bound hand and foot to the bedframe with leather straps and gagged with a cloth. It was the way he had dreamed of seeing her ever since the beginning. Now was the opportunity . . .

He took another long gulp of the scorchingly bad brandy, and reached for a small leather whip. Her eyes went wide with alarm as she watched him play with the tassels. She tried to scream something, but the cloth in her mouth prevented that. However her aggressive action surprised him.

"You are not supposed to resist . . ." he said, drunkenly slurring the words. "You are here to be taught a lesson . . ."

She started to thrash about, hurting her arms and wrists where they were so securely tied to the bed. For his part he felt a guilty pang of true pleasure shoot through him as he watched her breasts and hips move back and forth

"Oh, my dear," he said, slobbering a smile. "Don't you realize that all this . . . this moving and gyrating . . . is futile?"

She tried to scream a second time, but her cry was once again muffled by the gag.

He leaned over toward her, his lips just inches from her lovely well-formed breasts. "You defied me today, my sweet," he said in a weird, inebriated sing-songy whine. "It is almost as if you don't understand who you are dealing with here."

He dared reach out at that point, putting his leather glove on her right breast. He suddenly felt as if he had made history, and in a sense, he had: It was the first time in his 42 years that he had touched a woman's naked body.

She squirmed hard again, trying to force his hand from her, but she couldn't. He pinched her nipple tightly, causing her to arch up and back.

"You . . . you actually *enjoyed* that, didn't you?" he asked her, completely misreading her action.

He then put his hand between her soft white legs, feeling the smoothness of her thighs even through the leather glove. Again she tried to stop him from touching her by moving about, but again it was no use.

"And that?" he said, taking a swig of brandy, half of which wound up on his chin and neck. "You liked that too, didn't you?"

She violently shook her head from side to side.

"You didn't?" he said, his voice now approaching the timber of an elderly woman. "Well, that's good . . ."

Another gulp from the brandy and his uniform pants were down. He ripped open his jacket to reveal a hairless, almost feminine chest.

"Prepare yourself, my dear," he said, fighting off a violent series of hiccups. "Prepare to feel the sting of some long overdue discipline . . ."

Just then he reached down for his whip and for the brandy bottle at the same time. The complicated maneuver caused him to lose his balance. He came crashing down on top of her, cracking his head on the metal bed frame as he did so. Suddenly he rolled off her and fell to the floor, completely blacked-out, a nasty gash bleeding on his nose.

She prayed he was dead . . .

Part II

Chapter 27

"I suppose there's no way I can talk you out of this?" Jones asked Hunter as they walked down to the edge of the Potomac River.

Hunter didn't answer. He simply shrugged and readjusted the large, overfilled knapsack he was carrying.

"How about if I gave you a direct order *not* to go?" Jones continued.

The Wingman stopped and looked the general straight in the eyes. "Then I wouldn't go . . ." he said. He took a deep breath then asked: "Are you going to give me such an order?"

Jones stared at him for a moment then shook his head.

"No, I'm not, Major," he said. "But I want you to convince me that you know just what you're getting yourself into."

"I don't know what more I can say, General," Hunter told him as they resumed walking toward a small, riverside pier. "I promised Sandlake that I'd find his daughter. I feel I have to make good on it."

"But look at the monumental task you've taken on," Jones said. "Trying to find one person? In Central America? These days?"

"I know it's crazy," Hunter replied. "But I can't go back on my word. Besides, I've been holed up with Sandlake for the past five days, going over every possible Mayan or Inca site where they may have taken his daughter. It's really just a question of tracking them down to the right place."

"And then what?"

"And, then I'll try to snatch her back," Hunter said. "Just how will depend on the circumstances."

Jones let out a long, gruff sigh. "We don't have much time, you know," he told the pilot.

"I know that, sir," Hunter replied. "But we do have *some* time. We have to prepare the strike force, draw up the battle plans, do the logistics . . ."

"All true," Jones said. "But we are moving ahead very quickly to accomplish all that."

As if to underscore his point, he nodded to the long column of United American M-1 tanks that was rumbling down nearby Independence Avenue on their way to Fort Meade in old Maryland. Several of the tank commanders recognized Jones and Hunter and offered friendly waves and salutes.

"The Texans and the Free Canadians are on board," Jones continued. "And we're gathering the airlift capacity and putting everyone through a quickie course in jungle combat training."

"That's all great," Hunter said. "But we also have to take into consideration that Sandlake is still a way from completing his deactivating device."

"He seems to be progressing well," Jones said, watching two United American A-7 Strikefighters pass overhead and turn south. "Christ, we've got more than twenty engineers working with him and his rather lovely assistants."

"Again, that's super," Hunter replied. "But I've gotten to know the guy pretty well. He's really not a well man. He goes in and out. Flashes of brilliance, sure. But there are a lot of dark spots in there, too."

Jones nodded sympathetically. "Getting shot in the head does that to you," he said.

"So does missing part of your family," Hunter replied. "And frankly, that's not something that I myself have thought a lot about—until this past week, that is. Now I know what they mean when they say that having someone close to you turn up *missing* is worse than having them *die* on you . . ."

They walked without talking for the next few minutes. Jones had the feeling Hunter was stepping into uncharted psychic territory; a very personal place in his mind.

Two more A-7s streaked over, breaking the silence between them. Finally they had reached their destination, a small dock just this side of the Arlington Memorial Bridge.

Jones took one look at the contraption tied up to the pier and said: "Good God, what the hell is that?"

Hunter's mood lightened instantly. "I'm surprised at you General," he said. "I would have thought you'd recognize one of the best, most under-rated airplanes ever built."

"But it looks like it's an antique . . ." Jones said.

"It *is* an antique," Hunter replied. "And I can't think of a better airplane to take on this mission . . ."

It was a Vought OS2U Kingfisher, a World War II-vintage seaplane that Hunter and Fitz found packed away deep in the bowels of the Smithsonian's Washington, DC storage facility. Working with a crew of UA Air Force volunteers, they had it flying in just a few hours. Hunter then spent another half day souping up the single prop engine from 450 horsepower to 650, and adding extra fuel tanks. Another few hours went into installing three special mini-computers of his own design, plus a long range radio set, an infra red spotting device and a few more high-tech weapons systems, all modular construction.

"Why this airplane?" Jones asked, running his hand along the Kingfisher's smooth, all-metal frame. "We certainly have bigger and better aircraft you could use."

"I know that," Hunter replied. "But this baby has a few advantages over anything else we've got.

"First of all, it's a low maintenance bird. The engine is as simple as one in a '65 Chevy. It's durable and it will run well in hot, humid weather. The Navy used these airplanes in the South Pacific for the entire war as observation craft, air-sea rescue, things like that. They catapulted them off battleships and cruisers, or they took off right from bays and harbors. They took a real beating and kept flying.

"It's got a range of eight hundred miles and with the extra tanks I've added, I'll bet I get twelve hundred miles or more between fill-ups."

"But why a seaplane?" Jones asked. "You're going to the middle of the jungle . . ."

"Well, that's what I thought at first, too," Hunter replied. "Then I did some studying and some talking with Sandlake.

"It turns out that many of the Mayan sites are actually built fairly close to rivers or lakes. It makes sense because the people who built these places two thousand years ago needed water close by for construction and for drinking. And later, when the site was finished, they wanted to be near water for agriculture and so on."

"So you figure you can land this thing on any river or lake?" Jones asked.

"That's the topper," Hunter said, admiring the Kingfisher. "This airplane could land on a fair-size stream if it had to. And it's very maneuverable for something of its size and bulk. I think that's an option I'll need . . ."

Hunter could see Jones was slowly falling under the spell of the ungainly elegance of the Kingfisher. It was nearly 34 feet in length with a wing span of 35 feet, 11 inches. And with the float attached—it alone was more than 35 feet long—the OS2U stood 15 high on dry land. The pilot rode in a cockpit very close to the forward-mounted single engine. This pilot's compartment continued on two thirds of the way down the fuselage where it ended in a rear-facing gunner/observer seat. Overall, the airplane was somewhat similar in size and appearance to the more recognizable Grumman TBF-1 Avenger divebomber, one of the stalwarts of the US Naval Air effort against the Japanese. Except this airplane could float . . .

This Kingfisher now carried a very modern, very deadly Vulcan cannon contained in a weapons pod on its left wing; a small air-to-ground missile firing platform balancing the load on its right. Jones noted that Hunter had also somehow managed to hook up two air-to-air missiles to the Kingfisher's wingtips—"mini-Sidewinders" was what the pilot called them.

Jones peeked inside and saw that Hunter had arranged his minicomputers along one side of the pilot's compartment, his advanced weapons firing systems along the other. The tunnel between the pilot's seat and that of the observer/gunner was now adorned with a simple hammock and some boxes of food. A .50 caliber machine gun was attached to the gunner's post.

"Original equipment," Hunter told him pointing to the big fifty. "Believe it or not they used to shoot down Zeroes with those things . . ."

Jones took a step back and took in the whole package. It *was* a beautiful-looking airplane, much in the same manner as a Tucker had been a beautiful-looking automobile.

"What can I say?" Jones asked. "It looks like you've covered as many bases as possible."

"Well, I've tried . . ." Hunter replied, giving the airplane an affectionate pat on the rear. "But, then again, you never know . . ."

Jones checked his watch. "The staff is meeting in two hours," he said. "I understand you wrote out a list of recommendations for pre-strike activities?"

Hunter nodded, throwing his gear inside the airplane. "They're just suggestions, but I think they can only help us in the long run," he said. "We should establish a strong link between us and those chopper guys in Panama—the CATS. They're good at what they do, they know the terrain and they've been a thorn in the side of The Twisted Cross before we even knew what the hell was going on down there."

"Sounds like a good idea," Jones said, making a notation in his ever-present notebook. "What else?"

"Local involvement," Hunter said. "There are a lot of native Panamanians and Indians in that area who have been virtually enslaved by The Twisted Cross. If we could somehow get them informed, they'd be a tremendous help when the time comes to move."

"Again, another good idea," the general agreed. "Perhaps the CATS can help in that regard also . . ."

"The only other thing is the deactivator itself," Hunter

said, giving the Kingfisher one last look over. "JT and Ben are working closely with Sandlake, as is Fitz. If I understand the good doctor correctly, his device works on a high frequency radio burst system. Blasting the mines with short, quick bursts of radio waves screws up the timing devices."

"Sounds complicated," Jones said. "But once the device is completed, how the hell do we get it down to the Canal and working?"

"That's the sixty-four thousand dollar question, General," Hunter replied. "We're hoping Sandlake can rig something that can be installed onto the F-16. And then it would be a matter of me overflying the Canal and just blanketing it with the deactivator's radio bursts . . ."

Jones suddenly looked very worried. "That sounds extremely dangerous," he said. "Especially with the firepower they've assembled along the Canal."

Hunter shrugged. "That's my last recommendation," he said. "The only way I can think of pulling it off is for me to go in on the first wave of the attack, and while everyone and his brother is covering my ass, I just zip through and disarm all the warheads . . ."

"My God," Jones said. "Do you think you can actually do that?"

Once again, Hunter could only shrug. "Do we have any other choice?" he asked.

Completing his last visual inspection of the OS2U, Hunter knew it was time to shove off.

Jones shook his hand. "Good luck, Hawk," he said. "Don't forget to give us a yell if you need help . . ."

Hunter firmly grasped the man's hand. Jones was his superior officer, but he also considered him one of his closest friends.

"You'll hear me loud and clear," he said. "And believe me, General, I'll be back before you know it . . ."

With that he jumped into the Kingfisher and started its old but reliable engine. With the help of Jones and two dock hands, he cast off from the pier and floated out to the center of the river. Then, in one great burst of power, he gunned the floatplane's engines and took off in a great spray of smoky exhaust and water. He slowly gained altitude and circled back over the dock.

Then, with a wag of his wings, he turned south and soon disappeared over the horizon.

Chapter 28

Colonel Frankel swatted a swamp fly with his cap and watched as the large cruise liner sailed by.

It was the *Big Easy Princess*, once again transitting through the canal on its way to the west coast of Colombia. He envied the days when he had something to do with its passage. The luxury vessel usually carried more than its share of high-rolling gamblers and drug lords and these people weren't above giving top officers of The Twisted Cross something "extra" for allowing them to pass through the canal.

For Frankel's part, he missed the occasional bottle of fine Scotch he'd usually received from one of the *Big Easy*'s charter members, a fat slob of a man named Jean LaFeet. But Frankel had heard from a Party spy that LaFeet was in jail in New Orleans, awaiting trial, and so he would not get his bottle of hooch this trip.

A cool breeze came by and Frankel once again congratulated himself for the foresight to build this small but comfortable "office" atop of the hill close by the waterway. Better than the quarters originally given him halfway down the hill, from this height, he could see a full ten miles in either direction — a good vantage point from which to keep an overall eye on his slaves, his troops and the gold panning operations.

It was also *very private* . . .

The panners had been at it for sometime now and surprisingly enough, they had come up with a fair amount of gold. Not enough to make the whole silly operation worthwhile in Frankel's estimation, but just enough to keep the smelly little man named Strauberg off his back.

He leaned back and took a sip of his rum-laced iced tea. It was almost noontime — soon he would eat his lunch. But as he did most days when he was bored, he decided to have a little "appetizer" before eating.

He clapped his hands twice loudly. His sergeant of the guard suddenly appeared.

"How many are down there today?" he asked the man.

"Five or six, sir," was the reply.

Frankel nodded. "Bring them all up here at once," he said.

The sergeant saluted and quickly left, running down the road from Frankel's house to a small cabin located next to the compound's guardhouse. By the time Frankel had mixed another rum and ice tea, the sergeant had returned with two privates and five young women, all of whom were tied to each other by the ankle.

"Dismissed!" Frankel growled at the enlisted men, quickly dispersing them. Then he beheld the females before him. Each one was dressed in the same one piece shirt/skirt and rubber sandals. Not exactly glamorous clothes, but at least they were clean.

He pointed to a petite redhead, the second one in line.

"Your name?"

"Christine . . ." was the answer.

"Have you been up here before?" he asked.

The girl meekly shook her head no.

"Come up here," he ordered, taking a long swig of his drink.

The redhead did so, shyly standing before him. He reached out and put his hand under her dress, his fingers quickly finding their way beneath her underwear. He liked what he felt. Taking his hand out, he pinched her left breast. Once again he liked the touch.

"Go inside," he commanded her. She nervously swept back her long red hair and did as he told her to.

Once again he surveyed the line of females.

"You . . ." he said pointing to a dark, native beauty. "Up here . . ."

The woman was soon in front of him and he put her through the same intimate inspection.

"No," he told her. "Not today . . ."

He singled out a third girl, a svelte brunette, brought her to the porch and felt around her privates.

"And what are you called?" he asked.

"Sandra . . ." came the meek reply.

"You'll do," Frankel pronounced. Then he clapped his hands again, an action that brought his sergeant of the guard running once more.

"Take the rest away," he said to the man. "And don't disturb me for anything for one hour. Understood?"

"Completely sir!" the man said, quickly herding the four remaining girls away.

Frankel went inside the cabin and locked the door. The two girls stood in the center of the room, not quite knowing what to do.

"Take your clothes off," he ordered them, retrieving a can of oil from a nearby cabinet. The two girls had no choice but to do as he told them. Soon both stood naked before him.

He sat on the cabin's large overstuffed couch and undid his uniform's belt buckle, motioning the two girls over to him.

"Take the oil and rub me," he said to them.

The red head, probably the more innocent of the two, asked: "Where?"

He looked at her and laughed. "Where do you think, my dear?" he asked, at the same time forcing her hand down his pants and between his legs.

He soon had his pants completely off. Both girls dipped their fingers into the scented lubricating oil and nervously started smearing it on his privates. The warm slippery oil in the hands of the two young girls had the desired effect. Frankel leaned back and enjoyed the moment, trying to decide which girl he would screw after lunch, once he had rejuvenated himself.

166

Suddenly the door to the cabin burst open . . .

Frankel's eyes, nearly closed in climax, were now wide open in surprise and anger. In a split-second he vowed to shoot the sergeant of the guard for disobeying his orders to be left alone.

Just a moment later he realized the person who had so rudely kicked open the door was none other than the *smellmeister* himself, the man named Strauberg. He was accompanied by two, well-armed, black-uniformed Party lieutenants.

"So this is how you oversee the panning operations, Frankel?" the disgusting little man squeaked at him.

Frankel was on his feet now, embarrassed that the three men had seen him naked from the waist down and in such a vulnerable position. "I am taking my noon meal time, Herr Strauberg . . ." he offered in a weak defense.

Strauberg whispered something to one of the guards and soon the girls were quickly hustled away.

"This borders on desertion, Colonel Frankel," Strauberg said to him in his ratty little voice. "There are more important things afoot than masturbating with young girls!"

Frankel was absolutely mortified. Strauberg wasn't even an officer of rank in the Twisted Cross or the elite Party. But there was no doubting that the obscene little man carried a lot of power within both organizations.

"We have recovered much gold today," Frankel told him. "The panning operation is going extremely well . . ."

Only one of Strauberg's eyebrows went up in excitement upon hearing the news. For the first time since Frankel had become associated with the man, it appeared like he had something else on his little mind than gold.

"We have trouble . . ." Strauberg finally told him sternly. "Our whole operation here in the canal may be in jeopardy."

"What has gone wrong?" Frankel asked, legitimately concerned.

Strauberg thumbed the other guard out of the room. Once he was certain they were alone, he wiped his brow and stepped closer to Frankel.

"Do you remember that doctor you and your men sup-posedly killed up in El Paso?" he said.

Frankel nodded weakly.

"Well, he's *alive*, you fool . . ." Strauberg said, his face twisting into a grotesque mask of crimson rage.

"That's impossible," Frankel said. "I fired the shots myself!"

"And did you check for a pulse?" Strauberg asked, his voice taking on a very scary inquisitive tone. Suddenly Frankel felt as if he was on trial.

"I didn't *have* to," Frankel countered. "The man took two bullets in the base of the skull."

"It wasn't good enough!" Strauberg screamed, pounding a nearby table for emphasis. "He's alive and now our spies think he is in the hands of those flag-wavers in Washington, working for them."

Frankel thought it over for a moment, but maybe he was missing the point. "Why is that a disaster?" he asked Strauberg. "We have the mines. They are all nearly planted. What's the crisis?"

"The 'crisis' is that he may be able to give those sickening retro-heroes some information that could threaten the integrity of the mines," Strauberg said, his agitated voice going up an octave with every few words.

If Frankel had had a gun at that moment, he would have shot the smelly man. As it was, he had to step back a few paces, so intense was the body odor.

"*Herr* Strauberg," he said, trying to calm his voice. "Even if the engineer is working for them, what good would he be? We have nearly fifty mines strung out all along the canal. Even if someone tried to sneak in here—saboteurs or whatever—they would never be able to disarm every *single* one of the mines. Or even *half* of them for that matter. And as we both know, two or three of the mines exploding would be sufficient to destroy this canal forever.

"Besides, what do we have to fear from these United Americans? They're nothing but a bunch of movie stars. They belong in the comic books."

"Stop preaching to me, you ass!" Strauberg screamed at him. "Those United Americans were able to destroy the

Circle Army, a force which I'm sure I don't have to remind you had substantial Soviet backing and at one point controlled half the North American continent!"

"You face the facts!" Frankel screamed right back. "Even the United Americans wouldn't risk coming down in here in force. Eventually they will learn the extent that we have mined the canal with nuclear weapons and they'll realize they will have to deal with us. It will only mean more gold in our coffers . . . We can bleed them dry."

"You paint too rosy a picture," Strauberg said, his right eyebrow once again going up in a salute when he heard that magic word. "And you assume too much. What's to prevent those glory hounds from coming down here and launching a surgical air strike on us?"

"We have hundreds of SAMs for just such a possibility!" Frankel answered.

"And what would happen if they teamed up with those helicopter jockeys who keep harassing us?" Strauberg bellowed, trying to yell louder than Frankel. "Do you realize those bastards actually shot down one of our Phantoms! And damaged another?"

Frankel held up his hand in motion for Strauberg to stop. "The chances of those chopper thugs and the United Americans even *knowing* about one another are very remote," he said. "It would take an unbelievable coincidence . . .".

"Don't talk to me about coincidences!" Strauberg shouted back at him. "We've played out a string of coincidences just to get to where we are right now."

Frankel let a sinister smile spread across his face. "Why *Herr* Strauberg, I'm surprised at you," he said, turning the tables on the man. "Are you actually attributing our successes to mere coincidence? I would have thought that a person like you would believe in Fate as our movement's guiding hand."

Taken aback by Frankel's questioning of his Arayan resolve, Strauberg lowered his tone a notch.

"It would be very unwise for you to question my loyalty to the cause," he said in a stern whisper. "I came here because there are questions the High Commander wants answered.

By you, Colonel. The foremost is: how do we know the United Americans would be so willing to deal with us?"

"Why come to *me* with such a question?" Frankel asked. "How would I know? I'm just in charge of this nickel-dime panning operation. You can't order me to answer questions I know nothing about . . ."

For a moment Frankel thought Strauberg was ready to reach for *his* gun and shoot *him*, so infuriated did the odorous man become when Frankel asked him the question.

"You are an officer of The Twisted Cross!" the little man screamed. "You will do what you are *ordered* to do! Find the answers or I swear I'll put you on trial for insubordination!"

At that moment Frankel decided it was time to take a different tack. "All right, *Herr* Strauberg," he said as calmly as possible. "What is it you want me to do?"

Chapter 29

Colonel Krupp had spoken not one word to his driver the entire day.

The officer, his head sore and swollen from the gash on his nose, was also suffering with exploding intestines, the after-effects of the horrible banana brandy.

The uncomfortable silence made the slow, grinding journey across the devastated forest floor even more painstaking. The two heavy-duty troop transport trucks up ahead of Krupp's command vehicle had broken down frequently throughout the day, their plow-like front ends sometimes becoming stuck in a fallen tree or a particularly solid vine that had somehow been missed by the blockbuster bombs.

It was dusk when the convoy slowly passed around the last major obstacle and completed a turn which brought them descending into the hidden valley itself. Now, for the first time, Krupp could actually see the first few open structures at the Uxmaluna site.

"Splendid," he whispered to himself. He suddenly managed to forget about his embarrassment the night before. He had promoted the sentry who helped bandage him up in the middle of the night. The same man returned the woman back to her holding room in one of the bigger trucks. Still, Krupp was certain that word of some kind had spread around the convoy. Throughout his hangover, he was shaken with paranoid shivers, thinking that everyone was laughing at him behind his back.

But now they had reached this, their most important site

in Central America. It was here he hoped to lay to rest forever his image as a mediocre officer of The Twisted Cross. It was a coincidence that he was in charge of the recovery mission. Now here he hoped to find the treasure trove of gold that would vault him right into a high position of The Party.

So he even managed a grin as the first trucks rolled into the partially-uncovered ancient Mayan site.

Maybe tonight I will try again with the woman, he thought.

Chapter 30

Her name was Elizabeth . . .

She was five-foot-six and a half, deep brunette hair worn long. A magazine model's facial features: wide mouth and lips, a longish, thin nose and oval blue eyes. The photograph revealed unblemished skin, highlighted by a permanent suntan that was an occupational hazard for most archaeologists.

Over and over, Hunter had studied the photo and the brief written description that Sandlake had provided on his missing daughter. Studying her features was important. The Wingman felt that if he concentrated enough — and sent a mental message out over the ethers — then maybe, he would be drawn to her location . . .

. The trip from Washington to the very northeastern edge of the Yucatan peninsula had taken 15 hours hours in all, counting the time spent stopping for fuel in New Orleans and Corpus Christi. Flying 130 mph at 5000 feet, Hunter got to see parts of the continent that he usually sped above at speeds ten to fifteen times faster than his present velocity. He was amazed how peaceful it all looked — the forests of old Virginia, the hills of what used to be called Tennessee, the reddish farmland of Mississippi Free State. It was as if nothing had changed — as if there were no New Order. No treacherous skies filled with air pirates. No Nazis with a stranglehold on America's vital ocean-to-ocean shortcut . . .

He had to shake himself out of this unrealistic haze every once and a while — a touch of his hand to the breast pocket of his flight suit usually did the trick. The critical—almost desperate—nature of the task at hand would always come flooding back to him whenever he felt the folded bulge of the American flag he always kept over his heart.

As for the photo of Dominique wrapped inside it—he hadn't dared to look at it in days . . .

Hunter's first stop was the coastal town of Cancun, a former high-priced vacation spot located on the northeastern tip of the Yucatan peninsula.

Mexico had been a mystery to the democratic forces in North America since the imposition of the New Order. Intelligence from the country was always very sketchy at best—and if border activity with Texas was any indication, then most people believed that the entire country was now populated with murderers, rapists, white slavers, drug lords and thieves.

But Hunter knew it was neither wise nor fair to make such generalizations. The major border towns between the old State of Texas and Mexico had always been magnets for shady characters on *both* sides. By the same token, the southern half of Mexico—that territory beyond Mexico City—had always been quite different from the northern half.

It was almost as if Time had stopped in the Yucatan and in the other nearby Central American countries of Belize and Guatemala as well. But less settled didn't always mean less civilized and Hunter knew that these lands in the Yucatan and close by were once inhabited by some of the most civilized people on Earth . . .

Nearly two thousand years before, while the rest of the world was still counting on its fingers and toes, the Mayans were breezing through all kinds of advanced mathematics. While the rest of "civilization" was living in glorified animal stables, the Mayans were building incredibly complex city states—complete with elaborate pyramids and temples, causeways, marketplaces, sports stadiums and housing for tens of thousands.

174

The Mayans knew of astronomy — that the Earth circled the sun and not the other way around. They had calendars and were able to conceive of the notion of years that had passed and years that were yet to be. They devised an incredibly complex and sophisticated writing system. They knew enough about their environment to institute workable soil and water management systems. They created networks of trade routes. They built canals. They had organized health care for their citizens, built schools, hospitals, even billboards.

But all this couldn't prevent their downfall — or a better term for it was their *disappearance*. Despite years of study and many theories — ranging from invasions to natural disasters — no one quite knew just what had happened to the Mayans and why their great culture suddenly collapsed. There was even a theory that they had been visited by beings from outer space — ancient astronauts who brought them all for a ride they never returned from.

Whatever the reason, the Mayan civilization simply vanished, leaving behind just hints of their magnificence and one hell of a mystery.

That seemed to be the normal state of affairs for the Yucatan . . .

Hunter wasn't too surprised to find Cancun deserted.

He landed the Kingfisher easily enough in a man-made bay, next to a huge, abandoned luxury hotel, that was shaped, ironically enough, like a Mayan pyramid. He spent three hours wandering around the hotel and the surrounding resort area, some of it still showing signs of damage caused by a whopper of a hurricane called Gilbert years before. He was intrigued by the good condition of everything — beds in the hotel were made, there was liquor in bars and food in the ice chests, though long ago frozen over. There was even electricity in some parts of the modern pyramid, though he couldn't imagine where the power was being generated from.

All this struck him as being very odd. Just like the Mayans many centuries before, it looked as if the people who had inhabited *this* pyramid had simply vanished too . . .

He spent the night in a swanky suite located at the very top of the hotel. The next morning he lucked out when he found a holding tank full of non-contaminated fuel which was compatible with the Kingfisher's engine. He topped off his tanks, "borrowed" two bottles of Scotch from the hotel bar and took off, heading south to a place called Coba.

Chapter 31

Colonel Krupp had found it nearly impossible to sleep the hot and humid night before.

He would have liked to believe the insomnia was due to the excitement of finally reaching Uxmaluna, the most important of the Mayan sites.

But he knew this was not the case.

Not entirely, anyway. True, tossing and turning on his sweaty bedclothes, his cabin hot and filled with mosquitoes, he found he couldn't stop thinking about the place. Even an educated yet jaded mind like his couldn't deny the magnificence of the Mayan ruins was almost overwhelming. As the original second-in-command of the Recovery Operation, Krupp had spent three months in hiding on Bermuda rereading many of his old textbooks on the Yucatan and the various sites his unit would plunder. It had seemed like such a waste of time then, especially under the shady circumstances that had he and the other staff officers going to Bermuda in the first place. But now that he was in charge, he was glad he had taken the clandestine refresher course.

To the uninformed observer, Uxmaluna simply looked like a square-mile clearing in the middle of the dense jungle — a clearing that contained 12 massive earthen mounds, most wearing a cover of small trees and scrub bushes.

If it weren't for their square-to-square pattern, one might have dismissed the mounds as a natural part of the rugged terrain. In reality, a meticulously-planned city lay hidden beneath the dozen hills.

Built near a massive outcrop of limestone—the material of its construction—Uxmaluna was once the home to tens of thousands of people, maybe as many as 100,000. On the surrounding land that was now covered with nearly impenetrable jungle, these people grew beans, chili peppers, squash and early corn. For water, they built drainoffs and manmade reservoirs, some of which were layered with lime on the bottom—a primitive, but effective means of water purification.

The buildings and pyramids themselves—several partially uncovered by a pre-war expedition—were constructed of limestone covered with stucco. A reddish pigment called ferric oxide was washed over the stucco to hold off erosion. Around the structures were open plazas and concourses with many platforms and causeways built throughout—all this no doubt needed to handle the huge crowds of people who lived, worked, did business and worshipped in the city.

All in all the place was a tremendous architectural feat, one that would be difficult to duplicate even in pre-war times. And now it was inhabited only by the jungle animals, the insects, the birds and the ghosts of those who once lived here. Even to the unimaginative Krupp there came a feeling that in walking amongst the ruins, one was treading on hallowed ground.

But it was what lay beneath these buildings, in the deep mud-lined caves, that brought Krupp and his small army to the place. Perhaps the Mayan leaders had been clairvoyant; maybe they knew that some day strangers would arrive and lust after their gold. Assuming that it was their gold. Whatever the case, the Mayans decided to hide the bullion—and they hid it so well that it stayed concealed despite the flood of expeditions of legitimate explorers, archaeologists and grave robbers. It was only with the advent of Deep Zone Archaeology were the secret treasures found at sites like this.

Krupp had spent a long time lying in bed that night thinking about the gold that almost definitely lay hidden nearby. It excited him, no small feat. In the dead of night, sweating bullets and still wide awake, he tried to convince himself that perhaps he too was catching a bit of the gold fever, and that it had contributed to his sleeplessness.

But try as he might, he couldn't fool himself. He knew the *real* reason he hadn't fallen asleep. It was because of the woman . . .

He had wrestled with the idea of ordering her back to his truck and finally forcing himself on her. Drinking too much the time before had been an incredible blunder on his part. His virility, whatever of that he might have, had been quickly sapped by the bad brandy. He knew that even if by some miracle the woman had been willing, he would not have been able to perform.

What was worse, he was certain she knew this, and in her own way, was laughing at him behind his back, too.

So he had begged for sleep. But when it finally came, in the guise of a fitful slumber, things just got worse. He dreamed he saw Heinke, his missing commander, standing on the edge of the Uxmaluna clearing, beckoning him to join him in the woods . . .

Once again he was up and awake like a shot. He was trembling and having difficulty catching his breath. *What was happening to him?* It was as if something very evil was haunting his brain cells and would not let go.

Four aspirins and a glass of the vile brandy was what it took to settle him back down.

"Foolish men dream foolish dreams," he whispered, afraid to close his eyes again.

Krupp was by himself, sweating and hacking his way through the dense jungle. Five sentries posted to watch this southern rim of the encampment were missing, unaccounted for in the rugged blood-red piece of terrain that seemed miles away from the blasted-out corridor leading out of Uxmaluna.

It was unbearably hot. The more Krupp chopped away at the vegetation, the more it surrounded him. He was covered with hordes of gigantic, blood-sucking mosquitoes. They were biting him all over his face and wrists. They were flying down his backside, up his pant legs and even up his nostrils.

Suddenly his second-in-command was standing beside him, holding a radio.

"They've found them, sir," the man told Krupp. "Not far from here . . ."

Krupp wondered why the junior officer was not sweating or covered with mosquitoes. "They were lost?" he asked.

"They're dead, sir," the man answered, his voice showing absolutely no sign of emotion.

The next thing he knew, Krupp had reached the spot from where others in the search party had called. He found six of his soldiers sitting passively by a small stream. Two of them were naked. Occasionally one man would reach down and splash water into his face, as someone just getting out of bed might do.

"Where are they?" Krupp asked the soldiers.

One man looked up at him and smiled. He opened his mouth, but did not speak. Another simply pointed to a clearing on the other side of the narrow stream.

Krupp splashed into the stream which suddenly seemed too deep for its width. The water was moving too fast and he felt as if it were sucking him down. Several times he almost lost his footing, terror gripping him because he knew if he fell, he might not be able to get back up again.

Finally he blundered out of the water and into the clearing. Suddenly he felt something sticking to his boot. He looked down and realized that he had nearly stepped right into the open chest of one of the dead men.

They were all there. Five of them. Decapitated, disemboweled, hacked to pieces like the jungle vines. Most were missing arms and legs. Each man had had the heart torn right out of his chest. The soil beneath the bodies was already turning black with the release of blood and other body fluids.

Krupp couldn't move. He wanted to shut his eyes but they refused. He stared at the severed head of one of the soldiers and realized that he had spoken to the man just the night before. A look of unspeakable horror was frozen on this soldier's face. His eyes were wide open, his mouth agape in shock. Already the insects were feasting on his flesh.

Then the man's eyes turned and looked right up at him.

"Why did you bring us here, Colonel?" the decapitated man asked him.

Krupp woke up screaming . . .

Chapter 32

Hunter was 15 miles out from Coba when one of his minicomputers started buzzing.

He twisted around in the Kingfisher's cockpit and pushed a series of buttons on a panel just above the noisy computer. Turning back, he looked down at a miniature TV screen that was bolted next to his right foot.

"Damn . . ." he cursed under his breath as he saw a green blip pop onto the screen.

The computer had issued a correct warning: Someone down there had a SAM.

He quickly rechecked his position. He was at 4800 feet, cruising into a brisk headwind at 160 mph. He had just turned inland twenty minutes before, overflying a city named Puerto Morelos after having followed the coast down from Cancun. Once he had spotted a place called Playa Carmen off to his south, he determined that the ancient Mayan site of Coba was a little more than a dozen miles away to his southwest.

His computer started buzzing once again, this time with a higher, shriller tone. This meant the Kingfisher would soon be within striking distance of the SAM.

He immediately put the seaplane into a dive, cranking up his small Electronic Counter-Measures package and arming all his weapons in the process. Just because there was a SAM in the area, it didn't mean that the person with his finger on the trigger wanted to shoot it at him. Still, he couldn't take any chances . . .

Once he was down to a safer 1500 feet, he switched on his radio and pushed the frequency scan button. There was an immediate crackle of static as the radio started to run through the frequency range, seeking the nearest, strongest signal. It found one a few seconds later.

"West wall is about to go!" Hunter heard through the garble of static and atmospheric interference. "We need men . . . on the west wall!" "Mortar teams . . . to the battery!" he heard a different voice cry out. *"Hurry!* . . . they're breaking through!"

Hunter reached down and pushed the radio's signal amplifier to maximum, at the same time straining his ears to make some sense out of the confusion and static. Not only was the signal garbled, it also sounded like there was one hell of a firefight going on wherever the broadcast was originating from.

He dipped his wing and checked the landscape below. Sure enough, several columns of white smoke were rising from a point about nine miles off his port side. He confirmed that the radio signals were coming from this area by hand-cranking the Kingfisher's antenna in that direction, while simultaneously fiddling with the radio's tuner bar.

Immediately he knew he had stumbled across somebody's little war. The area of the conflict was still a good ten miles from the ruins at Coba, and so it would have been easy for him to just pass it all by.

But his body was beginning to tingle with a familiar sensation, sending a flood of messages via his nerves and bones to his brain. Someone down there was in trouble. Or more accurately, from what was coming over the radio, someone down there was in *big* trouble, surrounded and about to be overrun.

He was weighing the question of whether or not to check it out more closely when his radio suddenly came to life again. "East wall defenders!" he heard someone in absolute desperation yell out. "Fall back! Fall back to cover the women and kids!"

That did it. Soldiers fighting soldiers was one thing. Disputes and little wars come and go, and no quick decision could ever be made as to which side was right or wrong.

But women and kids in danger was a different matter . . .

"What in heaven's name is that?"

The man named Brother David had spotted just a glint of silver coming straight at him through the smoke and flame-filled sky.

"Is it a Phantom?" the man on his left, Brother Paul, asked. "It seems to be moving too slowly."

"I cannot tell," Brother David shouted back to him, his voice becoming lost in the sounds of the battle raging around them. "But we have just one SAM left. I should not waste it, even now!"

They *were* hopelessly surrounded and being overrun. Their small church mission — nothing more than a tiny chapel and a few buildings with a high stucco wall around it — had been under attack for two days by the bandit gang known as *Dos Chicos*. The Fighting Brothers — a 55-man order of highly-religious soldiers — had been battling back with small arms and the few mortars they had. But now it appeared as if the better-armed, numerically-superior *Dos Chicos* were about to overwhelm them for good.

The bandits had had some outside help and it appeared to have turned the tide in their favor. An airstrike by a lone Phantom earlier in the day had sufficiently weakened the west wall of the mission to allow the *Chicos* to batter it down with recoilless rifle fire. Now the enemy was swarming through the gap they had made and were climbing up to the roof of the church itself.

In the basement of the chapel, the women and children of The Brothers were huddled, awaiting their fate . . .

Brother David and Brother Paul both knew what that fate would be. Once the *Dos Chicos* overwhelmed the last of their Order's defenders, wholesale rape and massacre would surely follow.

But now, almost like an angel from heaven, the strange-looking airplane appeared overhead.

"It is a seaplane!" Brother Paul yelled out after shooting at point blank range two bandits who were trying to scale the still intact east wall. "Is it here to attack us?"

"Our last prayers should be to hope not!" Brother David hollered back, himself plunging a long sword into the neck of yet another bandit.

Suddenly the silver seaplane was upon them. It roared over, no more than 20 feet above the mission, its full-throttled engine making so much noise that bandits and defenders alike stopped to watch it pass.

The airplane quickly climbed, turned and came around again. Brothers David and Paul both saw it wag its wings noticeably. Somehow, Brother David got the message.

"Everybody down!" he screamed at the top of his lungs. *"Everyone! Get down!"*

Instantly those defenders on the parapets and in the courtyard fell flat out, their hands over their heads. The seaplane thundered in, the huge gun under its left wing suddenly erupting in a tremendous flash of smoke and fire. Seconds later, Brother David saw that half the roof of the church had been blown away, taking a third of the attacking bandits with it.

"My God!" Brother Paul cried out. "He has sent us a miracle!"

"Get down, Brother!" David yelled, yanking the man back down with him.

The airplane had turned and was coming in again. This time its right wing erupted, a flash of missiles shooting out from under it. In an instant, the fiery barrage demolished what remained of the heavily-damaged west wall, killing a dozen bandits outright and trapping many more under tons of smoldering rubble.

"It's the Angel of Mercy!" Paul cried out again.

Two passes of the airplane was enough for *Dos Chicos* — they wanted no more. Those who had survived quickly retreated across the fields surrounding the mission and into the deep woods beyond.

Brother David sighed in relief as he watched the enemy flee. "The Lord has certainly looked down upon us this day," he said.

Twenty armed men were waiting for him when Hunter put the Kingfisher down on the small man-made lake close by the mission.

He climbed down out of the cockpit and onto the plane's float, a long rope in hand.

"I'd appreciate some help," he called over to the soldiers, men he was certain were the defenders of the mission. A few of them would have to grab hold of the rope and pull the airplane to shore.

But the Brothers did him one better. As one, fifteen of them leaped into the water, moved to positions around the airplane and literally carried the Kingfisher to the bank. All the while the soldiers were bellowing *hurrahs!* at the tops of their lungs.

Brother David, the commander of the religious fighters, was on hand to greet him as he stepped from the float to dry land.

"Friend, I don't know who you are, but this day you have caused us to be blessed," the big, moon-faced monk told him after introducing himself. "I thank you for all of us . . ."

Hunter shook his outstretched hand. "Just heard that you were having a little trouble," he said. "Thought I could help."

"Help, you did, sir," David said. "And the Bible says that good works should be returned in kind. Thus, we must repay you."

"No," Hunter said, holding up his hand. "That's okay. No payment necessary . . ."

Brother David looked legitimately hurt. "But we must," he said. "It is our way. At least, you will come and eat with us?"

By this time the rest of the fighters had gathered around them. Their uniforms could only be described as "modern contradiction." Each man wore a brown sackcloth, right out

186

of Little John's Sherwood Forest wardrobe. Yet holding the garment to their waists were numerous ammunition belts and bandoleers. Also each man was carrying some kind of weapon, be it an M-16 or a AK-47, and more than a few also carried rocket-propelled grenade launchers. Nearly every weapon had some kind of religious medal or scapula hanging from it. The RPGs he saw had several small crucifixes dangling from their stocks.

All in all they looked like a tough, but pious bunch of guys.

"Sure, I'd be glad to eat with you," Hunter said finally.

A spontaneous cheer went up from the fighters and the small group moved back toward the partially destroyed, still-burning abbey.

"Whatever brought you to us, Brother?" David asked him.

One man, the fighter David introduced as Brother Paul, was carrying a battered Blowpipe SAM launcher.

"That did," Hunter told him, pointing to the shoulder-launched weapon. "I picked up your SAM's targeting signals on my airplane's computer. I'm glad you decided not to fire that at me."

"We definitely had the feeling that we shouldn't," Brother Paul said. "After all, one does not fire a missile at the hand of God."

Hunter was still rolling that statement over in his mind when they reached the mission. The place was in a kind of controlled chaos. Surviving Brothers were hastily removing the bodies of the bandits killed during the battle, as well as caring for their own dead and wounded. Others were already moving pieces of the smashed west wall back into position. At the same time Hunter watched a slow parade of women and children stream out of the basement of the chapel.

"Sorry about your church," he said, eyeing what was left of the still smoldering roof. "I wouldn't have cut it so close if I'd known your people were hiding inside."

"Don't think another moment about it," Brother David told him. "We are a small but determined ministry. We have been out in this Godforsaken country for several years and we've battled back from worse things than this. A roof we resurrect. Our lives we cannot . . . Only He could do that."

"Besides," Brother Paul told him, "it is a concrete shelter under the church. None of the dependents was hurt."

But Hunter had just barely heard Paul say this. Instead his eyes were glued on some of the women who had just climbed out of the shelter. He had expected them all to be dressed like nuns or something. Instead, most of the young ones were wearing tight jeans or even justs bathing suits — very *skimpy* bathing suits.

His thoughts were disturbed by a tugging on his pant leg. He looked down to see a small boy, no more than five or so, looking up and pointing at him.

"I know who you are," the boy declared. "You're The Wingman, aren't you?"

At last, Hunter thought, someone who knew he was still alive.

"Yes, I guess I am," Hunter said, bending down on one knee to shake hands with the boy.

"Surely, you are not serious?" Brother David asked him. "You are not Hawk Hunter, are you?"

Hunter straightened up and smiled. "Yes, I am," he said. "Major Hawk Hunter of the United American Air Force."

"I suppose I should have known, the way you handled that airplane," Brother David said. "But it is truly a work of God that you are here. For you see, there is someone here with us who knows you well. In fact, he speaks about you all the time."

Hunter was astounded. He couldn't imagine who it could be.

Just then he heard someone call out his name: "Hunter! *Paisano!*"

He turned around and thought he was face-to-face with a ghost.

It was none other than the Commodore Antonio Vanaria.

"Jesus Christ!" Hunter blurted out, at once hoping he hadn't offended any of the Brothers. "Commodore! I thought you were dead!"

They embraced, the short, wiry little man kissing Hunter twice on each cheek in impeccable Italian style.

"Me? *Dead?*" he laughed, beating his chest with a boastful motion. "Impossible!"

The commodore had been part of the flotilla that helped tow the *USS Saratoga* across the Mediterranean to the Suez in an effort to halt the onslaught of Viktor's Lucifer armies. The last time Hunter had seen the man, he and his small navy of boats — the *Liberte Marina* — were sailing off to a climactic mid-canal confrontation against the vanguard of Viktor's surface fleet. It was a battle everyone assumed had no survivors.

"How in hell did you get here?" Hunter asked the man, good-naturedly shaking him. "We all thought . . ."

"You all thought I was killed," the commodore finished his sentence for him in broken, heavily-accented English. "I thought I was killed too! My ship — it was blown right out from under me. My crew — all gone! I wake up — it is two days later. Above me, all around me, there is fighting. The Modern Knights against the Lucifer Army. Tanks. Rockets. Big guns. *Boom!* But I cannot move. My legs are broken. My hand is fractured in thirty places.

"The Modern Knights, they find me. Their doctors patch me up. They send me back to Italy. But I stay there for only a few months. I get restless. Then I get invitation to sail across Atlantic on nice ship. A luxury ship and I will have the best cabin. I know I want to come to America. I want to find you and my friends again! But there is fighting going on, we hear. The captain decides to go to California as he wants to see the beaches. But before we are to go through Panama, something in my head says: *Get off this boat, Antonio*. I do. Later I hear, she's been sunk by Nazis!"

Hunter listened to the story, shaking his head. The guy was just like old Captain Pegg — they both could spin a damn good yarn. It was just that the commodore's came with Italian subtitles. Only later did Hunter learn that his *paisano* had actually stolen away on a ship, one of very dubious character sailing out of Sicily. Having been discovered mid-route, the commodore just barely saved himself from being thrown overboard by promising to cook for all those on board. (Hunter knew from experience that the little guy was an excellent cook.) In no time at all the commodore was able to ingratiate himself with the bulge-over-the-left-side-pocket crew, whipping up gourmet Italian feasts for them on a nightly basis.

However, once they had made landfall, the commodore *was* tossed overboard, not too far from Cancun. The Brothers found him washed up on the beach and soon thereafter, the commodore found God.

The two Fighting Brothers and the commodore led Hunter to one of the mission's houses and soon the pilot found a large goblet filled with wine sitting in front of him.

The commodore offered a toast to him, then downed his entire glass of *vino* in no more than three gulps.

"I'm really glad to see you alive and well, Commodore," Hunter told him, taking a healthy swig of the wine himself. "What a coincidence that we should meet again, and here of all places."

"Hunter, my friend," the little man said with a wink, pouring out another glass of wine, "the Lord truly does work in mysterious ways . . ."

Hunter then told the commodore as well as Brothers David and Paul about the crisis situation in Panama and his mission to find Sandlake's daughter.

"We know all about these Nazis," Brother David told him. "In fact, they have given air support to the *Dos Chicos* gang, the people you saved us from today."

Hunter was surprised to hear this. In the grand scheme of things, it would seem that a battle between *Dos Chicos* and the Fighting Brothers would be small potatoes to the Canal Nazis.

Brother David read his mind. "I know what you're thinking," he said. "Why would The Twisted Cross become involved in our little war?

"The answer is they get involved in *every* little war they can find. It's part of their destabilization program. We know they have special units, made up of the worst of their lot. The dregs of their own twisted society. Criminals, perverts, homicidal maniacs, and not all of Aryan origin either. These people are highly trained and conditioned to operate either behind enemy lines or in neutral territories. Their strategy is to create trouble, simple as that. And they are fanatical about it. They help heathens like *Dos Chicos,* whether it be with an airstrike or a long-range artillery barrage or even a direct infusion of troops. They are utterly ruthless. Their sole purpose is to weasel their way into any disruptive situation and tip the scales to the criminal side. Always using the means of ultra-violence to achieve their aims."

Hunter was genuinely surprised. "You mean the Canal Nazis have a *third* arm in addition to its regular military units and The Party?" he asked.

Brothers David and Paul nodded glumly.

"They're called the Skinheads," David said. "And for obvious reasons: each one has a shaved head. It's a sign of their resolve, if you will . . ."

Hunter felt yet another piece of the puzzle drop in, though quite unexpectedly. Now he knew why Pegg's wouldbe assassins and the Nazis he and Fitz iced near Sandlake's ranch all sported bald domes.

"Before the Big War there were fringe groups in the States and in England that called themselves Skinheads," Hunter said. "If I recall, they did have a neo-Nazi bent. Are you saying that this third arm of The Twisted Cross is an outgrowth of those movements?"

Brother David nodded again. "A tremendous outgrowth," he said, anger creeping into his normally pastoral voice. "A downright cancerous outgrowth. The Skinheads are no longer a fringe group. Now they are a well-equipped, organized army on their own. They are specialists. They have access to everything from Phantoms to sniper rifles. They're terrorists — car bombs, letter bombs, they even poison water supplies. The last thing they want here or anywhere in this hemisphere is stable, peaceful settlements. The Cross just lets them run wild, spreading destruction, murder, rape and misery everywhere they go.

"For instance, the *Dos Chicos* gang was no more than a bunch of drunken petty thieves until the Skinheads made a deal with them. They gave them weapons, radios, logistical support. Now when *Dos Chicos* goes to work, on us, or on some of the small villages nearby, they know they can count on air support from Skinheads. It's really an insidious marriage."

"How widespread are these Skinhead teams," Hunter wanted to know.

"Very widespread," David said with a sigh. "In fact, they seem to be everywhere *but* in Panama. I don't doubt that even The Twisted Cross High Command are nervous dealing with them. So that's why the Skinheads are entirely self-supporting. We know they are all over South America as well as up here in the Yucatan. In fact, I wouldn't be surprised if some of them had made it up to North America as well."

"I'm afraid you're right," Hunter said grimly. He wouldn't have been surprised to learn that Skinheads were piloting the Phantoms he fought in the skies near New Orleans that day.

"They must be good at what they do," Hunter said.

"They are *damn* good at what they do," Brother Paul said, adding, "Lord excuse the language . . ."

"In many ways these Skinhead teams are more dangerous than The Twisted Cross's regular military units," Brother David continued. "The Skinheads are like the Gestapo of old, only worse. As I said, they operate on their own, entirely independent of The Twisted Cross High Command. No matter what the outcome in the Canal is, you can be sure that one or two or more of these Skinhead teams will be out there on the loose somewhere."

"That's a sobering thought," Hunter said. "And this is all good information. Frightening, but useful.

"However, I am curious: How do you know so much about all this?"

Both Fighting Brothers suddenly became very nervous. Even the commodore lowered his eyes and tried not to look at Hunter.

Finally Brother David spoke up. "We know it because we captured one of them," he said. "He was attached to the *Dos Chicos* as an advisor and during one of their raids, we wounded him and took him prisoner. And we made him talk, God help us . . ."

"Well," Hunter said. "Where is he now?"

"He's gone on to his Judgment," Brother David said, trying to be matter-of-fact about it.

"How?" Hunter asked. "Did he bite on a cyanide capsule? Or shoot himself in the head?"

Once again, both monks avoided his eyes.

"No," Brother Paul said finally. "We executed him . . ."

Chapter 33

Colonel Frankel had never met the High Commander.
Few people had. They said even his closest military advisors only talked to the man on the phone or through intermediaries. Now sitting in an antechamber on the top floor of the Panama City skyscraper that served as home to the High Command, Frankel was getting nervous. He suddenly longed for his boring but effortless old job. His hill, with its cool breezes and young women for taking, was heaven compared to this. The stress alone was already killing him. Here, in the High Temple of the Twisted Cross, he was just too damn close to the seat of power.

Few people knew what the High Commander looked like. Even fewer knew his real name. The high echelon of The Twisted Cross was cloaked in an almost impenetrable shroud of secrecy, attended to by the shadowy figures of The Party. And this, the top floor of the High Command was the Black Hole of that power — so intense not even the slightest ray of light could escape.

Frankel had no idea why they had picked on him. He was not expert in anything. His own secret past included seven years as a low-level officer in the East German Army, a communist affiliation he dared not breathe to anyone. Now, suddenly, Strauberg was saddling him with questions and problems that required a broad sweep of politics and history, not to mention military intelligence to solve. *Why him?* he had wondered over and over. Why did they think he had all the answers?

Suddenly the door to the High Commander's chamber opened and a black uniformed officer stepped out.

"Colonel Frankel," the man said. "The High Commander will see you now."

Frankel gulped so loudly, the officer heard him.

"You know the requirements?" the officer asked him. "You will repeat them to me?"

Frankel closed his eyes and rattled off the words he had memorized the night before: "I am an officer of The Twisted Cross. All that I do is for the Cause and our Leader. I will fight where I stand. I will never surrender . . ."

"Very good, Colonel," the officer replied without a hint of emotion in his voice. "And you realize that should you speak to any unauthorized individuals about your discussion with the High Commander, the penalty is death."

"I understand, sir," Frankel replied.

"A long, slow, *painful* death . . ." the officer added for emphasis.

Frankel gulped again. How he wished for those days of panning for gold . . . .

The black uniformed officer led Frankel through two inner rooms, finally stopping in the middle of a third. At its far end was a set of large black teak doors.

"Wait here," the officer said, before walking the ten paces to the doors and disappearing behind them.

In the scattering of seconds that followed, a hundred scenarios shot through Frankel's anxious mind. Normally cool and collected, he found himself uncharacteristically making up wild and disturbing flights of fancy. He imagined that the man sitting behind those black doors—the High Commander himself!—would be wrapped in a dark, fully curtained room. Ornate but in only the murkiest sense. And he would be wearing the blackest uniform of them all, patent leather black. And he would have no compunction at all against shooting Frankel on the spot should he not have the correct answers to his questions

Frankel tried to shake away the nightmarish thoughts, but they were coming like rain now. He had heard so many dark rumors about the High Commander, it was impossible to prevent his imagination from working overtime. The man behind the door would be disfigured in some way, Frankel was sure of it. His face was burned to point of disgust, or his limbs were missing, or his torso bent and twisted. Maybe he was blind. Or maybe he drank blood or ate flesh.

Or maybe, the man behind the doors was Adolph Hitler himself . . .

The door squeak echoed several times through the large empty waiting room before Frankel looked up. The officer was beckoning for him to come forward. Oddly, Frankel felt nailed to the spot. He just *couldn't* move. Come, the officer beckoned again. But Frankel's legs wouldn't respond. It wasn't a dream — he had already checked. Yet he couldn't speak, couldn't make a damn sound. Over and over the man at the door told him to come — he was even smiling, though a bit strangely. But Frankel was frozen. There was terror in his boots. Behind those doors he knew there was weird black-hearted craziness that this human wanted no part of. Yet, he had no choice. He *had* to go in.

A variation on Shakespeare suddenly popped into his head: *Hell is empty*, the bard had said. *"Because all the devils are here . . ."*

He walked slowly toward the door.

"Come in," the officer urged him with the suddenly friendly demeanor of a pub owner on opening night.

Frankel actually closed his eyes walking through the door, thinking this would somehow keep him in the real world just a bit longer.

It didn't work.

He looked up and saw that contrary to being dark, the room was so brightly lit, it hurt his eyes. Between the hot Panamanian sunlight flooding into the room through its enormous windows and the bath of fluorescent glow pouring down from the lights on the high ceiling, Frankel found himself blinking a dozen times, just to get his eyes adjusted.

Through the million reflections he could see a man standing behind a desk, which was set before the largest window of them all. He wasn't wearing patent leather black. Nor was carrying a gun or crippled in any sort of way.

In fact, he was wearing a suit and tie, a dark gray flannel Brooks Brothers and a red cotton Pierre Cardin tie, pinned neatly with a subdued tie tack. His eyeglasses were designer horn-rims and he looked as if he had just had a haircut in the last hour.

"Colonel Frankel?" the man asked in a positively upbeat tone of voice. He was out from behind the desk now, coming right at Frankel, his hand outstretched.

"Colonel, thanks for coming," he said through a well-brushed smile, shaking Frankel's hand in the correct manly style. "I'm your High Commander. It's good to meet you. And thanks for coming. Sit down. Can I get you some coffee? Or tea?"

Chapter 34

"Oh my God!" the woman cried out.

A breath had caught in her throat and she put her hands up to her mouth as if to keep it in. Her head was shaking from side to side and she couldn't have stopped it had she wanted to. The reflections of the hand lanterns were so strong, they almost hurt her eyes.

"I . . . I've never . . ." she couldn't say any more. The whole world suddenly appeared as if it were made entirely of gold.

Krupp was also speechless, as were the seven troopers with them. Almost at the same instant they had dropped their picks and shovels, and unconsciously wiped their dirty faces with their dirty hands.

"Is it all . . . *real?*" one of them finally managed to ask.

No one answered. No one could. No one had seen this much gold in one spot at one time.

They had broken through and into the tunnel beneath Uxmaluna's second Grand Pyramid about noon earlier that day. A 90-minute, single file, bent-over journey through the low-ceilinged cave tunnels followed, Krupp pushing the woman in front him, the seven laborers, shovels and picks resting on their shoulders like rifles, obediently following behind.

At the end of the tunnel they had reached a portal, one that had been sealed with a stone 1400 years before. It took Krupp and his men more than three hours to move it — four men pushing, four men working the hand tools. Finally it rolled, just missing an opportunity to crush Krupp's right foot by inches. Once removed, the stone only revealed another tunnel, this one blocked with dirt. Two more hours of attack by shovel and pick produced a four foot clearance in the tunnel and yet another stone.

But this one was thin and flat and made of soft limestone. Three blasts from the pick and it exploded into a thousand fragments. On the other side was a chamber — a large chamber.

And they found it filled to the top with gold.

"This is an incredible discovery!" the woman cried out, forgetting for the briefest of moments that she was a prisoner. "There has never been a find like this — *ever* . . ."

They stood at the entranceway for a full five minutes, as if to walk into the chamber would be unholy. Krupp was the one who finally took the first step. He played his lantern around the large, man-made cavern, its powerful beacon actually dimming before it reached the far wall or the ceiling.

"It's enormous," he uttered. "There must be *tons* of gold in here . . ."

"At least a hundred tons," the girl whispered, at the same time realizing that, with this treasure now in their hands, the Nazis would have no further use for her.

And it was all pure bullion. There were no goblets or chalices or necklaces. Rather the gold was laid out in odd, bowl-shaped ingots, each one looking to weigh at least fifty pounds. And there must have been four thousand of them, neatly stacked ten deep against the side and back walls and in an orderly laid-out center aisle.

"We must get the others," Krupp said, still not quite able to fathom the implications of what they had found. "We must call the helicopter here immediately."

"My colonel," one of the troopers spoke up bravely, as if the tons of bullion were brilliant enough to make such things as rank and bearing petty by comparison. "We will need a fleet of helicopters to take it all out. And a full battalion of men!"

That's when it hit Krupp. Right between the eyes.

"You're right," he said. "You're absolutely right."

"I will go back and tell the others!" one man announced. "I will tell all of them to get down here. Now!"

"No!" Krupp yelled, turning on the lowly private. "No, you will *all* go back . . . And each one of you will carry one ingot. We must show proof of this place. And while you are out there, you will radio headquarters and tell them to send the helicopters immediately, every one of them they can spare! And then come back down here and bring one hundred of the others. We will do this in shifts . . ."

Although the order didn't make much sense in a logical way, the troopers nevertheless rushed forward to grab one bowl of gold apiece.

"They are much heavier than I would have thought," one trooper said.

"The heavier the better," Krupp told him, the thought not entering his mind that the trooper would have to carry the 50 pounds of metal nearly a mile in the dark through the twisting, low-ceilinged cave.

The seven men, holding their gold ingots like children would hold large bowls of candy, each stepped through the opening and back out into the tunnel.

"And you, my colonel?" a sergeant asked. "You will carry two?"

"No," Krupp answered. "Someone must guard this place. I will stay here until you return."

The sergeant looked concerned. "And the woman, sir? shall we take her with us?"

Krupp turned and looked at her. It hadn't even entered his mind what to do with her.

"No," he said again. "She will stay here with me . . ."

Chapter 35

"They were here," Hunter said, picking up a handful of dirt at the base of the grand pyramid of Coba. "Not too long ago . . ."

Brother David nodded in agreement, himself inspecting an area to the left of the pyramid. It had obviously been used as the Canal Nazis' mess area as it was strewn with hundreds of pounds of litter. "The Fourth Reich appears to be as messy as the Third one . . ."

Hunter walked over to the spot. "I guess I'm not surprised that they wouldn't pick up after themselves," he said, looking at the mess. "What a bunch of fucking slobs . . ."

The ride from the Fighting Brothers' abbey to the ruins of Coba had taken just an hour by truck. Brother David and the commodore made the trip with him, along with a dozen of the biggest, toughest soldiers in the Order.

"The food they left behind has not been eaten completely," Brother David pointed out. "Maybe the animals won't touch it."

"Look over here," the commodore shouted at them, standing on the other side of the mess area. "Here was where they fueled their vehicles. See the oil spots? Still moist. I say four weeks ago at the most."

"And they brought this fuel in by barrels," Brother David pointed out. "Probably delivered to them by chopper . . ."

"Damn," Hunter spit out. "Four weeks is still long enough to leave a cold trail."

They walked the area three times, looking for any clues,

any possible indications, of where the Canal Nazis had gone next. All that time, Hunter was working on a theory. After a while, he began to spell it out for Brother David and the commodore.

"Maybe it's too logical," he said. "But try this: We know they're moving by truck. Judging from those tire tracks, they look like R75-18s, I'd say they're driving ton-and-three-quarter rigs. Probably six-cylinder diesels. Fuel tank of, maybe, thirty gallons . . ."

"You have an idea, Brother Hunter?" Brother David asked.

"Well, what's the fuel range of a truck like that?" he asked. "I can't believe they get more than a couple, three miles a gallon, loaded down. More likely two, don't you think?"

Both David and the commodore nodded in agreement.

"So, we assume they just fuel up at their next destination, as opposed to along the way. All we have to do then is figure out what their vehicles' fuel range is and look for the next logical Mayan site within that radius."

"Say no more, Brother Hunter," David said, his moon face brightening. "Chichen Itza . . . *That* is where they went, I'm sure."

Hunter recalled the name as another spot on his map. "It's about sixty miles from here, straight," he said. "How many by road?"

"Twists and turns, some mountains," Brother David said. "But no more than eighty-five miles . . ."

"My heart tells me this is where they are, Hunter," the commodore said.

Hunter nodded, still fuming at the extent of the desecration of the Mayan site. "Mine, too," he said.

Hunter took a few photos of the site and then they all loaded onto the truck and headed back to the mission, hoping to reach the abbey before dark.

He spent the ride back squeezed in the truck's cab between Brother David and the commodore. Not five minutes into the trip, Hunter heard the commodore commence snoring—he was fast asleep, using the hood of his monk's robe as a pillow. Brother David too was quiet, murmuring his evening prayers as he drove carefully and slowly along the jungle road.

Hunter used this quiet time looking at the photo of Sandlake's daughter, Elizabeth. It was almost spooky for him to think that she had been there, at Coba, fairly recently. If only time and space weren't so damned connected, he could have saved her. Now, he just had her photo. She had lovely features, pretty hair, pretty smile. And educated too. Someone he'd like to know . . .

"Hang on, Elizabeth," he thought, almost speaking the words out loud. "Someone's coming to the rescue."

In the next instant he heard a tremendous *crack!* He looked up and found himself suddenly staring right into the bloodshot eyes of a man who had somehow jumped up onto the hood of the truck. This person had landed with such a thud, his face was pressed up against the windshield, grossly distorting his features. But Hunter recognized one part of his makeup. The man's head was shaved . . .

"God help us!" Brother David yelled. *"Skinheads!"*

In a split second, Hunter's M-16 was up and cocked. He squeezed the trigger and instantly both the windshield and the man pressed against it were blown away in a glass-splintering stream of yellow-red fluorescent bullets.

The commodore was awake in a shot, his pistol out and firing into the left eye of a Skinhead who had leapt up on to the truck's running board.

"Boot it!" Hunter yelled to Brother David. He could hear crashing and banging in the back of the truck as the soldier monk put the vehicle's accelerator pedal to the floorboard.

In a matter of two seconds, Hunter was crawling over the commodore and out the door and onto the truck's running board. He picked off two more Skinheads who were clinging to the side of the truck's canvas covering, shooting blindly at the soldiers riding inside. Two more were following close behind the truck on a large motorcycle with a sidecar. Hunter sent a tracer barrage their way, causing them to veer across the road and fall back a little.

Hunter would learn later that the reason the soldiers riding in the back of the truck didn't respond quickly was that they, like Brother David, had been saying their evening prayers together, an act that called for them to put down their weapons, if only for the time being.

But now the soldiers realized they were being attacked and they all started firing out of the canvas covering at once. Confusion reigned as the covering was quickly shot away. There were a number of Skinheads who were actually hanging on to the top of the truck's roof.

With one hand locked around the commodore's arm for balance, Hunter leaned out of the truck as far as possible and opened up on the rooftop Skinheads. He got one in the legs, the burning tracer rounds scorching the man's knees and ankles to the extent that he fell over backward and was caught in the truck's frame. Hanging there upside down no more than three feet from him, Hunter got too upclose a look at the Skinhead. The man was wearing a black leather, cut-off vest, a camouflage T-shirt and regular-issue black jungle pants.

The 'Head actually smiled a toothless grin at him while raising his rifle to shoot. Hunter simply reached over and pulled on the man's collar, ripping him from the truck and throwing him to the speeding ground below.

Meanwhile another Skinhead had a bead on Hunter and was ready to pull his AK-47's trigger when suddenly the man's crotch exploded like a balloon filled with blood. The Fighting Brothers inside the truck were now firing their weapons straight up at the Skinheads on the roof, and this particular Nazi paid as a result. Hunter then turned his attention back to the motorbike, firing off a long spectacular barrage that surprised the driver. Instead of zigging, the driver zagged right into the deadly tracer stream and was blown out of the seat of the bike. Now driverless, the motorcycle careened off the road, slamming the bike's side compartment passenger full-force into the side of a large tree.

In the course of a few more seconds, the Fighting Brothers soldiers had shot off the four remaining attackers. Hunter continued to hang out of the truck cab as far as he could, checking the road behind them for any signs of vehicle pursuit. There was none. He climbed back inside the truck cab and settled down, much to the relief of the commodore who had been in danger of dislocating his shoulder while trying to hold Hunter steady during the action.

"Jesus Christ!" Hunter swore, the adrenaline from the brief but violent clash pumping through him at the speed of sound. "Excuse my language, Brother, but those guys are about the craziest fuckers I've ever run into!"

David looked into his rear view mirror and, upon catching a last glimpse of the smoke and fire left back down the road from the ambush, turned to Hunter and said: "Amen to that, Brother . . ."

Chapter 36

Colonel Frankel had just finished his second cup of tea.

"So that's the story, Colonel," the High Commander was telling him. "We think that we may be able to make a deal with the United Americans and we think you're the guy who can do the job."

It had been a very strange few hours for Frankel. The High Commander, who Frankel thought looked like some pre-war American politician whose name escaped him, couldn't have been more congenial to him. He had systematically laid out nothing less than the Twisted Cross's entire strategic plan—from occupation of the Canal to the plundering of the ancient Mayan sites and everything in between, using several charts and an overhead projector to illustrate his talking points.

"It's all business," is what the High Commander had said to Frankel over and over. "The Canal, the revenues, the protection money we get from the surrounding countries, the gold recovery units out in the field. Even the gold panning operation. It all flows back to one thing: Business."

Frankel hadn't uttered a word once during the presentation. Instead he just sat back, amazed at the charts showing not only the Cross's troop strengths, number of airplanes, tanks, gun emplacements, and SAM sites, but also projections for the organization's expansion for the next year, the year after that, five years hence and a full decade in the future. By that time, the High Commander had made it quite clear that the Cross would be running the entire world.

A chart showing the Twisted Cross's projected revenues for the next five years wrapped up the presentation.

"We hope that, five years we'll have a gold reserve totaling one hundred and forty-one tons," the High Commander told him. "It will be at that point that every working country in the world will have to deal with us. Not as manufacturers or agribusinessmen, but as the world's financial brokers. When we control almost half the processed gold in the world, we'll control how much the rest of the world's gold is worth. So, Colonel Frankel, when you hear all this talk about 'The Cause' and 'Our Cause,' well, hell, now you know what we're talking about."

Frankel was still speechless.

"And if anyone gives us any static," the High Commander went on. "And I mean *at all*, we come down on them like a ton of bricks. Because, along with our financial growth, we expect a simultaneous growth in our armed forces. If all goes according to the plan, the day we reach one hundred and forty-one tons, we will also have the world's largest standing army. Am I going too fast for you?"

"No, sir . . ." Frankel said, by force of habit. "But if I may, where do the nuclear mines in the Canal come in?"

"Well, Frankel, they're our ace in the hole, you see," the High Commander answered. "They provide leverage. We want their existence to be the worst kept secret in the world. Get it? No one in this hemisphere will screw around with us if they know we've got this nuclear underwater capability thing. And once the economy really gets chugging in this part of the world, they'll be backed up and taking numbers—itching for a chance to get through the Canal.

"Of course we have a fall-back position. Should a hostile takeover seem imminent, well, we'll just pull the plug."

"Pull the plug, sir?"

"Sure, Frankel," the High Commander said, sipping a glass of mineral water. "I mean, push the button. Light 'em up. *Liquidate* our assets along with half of Central America, cut our losses and, well, start all over again."

"It is brilliant, sir. Simply brilliant . . ." Frankel heard himself saying.

"So, you agree then that we should move at a constructive, yet conservative pace for now?" the High Commander asked, walking over to the edge of his desk and sitting down. "That would be solidifying our position here in the Canal, working the Mayan sites, and keeping the United Americans at bay with some long, protracted—oh, what shall we call them?—discussions of mutual security interests. How does that grab you?"

The man leaned forward, eager for Frankel's reply.

"Brilliant!" Frankel repeated, not knowing what else to say again. "A very workable plan!"

The High Commander put his suit jacket back on and sat down behind his desk. "Well, I'm glad to hear you say that, Frankel," he told him. "Because, for us to pull this off, we *have* to cut a deal with the United Americans, just to decoy them. And to do that, we have to send the right person to talk to them. Someone who looks convincing, acts confident and knows how to deal."

The High Commander leaned forward on his desk for emphasis and smiled tightly. "We think you're that guy, Frankel."

Frankel was astounded. "Me, sir?" he asked, unconsciously pointing at his own chest for emphasis. "But why me?"

The High Commander allowed himself a legitimate laugh. "Well, because Frankel, I just keep hearing so many damn good things about you, that's why. We liked very much how you handled that duty out on the entrance island. 'Operation Choose It or Lose It' is how we used to describe it back here. But you didn't screw up once, Colonel and that's not something that goes unnoticed around here.

"And let me tell you right now, that gold panning thing was just a smokescreen. We just wanted to get you back over here on the mainland. Close by while the others and I were tossing ideas around. It's an important assignment, Frankel, there's no reason to downplay that. But if you come through and really knock 'em dead, well, I can guarantee, you'll be up to major general in a snap."

Stunned, Frankel wondered if he had it in him to speak

more than two sentences at once.

"But why me, sir?" he finally managed to say again. "There must be a thousand other men here who could do the job better than I. Men who are schooled in politics, or debating or foreign affairs. I am not an expert in any of those things."

The High Commander chuckled once again. "Now, Colonel," he said, following in a sing-song voice: "Don't you think that we know that?"

Frankel could only nod.

"Well, of course we do," the Commander went on. "But you see, we want you Frankel, because, well, I don't know any other way of saying it other than you looked so damn good, Colonel. You *look* Aryan, man. Your face could go on a poster. We need someone who *looks* good, Frankel. Someone who can communicate to those United Americans that we mean business. And I mean Business with a capital 'B' . . . Do you think you can handle it, old boy?"

"I . . . I will do whatever you ask," Frankel told him, his voice still a bit shaky.

"Now that's what I *really* want to hear," the High Commander said with a loud clap of his hands. "Let's drink to it."

He moved over to his substantial liquor supply and poured out two banana brandies. "A toast!" he said. "To our Cause and your mission."

"Will I be briefed, sir?" Frankel asked, holding the drink numbly in hand. "Given information I can study up on?"

"By the best we have," the High Commander said, giving him a friendly jab to the shoulder. "Now drink up, Colonel. Tomorrow we'll have lunch with some of my people and bounce around something solid . . ."

With that, the High Commander took a long swig of his banana brandy. "Ahh," he said, smacking his lips in delight. "I just can't get enough of this stuff . . ."

Chapter 37

"Well, aren't you going to rape me, Colonel?" the woman asked him defiantly. "Or do you have to get drunk first before you can be with a female?"

"Silence!" Krupp screamed at her. "Or you will be shot in a minute . . ."

"I would prefer *that* to being here with you one more moment!" she snarled at him.

They were sitting in the entrance way to the fabulous chamber of gold, their two dimming lanterns casting grotesque shadows on the walls and on the rows of gold.

His men had been gone for hours and Krupp had spent much of that time berating himself for giving them such inane orders. He had made several huge mistakes: First of all, he had been blind to the fact that they had been in the tunnels for so long, it was now night outside. This would mean that, assuming the seven troopers found their way out all right, it would take them twice as long to rouse the others, then lead them on the trip back in.

Secondly, he knew it would probably be more than seven hours before anyone reached them again, and he wasn't certain that he could fight off sleep that long. And third, the biggest mistake of all, he had no gun—no weapon with which to hold the woman.

"How long have you been using whips, Colonel?" she asked him in an overtly mocking tone. "Did your mother use them on you?"

"*Silence!*" Krupp screamed so loudly his voice echoed around the cavern for a full ten seconds. "Or I swear I'll execute you right here and now . . ."

"And how would you do that?" she asked with a slightly deranged bravado. "Slap me to death? Beat me up? Do you really like those kinds of things, Colonel Krupp?"

He reached over and grabbed her by the hair. "I'll wring your Goddamn neck," he hissed.

"Ha!" she laughed and cried out at the same time. "It takes a man to commit cold-blooded murder, Colonel. You haven't got it in you . . ."

He shook her head violently once again. "You must be insane," he said to her. "How dare you act so defiant?"

Again, she laughed hysterically. "What have I got to lose?" she screamed at him. "Do you really think your goons found their way out of here? As tired as they were, carrying those pieces of gold? How heavy do you think they feel to them now? Maybe one hundred pounds. A hundred and fifty?"

Krupp reached over and slapped her hard across her face. Her months in confinement had obviously altered her mental capacities. "Don't *provoke* me!" he screamed, sounding a bit deranged himself. "I'll kill you, I swear . . ."

She spit right in his face. "Go to hell, you fucking Nazi," she snapped. "You're gutless . . ."

Krupp put his hands to his ears and tried to block out her words. Why was she doing this to him? How dare she? He was in command here, but at the same time, he felt something in his mind slipping away. It was her fault—she was hitting every panic button he owned at point blank range.

At that moment, his lantern blinked out.

It was mistake number four. The batteries on his light were now gone.

"Give me your light," he demanded of the woman, grabbing for the lantern that was slung around her shoulder. She had periodically shut it off during the trip into the caves, and therefore, its batteries were fresher.

"No . . ." she said, pulling the lantern away from him.

He reached out and grabbed her hair again and started yanking on it. But in retaliation, the woman threw the lantern against the cavern wall, smashing its bulb and lens.

Suddenly they were plunged into an absolutely terrifying darkness.

"Now Colonel," she said, openly mocking him. "Let's see how brave you are in the dark . . ."

Chapter 38

Hunter woke up in the middle of the night with one girl lying across his chest, another nestled under his left arm.

It took him just an instant to remember where he was and who his bunk guests were.

He was in the mission's guest house and the two women were members of the flock. The day before he had gotten a brief glimpse of a couple dozen scantily-clad women emerging from the Fighting Brothers' concrete shelter. At the time there had been no introduction, no explanation as to why 24 bathing beauties would be part of the Brothers' milieu. But after returning from the Coba site and the lightning quick battle with the Skinheads, these oversights were corrected.

The women, actually a company of "entertainers," had fled the island of Cozumel, which was just a stone's throw offshore from Cancun. Just why they were on the resort island in the first place was never really explained to Hunter, but the drift he got was that the women represented a personal harem for a crackpot who had set up his own little kingdom on Cozumel.

In any case, it had all happened about a year before and The Brothers kindly took in the women, on humanitarian grounds, of course. The act of kindness turned out to be an odd arrangement. While the Brothers took no vow of celibacy from the Order, most practiced it anyway. Of the 55 monks, only ten had wives (which explained the fifteen or so children that Hunter saw running around the compound). The others had decided to give up sex for religion before journeying to the wild lands of northeast Yucatan, but the appearance of the "entertainers" had gradually changed that decision for some. At last count, fourteen of the Brothers had matched up with one of the women and several more romances were reportedly in the works.

That still left a few unattached women and Hunter had met these two—Janine and Lori, he thought their names were—at a rousing banquet the Brothers had thrown together the night before. Hunter hadn't seen a feast quite like it in many a moon. The Brothers bottled their own wine and tasting it was the commodore's daily chore. It was powerful stuff—a half dozen glasses full and Hunter was into the spins.

At some point Brother Paul introduced him to the two women and the rest was history . . .

He reached over and gently moved Janine off his chest. Then he pulled Lori closer to him and began stroking her fine blond hair.

"Are you awake?" Lori asked him.

"Only if you are," he replied.

She laughed and let her hands wander all over his body. "So you're really this Wingman guy?" she asked.

"I'm beginning to wonder myself," he said. "For some reason people just don't want to believe it these days."

"The world is a crazy place," she sighed. "Lot of people just don't know what to believe anymore."

She snuggled even closer to him, allowing him to place his hand on her well-formed breast. "But I have to admit," she continued, "that in spite of everything, it can be very peaceful here with the Brothers. When those Chicos aren't running around like mad dogs, this place can be like paradise. I never thought I could find such serenity. I mean, I would never consider going back to the States now, or what used to be the States, I should say. I don't know how you can live up there. From what I hear, it's like cowboys and Indians everywhere, night and day. Is that true?"

"That's close," he answered. "But maybe some day it won't be as bad. If the government were able to get a handle on things, would you go back then?"

She thought it over for a moment, then answered: "I'm not sure. It's my country and everything, but nothing was ever the same after the New Order went down."

He pulled her very close to him. "Well some day, things will be better," he told her, a bit wistfully. "That is, if some day ever comes . . ."

Janine had woken up by this time. She adjusted her pillow and gave him a long series of kisses down his neck to his chest.

"Do you always manage to get two girls in bed with you at once?" Janine asked in her sweet, smart-ass style.

"No, not always," he answered. "I'm just lucky that way, I guess."

"Lucky, is it?" she said. "Well, let me ask you something else Mr. Bigshot Wingman: If you're this super flyboy hero we keep on hearing about, how come you don't have a steady girlfriend?"

Hunter felt as if he'd just been hit with two barrels of buckshot in the ass.

"That's a good question," he answered cheerlessly.

Chapter 39

It was so dark, Krupp didn't know if he was asleep or not.

His uniform was soaked through with moisture and the small mites crawling in his hair seemed real enough. Yet he couldn't feel his one hand with the other. He couldn't hear himself breathing and nor did he have any sensation of a heart beating in his chest.

"Maybe I'm dead," he thought.

He had no idea where the woman was. For all he knew, she had slipped away three hours ago when the lights went out. Since then he had gone through two fits of claustrophobia and at least a half dozen panic attacks. Since then, a strange white foam has been forming in his mouth and in his nostrils.

He had tried to count the seconds, thinking that if he kept it up, he could better judge when his troopers would return. But he gave up this futile, desperate exercise after realizing that even if he counted all the way up to 20,000, the earliest the relief party would arrive would still be four hours — or 14,400 seconds — away.

"Colonel Krupp?"

He froze. Had he really heard someone call out his name?

"Colonel? Answer me . . ."

It wasn't the girl's voice — it was that of a man, and it was vaguely familiar.

"There's no sense in not answering, Colonel. I know you are out there, somewhere . . ."

Krupp was absolutely paralyzed. The voice was so

strange, so *unearthly*. He knew it didn't belong to anyone in a relief party. Nor was it coming from any specific direction. At first it sounded as if it was in front of him. Then behind him. Then off to one side, then to the other.

"Colonel, it is time that you face the facts . . ."

Once again, Krupp put his hands to his ears in an attempt to block out what he didn't want to hear. But, if anything, the voice was louder.

"Colonel, you are just denying the inevitable . . ."

"Why is this happening?" Krupp cried softly. "Why me?"

He looked up and saw a faint glow no more than two feet from him. As he watched in terror, it grew closer and solidified into a man's features.

"Recognize me now, Colonel?"

Krupp stared in absolute horror and disbelief. He felt his stomach do a flip, a gut full of vomit traveling two thirds of the way up his esophagus before he was able to force it back down again. His eyes suddenly watered up in fear.

"Remember me, Colonel?"

At that instant, Krupp knew he had gone insane. The face before him was that of Heinke, the man who had walked into the woods at Chichen Itza and never came back . . .

"Having problems, Colonel?" another voice asked.

Krupp shook himself awake. He stared straight ahead and saw another face glowing in the dark.

"Sorry, I can't help . . ." the woman said, shining a barely-burning lantern up to her face.

Krupp looked at his hands in the faint glow of the dim lamp. They were sticky and streaked with blood. He put a finger up to his eyes and this came down covered with more, fresher blood. The strange white foam was all over his chin.

"How?" he asked the woman weakly.

"The light, you mean?" she asked. "Well, Colonel, your problem is you panic too quickly. This is your light, and sure, the batteries wore down. But after letting them rest for a few hours, they come back a little. See?"

She waved the lantern around the gold-filled room like a

child with a sparkler.

"Stop it!" he screamed. "And tell me, why am I bleeding?"

"You tried to scratch your own eyes out," she told him with a laugh. "Don't you remember?"

"But you *saw* him, didn't you?" he pleaded with her. "*Tell* me you saw him . . ."

She waited a few moments before replying. "Heinke, you mean?" she asked.

"Yes, yes!"

"Sure, I saw him," she answered cleverly. "You and he had quite a conversation."

"He *was* here then!" Krupp cried. "Somehow, he got in here with us, right?"

"Yes, Colonel," she said, turning out the lantern again. "Whatever you say . . ."

The relief party finally reached Krupp and the woman three hours later.

By this time Krupp was only semi-conscious, a regular flow of the foamy white substance oozing from his mouth and nostrils. The recovery mission's second-in-command, a captain named Gmund, arranged to have both Krupp and the woman carried out on stretchers. He then posted six guards at the entrance to the gold chamber, and strung a radio line back to the cave's opening at the base of the Uxmaluna's Grand Pyramid.

By this time, it was morning. Only then did he call his superiors in Panama City to report the enormous gold find.

Chapter 40

Back in Washington, things had just turned upside down.

"They want *what?*" Fitzgerald asked in disbelief.

"They want a summit meeting," General Jones repeated himself. "They want to sit down and talk. Negotiate. Discuss 'issues of mutual security,' is how the message puts it."

"I can't believe this," Fitz said. "These Nazis actually think we're going to sit down and talk rationally with them?"

"That's the offer," Jones told him. "We'll have to send some sort of reply back to them by midnight tonight, our time."

It had been a crazy few days for the top staff of the United American Army. Most of the time had been devoted to gearing up their land and air forces for the anticipated strike on Panama. An entire airborne division — a total of 15,000 men — had already deployed to a secret base in southern Texas.

Moving south with the paratroopers were seven squadrons of United American fighters and fighter-bombers. Unified under one command, the aircraft included Football City's 12 famous F-20 Tigersharks, 18 of Mike Fitzgerald's F-105X Super Thunderchiefs, known informally to all as the Shamrock Squadron, 24 Free Canadian CA-10 Thunderbolts, plus a large contingent of various aircraft belonging to the old PAAC including several AV-8B Harriers, 36 A-7D Strikefighters, and 18 A-4 Skyhawks, the small, laser-equipped attack jets that had worked so well in the recapturing of Football City in the last war against The Circle.

Also deployed to bases in Texas were nine of the United Americans B-52 Stratofortresses, the two enormous C-5 gunships known as *Bozo* and *Nozo,* and the super-secret *Ghost Rider* air unit which was made up of five, electronically jam-packed B-1B supersonic, near-Stealth, swing-wing bombers.

It had been a major air movement; counting various support aircraft such as the United Americans' fleet of KC-135 aerial tankers as well as three dozen C-130 Hercules cargo ships — including 12 from the famous New York Heavy Lift Corporation known better as the New York Hercs — nearly two hundred fixed-wing aircraft had been transferred, virtually overnight, to the Republic of Texas. There, they would be additionally complemented by the Texans' own five squadrons of F-4X Super Phantoms.

Moving the United Americans various ground units had taken longer. Two armored divisions — equipped mostly with nearly 200 M-1 and M-60 tanks — were traveling at that moment on rail cars that would eventually bring them to the port city of Galveston, Republic of Texas. There they would be loaded onto anything that could float — Free Canadian amphibious assault ships mostly. A total of ten ships, converted container-carrying vessels, would be devoted just to carrying the United Americans' substantial helicopter force. Forty-eight hours before the operation was to commence, these seaborne units would set sail. If everything ran smoothly, they would be waiting somewhere off the coast of Panama when the first bombs fell.

That all this had to be done as secretly as possible was only half the problem for the United American Command Staff. The biggest challenge was that it had to be done in less than a few days.

And it was . . .

"And now after all this, these guys want to talk about it?" Fitz asked, still astounded that the Canal Nazis had actually offered to negotiate.

"That's the purpose of the message," Jones told him again.

The message, which was first intercepted by an United American advance listening post down on the Louisiana coast, proposed that a representative from The Twisted Cross fly to Washington and "start a dialogue" immediately. Jones had received the communique just about midnight and now, at 0900 he was discussing it with Fitz, Ben Wa and JT Toomey in his Pentagon office.

"This is nuts," Toomey said. "One day these guys are all into cloak-and-dagger and now they want us to throw them a coming out party. I say we tell them to go take a fucking leap."

"I agree," Wa said. "The time for them to talk was before they started planting the underwater nukes. These guys are vicious. They're murderers."

"Most likely they caught wind of our deployments," Fitz added. "Now they're either scared, stalling for time or a little bit of both . . ."

"In other words, now's the time to zap 'em!" Toomey said.

"No," Jones said firmly. "Now's the time to listen to what they have to say."

All three men were taken aback.

"Are you serious, General?" Fitz asked. "Sit down and diddle with Nazis?"

"Not 'diddle,' " Jones replied. "I said talk to them."

"But why?" JT asked. "You know they're just trying to screw us over."

"Maybe," Jones said. "But I have the lives of nearly sixty thousand people in my hands — you three included — not to mention any civilians down in the Canal Zone who could get killed if we attack. I owe it to all of them to at least listen to what these guys have to say."

Fitz, Ben and Toomey were speechless.

"I'm sending a reply back to them right now," Jones said, concluding the brief meeting. "I'm telling them that we accept their offer."

Chapter 41

Major Dantini, commander of the Central American Tactical Service, took a sip of tequila then went back to strumming his well-worn Martin guitar.

Things had been so slow lately, he had even found time to play the old six-string. They had not attacked the Cross in what seemed like years now, at the request of Hunter and the United American Command. He supposed the fear was that any fighting around the Canal Zone could accidentally set off one or more of the underwater nuclear mines. It was unlikely of course, but Dantini knew now was not the time to take any risks. Not when he and his one hundred chopper troops were about to gain 60,000 allies.

They were now camped near the deserted town of Bocas del Toro, which was on an island some 150 miles west of the Canal on the western end of the Mosquito Gulf. The terrain here favored them. There were dozens of tall hills surrounding the city and Dantini and his men had claimed two of them as their temporary base. The height advantage worked in two ways: first it would help should the whole 15-chopper force have to move quickly, and second, it gave them a clear view of the Panamanian mainland, both to the south and to the west. Even a fast-moving jet coming out of Panama could be spotted far enough away to give ample warning for everyone to get to shelter.

Still strumming his guitar, Dantini continually scanned the horizon, looking for anything unforeseen. Several minutes passed, but then he did see something approaching from the southwest. He didn't miss a note on his instrument, however; it was one of the Flying Cranes returning from the only kind of mission they were able to carry out these days.

He watched as the big ship hovered just off to his left, preparing to set down on the large, flat wooden platform set up on top of the hill. The Crane was straddling one of the group's purpose-designed containers; this particular PDC was the one bristling with various radio antennas, including one for broadcasting on AM and FM frequencies.

The Crane finally landed, kicking up a couple of pounds of dust as it did so. A few moments later, the door on the Radio PDC opened and two men climbed out, their uniforms disheveled, beer cans in hand.

Dantini shook his head in mild disgust at the pair. The two men were probably the only people left in the New Order world who could actually get beer in cans. "I thought there was only supposed to be *one* in every bunch," Dantini murmured to himself. "I've got to get stuck with trouble times two . . ."

By this time the two had walked over to him. "Mission accomplished, Major," one of them, a man called Masoni, told him in a voice so gravelly, you could pave a highway with it.

"Any problems at all?" Dantini asked.

"Negative," the other man, a sergeant who went by the stage name of Gregg O'Gregg, reported between swigs of beer. "We put out two solid hours right near El Cope, then another ninety minutes just outside Nata. Didn't see a soul out there."

Dantini breathed a sigh of relief. Despite their appearance and general demeanor, Masoni and O'Gregg always came through. That was the only reason why Dantini was so tolerant of their less-than-proper military behavior.

The PDC was actually a flying radio station, and together, Masoni and O'Gregg made up the entire CATS psyche-war section. They worked via a dangerous MO. The Flying Crane would carry the PDC — known as Radio

CATS—to various isolated parts of Panama and once set up, the two men would start broadcasting clandestinely. Like a mini-Radio Liberty or Radio Marti, Masoni and O'Gregg would play Panamanian national music and any music hits that were popular in Panama before the Big War. Interspersed between the songs, the men would read carefully prepared statements urging the Panamanian natives not to give up, that the Canal and their country would be liberated one day from The Twisted Cross.

The tactic was effective—Dantini and his men were always greeted with open arms by any natives they happened to run into. While it was dangerous to carry a radio in or near the occupied Canal Zone itself, many people who lived out in the Panamanian hinterlands still had their trusty transistor sets and boom boxes. Everyday, they would click them on, hoping to hear an hour or two of the music from the old days.

The tactic also served to drive the Canal Nazis batty. To this day Dantini was convinced that the Nazis believed the radio was actually carried by truck, and not by helicopter. That was why whenever they set up camp, the first PDC to be camouflaged and hidden away was Radio CATS.

"Okay," Dantini told Masoni and O'Gregg. "Get something to eat and then check back with me this afternoon. We'll pick your broadcast posts for tomorrow then."

They both offered wide-smiling, snap salutes. On cue, they guzzled the rest of their no-name beers and symbolically crushed the beer cans on their foreheads. Then they turned on their heels and marched away, leaving Dantini as always, shaking his head.

"If I thought too much about it I'd go nuts," he said to himself.

He sat back down and picked up the Martin six-string again. Suddenly, the radio at his feet burst to life. He heard Burke's excited voice on the other end.

"Major! We've got company coming . . ."

Dantini immediately reached down, picked up the radio and punched the send button. "Who and where?"

"Choppers," Burke, who was over on the other hilltop,

reported. "Two of them coming in from the north. They look like Cobras."

"Cobras?" Dantini wondered out loud. "Are they blinking?"

"Three reds, two whites," Burke called back. "Is that today's sequence?"

Dantini hastily retrieved a piece of folded paper from his boot. He unwrapped it and quickly read the scrawled list of what were called "approach sequences." These were messages sent by using the navigation lights of an aircraft, thereby eliminating the use of intercept-prone long-range radio messages.

"Three reds, two whites," Dantini confirmed, checking the sheet he and Hunter had drawn up before the pilot headed back up north. "Yep, that's the password."

He carefully laid his guitar aside and ran down the hill to the beach. Burke arrived at the same time, and together they watched as the two Cobras roared in over the wavetops.

"These have got to be the guys Hunter was talking about," Dantini said as the two gunships set down on the beach about 150 feet away.

Through the swirl of sand and seaspray, Dantini saw one man emerge from the first helicopter. He and Burke met him halfway.

"Major Dantini?" the man from the Cobra asked. "I'm Captain Jesse Tyler, United American Army."

"Are you one half of the famous Cobra Brothers?" Dantini asked shaking hands with the man.

"Yes, I am," the man answered through his thick Texan accent. "Hunter told you about us?"

Dantini and Burke both nodded. "Did he ever," Burke said. "Had us up all night once, telling about how crazy you guys were."

Tyler laughed. "Well, he can spin a tale as well as the rest of us," he said. "Better, even . . ."

By this time the three other members of the Cobra team had joined them. "This is Captain Bobby Crockett, and Lieutenants John Hobbs and Marty Baxter," Tyler said over another orgy of handshakes.

"So I suppose I don't have to guess what the purpose of your visit is," Dantini said. "I assume the United Americans are ready to attack. When is H-Hour?"

Tyler took off his helmet and ran his fingers through his hair.

"Major," he said, "let's all go someplace quiet where we can talk . . ."

Chapter 42

The Fighting Brothers' long-range patrol was back at the mission before noon.

They had left one hour before sunup, walking back to reconnoiter the place were the Skinheads had attacked the mission truck. Thirty minutes after the patrol's return, Brother David met Hunter at the small lake's shoreline. They talked as the pilot went through a list of routine preflight maintenance checks on the Kingfisher.

"My Brothers confirm that it *was* a full squad of Skinheads that we tangled with yesterday," David told him.

"Is that unusual?"

"Yes, it is," the monk said. "We know of Skinhead advisors traveling with gangs like *Dos Chicos*. But this is the first time we've encountered a force made up entirely of Skinheads."

Hunter opened the plane's engine cowling maintenance door and peered in at its power plant. "What does that tell us?" he asked. "So many of them in the area at once . . ."

"I'm afraid it means they have suddenly attached a new importance to us," David said.

"Maybe they know I'm here," Hunter said quietly.

"I'm sorry, but I think I have to agree with you," the monk replied. "It's really the only explanation. They were content just to arm the *Chicos* before. Now, this . . ."

Hunter saw that everything inside the engine checked out, so he closed the small door and wiped his hand with a rag.

"Well, I won't be here much longer," he said. "But how will they know that?"

Brother David shrugged. "They won't," he said. "And there's a more frightening aspect to this. Our patrol found a Hind helicopter out near where the 'Heads set upon us. It was destroyed, burned."

"Really?" Hunter asked. "By who?"

"By the Skinheads themselves, I would guess," David answered. "It can only mean one thing . . ."

Hunter didn't have to have it spelled out for him; he knew what the burnt out chopper meant. "They were on a suicide mission," he said. "They burned their own means of transport before setting out to get us."

The Top Monk nodded. "Yes," he said. "We have definitely caught their attention. These pagans don't just send their hari-kiri squads after anyone . . ."

Hunter thought about it for a moment, then said: "Okay, I feel responsible for this. I think you'd better consider evacuating your people."

"I agree, Major," David said. "But where can we possibly go where it is safe? And where it's big enough to accommodate us all?"

Hunter flashed a smile. "I have just the place in mind," he said.

It only took about ten hours in all to move The Brothers, their families, their girlfriends, their weapons and their equipment to the abandoned pyramid hotel at Cancun.

Hunter rode shotgun in the sky as the long convoy of trucks wound its way the sixty miles to the resort city. By midnight, the Fighting Brothers had christened their new abbey. The beauty of the place—in addition to its lavish space and easily defended location—was that to its rear was an entire fleet of luxury yachts, most in running condition. So should the Brothers come under attack from a superior force, they always had the option of taking to the boats and escaping.

All these precautions made Hunter feel better about the safety of the monks and their people, and by the end of the long day, he was bushed. He spent the night with Janine and

Lori again, making love to both then letting them massage his tired muscles to sleep.

The next morning dawned bright and hot. Hunter wolfed down a quick breakfast, then was down on the docks, getting his airplane ready for flight again. He was heading for Chichen Itza, most likely the next set of ruins on the Canal Nazis' plunder list.

He was just about to load on his dufflebag of gear when he saw Brother David walking down the long dock toward him. Oddly, he was carrying a full knapsack and his rifle.

"I was just coming up to say *adios* to you, Brother David," Hunter told him.

"No need for that, Brother Hunter," David replied. With that the big man threw his knapsack into the pilot's compartment of the Kingfisher. "We still have a long road to travel together . . ."

"You're not actually thinking of coming with me," Hunter said.

"I am," was the stoic reply.

"But, your people," Hunter said. "They need you."

"But, Brother Hunter, you need me more," the monk replied, matter-of-factly. "I can't expect you to face these fascist infidels alone, not after you saved us the other day. It was an act I must replay."

Hunter shook his head. "I told you that repayment wasn't necessary, Brother," he said. "Besides—"

"Besides nothing," the monk told him, lowering his M-16 into the airplane. "Paul is capable of watching the flock for awhile. As for myself, I am a trained soldier. I can hold my own. I will not be a burden to you."

Hunter was about to counterpoint the man's statement when he saw the commodore strolling down the docks toward them. He too was carrying a full knapsack and a weapon.

"Now what the hell is going on?" Hunter asked.

"I am going too," the commodore declared.

"This is getting out of hand . . ." Hunter said.

"No," the feisty little Italian said. "I am a trained soldier. I

229

can hold my own. I will not be a burden to you."

The litany sounded very familiar — too familiar. David and the commodore had obviously rehearsed the little scene several times. Hunter at once realized that he was victim of a conspiracy of friends.

There was no sense arguing with them — two more stubborn people did not exist.

"Okay," the pilot said. "It's going to be crowded, but I appreciate the help . . ."

The commodore slapped him twice on the back. "We knew you'd feel that way, Hawk, old friend."

"Let us be off," Brother David said. "The Lord's wind will guide us."

Brother David took his place in the Kingfisher's rear-facing gunner's seat, while the commodore strapped himself in the hammock just behind Hunter pilot's seat. The take-off went smooth as silk. Hunter slowly put the Kingfisher into a climb out over the ocean. Then he turned inland, flying directly over the pyramid to see the entire congregation gathered on the roof and waving goodbye.

Chapter 43

"Negotiations!" Dantini said angrily.

"That's the word," Cobra Captain Tyler told him for what seemed like the hundredth time. "We heard it on the way here, and we got it so quickly only because we have scramblers on board. But they thought it was important that you guys know."

They were sitting in Dantini's command tent high on the island hill. Coffee had been the drink of preference — up until Tyler broke the news to Dantini and Burke. Now the tequila had been going around non-stop for hours.

"But what in the world is there to talk about with them?" Dantini asked again. "They're Nazis and they've got nuclear bombs floating around in the Canal, for Christ's sake. What's to discuss?"

Tyler took a long swig of the Mexican firewater. They had been arguing the same points over and over all night. Now the sun was coming up. "It's more complicated than that," he said. "They're entrenched and the bulk of our forces are hundreds of miles from the Canal Zone. Whatever action takes place, there is undoubtedly going to be a heavy loss of life. Our top man, General Dave Jones, is the kind of guy who would do anything humanly possible to prevent unnecessary bloodshed."

"Does that include playing footsies with Nazis?" Burke asked sarcastically.

Now it was Tyler's turn to get angry. "You're out of line, Lieutenant," he told the man sternly. "You don't know Jones. The fucking guy is George Washington, Abe Lincoln and

FDR all rolled into one. You couldn't have a better guy in your corner . . ."

"Is that right?" Burke drunkenly spouted off again. "Then what about your famous Hawk Hunter? Where the hell is *he* during all this?"

Tyler eyed his partner Crockett and shook his head slowly. "Like we told you, he's on a very sensitive mission," Tyler said finally. "We really can't say anymore than that."

"This is *bullshit!*" Burke exploded. "I knew it was a big mistake listening to these guys."

"Hang on, Lieutenant," Dantini interrupted. He then turned to Tyler.

"You've got to remember that we were hired to do a job here," he said. "We have people—landowners, businessmen—both in Panama and in Big Banana, who are laying a lot of money on us, for the sole purpose of us attacking the Nazis. What are we supposed to tell them? The Big Powers are negotiating, so it's 'fuck you?' "

"No," Crockett said. "You tell them to be patient. Hang on. See what happens . . ."

"How long?" Dantini asked. "How long do we wait?"

"Until we get the word from DC," Tyler said. "Whatever it may be . . ."

"Great," Burke huffed. "So now we have to sit around for what another two weeks? Or two months? Or two years? Doing nothing?"

"No one said anything about 'doing nothing,' Lieutenant," Tyler told the man. "In fact, there are some very important things we have to do while these talks are going on.

"In fact, that's why we're here . . ."

Chapter 44

Elizabeth was amazed that she had actually been allowed to take a bath.

Like Krupp, she too had been carried out of the caves on a stretcher, and given first aid by the camp doctor. Truth was, there was nothing really wrong with her as a result of being in the cavern for nearly 24 hours—many times in her school work, she'd stayed in caves up to four to five days at a time. But the doctor, who was actually a South African, was hard-pressed yet compelled by his profession to recommend *something*. So he prescribed that she should take a bath and be fed a hot meal.

To this end, her guards somehow rustled up a plastic three-foot tub and set it up behind the doctor's tent, which was right beside the Grand Pyramid at Uxmaluna. They even erected a hastily-built curtain and some sheets, then provided her with three, five-gallon drums filled with lukewarm water. When she lied to one of them and said that the doctor insisted she use soap, one man went off and returned five minutes later with a bar of strong laundry soap. She didn't mind—at that point she would have bathed in pure lye.

So she scrubbed herself over and over again until the water was cool and murky. Then she rinsed and dressed in the size-small uniform they had provided for her. Well-clothed and clean for the first time in weeks, she stepped out from behind the curtain, expecting her guards to be waiting with handcuffs and hood once again.

But they weren't . . .

The guards had left her. They were gone, hoping to be

closer to the activity near the entrance to the tunnel which led to the chamber full of gold.

It was amazing what the fever could do to people, she thought.

Before she had led the Nazis to the huge gold find, she was dirty, beaten, starved, always in handcuffs, always hooded and nearly raped on several occasions. It had been a group effort on their part. But now there was a new "crowd mentality" at work. Drying her hair, she walked, casually and unescorted, back to the truck that had been her prison. Guards and officers passed her, yet no one said a word. The tons of gold in the tunnel cavern deep beneath Grand Uxmaluna were all that mattered. It had become their whole world, their entire existence. For the moment at least, they didn't even know she was there.

She was fascinated at the flip-flop in group dynamics. Testing the theory, she walked, again unescorted, to the mess tent, and simply told the cooks that the doctor had prescribed a hot meal for her. To her amazement, they not only rustled her up a plate of scrambled eggs and a pot of black coffee, one of them even carried it back to her truck for her! She dismissed the man with as much authority as she could muster. Then closing the curtains on the back of the vehicle herself, she dove into the meal with giddy abandon.

Ever since she had been taken out of the cave, the camp had been a beehive of activity. Helicopters carrying Party bigwigs were shuttling in and out. A TV video crew had arrived and were trying to figure out how much cable they would need to get a direct feed from the chamber to the satellite dish they had brought in on a giant Soviet-made Hook helicopter. From there, the video signal would be bounced back to Panama City and presumably, to the High Commander's personal set.

She had briefly considered bolting into the woods and escaping, but in the same instant knew that even the thought of it was foolhardy. She wouldn't have made it a mile before she would have been caught — not by the Nazi guards but by the mortal dangers of the jungle itself. If some poisonous snake or spider didn't get her, then the deep underbrush, with its many opportunities for breaking arms or legs, or for ripping flesh, would have. Once lame or bleeding, a larger animal would seek her out. Once thirsty, only disease-bearing water could be drunk. Once hungry, nothing could be eaten.

So she had to stay—but not only to survive. There was a cloud of an idea forming in the dark recesses of her mind. Didn't some measure of retribution have to be delivered here? Had the tables so turned? Something had happened to her down in that cave with Krupp, something she could feel but not describe. It had started with a noise. Something went *snap!* deep within her brain. She had heard it—clearly, distinctly—in between the time Krupp passed out and when she had been able to revive the failing lantern. She had sat in the complete darkness all that time, reliving the horrible hours that they had forced her to stay in the caves, tied and blindfolded.

But this time, she heard something go *snap!* And she was never the same after that . . .

Suddenly it all made sense. Together, both she and Krupp became a little madder than they had been before. It was how they reacted to it that made the difference. When plunged into total darkness, the Nazi officer had started hallucinating. Then he had tried to scratch his eyes out.

Accustomed to the inky black, she had started plotting . . .

Having finished her meal, Elizabeth sat on the tailgate of her truck and watched the strange show around the entrance to the cave. It looked just like a beehive, people flitting in and out, each one with the mask of joyful determination on his face. What was it? Did the guards and the underlings think The Twisted Cross was going to split the booty evenly among them? Did any of them actually think they would get even a nugget of the gold? She didn't know. She just sat and watched.

Ten minutes went by when she saw a very curious, almost humorous sight. It was another person being brought out of the cave on a stretcher. A closer look revealed that the person was the smelly little man named Strauberg. She would learn later that upon seeing the tons of gold in the chamber, the man had fainted dead away.

Also coming out of the cave entrance were two Party members who were obviously well-schooled in archaeology. She knew this because they were the only ones to go down to the chamber dressed in the right apparel and carrying the right equipment. Now these two men were approaching her, accompanied by a pair of guards who were carrying two of the gold bowl-like ingots.

"We need your advice," one of the men said, even pausing to tip his hat to her. "These ingots were found at the top of the first two stacks along the far wall. You can see there are inscriptions on both of them. We believe the top ingot in each pile is marked this way. But these are glyphs we cannot possibly hope to read."

She took the first ingot and set it down on the tailgate. Sure enough, there were several lines of glyphs imprinted into the gold. The second ingot had identical writing.

"Can you read them?" the second officer asked.

"I'm not sure," she lied, running her finger over the animal-like figure writing. Actually she could read the Pre-Classic Mayan language almost as easily as she could read English. Still she said: "I will need some time with them . . . alone."

The two officers looked at each other and shrugged. "Study them, please," the man who tipped his hat to her said. Then he nodded to the guards and all four men left.

"And you'll call us when you have something?" the other officer asked as they walked away.

"Of course, I will," she answered with a smile.

Time passed and a ominous dark thunderstorm blew up. The wind whipped through the trees surrounding the grand pyramid, and the rain came down without mercy. The entrance to the cave seemed to be the shelter of choice for many of those at the camp. So few people if any took notice when Elizabeth left her truck and walked over to the one belonging to Colonel Krupp.

Reading the glyphs had been easy, as she knew it would be. *Interpreting* them was another matter. But in the course of twenty minutes she was sure she had it figured out. And the truth be known, she had made one of the most earth-shattering discoveries in the realm of Ancient American studies.

But this was hardly foremost in her mind at the moment. Self-preservation, or more accurately a return to self-*realization,* was more important. She was prepared to go to great lengths just to prove to herself that she was a person again. *Any* lengths. Her thinking was twisted, there was no denying that. But it was nothing new. The spiral had started during her three years of living with her father on the isolated ranch near El Paso. That would knock the flowers off anyone's wall. Being kidnapped by the Nazis, accumulating all those days bound and gagged, a hood around her head, sitting in damp caves, certain that death would be preferable, was all very traumatic. But, in the end, it had only drawn her closer to a madness she already considered an acquaintance.

"I don't want to die here," she kept telling herself. And she wasn't so delusional not to recognize that it was just a matter of time before one of the Twisted Cross high officials realized that she was still around and now *very* expendable. That's when things would revert back, she whispered to herself. And when it happened, she had little doubt she'd be led out to the woods and, like her father, shot twice in the back of the head.

And it was this that she vowed would not happen . . .

There was no guard at Krupp's truck.

She knocked three times hard on the door. There was no reply. Three more times, she heard stirring inside, but still nothing. A third series of knocks and she heard Krupp's whiny voice call out: "What is it, guard?"

"It's me," she said simply. Calling out her name wasn't necessary; she was the only woman in camp.

The door opened a crack and Krupp peeked out.

"What are you doing here?" he asked, obviously flabbergasted to see her.

"We have to talk . . . now," she whispered. "While there is still time . . ."

She would really never know exactly why Krupp decided to let her in. Under the circumstances, it seemed like a very foolish thing to do.

Yet she stepped inside and took a good, long look at him.

She knew he was almost gone — like her, almost over the brink. She would have to move fast.

"Did you hear that they found some writing on some of the ingots?" she asked him.

Surprised that she would talk to him in a civil tone, he stumbled to find words and couldn't. Finally he just shook his head no.

"Well, it's true," she said. "And you want to know something? I'm the only one here who knows what the writing means."

He was sweating, his eyes were dilated and there was still a hint of the foamy drool running from the sides of his mouth. In all, he looked disgusting. But she couldn't let that deter her.

"The writing actually tells where more gold is hidden," she began. "More than we found today."

"That's impossible," he said in a weakened voice.

"No, it's true," she said. "I know where there is more. Much more. And I want you to take me there."

She stunned him — it was all over his face. What was going on here? his eyes said. Didn't she hate him? Hate him enough to kill him?

"Take you there?" he asked. "Why would I want to do that? What benefit would it be for me?"

It was the question she had been waiting for.

She reached up and slowly began unbuttoning her shirt.

"What . . . what are you doing?" he asked, choking on his words.

She didn't answer him. She just watched his eyes go wide with her action. And when the floppy uniform was open, she slowly pulled it back to reveal her lovely, well-formed breasts.

"This is what *you've* wanted all along, Colonel," she told him. "So now take it . . ."

Chapter 45

The Kingfisher had just ridden out a violent thunderstorm when Hunter noticed the two blips on his radar screen.

"Damn!" he whispered. "I have a feeling this ain't going to be good."

The commodore crawled up beside him and also saw the radar blips.

"They come our way?" he asked.

Hunter did a couple of quick adjustments to the radar set, but he really didn't have to. His brain was buzzing in afterburner. The aircraft *were* coming their way—and fast. He could feel it in his bones. And his sixth sense was telling him that they weren't friendly.

"Strap in, Brother David," Hunter said, arming all the airplane's weapons. "We're in for a fight."

"Commodore!" the monk cried out. "Come back and help me load this gun."

Hunter switched on his ECM package and started emitting right away. But he knew it was too late to fool the oncoming jets.

"Christ," he murmured as he looked out on the southwestern horizon. "There they are."

Three seconds after he said it, two unmistakable shapes appeared over the horizon. The turned-up wings, the reverse-V tail section, the dirty brown exhaust. "And they're Goddamn Phantoms."

He put the Kingfisher into a dive—not a steep one, more slow and "routine." Within 30 seconds he was cruising just 50 feet above the jungle's treetops.

But this didn't discourage the Phantoms — nor had he thought it would.

Both F-4s spotted him at the beginning of his descent and now they peeled off and streaked down toward him.

"Brother David? You got a handle on that gun back there?" Hunter yelled back.

"I have!" came the reply.

"He has," the commodore added.

"Okay, here's the plan," Hunter told them. "They're going to come down for a look-see before they decide to blast us. Let's just play innocent until I give the word."

Sure enough, within ten seconds the two Phantoms had slowed and pulled up about a quarter mile in back of the World War II-vintage floatplane.

Hunter continued to fly straight ahead, pretending not to notice. "Get ready," he called back to David and the commodore. "Play dumb . . ."

The two F-4s moved up a little closer. "Are they Skinheads?" Hunter called back to the monk.

"No," came the answer. "These airplanes bear the emblem of The Twisted Cross. The Skinheads fly unmarked aircraft."

That was a valuable piece of information, Hunter thought, lowering his altitude even further. By this time both of the fighter-bombers were right up on them.

"Steady, boys," Hunter cautioned. "When I give you the word, Brother, open up on the nose of the nearest airplane."

"On the nose?" came the question.

"That's right," Hunter answered. "Make it quick and don't let up until you have to, okay?"

"Yes," came the stoic reply.

For Hunter's part he was just hoping that he could give Brother David the word to fire before the Phantom pilots noticed that his flying antique was carrying a Vulcan cannon, a few racks of air-to-surface missiles, a 50-caliber machine gun sticking out its back, two mini-Sidewinders on its wingtips and a bristle of radio, infra-red and advanced-seek radar antennas poking out at various points on the wings and fuselage.

Although he was flying low, he had the Kingfisher's throttle opened all the way. Still the Phantoms were now almost even with him. Soon they would realize that the strange black object sticking out the top of the fuselage's midsection was really a deadly 50-caliber machine gun. But even when Brother David opened up on them, they would still have to back off or peel away completely in order to get a shot back at the old airplane. And that would take time. Hunter planned to use every second of it to his advantage.

"Get ready, Brother . . ." he called out. "Steady . . . steady . . . *Now!*"

Instantly the noise of the big fifty going off inside the compartment nearly deafened them all. His ears ringing, Hunter immediately yanked back on the control stick and put the Kingfisher into a rivet-popping climb. All the while, Brother David was pouring fire into the lead Phantom. Before its pilot could pull away, the big fifty's bullets had luckily found the F-4's nosecone — the home for the airplane's radar and the brains of its weapons control system.

The wounded F-4 finally pulled up and away, for a second streaking right by the also-climbing Kingfisher. As Hunter hoped, the second F-4 started to climb also, slower than his companion so as to get a clean shot at the seaplane. That's when Hunter knew he had to play his ace card.

"Hang on Brothers!" he cried out, then he reached over and cut his engine.

All three of them suddenly felt weightless — as if they were floating in the air. The F-4 unintentionally zipped right by them, his quick attempt to lower his flaps only playing right into Hunter's hands. Just as the Kingfisher's propeller came to a dead halt, Hunter fired off both his mini-Sidewinders *and* pushed his Vulcan cannon trigger.

The combined cannon-and-missile barrage hit the F-4 point-blank on its mid-flanks. Even to Hunter's surprise, the jet fighter split right in half. Then its engine blew up, which ignited its underwing fuel tank. He wrestled with the Kingfisher's dead stick in an effort to avoid colliding with the skyful of debris. He made it — but just barely. Three quick pulls of his throttle choke followed, then he slammed the airplane's engine starter button. With a sputter and a cough, the Kingfisher's engine came to life. He had turned the plane completely over by this time and, gaining his power back, leveled out about 35 feet from the top of the jungle canopy.

There was still the question of the other Phantom, but Hunter knew it was no problem at all. The airplane came around on them, streaked by like an angry buzzard, yet fired no weapons at them. It couldn't. Brother David's quick but timely barrage had effectively emasculated the enemy F-4's firing systems. Even its cannon could not be fired. The Phantom buzzed them twice more, Hunter giving in to the temptation of flipping the finger to the pilots on the last pass.

"Fuck you guys," he yelled as the Phantom's pilot, unable to do anything but fly, booted his throttle and disappeared off to the south.

"Still with me, boys?" he called back to his companions. When he received no immediate reply, he turned back and saw both men were staring at him, mouths agape. The pair looked as if they had just endured an hour's-long roller coaster ride.

He had to laugh. "That will teach you to volunteer," he said.

Chapter 46

"But I insist on continuing this mission!" Colonel Krupp was saying, his voice loud but jittery. "There's nothing wrong with me."

"There will be if you continue that tone of voice!" Major General Udet told Krupp. "You are addressing a superior officer, Krupp. Don't forget that!"

Udet, the same high Party officer who congratulated Krupp with a linen and silver luncheon in the shadow of the Chichen Itza pyramid, now stood before him in the recovery mission's command truck, gritting his teeth. He had flown in at first word of the huge gold find and had just returned from seeing it himself. But what he had assumed would be a triumphant visit had turned sour just as soon as he visited Krupp in his command truck and got his first good look at the officer.

The man looked as if he had aged 25 years in a matter of weeks. The officer that Udet had commended at Chichen Itza had been a tall, if weak looking man of 42 years. The man before him now was hunched over, with bleary eyes and dark circles under them. Udet, a veteran of the Big War, had seen men with advanced battle fatigue, and still they had looked better than Krupp did right now.

"Colonel, there is no *reason* to continue the mission," Udet said. "The amount of gold found in that chamber exceeds anyone's wildest expectations. It will take all of our efforts just to retrieve it all."

"General, you don't understand," Krupp pleaded with the officer. "There is more gold to be found. At the other ruins . . ."

Udet was beginning to detest the man. "Look, Colonel," he said. "You've done a fine job here. Your work has been very successful. Why ruin it? You deserve the time off. To . . . recuperate. Get some rest down in Panama City or on one of the islands, and then, if the High Command recommends it, you can resume the recovery mission at that time."

"No!" Krupp screamed at the general. "No, we must push on *now.* To other sites. There is more gold there, can't you understand that, General?"

Udet thought of slapping the man across the face with the back of his leather glove. But even a criminal mind like the general's was able to feel pity — and slapping Krupp would have been nothing less than pathetic.

"Colonel," Udet began, his tone as hard as rock. "It's enough that the High Commander requested that I come out to this hellhole, I have neither the time nor the patience to listen to you. The recovery mission is hereby suspended. You will be flown to Panama City and report to our hospital there. And that is the end of this discussion."

Krupp wiped another bit of foam from his mouth, and dried his eyes on the sleeve of his uniform jacket. He was hearing voices again: *You must go on. The only reasonable thing to do is to continue the mission. You alone know that it's the only avenue that makes sense. Continue the mission. It must go on . . .*

"It must go on!" Krupp screamed at Udet.

The general was so surprised at the rising tone of Krupp's voice, he was speechless. For a moment, he considered calling to the guard. But by the look on Krupp's face, calling for the unit doctor would have made more sense.

"I'm the only one who knows, don't you see?" Krupp said, his voice cracking under the strain. He was crying now. "I alone know that continuing the mission is the only avenue that makes sense. You are a fool to deny that to me, General."

Udet never saw the knife until it had been plunged into his neck. He felt his whole left side go numb. He opened his mouth and tried to scream, but the knife had severed a vocal chord. He felt Krupp pull the blade from his throat and plunge it back into him, just above his clavicle. Then he was stabbed again below the rib cage, and in his last dying moments, he saw the contents of his stomach spill out on to the floor of the command truck.

"My commander," he whispered, his dying words saved for a man he had never really met. "For you and for our Cause . . ."

Udet closed his eyes and felt his soul start the long plunge down.

Chapter 47

The 737 airliner, the largest airplane belonging to The Twisted Cross, entered United American airspace over Louisiana at 0700 hours, barely eight hours after Jones had sent his acceptance to the Nazis' offer of "mutual discussions."

Three hours and twenty minutes later, the all-black aircraft and its five-plane F-4 Phantom escort, were circling the former National Airport just outside Washington, DC. The airport had been cleared of all unnecessary personnel, and a cordon made up of three reserve battalions of United American soldiers was thrown up around the airfield. The roads leading to the meeting place — the old National Press Club Building in downtown DC — were also blocked off and guarded at every intersection.

Jones had asked Major Frost to meet The Twisted Cross delegation at the airport. No handshakes were exchanged as the Free Canadian Air Force officer introduced himself to Colonel Frankel at the bottom of the airliner's access stairs and led him to a waiting limousine. The rest of Frankel's entourage, including the ten F-4 crewmembers who doubled as his bodyguards, were relegated to a battered Greyhound bus.

There was no one to meet the Cross delegation at the entrance to the Press Club Building; Frost served as guide as the Nazis were stuffed onto elevators and brought up to the top floor meeting room, a space once reserved as the Press Club's well-used bar.

Frankel entered the room first and saw that a long rectangular table had been set up, seven chairs on each side. Sitting in the center chair on the opposite side of the table from him was the small, tough-looking man of 60 that Frankel knew was General David Jones, commander in chief of the United American Army. Six other officers, of various uniforms and rank, flanked the general. No one stood up.

The Nazi walked to his seat and reached across the table to shake hands with Jones. But this too was met only with icy stares.

Chapter 48

"Landing coordinates are two-four-zero.. . ." Cobra Captain Jesse Tyler heard in his headphones. "Come in nine-by-six. No wind at LZ . . . Over."

"Roger Foxhound, I read you, over . . ." Tyler replied. "We'll give it another try."

He switched his radio over to internal and called ahead to his front gunner. "Hey, Bax, you see anything down there?"

"Not a thing, Captain," came his gunner's reply. "I knew these guys were good at camouflage, but this is ridiculous."

They had spent the last 20 minutes circling a dark, heavily wooded area just 25 miles north of Panama City. It was the middle of the night and they were looking for the Radio CATS PDC, code-named Foxhound. It was down there somewhere, hidden in the moonless darkness, down beneath the dense jungle growth particularly suited for broadcasting its clandestine radio programs.

"Let's give it another sweep," Tyler said, activating his NightScope goggles and bringing the Cobra gunship down to treetop level once again, looking for the elusive two-four-zero landing coordinates.

"Hold on, Captain," Baxter called back. "I think I see it . . . Down in that gulley at nine o'clock. Isn't that leaf netting?"

Tyler dipped the Cobra slightly to the left, turning a wide arc. He increased the power to his infra-red glasses and scanned the area off to his portside.

"Christ, that *is* them," Tyler drawled, checking his map against the terrain and coming up with an approximate two-four-zero bearing. "Those sons of bitches really know how to hide that thing."

They could just barely see the outline of the large container, sitting at the edge of gulley, hard by a small stream. Sure enough, there was a clearing about 20 feet beyond that that was large enough to handle the gunship.

"No wonder the Canal Nazis have never found them," Tyler said, heading for the LZ.

Ten minutes later, Tyler and Baxter were sitting inside the portable radio station, both of them drinking black coffee.

"So, this is the latest?" the gravel-voice man named Masoni asked.

"Hot off the presses," Tyler told him, sipping his java. "It bounced down from DC, to Texas, to Cobra Two off the coast of your island, to us, and now to you. Each time it got scrambled a little more."

They had been following this pattern for the past 12 hours. For reasons really only known to Jones and maybe a few others, messages to be broadcast between the music on Radio CATS were being written in DC and "bounced" all the way down to Panama. It was up to the Cobras to relay the messages because their aircraft carried scrambler equipment and the choppers of the CATS did not.

But to keep the integrity of the system, the messages had to be delivered from the Cobras to Radio CATS by hand. This was the fourth such message of the day, the first three had been ferried in by Cobra Two.

"Wow," Masoni said, "this one's a whopper."

"Those are the orders," Tyler said. "Sounds nutty, but what the hell—I'm no expert in psyche-ops. Not like those guys up in DC are, anyway."

A selection of pre-war Panamanian pop music was just ending. Masoni's partner, Gregg O'Gregg, faded the music out and said: "And now, another news message for our listeners . . ."

He gave Masoni the "Go" sign, and the other man moved closer to the microphone.

"Here's the latest on the peace negotiations in Washington," he began. "Representatives of the United American Army and of The Twisted Cross have met for a second time, and at the end of the two-hour session, both sides expressed optimism in reaching a peaceful solution to the crisis here in Panama.

"As you know, we've been keeping you informed on these very important negotiations by the hour and we will continue to do so . . . And now, here's some more Carlos Santana."

O'Gregg hit the turntable control button and the first strains of Spanish-tinged electric guitar filled the small PDC radio studio. He lowered the in-studio volume and poured he and his partner another coffee.

"There you go, boys," Masoni said. "Mission accomplished. By the way, we've got to stay on the java until we get off the air, but you guys can lift a beer before you go."

Tyler and Baxter looked at each other and shrugged. "Better not," Tyler said. "We've still got some night flying to do."

Masoni laughed and reached into his cooler. "Well, here," he said, retrieving two cold ones. "Take a couple for the road."

Chapter 49

Elizabeth had helped Krupp hide the body.

They tried putting it into a steamer trunk first, but it was already stiffening and refused to fit. Instead they squeezed it into the command truck's Lilliputian lavatory. She left cleaning up the body's leftover mess to Krupp.

Now that this gory detail was attended to, they sat at the truck's small table and their strange plotting session continued once again.

"This is actually a wonderful coincidence," Elizabeth told him. "It eliminates one big problem for us."

Krupp ran his fingers through his hair. "Udet just didn't understand," he said, looking back toward the now sealed-up bathroom.

"Of course, he didn't," she said. "Now, let us talk it over again. How will we get a helicopter? How will we get someone to fly it?"

"That is not a problem," Krupp said, still not quite believing that they were having this conversation. "You see, by orders of the High Command, at least one helicopter at the recovery site must be ready to take off at a moment's notice."

"But why is that?" she asked, legitimately curious.

Krupp smiled. "It's really ingenious," he said. "We call it the blitz copter, as in lightning quick. It's always ready to go in case we are attacked or whatever. You see, anytime we recovered gold from any site, we immediately loaded it on to a designated chopper. That way, if something went wrong, the gold we recovered would get out safely."

"And that helicopter is ready? Right now?" she asked.

"Yes," he said. "No one has rescinded that order."

She smiled. That *was* good news.

"And the pilot?" she asked. "Will he be willing?"

Krupp started to answer, then literally bit his lip. Suddenly the expression on his face changed. "I must ask *you* for something," he said.

"Yes?"

"Before . . ." he said meekly. "Before Udet came here, you had . . . I mean, your shirt was . . ."

She immediately knew what he was getting at.

"You mean, my shirt was open?" she asked.

He nodded energetically, wiping quickly-formed beads of sweat from his brow. "Yes . . ." he said. "Yes, it was . . ."

"And you want me to open it again?" she asked, feigning innocence.

"Yes, I . . . I would like that very much," he answered, another nasty stream of foam appearing in one corner of his mouth.

She laughed a little, then slowly undid her buttons again, watching his spasmatic reaction as each one came undone.

"There," she said when she had finished. "How's that?"

"It's just fine," he said. "Maybe open just a bit more."

She shook her head at him as if she was addressing a misbehaved schoolboy. "Just a little," she said, flopping the shirt tails slightly, exposing the majority of her lovely bosom.

He was using a white cloth to dab his sweat at this point. Elizabeth imagined that she could see a war going on inside his subconscious. So many confusing signals were being sent to his brain, he looked like he was about to blow a circuit.

"All right," she said. "We must move on. The pilot of the helicopter. Will he be willing?"

Krupp wiped his mouth. "If he's not, I'll simply hold a gun to his head." He pulled up Udet's pistol and showed it to her for emphasis.

"Very good," she said. "And how about fuel? Do we have enough to get where we are going?"

"That may be a slight problem," he said. "I know the chopper is supplied with extra fuel tanks. Just how far they will carry us, I'm not sure . . ."

"Beyond Panama?" she asked, pulling back her shirt a little more, and re-exposing one of her soft, pink nipples.

"Not quite," he said. "But I don't see it as being a problem. There are many places to buy fuel between here and the Canal and certainly south of it. Our pilots do it all the time."

Once again she nodded her head approvingly. And now for the final question: "And the ingots recovered already? They will come with us?"

Krupp nodded gleefully. "Except for the two we will get from your truck, the five others have already been loaded onto the blitz copter. Orders, you see . . ."

"Well, isn't that fine?" she said. "It seems like we have everything covered? Are you ready?"

"Oh, yes, I am," he said. "More ready than I've ever been in my life."

They both stood up, she glancing out the window to see that the sun was about to rise. Her timing had been perfect.

She purposely backed up against the door and not without flair, opened her shirt wide.

"Come here," she said.

He nearly stumbled as he moved up close to her. She took his hands and placed them on her breasts. His breathing became so labored, she thought he might hyperventilate.

"Kiss them . . ." she whispered in his ear. "Kiss them hard and tell me how much you want to go through with our plans."

He put his mouth to her right breast and began slurping over her nipple.

"That's right," she cooed in a low voice, reaching between his legs to find the area still soft. "That's right, keep doing it just like that . . ."

Chapter 50

Hunter sat at the head of the long table and fingered the finely-woven linen tablecloth.

"What the hell is this all about?" he asked, turning in his seat to look up at the giant Grand Pyramid at Chichen Itza. "A banquet set up, way out here?"

The commodore slid into the chair to his right. "It is like a Fellini movie, is it not?" he asked excitedly. "The clash of sensibilities. Of styles! There's a surrealistic touch in it all."

"Well, those Nazis sure eat damn well out in the field," Hunter said, shaking his head as he surveyed the still-set, yet dusty table.

"It's been exposed to the elements for awhile," Brother David said, sweeping a quarter inch of dust from the top of the table. "See? It's been rained on and dried out a few times."

As usual, the Nazis had left a half ton of litter behind after evacuating the ruins. They had also left scarring holes in the sides of the precious Mayan architecture, spilled oil everywhere and had generally desecrated the ancient site. And they had left behind this table, set at one time for a king's evening meal, as one last bizarre symbol of their short, but destructive visit.

"Still, I think not long ago, they were here," the commodore said. "I can still smell them."

"A week," Brother David said, surveying the length of the table. "Two at the very most. For some reason, they decided to leave this behind."

"There's a big difference between one week ago and two," Hunter said. "If only we could find out for sure."

He stood and walked slowly through the site. It was much bigger than Coba and much more elaborate. He could feel an electricity in the place, a strange ethereal sensation. What did go on here, not just two weeks ago, but two *thousand years* ago. Where *did* the Mayans go?

He walked past the last unexcavated structure and was soon on the banks of the ancient, but still flowing Casa Casa canal, where the Kingfisher was docked. He retrieved his video camera and turned to go back and take some footage of the site.

But before he could take one step, he was surprised to see the commodore running at full throttle toward him, Brother David right at his heels.

"Start the plane!" the commodore was yelling. "Start the *damn* plane!"

It took only an instant to see what his two comrades were running from. Close behind them was a hundred, no *two* hundred, extremely angry people.

Hunter was in the plane's cockpit inside of three seconds, punching the starter button with one hand, the engine's throttle choke with the other. The propeller suddenly sprang to life, sending a jolt of vibration up and down the fuselage.

By this time, the commodore and Brother David had reached the shoreline, the crowd of angry people not more than 25 feet behind.

"Jump on the wingfloat!" Hunter yelled, even then backing away from the shore. Both Brother David and the commodore took one giant leap and landed squarely on the left wing's float. Once Hunter was certain they were on and holding tight, he gunned the Kingfisher's engine and started it moving forward, down the canal and away from the Chichen Itza site.

The mob followed, right along the riverbank, hurling rocks and spears as they ran. Hunter was able to catch only quick glimpses of them. They all appeared to be wearing some kind of native costumes — bright red and yellow tunics for body garments, orange feathers on their headdresses. Yet he had the strange feeling that the outfits were more ceremonial than anything. They just didn't *look* like everyday wear.

But the fashion of their pursuers quickly slipped in importance in his mind. At the top of the list was getting away from the mob.

He gunned the engine to near take-off speed but quickly realized that the jungle wasn't going to cooperate. In this direction, the trees formed a canopy over the old Mayan canal making a take-off for at least the next mile an impossibility.

"That's it," Hunter said, reducing his speed so as not to capsize from the engine's torque. "I've just got to stop dropping in on places unannounced."

He had to slow down to about 25 knots, enough to get away from the oddly-dressed mob. Or so he thought . . .

"They're all along the riverbanks!" Brother David cried as he crawled up onto the wing and into the compartment. He reached back out and lifted the commodore inside by the collar of the little man's jacket.

"They are millions of them!" the commodore cried out before he even hit the compartment's deck.

After taking another scan of the riverbanks, Hunter was almost inclined to agree with the commodore's estimation. Both banks of the river were crowded with the natives for at least a mile ahead.

"Jesus Christ!" he yelled. "Where the hell did everyone come from?"

He continued plowing down the canal, at times becoming airborne just for a few seconds to clear the occasional set of rapids. All the while, there was a steady rain of clunks on the airplane's outer skin, the result of the hundreds of spears being thrown at them. Most bounced off rather harmlessly, but Hunter knew that a spear in the wrong place could do a job on the Kingfisher's engine.

"I'd turn the gun on them," Brother David cried out, "but I can't bear to shoot them."

"I agree, Brother," Hunter yelled back to him. "After all, we were trespassing on their turf . . . Take pictures instead."

"Pictures?" the commodore asked. "Now?"

Hunter already had the small video camera up and turned on. He handed it the commodore. "Just press this button and point it out the window," he said. "We might be able to use the footage later on to figure out who these guys are!"

Timidly at first, the commodore held the camera up to the Kingfisher's canopy and started it whirring. There was no letup in the barrage of spears thumping on both sides of the airplane — if anything, it became more intense.

When one spear came within inches of crashing through the canopy, the commodore's career as a cinematographer came to an abrupt end.

"Cut!" he yelled out, ducking down and shutting off the camera. *"Cut . . ."*

It didn't matter as the escape scene was drawing to a close anyway. Up ahead Hunter could see a large beam of light streaming through the jungle's green roof. It wasn't much of a hole, but it would have to do.

"Hang on, compadres!" he called out.

Having learned their lesson the last time, both Brother David and the commodore grabbed hold of something solid and became glued to it. Hunter gunned the Kingfisher's engine, pushing the throttle to the maximum. With an ear-splitting whine, he yanked back on the control stick. There was a rush of spray and smoke, then the seaplane roared up out of the canal and through the opening in the trees.

They were back down just twenty minutes later, Hunter finding a rare shallow lake about 45 miles from Chichen Itza. The plane was pulled to the shore and the commodore started a small fire and heated up some old coffee.

"Where did all those people come from?" Brother David asked. "They couldn't possibly live in the jungle around those ruins."

Hunter sipped the thick day-old coffee and shook his head. "No way," he said. "They must have moved into the area after the Nazis moved out."

"Maybe they were ghosts," the commodore said in all seriousness. "The people from long ago, risen up to claim their land back."

At that point, Hunter would have believed anything, including the rising of ancient Mayan spirits from the dead.

He walked over to the airplane and pulled out a long electrical extension cord. Then he retrieved the mini-video camera, plugged it into the cord and switched on the Kingfisher's auxiliary generator. A soft mechanical noise drifted out from under the engine cowling as electricity flowed into the video camera. Hunter then rewound the small video cassette, and with the other two leaning on his shoulders, they watched the playback of their escape on the tiny TV screen that also served as the camera's viewfinder.

"Look at them all!" Brother David exclaimed.

Sure enough, the replay clearly showed that there were many more of the mysterious natives farther back in the woods as well as on the banks of the narrow canal. But it was their style of dress that fascinated Hunter.

"Look at their get-ups," he said, freezing a random frame and pointing out the brightly colored feathers and body garments. "I tell you I have the feeling that they were there for some kind of ceremony. I mean, those outfits are pretty wild even for this nutty place . . ."

"Look!" the commodore said just after Hunter unfroze the video. "That one—is he dressed in a uniform?"

Neither Hunter or Brother David saw it on the first run. But turning the video back a way, they replayed it again. Sure enough there *was* a man who appeared to be wearing a uniform standing on the bank of the Canal with the natives.

Hunter froze the image and they studied the blurry frame. They couldn't key in on his face—the speed of the airplane and the resulting jiggling of the camera prevented that. But the uniform was more clearly defined. It was khaki in color and featured many pockets on the breast and sleeves. The pants were the same color. A holster hung from the waist and the man was wearing military-issue combat boots.

Hunter had seen this type of dress before. "It's a Twisted Cross uniform," he said. "Same as the jokers down in the Canal wear."

"Do you really think?" Brother David began.

"That this guy is a Canal Nazi, whipping up some locals?" Hunter filled in. "No . . . I don't think so. It's almost like that would be too convenient for us. Too easy an explanation . . ."

Hunter studied the ghostly image of the man in the uniform. He thought he could see some officer's rank emblems on the shoulders, but he couldn't be absolutely certain.

"Then what could the explanation be?" the commodore asked.

"I don't know," Hunter confessed.

Chapter 51

It was a half hour before sun-up when Elizabeth left Krupp's command truck.

Remarkably, no one had come looking for Udet — yet. Those in the encampment just assumed the officer was deep underground in the gold chamber, and those in the gold chamber just assumed the officer was topside. The majority of soldiers in the recovery mission were more concerned about other things anyway. Half of the reinforced work party was involved in laying down a crude rail system that would, when completed, stretch from the entrance to the cave all the way down to the gold chamber itself. On these rails would ride small four-wheeled dumper cars, in which the gold would be placed and then moved from the chamber to the surface.

Those not working on this South African-designed system were laboring in the chamber itself. Marking each ingot, checking it for any inscriptions, weighing it and restacking it closer to the chamber entrance for easy moving to the mini-railway. In amongst all this was the TV crew, still trying to get a clear signal out to their dish and thus, back to Panama City. The problem was finding a still-functioning satellite in orbit off which to bounce their signal.

Also on hand were several of the High Commander's personal still photographers, they being responsible for recording the event in purely "artistic" terms, and a slew of actual and make-believe Twisted Cross "scientists," each one claiming to know more than the other about ancient Mayan sites and how the gold happened to get so deep into the ground in the first place.

But in reality, only one person knew the true answer to that important question. And at that moment, she was calmly walking toward the gigantic Hook helicopter, Krupp at her side, struggling to carry the two inscribed ingots.

Just as Krupp had promised, the big Hook chopper was sitting at the far edge of the encampment, its generators turning, its engine just a pushbutton away from starting up. In its hold were five additional ingots — counting the ones Krupp was lugging, there were more than 350 pounds of pure gold in the chopper.

Elizabeth was the first to climb aboard. The pilot looked at her strangely, but the appearance of Krupp quelled his suspicions for the moment.

"Start the engines," Krupp told him. "We must get to Panama City immediately."

The pilot did as told, somewhat anxiously calling back over his shoulder: "Are we about to be attacked, Colonel?"

"No . . ." Krupp answered, adding hastily: "But this *is* an emergency."

The pilot continued preparing the big chopper for lift off, but still expressed concern. "My orders are to take off only if we are being attacked," he yelled over the growing noise of the copter's slowly-turning rotor blades. "Has another aircraft been designated as 'the blitz?'"

"Well, of course," Krugg snapped at him. "Look out there, what do you see?"

The Hook pilot looked back toward the encampment and the grand pyramid. He saw dozens of people scampering around the cave entrance, technicians fiddling with the satellite dish, and scattered just about everywhere, at least two dozen Twisted Cross helicopters.

"Now get going!" Krupp screamed in the man's ear.

Convinced, the pilot pushed a few more buttons, threw a couple of switches and prepared to take-off. But just then, he saw a small figure running toward the aircraft.

It was Strauberg . . .

"Is Herr Strauberg also making the flight?" the pilot called back to Krupp, indicating the man running toward them.

Krupp froze; he had no idea what to do. Suddenly, the woman grabbed his shoulder and yelled close to his ear: "Let him come on board. He may be helpful to us."

"Yes, Strauberg is making the trip," Krupp instantly called to the pilot. "You can see he wants to lift off immediately."

It made sense to the pilot, so he actually pulled back on his control stick and lifted the big copter a few inches off the ground.

By now, Strauberg, his face red from a combination of anger, confusion, and just plain full-out running, reached the Hook's open door. He was screaming at the top of his lungs, but of course, no one could hear him over the enormous racket of the copter's now-whirring rotor blades.

In one swift motion, Krupp reached out and pulled the surprised Strauberg on board, yelling to the pilot to take off at the same time. The smelly little man found himself half-way inside the copter, the vibrations of the old helicopter's take-off running through him like a dozen jackhammers.

"Krupp!" he was yelling, holding on for dear life as his legs were still dangling out of the aircraft's open door. "Krupp, pull me in, damn you!"

Krupp grabbed the man by the back of his belt and pulled him in another foot. By the time Strauberg had rolled over and was up on his knees, the helicopter was 200 feet above the encampment and gaining speed toward the south.

Strauberg looked as if he were about to blow a blood vessel. "What the *fuck* are you doing, Krupp?" he demanded in a voice so loud, it could be heard above the racket of the Hook's engines.

His answer was a pistol nuzzle in his face. Krupp was smiling at the other end of the gun, and for the first time, Strauberg realized that Elizabeth was on board.

"Krupp! You *fool* . . . Turn this helicopter around!" Strauberg screamed. "This is desertion! You'll be shot!"

Suddenly a boot came out of nowhere and hit Strauberg hard along side of his head.

"Shut up!" Elizabeth screamed at him, kicking his face a second time. "*We* are in command here!"

The pilot was watching all of this over his shoulder, wondering what, if anything, he should do. Strauberg was a powerful member of The Party, but he held no rank in the army of The Twisted Cross. On the other hand, though Krupp was technically the pilot's superior officer, the man's actions were very strange at the least.

Caught in between, the pilot considered whether he should just stay smart and to keep his mouth shut, or speak up and ask what the hell was going on.

He decided to ask questions. But before he could get the first syllable out, Krupp had the pistol up against the side of his head.

"Just shut up and fly!" the colonel yelled in his ear.

Chapter 52

They were called the *Tulum Dzibilchaltun*.

Scattered throughout the upper Yucatan, they were tribes of rugged individualists — no more than twenty or thirty lived in the same settlement at one time. For years — centuries even — the *Tulum* Indians had kept to themselves. They avoided the so-called "civilized" areas of the peninsula and also the areas belonging to other *Tulum* tribes. It was not rare for first cousins to live just over the next hill from each other but never in their lifetimes meet.

When government-sponsored social workers came into the territory, most of the *Tulum* would simply melt away into the bush and wait for the strangers to leave. Those who did stay in the village would rarely talk to the outsiders, sometimes not even acknowledging their presence. It was in the make-up of the *Tulum Dzibilchaltun* to be left alone, a trait ingrained in them 1400 years or more before.

The *Tulum* were great believers in the underworld. Ghosts and devils were regular inhabitants of their everyday lives. They were also highly superstitious — a typical male of 30 years old would perform as many as 80 to 100 minor rituals a day, just to keep on the right side of the gods. They rarely carried weapons for anything more than ceremonial purposes — they were not meat-eaters, so they needed no clubs or spears or arrows.

Even in days past when battles *would* break out, their first line of weapons were nothing more than their eyes. The *Tulum* believed, with no small fervor, that by simply staring and thinking ill of an enemy, that enemy would be so afflicted. It was an ancient form of mind over matter, one that for whatever reason, had worked for the *Tulum* for more than a millenium.

But events had changed the Yucatan peninsula over the past season — invaders, more brutal, more destructive than the usual archaeologists, had appeared. They had raped the land like no other conqueror since the Spanish. To these invaders, the *Tulum* did not exist any more than a barely seen set of pupils staring out of the woods and into the encampments in the dead of night, if at all.

It was these circumstances that led one *Tulum* village leader to take an unprecedented step. He walked over that nearest hill and asked to talk to that first cousin he had never met. Their discussion was about the new invaders, the ones who were desecrating the ancient sites at Coba and Chichen Itza. And these two men agreed something had to be done. So, together, they walked over the next hill, and spoke to that village's leader, and he went and talked to others, and they to others. And soon, all of the *Tulum* that were spread across the Yucatan knew that for the first time in 1400 years, they would gather and talk over what to do about the new invaders.

The gathering called for the highly-superstitious *Tulum* warriors to wear their ceremonial dress and carry their one-and-only ceremonial spear. And it was to be held at the *Tulum*'s second most sacred site, Chichen Itza . . .

But the meeting started later than scheduled as the *Tulum* warriors found their sacred site had been invaded again — this time by three men and a strange water machine. Bravely, the *Tulum* caused them to flee. And now, as a mid-morning thunderstorm rolled in from the west, the ceremonial warriors — all 650 of them — sat at the base of the Grand Chichen Itza Pyramid and started a prayer service to purify the ruins.

Not a minute into the service there was a crack of thunder, followed closely by a streak of lightning. This bombast of Nature barely ruffled the *Tulum;* they were citizens of the jungle, masters at working with the ecology of the place. A little thunder and lightning didn't bother them. •

But the man who had suddenly appeared at the top of the

excavated pyramid did . . .

Several warriors had seen him at once. "Look!" they screamed in unison in their guttural *Tulum* language. "On top of the great temple!"

Within seconds the whole congregation saw the figure, his arms raised above his head, another crack of thunder adding the right touch of special effects.

"It is the ghost of *Balankanche!*" one man yelled, referring to the Mayan king high priest that legend said was buried deep below the Grand Pyramid.

A wave of confusion and panic rippled through the gathering of *Tulum*. Human threats they could deal with—ones from the underworld were beyond their control. The prayer leaders urged calm. Some of the natives fell prostrate, others jumped up as if to flee. Most were just frozen in their kneeling positions, wondering what to do.

There was another boom of thunder and three quick bolts of lightning split the sky. The winds were swirling around the ancient site at near hurricane speeds—yet not an eye was taken off the mysterious figure standing atop the Grand Pyramid.

Then, suddenly, the figure moved . . .

"He is coming to reclaim his soul from us!" one of the *Tulum* cried out.

"He will blame *us* for the desecration down here!" another screamed.

As those gathered watched in horror, the figure started to slowly descend the steps of the pyramid. The storm seemed to grow in intensity with his every movement.

"Get down!" one of the prayer leaders finally yelled to the ceremonial warriors. "We must not upset him!"

"Pray!" one cried out. "We must pray that he leaves our souls untouched!"

"We must listen!" a third leader declared. "He is here with a message from the gods themselves!"

All the while the figure had dramatically descended the worn steps of the pyramid. Now he stopped and raised his outstretched arms up over his head. A strange silence suddenly enveloped the site. Lightning was still flashing but there was no thunder, no wind or rain . . .

The figure turned to the left and the right, then he lowered his arms as if to take in the entire congregation of *Tulum*.

Then he opened his mouth to speak.

"Paisano!" he cried out in an odd heavily-accented voice. "Paisano . . . Fung-goola . . . Goombah . . . *Goombah!"*

"He speaks in a strange tongue!" one of *Tulum* priests declared.

"He is not one of us!" another cried.

"He is one of *them!*" a third yelled.

"Kill him!" a dozen warriors screamed in unison.

For the *Tulum,* this meant nothing more than grabbing the man and staring at him until he died. But before the congregation could move, there was a loud *crack!* behind them. They turned to see that two other men had managed to walk up behind them while their attention had been drawn to the smaller man who had descended the steps. Now one of the two strangers was firing a weapon into the air that emitted frightening yellow-red bullets.

"Stop!" the man with the gun yelled.

"We are friends!" the other man boomed, he being dressed in a monk's robes with two bandoleers of ammunition crossed over his chest.

The gathering of 650 *Tulum* were frozen in their places, confused as to just what the hell was going on.

"We are here to help," the man with the gun yelled. "We are here to catch the people who desecrated this place!"

"So are we!" came the reply from the middle of the crowd. In English, no less.

"Then let's talk," the man with the gun called out.

A murmur went through the crowd as this proposal was hastily discussed. Finally one of the priests called out in English: "All right. Let us talk . . ."

The first few minutes of discussion with the *Tulum* went badly for Hunter, Brother David, and the ghost of *Balankanche,* otherwise known as the commodore.

The *Tulum* were convinced that Hunter and his colleagues

267

were part of a grand scheme cooked up by the "jackals" — that being the name the *Tulum* had bestowed on the Canal Nazis. They were also hurt that the three would play such a dirty trick on them.

It was Brother David, using his remarkable skills as an orator, who finally began to turn the crowd on to their side. He did this by telling them first that he, like their priests, was a religious leader too, and second, that the blasphemous jackals who had trashed the sacred site had to be caught and punished.

Hunter's already substantial admiration for the Fighting Brother increased as he listened to the man's sermon. Like many great speakers, it wasn't *what* he was saying as much as *how* he was saying it.

The soldier monk walked through the crowd, his arms raised, his hands emphasizing certain points, downplaying others. He smiled, he growled, he raised and lowered his voice in a series of crescendos. All the time emphasizing that they, like the *Tulum*, were upset and angry about the destruction at the Yucatan Mayan sites.

When his 15-minute speech ended, the *Tulum* gave him an ovation of hoots, their version of whistles and applause.

"Brother David missed his true calling," Hunter whispered to the commodore. "In the old days, he'd have been elected President."

"Or pope . . ." the commodore added.

The three prayer leaders urged Hunter, David and the commodore to sit with them at the front of the gathering. Together they discussed the whereabouts of the jackals.

One man claimed that the Canal Nazis had moved on to a place 80 miles from Chichen Itza. "The hidden place" was how he described it. He was a representative of a very isolated *Tulum* village near a valley that was the most sacred of all the *Tulum*'s holy places.

The man told a strange tale — one so odd that Hunter at first thought it was a complete fabrication. The man claimed that starting one night and lasting all the next day, the "silver birds" had come and started eating up the jungle leading into the hidden valley. They used "tongues of flames" to do this.

268

The smoke from the fires alone choked five people to death in his village and the small streams the man's village depended on for water were poisoned. Many animals were also killed and injured as a result of this. Several badly wounded animals wandered into the village and attacked the people, killing two more.

What convinced Hunter in the end that the storyteller was recounting some variation of the truth was the tears that welled up in the man's eyes as he talked about the destruction the silver birds had caused. The Wingman knew emotions like that couldn't well be faked. The man also claimed that after the fire and explosions had died down, an army of jackals appeared and they rode through the flattened, burned-out forest in order to reach the lost city in the hidden valley. And they were still there.

"And what is this place called?" Hunter asked the man.

"Uxmaluna," was the reply.

The discussion went on for about another hour. The storm had passed by this time, and the *Tulum* shared their meager supply of corn and honey with Hunter and his friends. Brother David ended the meal by telling the warriors through the translator that a day was coming soon when they could get their revenge on the jackals. He urged them to stay organized and stay ready, that one of his "white friends" would be back and tell them more news.

It was at this point that Hunter happened to spot the *Tulum* warrior who was wearing the uniform in the video. He walked over to him, and the rest of the crowd gathered around them.

"How did you get this, friend?" he asked the man. The question went through one of the gathering's two translators. The man replied that he was the first ceremonial warrior to reach Chichen Itza for the prayer meeting. The uniform was hanging from a tree near where the strange banquet table had been set up. The warrior knew it belonged to one of the jackals, so he had taken to wearing it in an effort to steal the man's soul.

Hunter asked to look at the jacket and the man took it off and handed it to him. Hunter had no idea how or why the uniform was left behind at the Chichen Itza site, but by examining it thoroughly, he was convinced that it was a standard Twisted Cross issue uniform. The stripes on the jacket's lapels also confirmed that it had belonged to a high officer in the Cross, most likely a general.

"See, the man's name is sewn on it," the commodore pointed out, indicating the ID tag stitched over the left breast pocket.

Hunter ran his finger over the embroidered letters. The name stitched onto the uniform was: *Heinke*.

Chapter 53

"This is absolutely fabulous!" the High Commander said, clicking his heels with glee.

He struggled with the VCR's remote control device again, finally finding the spot on the videotape that he had been watching over and over for the past two hours.

"Tremendous . . ." he whispered again. "Just incredible . . ."

The TV techs at the Uxmaluna site had finally found a satellite in orbit that still had some life to it. With no small effort, they were able to broadcast an 11-minute show back to Panama City. Forewarned the transmission was coming, the High Commander's staff rustled up a pair of VCRs and had them on "Record" when the feed came over.

Now the High Commander was watching the tape for the fifth time, a number which would have been greater had he been able to master the rather simple Rewind-Play remote control device.

"Super, just super," he exclaimed as he watched the video sweeps back and forth of the large gold chamber. "The stacks!" he cried out. "Look at those stacks!"

The very inner circle of the High Commander's staff collectively rolled their eyes as their boss grappled to get the tape to rewind again for the sixth time.

"Those guys up there in the jungle are just doing a super job!" he said with a hint of wilting enthusiasm. "Promote them all!"

"All?" one of his aides asked. "There are more than two hundred and eighty men in the recovery mission."

The High Commander stopped struggling with the remote control device just long enough to straighten out his handknit mauve tie and adjust his tortoise-shell glasses. "Not the soldiers on the recovery mission," he said, wondering if it was only he who was confused. "The TV guys . . . They did one hell of job here and I think they should be rewarded. Don't you?"

There was an immediate chorus of "Yes, sir," with one "Definitely, sir" thrown in by some brash up-and-comer.

"Darn straight," the High Commander said, returning his attention to the rewind button once again. "When they get back here, make arrangements for them to join me out on the yacht. Chill some shrimp for that trip, too—"

He was interrupted by another aide coming into the room.

"Great news, my commander," the officer, a major said. "We've received word from Colonel Frankel . . ."

After several tries, the High Commander managed to freeze the frame of the gold chamber videotape. "Frankel? How did he get through to us?" was the man's first question.

It was the only problem The Twisted Cross High Command had not been able to figure out in the short amount of time they had been given to plan Frankel's trip to Washington. It was obvious that Frankel couldn't just pick up a phone and call in a report. Nor could non-secure radio links or couriers be used. Before the man left, he promised that he would work on somehow getting a message back to Panama—possibly through a spy in Washington—on the progress of the negotiations.

"He was able to send a telex message to the old American Embassy here in Panama," the aide reported. "The machine was still operating, and, best of all, so was its scrambler. So he was able to get a secure message in."

For the second time in less than two hours, the High Commander looked as if he was about to overdose on glee.

"Well, read it out!" he yelled to the aide, a wide smile spreading across his thin lips.

The aide cleared his throat and began: "My dear Commander. Happy to report that negotiations are going well. I have had a series of meetings with United American staff. I believe they are beginning to come around to our point of view. Several more meetings have been scheduled. I'm confident that a formal sovereignty agreement can be reached soon. Weather is fine. Your humble servant, Frankel."

"Can you believe this?" the High Commander asked those assembled, a look of awe on his face. "Can you believe that we are *this* lucky? First we find the largest cache of gold in the history of mankind and now it appears as if the United Americans are about to back off.

"This means our plans have just been accelerated by at least two, maybe three years. If the United Americans agree to our sovereignty here, then we'll have nothing to fear from them or from anyone else."

The gathering of aides broke into a syncopatic round of applause.

"This calls for a toast!" the High Commander, once again switching the gold chamber videotape to Play. "Let's try that new Chablis I just got in . . ."

Chapter 54

The giant Soviet-built Hook helicopter was running low on fuel.

"We have twenty-five minutes," the pilot yelled back to Krupp. "Then, like it or not, we're going down."

He was leaning over the pilot's shoulder, watching as the miles of jungle rolled away beneath them. They had been airborne almost three hours now and so far, the flight had been uneventful. Strauberg was bound and gagged back in the chopper's rear compartment; Elizabeth was back there too, studying the gold ingots.

Krupp had also been monitoring the chopper's radio, listening for any report of them stealing the big Hook. But he heard nothing more than the routine chatter. As far as he could tell, the people back at Uxmaluna didn't even know they were missing — yet.

Krupp wrestled with a map, trying to fix their approximate location.

"I'd say we are five miles north of Coban," he said finally. "That means we are still about one hundred miles from Guatemala City."

Krupp knew they could get fuel in Guatemala City — you could get *anything* in Guatemala City. It was a regular refueling stop for all the Twisted Cross choppers transitting from Panama to the Yucatan and back. But at the chopper's current rate of speed, which was approximately 180 mph, and its remaining fuel, the calculations said they would wind up some 10 to 15 miles short of their goal.

"How can we make sure we get to Guatemala City?"

Krupp asked the pilot, nudging the man's ear with his Luger. "Will flying slower help?"

The pilot shook his head, feeling the cold sting of the pistol's muzzle against his neck as he did so. "No," he answered. "Flying slower actually uses more gas."

He pushed the pistol further into the man's ear. "Tell me how we can make it," Krupp said nervously. "There's got to be some way."

The pilot turned and gave him a gruesome smile. "There's only one way to do it," he said. "Lighten the load."

Krupp stumbled over a few words, but then realized exactly what the pilot was talking about. There were more than 350 pounds of gold in the Hook's cabin. Getting rid of some or even all of it would mean they'd made it to Guatemala City.

Krupp returned to the rear of the chopper cabin to tell Elizabeth the bad news. But when he arrived there, he was stung by what he saw.

Not only was Strauberg untied, his pants were down around his knees. He was stretched out on a fold-down bench seat arrangement, his eyes closed, his face red. And for the first time that he could remember, Krupp actually saw a smile on the creepy little man's face.

Elizabeth was on her knees beside the bench, her back to Krupp. She was fooling with her hair — apparently she had tied it up in back and now was letting it down again. She stood up and turned around and when she did so, Krupp could see that Strauberg's private parts were exposed.

"What . . . what is going on here?" Krupp managed to yell above the thunderous din of the chopper's engines.

Elizabeth looked up at him, a strange smile spreading across her lips. Her shirt was unbuttoned all the way again and the top buckle of her pants was undone. It was obvious that she had just performed a sex act on Strauberg.

"What are you doing?" Krupp blurted out.

"Does it bother you?" she asked, stretching to reveal her beautiful bare breasts to him.

"Well, of course it does!" he exploded, noticing that her lips and mouth were extra moist.

She just laughed in his face, sat down and continued fiddling with her hair. He felt as if his chest was about to cave in.

"We have a problem," he told her after a few moments. "We might not make the refueling station in Guatemala City."

She looked up, mild surprise on her face. He explained to her what the pilot had said. They were flying too heavy.

"He says the only way to make it is to lighten the aircraft," Krupp told her, eyeing the seven gold ingots, neatly stacked beside her.

"You *are* crazy," she told Krupp. "Don't even think about throwing them out."

"But why not?" he asked. "If your interpretations are correct, there'll be plenty of gold where we are going."

She shook her head and told him: "You just never get the message, do you?"

Then she got up and walked ahead to talk to the pilot.

In the meantime, Strauberg had sat up and was adjusting his pants. He had been listening in on their conversation. His eyes caught Krupp's and the two men stared at each other with equal amounts of embarrassment and hate.

Krupp started sweating. "When was the last time you took a bath?" he asked Strauberg the question that was on the lips of everyone who met him.

Strauberg took the comment like a knife in the heart.

"You know nothing about commitment!" he screamed at Krupp. "Or dedication. Or loyalty. I have served my High Commander faithfully — twenty-four hours a day. I cannot let my own personal interests interfere with that!"

Krupp began looking for the rope with which to retie Strauberg.

"This is a fool's errand you are on, Krupp," Strauberg said acidly. "Do you actually think you won't get caught? Do you actually think you can get away from The Party. Or the Skinheads?"

The last comment ran a bolt of panic through Krupp; the Skinheads were well known for their tracking abilities as well as their notorious interrogation techniques.

"You're out of your league, Krupp," Strauberg continued,

with a snide laugh. "What kind of fool would actually consider getting rid of all that gold?"

Krupp sat down and tried to ignore the man.

"What did she promise *you*, Krupp?" Strauberg asked him. "A house in the mountains?"

"Shut up, you fucking weasel," Krupp yelled at him with all the gumption he could muster. "She's none of your concern."

Strauberg put his hands between his legs and made an exaggerated motion as if he were adjusting himself.

"She is now . . ." he said.

Krupp had the pistol up and pointing at Strauberg's temple before he even knew it.

"I'll blow your fucking head off," he hissed at the little man. "You'll get yours just like Udet got his."

This statement gave Strauberg pause. "You want me to actually believe you killed your superior commander, Krupp?" he asked sarcastically.

Krupp didn't reply.

"You don't have the guts," Strauberg taunted him. "Not for that. Not for handling that gold. And *certainly* not for handling that woman."

Krupp drew back the hammer on the pistol.

"And you don't have the guts to shoot me either," Strauberg said with another snide laugh.

Krupp took aim. His finger felt the cold steel of the trigger. One squeeze away from eliminating yet another problem.

"*Stop!*"

They both turned and saw Elizabeth standing at the door to the rear compartment, next to the open cargo hatchway. The wind flooding into the chopper was blowing her hair around, making her look like a wild woman. It was also flapping her still-unbuttoned shirt.

"I've just talked to the fueling station in Guatemala City," she said to both of them. "We're ditching this helicopter and chartering an airplane."

Krupp was extremely upset that she wasn't talking directly to him. It was as if Strauberg was now in on their plan.

"But what about our fuel in *this* aircraft?" he asked, trying to appear that he had some control over the situation. "How are we even going to reach Guatemala City?"

She walked over and took the pistol from him. "You know the answer, Colonel," she said. "The pilot said we must lighten the load."

Krupp was suddenly paralyzed with fear. "How . . . how do you intend to do that?" he asked, literally shaking in his boots. "We must throw out the gold?"

She walked back to the door entrance and motioned Strauberg to stand beside her. Then she turned the gun on Krupp.

"I still can't believe how stupid you are, Colonel," she said, putting her arm around Strauberg's waist. "All that time while you had me locked away in those caves, I thought at least you had some brains. I thought you were as calculating as all real Nazis are.

"But you disappoint me. You're actually very spineless. You have no appreciation for the finer things. You have no idea about the beauty of gold, and what it can do for you. And you are carrying so much sick and emotional baggage, I don't know how you can sleep at night."

She had the gun up and pointing at him. "And," she said with a pitying shake of head. "We *do* have to lighten the load."

She looked at Strauberg and smiled. Her free hand reached down between his legs, causing him to catch his breath.

"A little while ago, was it good for you, baby?" she cooed, her tongue flashing out and dramatically licking her lips.

"Oh, yes," Strauberg replied, the excitement welling up inside him.

"Do you want it again?" she asked, continuing to fondle him.

"Oh, yes," he exhaled. "Very much . . ."

She smiled and backed him up right against the cabin wall, all the while keeping one hand between his legs, the other holding the gun on Krupp.

"Do you think you can take it again? So soon?"

"Yes," Strauberg replied, now almost breathless. *"Yes!"*

She turned and smiled at Krupp. "Now pay attention, Colonel," she said. "Watch how I take care of a *real* man . . ."

With that, she grabbed Strauberg's belt buckle and in one swift movement, flung him out the open hatchway.

Krupp was stunned as Strauberg seemed to hang in mid-air for an instant, a look of pure, unadulterated horror on his face.

Then the outside pressure sucked him out and down. Even over the racket of the helicopter's blades, they could hear his terrified screams.

It seemed like a very long time before they finally died away . . .

Chapter 55

It was noontime, but Hunter couldn't go to sleep.

All three of them on the Kingfisher had been up for 36 hours and now that there was some relative peace — floating in the middle of the Casa Casa canal, more than a hundred *Tulum* ceremonial warriors watching over them — he thought it would have been a good idea for them to get some shut-eye before moving on.

He was wrong — at least in his case. Brother David was curled up at the far end of the fueselage compartment, lying in a position of peaceful repose. The commodore on the other hand was swinging in the mid-section hammock, snoring loud enough to actually wake up some long-dead Mayans.

But for Hunter, stretched out in the crawl space just under the Kingfisher's pilot seat, sleep would not come.

Where is she? a voice inside him kept asking.

The irony of the question was not lost on him. In the past four years, he had heard it literally thousands of times. But then, he was wondering about Dominique.

Now he was wondering about this woman, Elizabeth.

He pulled out her photo and studied it for at least the 200th time in the past few days. Did his heart really skip a beat every time he looked at it? Or was it just his imagination? Was he being seduced by a simple photo? By her beautiful features? Of course not, he answered the inner voice. After all, he was a rational person. Calculating was a better word for it. It was demanded by his profession as a fighter pilot. Calculating, rational people didn't fall for women they've never met . . .

Did they?

Where is she?

Did his current situation — or better put, *non*-situation — with Dominique have anything to do with this? Had he really lost her for good? To a cult, of all things? Would she get his letter he left behind in Montreal? Would it make a difference?

Where is Elizabeth? Right now? At this moment?

He tapped his breast pocket and felt the flag he also kept there. But he just couldn't bring himself to pull it out, unwrap it and look at Dominique's photo. What the hell was going on with him? Pining over photos of women? Had it really come to that?

Was she safe? Was she even alive?

He shook away that disturbing thought — he *knew* she was still alive. Every sense in him told him so, and he had learned long ago that he, more than anyone, should trust his instinct. He tried to put his mind on the business of going to sleep. He still had work to do. He had to catch up with those Canal Nazis and soon. He had no idea just exactly what was going on up in Washington or down in Panama. Quite rightly, he felt like a man caught in the middle. And he knew that his overactive imagination had a tendency to take off on him — sometimes with all the finesse and control of a runaway loco-motive.

Will you kiss her when you finally find her?

Yes, *work* — that was the key! Finding the woman Elizabeth was acutally an intricate part of his job — her scatter-brained father was undoubtedly twisting some what-zit and powering up some doo-dad back in DC, getting that damn deactivator in shape. Then the real work would begin. And when the job was finished, he would go and find Dominique even if it meant he had to climb the Goddamn Canadian Rockies to do so. And he would hold her. And love her. And dream of her . . . Not some dame he'd never met.

And if he just kept on telling himself that, he might even start to believe it.

Three hours later, they were airborne.

It had taken a while to get understandable directions from the *Tulum* on how to get to the aptly-named hidden valley of Uxmaluna. Even the *Tulum* who could speak English had a hard time pinpointing exactly where the place was located. Those ceremonial warriors who lived near the valley and who had journeyed to Chichen Itza from there, traveled only jungle routes — snake-like passageways through the dense forests that were invisible from the air and therefore of no use to Hunter as navigation points.

But finally, after much discussion back and forth, Hunter thought he had a fairly good idea where to find the hidden valley of Uxmaluna.

They took off to the cheers of the 650 ceremonial warriors, who threw feathers at them this time. Their departure was duly recorded by the commodore on his new toy, the mini-video camera. Brother David had accepted a large basket of food from the *Tulum* for them to eat on the way. After throwing out anything he'd never seen before, the three of them feasted on apples, dried corn, and some almond-like nuts dipped in honey. The smell and stickiness of this last treat reminded Hunter of the repugnant Jean LaFeet. Where was that slob of a human being now? he wondered. Chowing down in a prison cafeteria somewhere?

Then his thoughts drifted back to old Captain Pegg — he hoped the old sea coot was recovering all right. From there he found himself thinking about Jones and Ben and JT, Fitz and the others. What the hell were *they* all doing right now? Still preparing for war?

Everything was moving to the brink. He could feel it . . .

Brother David saw it first.

"Good Lord and Savior!" he cried out so loud Hunter heard him over the roar of the Kingfisher's engine.

His exclamation caused Hunter and the commodore to immediately scan the terrain below. They saw it at once — it would have been hard to miss.

"Jesus, that is incredible . . ." Hunter said, anger welling up in his voice. "Those frigging destructive bastards."

It was still about twenty miles away — yet it was not in the least bit difficult to see. This part of the Yucatan was like an endless wave of rolling jungle. But in the middle of this pristine state, there was a rash, ugly scar.

"My God, it looks like they took a scythe to it!" Brother David cried out as Hunter put the Kingfisher into a slight lefthand bank.

It was an apt description. Cut into the jungle was a 12-mile long, quarter-mile wide swath. Like a bad blemish on a pretty face, or a masterpiece painting slashed by some kook, the blasted-out jungle passage *looked* evil in itself.

Hunter suddenly felt a particularly nasty anger explode in his heart. What kind of mentality would do something like this with simple greed as their only motive. Scarring a piece of the earth that would not grow back for decades? Was there no conscience left anywhere down here?

And if these people wouldn't hesitate to turn something this beautiful to something this ugly, what would they do to an innocent victim like Elizabeth?

Hunter banked again and saw a thin column of smoke rising from the end of the passageway. Even that was more than he needed to know.

"They're still down there," he said to the others. "Now *I* can smell them . . ."

Chapter 56

"And here's the latest on the negotiations in Washington . . ."

With that opening, the CATS radioman named Masoni began reading the most recent report to come down the secure line between Washington and the Panamanian jungle:

"General David Jones, commander of the United American Army, said earlier today that a 'Mutual Security Pact' is close to being worked out between his forces and those of The Twisted Cross.

"Jones congratulated the negotiating team of The Twisted Cross for their understanding and diligence in attempting to bring about a peaceful solution to the crisis here in Panama.

"He went on to say an official announcement will be made in Washington soon — and that a formal signing ceremony will take place in Panama City the following day . . ."

Masoni hit his cue button and faded up a Bob Marley record. Once he had switched off his own microphone, he reached for a handful of ice water and splashed it on his face.

"That was a tough one," he said to the Cobra pilots Tyler and Baxter. "Toughest one yet . . ."

"You did great," Tyler said. "Hardly a pause or anything. Real smooth . . ."

As his partner Gregg O'Gregg cued up another record, Masoni took a break and lit up a cigarette.

"Is it me?" he asked. "Or are things really getting tense in this whole situation?"

Tyler lit a butt of his own and nodded. "It ain't just you," he said. "Everyone's feeling like that, me included."

"Ditto," Baxter said.

Masoni took a deep drag from his cigarette and guzzled a half of cup of cold coffee. "We've been out here in the bush almost every day for a year and a half," he said. "Hiding from the Nazis. Moving around under that Goddamn flying monster, sweating off three, four pounds a night.

"But believe me, that was all child's play, compared to this . . ."

Tyler used a little bit of the ice on his own forehead. "Look at it this way," he told Masoni. "It won't go on much longer."

Masoni blew a long stream of smoke from his nose and mouth.

"Oh yeah?" he said in his two-pound gravel voice. "Can I quote you on that?"

Back on the CATS island HQ, Major Dantini was interrupted from studying his well-worn map of the Panama Canal by the sound of an approaching helicopter.

He had been around his own choppers so long, he knew the noise wasn't coming from one of his boys. Instead, he recognized the sound as being from one of the Cobras.

He walked out of his tent and down to the beach just as Cobra Two was hovering in over the water for a landing. The pilot, Captain Bobby Crockett, gave him a thumbs-up as the chopper's blades began to stir up a whirlwind of seaspray and sand.

Dantini liked the Cobras—both the helicopters and the guys who flew them. Just as the souped-up Cobra gunships were much more than the average chopper-for-hire machine, the Cobra Brothers were much more than just run-of-the-mill chopper jocks. They were *involved*—committed to the cause of the United Americans. As such, they had no compunction about flying at night or in bad weather or both. And Dantini, being somewhat of an expert himself on the machines, knew that most choppers were fair weather birds.

The Cobras had flown every night since coming to the CATS island, this in addition to ferrying messages to the radio station PDC. Dantini knew it was better not to ask too many questions, but he did know that the gunships were making a regular rendezvous with a ship of some sort about a hundred miles east of Panama. One night Cobra One would go out, the next night Cobra Two would make the trip. Each time they would come back with some kind of booty to share — a few bottles of booze, a carton of cigarettes. But each time, the pilots looked more worried than the time before. And Dantini had been in the military long enough to know what that meant, which was another reason he didn't ask questions.

This time would be different, though . . .

The Cobra's rotors finally stopped spinning, giving a rest to the mini-sandstorm. Crockett climbed out, soon followed by Hobbs, the weapons officer.

"Hey, boys," Dantini said by way of greeting. "What's shaking today?"

"A lot," Crockett told him point blank.

"More radio messages for my guys to read?" Dantini said off-handedly, assuming that was what the Cobras were talking about.

"Yes, we have another message," Crockett said. "But it's small potatoes."

Dantini had already turned to lead them as usual to the mess tent for a cup of coffee. But now he turned back, sensing in their tone that something big really *was* in the offing.

"Okay, guys," Dantini said. "What's up?"

"Pack a bag, Major," Crockett said. "And pick a temporary commander for your boys. General Jones has requested your presence up north immediately."

The High Commander had just finished his morning aerobic workout and was pondering a report on the previous day's revenues and activities.

It read:

1.) Four ships were challenged on the Pacific side of the Canal, two let through for a combined 300 bags of gold. Two sunk after failing to meet requirements.

2.) Twenty bags of gold were panned from the Canal over

the past week.

3.) Another delivery of Argentina's monthly "security payment" arrived via the usual route, i.e. Twisted Cross naval forces boarded the unsuspected courier's ship off Chile, taking the payment, sinking the ship, liquidating the crew.

On the red side of the ledger:

1.) The King of Brasilia is behind on his payments for the second straight month.

2.) No reaction from the Cubans about their increase in payment plan.

3.) Unexpected expenditures for the day exceeded the limit of 20 bags of gold, due to increase in food costs for prisoners/gold panners.

The High Commander scribbled three notes at the bottom of the report: "Plan air strike on Brasilia's fuel depots," "Do same for Cuban electric plants," "Trim food costs for prisoners and panners by most expedient means."

That done, he indulged himself in a laugh. Since the major gold find up in the Yucatan, the tolls and the panning operations suddenly seemed very nickel-and-dime.

He called for his aide-de-camp, who quickly appeared and took the marked-up report away for action. No sooner was he out the door when his top officer in charge of communications bounded into the office.

"A hundred pardons, my Commander," he said with a slight bow. "But Colonel Frankel had just reached us via short-wave radio."

The High Commander looked up at once. "Does that mean we can talk to him?" he asked.

"Yes, sir!" the communications officer beamed. "He's talking through a scrambler, so it may be faint but at least it's a secure line. We have him piped in over your squawk box, sir."

"Well, that's super!" the High Commander beamed back. "Let's talk to the man, then."

The communications officer quickly walked over to the High Commander's desk and flipped his phone speaker box on.

"Can he hear me now?" the High Commander asked.

"He should be able to, sir," the communications officer answered. "Hello, Frankel, are you there?"

A burst of static leapt from the small speaker. But then Frankel's voice came on.

"Yes, sir . . . Hello, sir . . ."

"Frankel, old man, this is the High Commander, how's it going up there?"

"Wonderfully," Frankel answered. "I really think they've come around to see our point of view. And it's really not that much of a surprise. The whole eastern half of the country is absolutely devastated."

"Glad to hear that," the High Commander said. "We've been monitoring the guerilla radio station down here for the past few days. They've been putting out very optimistic reports. They're doing our job for us, pacifying all the locals."

"Well, they are very good at that sort of thing, sir," Frankel said. "They believe in letting everyone — from citizens to their lowest soldiers — know what's going on at any given moment. They are very open about things like that."

"Well, don't you get spoiled, Frankel," the High Commander said with a laugh. "By the way, as this is a secure line, let me ask you something. Does this agreement you've worked out call for withdrawal of their forces from Texas?"

"Yes, it does, sir," was the reply. "The timetable now is for us to announce the terms of the agreement at a joint appearance tomorrow. At that point, they will start dispersing their air wings out of Texas. Their ground troops will also move as soon as they can muster up enough rail and road transportation.

"At that point, we will fly back down there to Panama for the formal signing ceremony. I will discuss the particulars of that with your staff, sir."

The High Commander's face was flushed with excitement.

"You've done an excellent job, Colonel," he told his officer. "And right after we sign that agreement down here, you can expect to attend another ceremony. One that will celebrate your elevation to major general of the Party."

There was a slight hesitation from the other end. Then they heard Frankel's voice say: "Sir, that is much more than I could ever expect. I am just glad that I was able to serve you and our

288

Cause."

Frankel signed off from the High Commander, and his call was rerouted to an office down the hall where he would give the High Commander's staff the lowdown on the signing ceremony preparations.

Meanwhile, the leader of The Twisted Cross could hardly contain himself.

"Do you have any idea what this means?" the High Commander asked the communications officer.

The officer had little choice but to shake his head no.

"It means there'll be *no* war with the United Americans," the High Commander said, slapping his knee with perky glee.

"No *war* . . . That is wonderful news, sir," the officer said.

"Darn it is," the High Commander replied. "This means we'll be able to annex Big Banana within a half year. Knock off those other small-timers in two, three months. Hell, we can be on the Mexican border this time next year!"

He reached into his desk drawer and came up with two cigars. "I don't usually do this, but will you join me?" he asked. Then he handed a cigar to the somewhat bewildered officer, and lit the other one for himself.

"Got these in Bermuda," he told the officer, blowing out a long stream of blue smoke. "Next to Cuba, they have the best cigars around."

Chapter 57

Some things require planning. For hours, days, weeks, even years. Details. Timetables. Contingency plans. Follow-up. Conclusion. Fuck it up and it's back to the drawing board.

Other things are just better done without planning. There *is* no time. No known details. No second chances. Nothing to follow-up on. Fuck it up and you're dead.

Deciding what to do when — plan it or improvise it — is usually a totally personal decision. Make the right choice, you're a genius. If not, well, that's what gravestones are made for . . .

By nature fighter pilots like to plan things out. It comes from being so protective of their fuel supplies. How far can I go and can I get back with this amount of fuel. That's all most of them care about — and rightly so. All the whiz-bang missiles, cannons, radars, HUDs, computers, and 45,000 pound thrust engines don't go anywhere if there ain't no gas in the tank. So the flight revolves around your fuel load; see how much you can carry and plan from there.

Hunter knew the value of good planning — but improvisation has its place too. On the football field, in a piece of jazz or when you come upon 300 Nazi scum who are vandalizing Man's collective past and are littering heavily in the process.

So you can plan an air strike right down to the last bomb. But sometimes, when you're mad and you have to kick some ass, it's better just to make it up as you go along.

Sorry, General Jones, that's just the way it is . . .

"Are you sure about this, Brother Hunter?"

"No, Brother David, I'm not," Hunter answered truthfully. "But my instinct is that we'd better move fast here. I've the feeling that these guys aren't going to be sticking around here much longer."

Brother David performed a lightning quick sign of the cross. "Only by the power of prayer . . ." he recited.

They were hiding in the woods no more than 50 feet from the perimeter of the Uxmaluna site. The Kingfisher, with the commodore on guard, was hiding under the branches of a large cedar tree next to a small, narrow lake, just a mile from their position. As always, the Mayans built their magnificent cities close to a source of water. Fourteen hundred years later, Hunter was using them as his landing strips.

"Look how the helicopters are piling in and out of here," Hunter said. "These guys don't all know each other. They're airmen—they don't mix with the ground help."

As if to emphasize his point, two Soviet-built Hinds roared over their heads, kicked up a storm of dust and landed side-by-side on the near lip of the blasted-out road. No sooner were they down when a larger and older Soviet-built Mil Mi-4 Hound took off and roared away to the south.

"They found something big time in that pyramid," Hunter said after observing the beehive-like activity around the cave entrance on the side of the Grand Uxmaluna Pyramid. "Maybe a big 'deep zone' gold find that Sandlake's daughter led them to."

" 'Gold robs the soul of life . . .' " Brother David said, quoting somebody.

"If that is the case," Hunter said. "If they did find a lot of gold, that means she's here with them. They're too dumb to do it on their own."

"They're certainly prepared," the mercenary monk said. "Isn't that a TV satellite dish over there?"

"That it is," Hunter said, lifting his head the slightest bit to get a good look at the piece of broadcasting hardware. "They must have somehow found a satellite that was still working in space."

"They're advanced, Brother," David said. "They're very high-tech . . ."

"Yeah, but high-tech doesn't always mean 'smart'," Hunter replied, taking a quick shot of the dish with his handy video mini-cam. "I mean, you'd think these guys would have learned by now. They don't even have a defense perimeter set up."

"They are all too busy with whatever is going on inside that cave," the monk said.

"And that's our 'in,' Brother," Hunter said. "They're just too busy . . . Are you ready? Any last minute prayers?"

"Ready, I am," the monk said taking a deep breath. "And I won't make any final peace with the Lord right now because, frankly, I don't want Him to know what I'm up to."

"Me neither," Hunter replied.

With that, they got down on their stomachs, and slowly crawled across the green, slimy ground, using the foot-high green, slimy underbrush as their cover. Hunter had never seen so many bugs in his life — some of them were the size of his fist. But what concerned him was that wherever one found bugs in the jungle it usually meant that a well-fed, always-hungry snake was nearby.

It was if Brother David had read his mind.

"Do not worry about the snakes," the monk whispered to him as they slowly made their way closer to the edge of the camp. "My middle name is Patrick. St. Pattie is my patron saint. You know what he was famous for?"

Hunter had to think. "Besides green beer?"

"He drove the snakes from Ireland," David told him. "There's not a one of the disgusting things in all of Eire. So don't worry here. He'll watch over us."

St. Patrick came through. Twenty minutes later they were hidden in the crown of a tree felled by the Nazis' scorched earth roadbuilding and there wasn't a fang mark on either of them.

"Okay, here comes a chopper," Hunter said. "Get

292

ready . . ."

It was another Mi-4 Hound—the rugged yet antique aircraft that looked like something from a 1950s newsreel.

"Take a good look, Brother David," Hunter said. "That chopper is older than we are."

The Hound was just setting down, its open cargo door facing away from the encampment and toward Hunter and the monk.

"We're lucky," Hunter whispered, seeing that the only people aboard were the two pilots. "It's a ferry ship—no other crew members."

They waited for the pilots to shut down the chopper's engine. "Okay," Hunter said finally. "Let's go . . ."

Within five seconds, Hunter had sprinted the 20 feet of clearing separating them from the copter and was climbing up into the open cargo bay.

The pilots didn't hear him come aboard, the noise of the engine winding down made sure of that.

"These guys are the lucky ones," he told himself. "All they'll get is a bump on the head."

The first thing he was able to grab was a huge lug wrench of the type used to tighten up and torque the chopper's power train. Two cracks later, he had two very unconscious Nazis on his hands. An extra added squirt from his chloroform water pistol insured the enemy chopper pilots would be out for at least five hours.

Brother David had arrived by that time.

"You take the big guy," Hunter said. "And hurry."

As quickly as they could, they stripped the uniforms from the pilots, including belts and helmet. Because these were one-piece Twisted Cross flight suits, the fit on the large-framed Brother David looked better than expected.

Once dressed, Hunter and the monk quickly went through the supplies that were stocked in the Hound's cargo bay. Once again, they were lucky.

"This is great," Hunter said. "These are extra supplies for the satellite dish. Extra wire, some diodes, a generator booster. Just what we need."

They dumped the knocked-out Nazis into the dense underbrush. Then Hunter loaded up Brother David with the awkward-shaped generator booster—a kind of supercharger for diesel-fueled generators. It's odd shaped served to hide that portion of Brother David's face not covered by his purloined helicopter helmet.

Hunter then took three rolls of standard TV cable and put one around each shoulder, and another around his neck. This one he had snapped off the bindings and held the loose end in his hand.

"Okay, Brother," he said, turning toward the monk. "Are thee ready?"

"Thee is," the monk replied. "I think . . ."

"Why not say a prayer to the patron saint in charge of kicking Nazi butt?" Hunter suggested. "And remember. We're TV technicians. We've got to act like they do . . ."

"And how is that?" the monk asked.

Hunter shook his head. It was too involved to explain. "Just watch me," he said.

He took a deep breath, patted his breast pocket and then went into action.

First he tied the end of the cable wire to the frame of the chopper's cargo door. Then, taking long, bold strides, he literally flew around the end of the helicopter and walked briskly right into the center of the encampment, all the while unreeling the length of wire. Brother David had no choice but to follow close behind, holding the booster as high to his face as possible.

"Hey watch it, there . . ." Hunter said to a pair of Nazi soldiers who dared to cross his path. "Watch it, hot stuff here . . ."

The two men, sergeants both, obediently hopped over the wire and quickly made way for Brother David. Hunter was already at the dish and down on one knee fiddling with something by the time the two soldiers had turned and started walking away.

"You're a brazen lad, Hunter," David told him, setting the booster next to the dish.

"Yeah, sure," Hunter replied as he meticulously did nothing to the dish's central control receiver.

They hung there for about a minute, Hunter getting the lay of the place. Above all, he was looking for any evidence of Elizabeth. But at the moment, he saw none.

What he *did* see was a bivouac for about 250 people, maybe 300 if they really crowded in. This was close to his previous guesstimate. There was no less than 25 choppers scattered about the place, and 27 trucks of all types and sizes. But the important thing was that, aside from a handful of fifty caliber machineguns attached to the Hind gunships, there were no major weapons installed in the camp. No artillery, no mortars, no SAMs.

"Okay," Hunter said. "Time for chapter two . . ."

Having attached the end of the loose wire onto something important-looking underneath the dish, Hunter once again started walking away like the guy who owned the place. The two rolls of cable still on his shoulders, he continued to purposefully unfurl the third one. A slight chill went through Brother David when he realized Hunter was heading right for the cave entrance.

The monk looked up at the magnificent excavated Mayan temple and wished he knew more about the Mayan's form of religion. Then he swore for the first time in two years. "If you're the same God," he said, looking to the various ornaments decorating the top of the pyramid. "Please save this crazy fucker. And me along with him . . ."

Once inside the cave entrance, Hunter went about his work charade like a TV repairman working overtime. That was, as slowly as possible.

Hunter helped David drop the booster at the cave entrance, then he handed him a roll of wire. It was just barely illuminated inside the tunnel—someone had strung what looked like a long string of white Christmas tree bulbs along the cave wall. As the tunnel ran nearly straight and down at a slight incline for several hundred feet, it looked like the lights stretched on for an eternity.

Carefully, Hunter and the monk started playing out the

roll of wire. They passed guards, Twisted Cross officers, even other TV men. Yet no one stopped to challenge them. No one even said a word to them.

One hour and fifteen minutes later, they were standing at the entrance to the gold chamber.

Chapter 58

Colonel Krupp's aide-de-camp, Lieutenant Boshe, was getting worried.

He hadn't seen the officer around for quite some time. This in itself was not that unusual — Krupp would frequently lock himself inside his command truck for hours at a time, usually to sulk. But even on those occasions, Boshe was able to rouse the commanding officer with three sharp raps on the command truck door.

But now he had been knocking at the officer's door for five full minutes with no reply.

Perhaps Krupp got drunk again and was deep in an inebriated slumber, Boshe wondered. He had looked very peaked when they pulled him out of the tunnel. Then another thought crossed his mind. He, like the rest of the men in camp, knew that Krupp had brought the woman to his truck several nights before and had engaged in some rather bizarre sexual behavior. On that night, one of the soldiers had found Krupp drunk, barely conscious, half-hanging out of his truck door, his nose smashed in, the woman tied up and various examples of S&M paraphernalia lying about the floor of the vehicle. Although the soldier had been sworn to silence by Krupp in return for a promotion, word about the incident nevertheless quickly spread around the camp to the delight of the troops on the recovery mission, most of whom considered Krupp to be a weak-kneed nincompoop.

But now Boshe noticed that both Krupp *and* the woman were not around. If the strange officer was trying once again to "kink it up" with the woman, he had certainly picked an odd time to do it — the Uxmaluna site was crawling with high level officers of The Twisted Cross and The Party.

Even Major General Udet was around, somewhere . . .

As Boshe was contemplating all this, he was approached by the two Twisted Cross archaeologists who had found the first set of marked gold ingots. Having just returned from the woman's truck and not finding her, or their unusual fifty-pound gold pieces, they decided to check with Krupp.

"Something doesn't feel right here," one of the archaeologists said after Boshe explained to him he hadn't seen Krupp or the woman in a while. "Where are the guards for the woman? There was no one at her truck at all."

For a moment Boshe considered telling the two about Krupp's "thing" for the woman, but decided against it. It would be safer to break into the command truck.

Boshe hit the door with his shoulder twice — and nothing happened. He kicked it three times, and still nothing budged.

"Wait a minute," one of the archaeologists said. "It opens from the inside out . . ."

He went off and soon returned with a crowbar-like digging tool. Two minutes later, they had the door pried open.

Boshe was the first one in. Everything looked in place in the cramped living compartment — the bed was folded up against the wall, the small all-purpose table was covered with various documents, but neat and clean nevertheless. Even Krupp's five pairs of muddy boots were lined up in one neat row.

Instinctively, Boshe tried to open the lavatory door. It was locked. He hadn't considered that the colonel might simply be on the pot all this time. He knocked politely. No answer. Once again. Still no answer.

"Kick the fucking thing in," one of the archaeologists commanded.

Boshe shrugged and kicked the flimsy door twice. It splintered, enough for Boshe to look in.

Staring back at him, eyes open, face utterly devoid of color, was the corpse of Major General Udet.

Chapter 59

"What are you doing here?" the voice bellowed around the gold cavern.

But Hunter and Brother David didn't hear it. They were too busy pinching themselves.

They had strung the cable as far as the gold chamber entrance, waited for an opportunity, then walked into the chamber itself. Now they had spent the last five minutes gawking at the tons of gold, as a squad of Nazi troopers scurried around the chamber taking inventory before the operation to move the gold out began in earnest.

"I said 'what the hell are you guys doing here?' " the voice asked again.

Hunter heard it this time. He spun around and instantly assumed his game face. "Stringing cable for the TV link-up," he said in a voice oozing confidence. Hunter saw right away the man he was addressing was no more than a lowly Twisted Cross lieutenant; he wouldn't be hard to handle.

"In fact, give us a hand, will you?" he brazenly asked the man. "We've got to get a beam up and back to Panama within the hour . . ."

A look of pained acceptance came over the officer. "Christ," he said. "What do you want me to do?"

Hunter handed him the very end of the long roll of cable wire. "Hold this here," he said. "We've got to go up the line and make sure there are no snags."

With that, Hunter whipped out the pocket-sized mini-video camera and took two quick sweeps of the place.

"Got to get the light level," he mumbled expertly while panning the chamber.

Then he and Brother David turned to leave.

"Wait a minute," the Cross officer said. "How long do I have to hold this thing?"

Hunter shrugged and said: "You know, until we tug on it. You'll feel it—three times real hard."

With that, he and the monk departed the chamber.

They were about halfway out of the tunnel when they saw a group of Twisted Cross soldiers running toward them.

"I don't like the looks of this," Hunter said as he and Brother David immediately started fiddling with the cable they had laid in the tunnel.

The soldiers—two officers and three sergeants—reached them.

"What are you guys doing here?" one of the officers, a captain, asked.

It seemed to be the most asked question of the day.

"We're working on the TV uplink," Hunter said. "Running cable down to the chamber."

"Forget that," the officer quickly commanded. "Did you come in a chopper?"

"Yes, sir," Hunter said with the right amount of reverence in his voice.

"Then get your asses up topside!" the officer said. "We've got an emergency and we need all the chopper pilots we can get up there now!"

Hunter and Brother David quickly saluted and started running up the tunnel.

"Wait!" the other officer said.

Hunter stopped in his tracks and spun around. "Yes sir?"

"We're looking for *Herr* Strauberg," he said. "Did you see him down in the chamber?"

Hunter had to think quick. "Not sure," he said. "What's he look like?"

The officer glared at him strangely. Instantly Hunter knew that this Strauberg was known to everyone in the Nazi

300

camp.

One of the sergeants piped up. "You know, the smelly little guy . . ." he said loudly.

Hunter just shrugged. "I don't know," he said. "There are a lot of people down in the chamber right now and they *all* smell pretty bad."

For some reason, the Nazis accepted the rather puzzling explanation and continued back down toward the chamber.

"That was close, *kee-mo-sabe* . . ." Hunter said to Brother David. "Let's get going before they reach that chump holding the wire back in the chamber."

It was odd how it happened, but the first thing Hunter noticed upon reaching the surface was a woman's bra.

It was hanging rather haphazardly on a tree next to the camp's mess tent which happened to be close by the entrance to the cave. On the tree next to it was a pair of women's underpants and a skirt. A soiled blouse was on the ground nearby.

"Jesus, what did they do? *Eat* her?" Hunter said, pointing out the articles of clothing to Brother David.

"Well at least we know she is here," the monk said. "Or *was* here."

They ran to the center of the camp and saw that just about every helicopter but "theirs" was warmed up and ready to take off.

A man ran by them. Hunter reached out and caught him by the shoulder.

"What's going on?" he asked, the soldier, a lieutenant.

"Are you guys pilots?" he asked in return.

Hunter nodded. "We just got in from Panama . . ."

"Okay, you'd better get back to your ship," the man said excitedly. "A couple of guys killed the top dog here. Murdered him. They found him slashed up in that truck over there. Whoever did it, took the 'blitz' helicopter and split."

"Wow," Brother David said involuntarily.

"More than just 'wow,' " the man said, obviously caught up in the excitement of the event. "They got away with a bunch

301

of gold, too."

"Wow," Hunter said this time. Then, without planning it, he took a big chance and popped out another question: "What about the woman?"

The man had already resumed running to the helicopters. "She's missing too!" he called over his shoulder. "The brass think she went with them."

Chapter 60

It was a strange aerial formation that formed up over Ux-maluna and headed south.

Eighteen helicopters—mostly Soviet-built Hind gun-ships—set off after the missing Hook "blitz copter." It was only because one of the TV technicians had seen the big Hook take off and head south, did the Twisted Cross officers even know what direction the missing chopper had taken.

It had been the two archaeologists who put the whole thing together. Seeing Udet's body, they quickly discovered that Krupp, the woman, Strauberg *and* the seven marked gold ingots were all missing. To them, it added up to a classic murder-robbery, with the Hook providing the getaway vehicle for the thieves.

"That pig Strauberg orchestrated this," one of the archaeologists told the other. "He's the only one of the three smart enough to pull it off."

So the dozen and a half choppers—including the Hound being piloted by Hunter—were dispatched in pursuit.

Three Cross officers, with a squad of armed soldiers, sat in the cargo hold of the Hound while Hunter steered the craft and Brother David pretended to play copilot. A constant wave of chatter was coming over the radio, most of it emanating from the lead Hinds, which were carrying the bulk of Nazi superior officers.

Early on in the flight, these officers decided to split their force. Theorizing that the blitz copter could only head for one of three possible refueling stations in the south, the officers ordered six choppers to Punta Gorda in the old country of Belize and six more to La Ceiba in Honduras.

The final six, Hunter's aircraft included, were ordered to head for Guatemala City.

Chapter 61

They were just about out of fuel by the time Hunter and the other pilots landed the six helicopters on the edge of the dilapidated airfield/aircraft refueling station which was about a half mile from Guatemala City itself. As usual, the Canal Nazis had flown in unannounced, not bothering to call ahead for landing clearance or any such trivialities.

But no sooner had he turned off his aircraft's engine when Hunter knew something was wrong.

These refueling stations were notorious for their wild drinking, wild whoring, anything-for-a-price reputations. Yet this place was unusually serene. There was a control tower, a handful of hangars at the far end of the runway and maybe a dozen buildings in between. The runway lights were on, burning a deep yellow, as were all the lights in the control tower and in the buildings nearby. Yet despite all this, Hunter didn't see a soul.

Three minutes later, he and Brother David joined the other Twisted Cross soldiers as they burst into the small control tower that doubled as the refueling station's business headquarters. And although the Nazis kicked in every door they found locked, there were no people to be seen anywhere. The place was dead empty.

"Spread out!" the Cross commander yelled, he too, feeling something was amiss. "Check every building on this base."

Hunter and Brother David saw this as an opportunity to separate from the rest of the group. As soon as the commander had yelled out the order, the monk and the

305

Wingman were running down the small airstrip to the hangars farthest away from the deserted tower.

Impressed by the enthusiasm of at least two of his men, the Nazi officer lambasted his other troopers, screaming at them to hustle "like those guys . . ."

In actuality, all Hunter and David wanted was a safe place where they could figure out just what the hell to do next.

The last building on the strip was a small shack, painted in wide, red-and-white barber pole stripes. Once inside, Hunter and the monk stopped and took a minute to catch their breath.

"I fear we are trapped, Brother Hunter," David told him, taking large gulps of air.

"Maybe," Hunter said, looking around. "Maybe not."

Brother David shook his head. "But could that large Hook helicopter make it this far? Even our aircraft just barely had enough fuel to make it here."

"I know," Hunter said. Then he closed his eyes and concentrated. "Sounds crazy, but I really feel like they were here. The woman anyway . . . Plus, *something* isn't right at this place. I mean, where is everyone? An operation like this needs a couple dozen people to keep it running."

"At least," the monk said. "But that's beside the point. Eventually, these Nazis will realize who we are—or rather, who we *are not*. At that point, they'll forget about who they are chasing. At least until they kill us . . ."

"Faith, Brother," Hunter said, peeking out the shack's doorway. Directly across from them was a lone airplane hangar, separated from the rest. One of its doors was ajar.

Hunter took a sniff of air, then said: "Let's check out that place."

Seconds later, they were both sprinting across the taxiway, toward the hangar. A quick look down the row of buildings told Hunter that the rest of the Nazis were still far away, searching each building with typical thoroughness.

He and Brother David reached the hangar and slipped inside. Right away, they both had the chills.

It was pitch black inside, yet Hunter picked out two distinctive smells. One was the unmistakable odor of airplane engine exhaust.

The other was the smell of blood . . .

He reached up for the light switch. "I'm almost afraid to do this," he told Brother David.

Then he flipped on the light.

The first thing they saw was the pile of bodies. There was at least ten of them—it was hard to put an exact number on it as they were sickeningly sprawled on each other, oozing blood everywhere. Judging by their clothes, the victims were technicians and control tower people. Each one looked as if they had taken two bullets in the back of the head.

"God help us!" Brother David said in a shocked whisper. He immediately fell to one knee and made the sign of the cross.

But already Hunter's attention was drawn to something else inside the hangar: the large helicopter sitting at the far end of the barn.

It was a Soviet-made Hook.

"Bingo!" Hunter said.

They quickly walked over to the aircraft and inspected its insides.

"This has got to be the one," Hunter said, feeling the roof of the aircraft. It was still warm. "And it's been here for only a few hours, if that . . ."

"If they *were* here," Brother David said, turning back to the grisly pile of bodies, "then they must have been responsible for this . . ."

"Yeah," Hunter said, "They blew in and out, and they didn't want to leave any witnesses."

Hunter walked over to the empty space in front of the hangar's second door, reached down and dabbed his finger in a small pool of liquid on the hangar floor.

"JP-six," he said, sniffing the fuel. "Still fresh . . ."

"And that means?" Brother David asked.

"It means they're probably in another aircraft," he said. "Prop job. One that was stored in here. It's a medium size plane and I'd bet they took off less than an hour ago."

"But where did they go?" the monk asked.

Hunter looked at the big Hook, and then back at the

bodies. "Now that's a *really* good question . . ." he said.

And it was the Nazis who answered it.

Hunter and David were leaving the hangar just as the rest of the search party reached the door. Bringing up the rear were two Nazi soldiers half-dragging a man between them.

"We found the Hook, sir." Hunter told the commander. "It's in there with a bunch of bodies. Pretty gruesome."

The commander waved the rest of his men into the hangar with him.

Hunter walked up to the two sergeants holding the prisoner.

"Who's this?"

"Found him hiding in one of the buildings," one of the guards answered. "The commander recognized him as the blitz copter pilot."

Hunter looked the man straight in the eye. "Is that true?" he asked.

The man, who looked beaten and was bleeding in several places, coughed once and said: "Fuck you . . ."

One of the guards slammed his rifle butt into the man's kidney as punishment for the comment.

"Why the rough treatment?" Hunter asked the guard.

The soldier shrugged. "The commander believes this man was in on the murder and the gold theft. He's about to execute him."

"Execute him?" Hunter was mildly flabbergasted. "Here?"

"Here and now," the guard said. "He's organizing a firing squad."

With that the guards hustled the man away.

"That's just like the Nazis," Brother David said. "They're about to shoot the only person who could tell them where those people went."

"Maybe he already has," Hunter replied.

Down the end of the runway, he could see that several other Nazis had commandeered a fuel truck and were in the process of refueling the half dozen choppers.

"Check that out," Hunter said, pointing out the refueling

operation to the monk. "Looks like they're planning on moving soon."

At that moment, the rest of the search party came out of the hangar, more than a few pale shocked faces in their ranks.

"Are you looking for volunteers for the firing squad?" Hunter suddenly asked the commander, causing Brother David to think that he was hearing things.

The commander looked around at some of his weak-stomached troopers. "You guys got experience?" he asked Hunter.

"A little," Hunter lied, wondering just how much training one would need to shoot an unarmed, bound and gagged man.

"Good," the commander said. "Follow me."

The commander of the search party marched the hapless prisoner past the control tower and up to a stone wall out of sight of the rest of the search party.

As Hunter predicted, the man was bound and gagged, but not blindfolded.

"Ready . . ." the commander called out to the 12 men in the firing squad.

"Aim . . ."

Hunter eyed Brother David, standing beside him in the firing line with a fully-loaded AK-47 in his hands. They hadn't had any time to verbalize their plan. Hunter was just hoping the soldier monk would know what to do.

"Fire!"

A furious barrage of gunfire followed. When the smoke cleared, the commander and the ten Nazis in the firing squad all lay dead.

The prisoner couldn't believe it.

"Who are you guys?" the man asked in astonishment as Hunter undid his leg bindings.

"Never mind," the Wingman told him harshly. "You just bought yourself a few extra minutes, that's all."

Both Hunter and Brother David roughly sat the man down next to the wall. Hunter put his still-smoking AK-47 muzzle up to the man's nose.

"Okay," he said. "Talk or we finish you right now . . ."

The man gulped hard. He was still shaking badly. "Jesus Christ, what do you want to know?"

"*Did* you fly that Hook here?" Hunter asked him.

"Yes," the prisoner answered immediately. "But I wasn't in on it. They made me fly them."

"Who is 'they?' " Brother David asked.

"This nutty colonel," the man answered. "Krapp or Krupp or something like that. I don't know, my base is in Panama. I was just assigned to blitz duty that day, right after they made the big gold find."

"Who else was with him?" Hunter asked. "The woman?"

The man shook his head. "Yeah, she was with him all right."

Hunter couldn't quite place the reason for the man's sudden insolent tone.

"And this guy, Strauberg?" the monk asked. "Him too?"

The man shook his head. "No, he's dead," he replied. "He went out the door at about four thousand feet."

"Where are they now?" Hunter demanded, pressing the gun muzzle in even closer to the man.

"They took a big plane out of here," he said. "They snatched two Afrikaner pilots at gunpoint and shot everyone else . . . I got away after they made me load the gold on board their plane."

"Well, ain't you the lucky guy?" Hunter asked the man sarcastically. "You've dodged the bullet twice today."

"Don't blame me," the man said defensively. "This colonel is really nuts. He forgot I was even here. So I hightailed it into one of the buildings. Until your pals here found me."

He looked back out at the remains of the firing squad.

"I didn't mean nothing by that," he added quickly. "I don't give a flying fuck *who* you guys are."

"Hey, watch your language in front of the monk." Hunter said. "And listen up. You better know what kind of airplane they took. Or you're going to need a priest — to bury you."

"Okay, okay!" the man said. "They've got a Fokker F-27M. It's an old cargo carrier these guys down here converted to an inflight refueler."

Immediately a profile of the airplane popped up in Hunter's mind: Pre-war West German manufacture. Two-engine propeller driven, converted medium-range airliner. About 300 mph as top speed. Max height at 30,000 feet. Most important, its range was about 2800 miles. With the extra gas on board for inflight refueling, the range might be up by another half or more.

Hunter put the rifle's nose right between the man's eyes. Unlike Jean LaFeet, this guy had no idea who Hunter was, and therefore had no doubt that he would pull the trigger.

"Okay," Hunter said to him. "The most important question of all: Where were they heading?"

Despite the circumstances, the prisoner managed a smile. "That I know," he said. "And I'll tell you just like I told those guys over there before you iced them. But first we make a deal."

Hunter didn't want to quibble. "Tell us and you get to live," he snarled at the man. "How's that for a deal?"

"Just fine," the prisoner said. "Okay, they're heading for a place in Peru, called Nazca . . ."

Chapter 62

"This is called 'appeasement!' " Masoni, the Radio CATS announcer said.

Cobra Captain Bobby Crockett shook his head. "Calm down, man," he said. "I don't make the rules."

Masoni looked over at his partner, O'Gregg, who could only shrug.

"I just feel like a traitor reading this," Masoni said. "I mean, we've been out here sucking jungle gas for almost two years, man. Do you know what that can do to you?"

Crockett held out his hands as if to say there was nothing else he could do. "Orders are orders," he said.

It was almost midnight and the CATS clandestine radio station was about to go off the air and be moved to another location. But before that happened, there was another message from Washington that had to be read.

"Do you guys remember your world history?" Masoni asked Crockett and his gunner, John Hobbs. "Remember Munich? And Chamberlain waving that piece of paper that he and Hitler signed? 'Peace in our lifetime' is what he said. It was actually a sell-out! They sold the Czechs and the Poles down the river. The Nazis ate 'em up for breakfast and the fucking world was at war two years later *anyway*."

"Things are different now," was all that Crockett could say.

"It's still called 'appeasement,' " Masoni repeated. "Dealing with the Nazis might be okay with you guys way up there. But how about us down here? The people who've been fighting those scumbags? And the people who live down here who have lost people in their family? Who gives them a say in this?"

"Does this mean you're not going to read it?" Crockett asked him. "Because if not, I will."

Masoni let out a derisive laugh. "You know, I get a kick out of you guys," he said. "You fly around in your kick-ass machines like you're Batman or Robin or Green Lantern or someone. But when it comes down to dirty work, all of a sudden, there's no more capes and masks and derring-do, you know? We've been reading this bullshit over the air now day and night, thinking there was more behind it. But now I know who the dupes are. It is us . . ."

He threw the piece of paper at Crockett and said: "So, sure, be my guest. Let the people down here get the news right from the source. Right from an authentic superhero. I want no part of it."

With that he got up and stormed out of the PDC.

Crockett picked up the paper, sat down and adjusted the broadcast microphone. The song that had been playing was just finishing up.

"Turn it on," Crockett told O'Gregg, pointing to the microphone.

"Fuck you," O'Gregg answered him. Then he too stormed out the door.

Crockett flicked a few switches and saw a red light blink on. He knew from this the microphone was "live."

"To the people of Panama and surrounding areas," he began in a deep southern-tinged monotone. "Here is an announcement from the United American Army headquarters in Washington, DC.

"At six PM, eastern time today, an agreement was signed between the United American Army and the forces of The Twisted Cross. This agreement states that both sides recognize and respect the sovereignty of the other and that neither side will commence hostilities against the other for a period of five years, at which time this agreement will be renewed.

"This means for the people of Panama and for the people of North America that there will be no war. I repeat, there will be no war. Both governments wish to express the fervent

313

hope that peace will be a benefit to all whose interests lie in this important region.

"An official signing ceremony will be held in Panama City within forty-eight hours. Residents along the Canal and in the Panama City area are hereby notified that a twenty-four-hour curfew is in force in your area starting immediately. It is the responsibility of those listening now to tell any neighbors who don't have access to a radio. They should know, as should you, that failure to obey this curfew will be dealt with in the harshest means possible."

Crockett reached up, turned off his microphone and let out a long whistle.

"That *was* tougher than I thought," he said.

Hobbs fiddled with a few control buttons. "Should I put on a record?" he asked.

Crockett thought for a moment, then said: "Don't bother. I can't imagine anyone out there wanting to hear music right now."

An hour later, Mike Fitzgerald walked into Jones's Pentagon office.

The room was dark except for one dim lamp. The general was sitting behind his desk, no less than a hundred different documents piled in front of him. Fitzgerald was struck by how old the man looked at that moment.

"Just got confirmation, general," Fitz told him. "The Texans monitored the CATS broadcast. The word is out."

Jones wiped his face with his hands. "There's no turning back now, is there . . ." he said.

Fitz shook his head. "No, sir, there isn't."

Jones sat up and shuffled some of the documents on his desk.

"No word from Hunter, I suppose?" he asked.

Again, Fitz shook his head. "No, sir. Nothing."

"Damn," Jones whispered. "This thing would have been a hell of a lot easier to do if he had been here . . ."

Chapter 63

The southern coast of Peru is made up of a range of low hills that run north to south. Squeezed between these coastal highlands and the first steps of the mighty Andes is a long low basin called *Pampa Colorada* or, to North Americans, the Plain of Nazca.

Nazca is a strange place—a mystical plateau that people were known to frequent as far back as prehistoric times. Most of the top covering material on the plain is made up of rocks, ranging in size from pebbles to good-sized boulders. These rocks, tumbling down on the basin through years of runoff from the Andes' foothills, were a strange shade of deep red—this the result of morning dew being burned off in the hot South American afternoons, thereby oxidizing the rocks.

But it was what lay underneath these rocks that made Nazca so odd. If one moved a rock or even scratched the surface under Nazca's top layer, they revealed another layer of fine-colored, almost luminescent soil beneath.

The archaeologists called it a "natural blackboard" and determined that Nazca had been like this for tens of thousands of years.

But these scientists weren't the first to discover this secret about Nazca. Fifteen hundred years before, a group of people, their origin unknown, carved out huge drawings on the plain's surface simply by displacing the top covering of red oxidized rock and sand and revealing the luminous soil underneath.

This alone had taken great insight on the part of those unknown Peruvians. The people at Nazca "drew" animals — monkeys, spiders, eagles, lizards — thirty enormous drawings in all. And these were intersected and surrounded by literally miles of straight lines, criss-crossing back and forth over the plain. To say that it must have taken an enormous effort in manpower to "dig" the figures and the lines would have been a gross understatement.

But it wasn't so much what the mystery people drew as to *why*, that had puzzled the experts ever since.

Because, the simple fact at Nazca was that the drawings on the absolutely flat plain can only be appreciated when viewed from the air . . .

Elizabeth knew the animal glyphs on the Uxmaluna gold ingots were the exact figures that were drawn on the Plain of Nazca. In doing so she had stumbled upon a startling "missing link" in the study of ancient peoples of Central and South America. That contact had been made between the mysterious people at Nazca and the Mayans, some 2500 miles to the north in Yucatan, was in terms of the accepted notions of archaeology, absolutely astonishing. The fact that the Nazca people had, for whatever reason, moved tons of pure gold over those 2500 miles to be hidden underneath the Grand Pyramid at Uxmaluna was even more mind-boggling. In her heart as a scientist, Elizabeth knew that should books ever be published again, then all the volumes on the Mayans and the ancient pre-Inca Peruvians would have to be rewritten.

But, sadly, other thoughts — deeper, darker — were circulating in Elizabeth's brain at the moment . . .

It was not lost on anyone inside the Fokker — not Krupp, or Elizabeth or the two captured pilots — that the Plain of Nazca, with its miles of straight lines, looked not unlike a present day airport.

The transport airplane had made the 2200 mile journey in less than eight hours — good time considering that they had to fly out and around Panamanian airspace, which added another 90 minutes to their trip. The pilot set the airplane down right near one of the drawings—that of a monkey with a long, curlycue tail. The landing was rough, bouncing the airplane as its speeding wheels hit the loose red rock covering of the basin. But the Fokker had substantial short take-off and landing capabilities, and the pilots were able to stop the airplane in a very short amount of time and space.

Yet this didn't satisfy Elizabeth. She ordered them to taxi here and there, all the while checking their location in relation to the carved out figures and those on the ingots. Finally, she told them to stop and to shut down the engines. They had arrived.

Krupp was the first one to climb out. He was instantly hit with an extremely hot gust of wind, typical of the waves of heat that swept the plain. Elizabeth was the next to disembark. She was holding another gun by this time—a .45 Colt automatic. They were also able to get a half dozen AK-47s when they had first landed at the Guatemala City refueling station. It was one of these weapons that was used to kill the station's crew in the hangar where they dumped the Hook helicopter.

Elizabeth motioned for the two pilots to climb out of the airplane also. These men were, like so many of the scum roaming Central America these days, fascist South Afrikaners. Under different circumstances, they and Krupp would no doubt be allies.

But not now . . .

Before landing she had had the pilots circle the plain six times. This allowed her to match up the ground drawings with those on the ingots. Once this was done, she alone knew that the lines on the Plain of Nazca were not dug out at random or for some kind of religious reason. Actually, they were a very elaborate puzzle, the key to which could be found on the ingots. What she had read from those gold imprints was simply the code with which to figure out this puzzle. The prize for doing so was finding a treasure of gold at least twice the size of that which sat underneath the pyramid at Uxmaluna.

"You, bring the equipment," she ordered one of the pilots, flashing the Colt around with some authority. "And you, carry the water bags."

The pilots had no choice but to obey her. With Elizabeth leading the way, the foursome walked about 100 feet from the airplane. She held up her hand when they had reached a point just off one of the larger "runways." It was close by the only point on the entire plain where eight lines intersected. It was as simple as that.

"Dig," she said to the pilots. "Right there where all the lines meet."

They resignedly took hold of the two shovels and did as told.

Krupp was already sweating profusely by this time, and the fact that he had to hold the heavy AK-47 on the two pilots didn't help matters any.

She noticed his plight right away.

"That heavy uniform is not the type of clothing for this place," she said to him.

"But, but you have the same clothes on as I do," he said, noting her Twisted Cross uniform.

"That's exactly my point," she said with a smile.

They walked back to the airplane and the relative shade of the cabin. Once inside, she undid her shirt and let her breasts become exposed. Krupp immediately felt his mouth go dry. He couldn't take his eyes off her beautiful chest and she knew it. She laughed at the expression on his face. She was playing him like a violin.

"You like them, don't you?" she asked.

"Oh, yes," he was just barely able to say.

"Do you want to touch them again?"

He was only able to nod his head, his excitement was growing so. "Yes, you know I do," he said.

She put her own hands to them and gave them a seductive squeeze. "Then tell me: what will happen once we get out of here?"

The question took him by surprise. "I . . . I don't know," he said. "We'll have a lot of gold, correct?"

"More than you can imagine," she said, looking back out

at the two pilots who were digging in the broiling sun. "But where can we possibly go? I know about the Skinheads. I know they won't stop until they catch you and when they do, they'll catch me too."

Krupp felt a long tremor of fear rip through him.

"There will be plenty of places to go," he mumbled. "Just give me some time to think about it."

She squeezed her breasts again and gave out an erotic sigh. Then, to his dismay, she rebuttoned her shirt. "Don't take too long thinking, Colonel," she said. "It might be dangerous . . ."

Meanwhile, 250 miles off the coast of Peru, a remarkable aerial operation was in its final phase.

For the third time in six hours, Hunter moved the AV-8BE two-seat Harrier jumpjet up and under the inflight refueling probe sticking out of the rear of a Texas Air Force KC-135 tanker.

"Contact . . ." he radioed the crew of the tanker. "And lock . . ."

"Roger, Harrier," came the reply. "Sit back and drink up . . ."

Hunter could use the rest. The past eight hours were a blur and he didn't expect it to get any better any time soon.

As it turned out, getting away from the Guatemala City refueling station had been the easy part. He and Brother David neutralized the Hook chopper pilot via a squirt from Hunter's water gun, and, after scattering the remaining Nazi troops with a few rounds from their AK-47s, carried him aboard one of the waiting Hind gunships and took off. With Hunter at the controls and Brother David at the big 50-caliber side gun, they made short work of disabling the five other Nazi helicopters, along with a good part of the refueling station itself.

At that point they flew barely ten miles, and set down right into the heart of the Guatemala City—the Dodge City of New Order Central America. Amidst running gunfights and non-stop terrorist bombings, Hunter and David dumped the unconscious pilot along the roadside and made their way to the city's one and only police station, which happened to be under attack at the time. Bribing a guard at the back door, they were allowed ten minutes on the station's shortwave radio set.

It took almost eight minutes but they were able to reach a friendly listening post in Louisiana. Speaking faster than he could ever remember doing, Hunter asked the radio operator to patch him through to Washington, DC. Another bribe and some AK-47 ammunition bought them five more minutes on the radio. Hunter spent all of it talking to Fitz.

He told him all he knew. The battle for the Fighting Brothers abbey at Coba. The ambush by the Skinheads. Meeting the *Tulum* at Chichen Itza. Seeing the massive gold find at Uxmaluna. Most important was the information that the woman and an unstable Nazi colonel were on their way to a deserted plain in southern Peru.

In the few seconds they had left, Hunter and Fitz hatched a bold plan. Hunter needed to get to Nazca and he needed to get there fast, before the whacked-out Nazi colonel did her harm. It was ten times the range of the Hind helicopter — they both knew he needed a jet, preferably a two-seat Harrier, as the mission called for a VTOL and he intended on bringing only one passenger back with him.

Fitz told him to sit tight for 90 minutes, an unbearable length of time for the impatient, anxious Wingman. But wait it out he did, he and Brother David managing to get out of the besieged police station and back to the Hind copter, taking time to stop at a street side cafe to pick up a half dozen tacos and a four-pack of beer.

It was a happy and well-fed pair that saw no less than a half dozen Harriers show up 89 minutes later. They were a mix of Texans and Football City pilots flying United American Harriers that had been deployed to Houston earlier. Only two Harriers landed — both of them two-seater versions. While Hunter helped strap an astounded Brother David into the back of one of the jumpjets, they started taking some fire from some buildings nearby. The four Harriers still aloft broke out of their hovering, four-sided protective cordon and, one by one, delivered a fire-suppressing barrage on the suspected location, courtesy of their powerful Aden cannons.

By the time the fourth Harrier got his plugs in, Brother David's jumpjet was up and gone, and Hunter's was taking off. The six VTOL aircraft didn't fly very far — they came back down again in an old soccer field about 20 miles from the town. There, they proceeded to play a game of musical cockpits.

First of all, Hunter prepared to take over the Harrier that had picked him up. His pilot took the rear seat in one of the other two-seaters.

At this point, Hunter bid farewell to Brother David. It was hasty — it had to be. Time was of the essence.

"Bless you, Brother Hunter," the monk had said, firmly grasping Hunter's hand. "I still feel I owe you for saving our mission."

"First of all, it is I that owe you, Brother," Hunter had told him. "I could never have got this far without your help. Secondly, you act as if we'll never see each other again. I promise you, Brother, we will."

That was all he could say. The Harrier's cockpit snapped closed and the jumpjet took off, straight up, Brother David waving like mad despite the force of the jet's vertical acceleration.

The other Harriers also took off at this point — two would proceed to the lake near the Uxmaluna site to pick up the commodore, then they would all form up and head for the safety of Texas.

Once Hunter was alone, he took off and headed west at full throttle. Off the coast of the most southern tip of Mexico, he met the first Texan aerial tanker and filled up. After breaking off contact, he headed due south, again at full throttle. Avoiding Panamanian airspace added 250 miles to his trip. About 400 miles off the coast of Big Banana, he met his second Texas tanker, which was actually accompanied by yet another tanker. Once Hunter took on his needed fuel, the tanker itself topped off its tanks from its companion, then turned for home.

Phase three had Hunter taking on his third fuel load at 250 miles off the coast of Peru. Once that was done, the Texas tanker did a U-turn and headed back north, Hunter knowing that the weary crew would have to rendezvous two more times to get enough fuel to make it back.

It had been a complicated operation, but it went off without a hitch.

Now Hunter could turn to the business at hand . . .

Chapter 64

The two captured Fokker pilots had dug down five feet when they came to a hand-carved chunk of limestone.

"Amazing," Elizabeth said on seeing the soft rock. "Mexican limestone in the Peruvian highlands."

"Now what?" one of the pilots asked, wiping his brow.

Krupp, standing by the edge of the hole, was wondering the same thing.

Elizabeth looked at the two pilots, then ordered the one who had asked the question out of the hole. Like his partner, he was tall and blond.

"Keep an eye on this one, Colonel," she said to Krupp. "Don't come near the airplane until I call you."

Mystified, Krupp nodded numbly and watched as Elizabeth led the pilot back to the Fokker.

Ten minutes went by. Krupp was sweating buckets in the afternoon heat. The pilot still in the hole was faring no better, trying to whack away at the limestone with the now-dulled blade of his shovel.

Then Krupp heard Elizabeth. "Colonel," she called out somewhat breathlessly. "Come here . . ."

Krupp half-heartedly told the man to keep on digging and walked to the airplane. Climbing inside, he got the shock of his life.

Elizabeth was naked. So was the pilot. He was lying on his back and she was on top of him, riding him like a young girl rides a horse. Her hair was going wild, her breasts were bouncing crazily. She looked completely caught up in the sex act — completely out of control.

"Jealous, Colonel?" she called to him, out of breath and laughing wildly. "Oh, but you like to watch, don't you?"

Krupp was absolutely speechless.

Elizabeth turned her attention back to the young stud of a pilot who was exerting himself like a lead role player in a hard-core X-rated movie.

"Give it to me!" she screamed in passion.

Their love-making got even more heated — Elizabeth was lost in her passion, alternating between orgasmic screams and moans and delirious bursts of laughter. Krupp couldn't move a muscle. She would occasionally glance over to him, flash a devious smile, then go back to her frenzied love-making. For his part, he had never seen such a display of obscenity.

When it was certain that both of them were reaching their orgasm, Krupp could take no more. Why was she torturing him so? He turned and quickly left the cabin, leaning on the wing, trying to collect himself.

Seconds later he clearly heard Elizabeth scream in utter delight, the pilot too cried out at his climax.

Then, suddenly, a gunshot cracked through the desert air!

Krupp spun around and ran back to the cabin, thinking that the pilot had somehow gotten hold of her gun.

But when he reached the door and looked in, he realized he had it all wrong. The pilot was dead — a single bloody gunshot wound in his temple. Elizabeth, gun in hand, was just climbing off his limp body.

She turned and wriggled her own naked body at Krupp and laughed. "I told you I could be dangerous . . ." she said.

Chapter 65

Krupp was still shaking when Elizabeth finally emerged from the airplane.

She was brushing back her hair and adjusting her clothes as if she had done nothing more than freshen up.

"Have you broken through yet?" she asked the remaining pilot.

Knowing full well the fate of his partner, the man was suddenly very accommodating.

"I've got a peephole in it," he said. "There's a tunnel below."

Elizabeth smiled once again and looked at Krupp. "Makes the trip worthwhile, no?" she said.

The pilot had kicked a larger hole in the limestone plate now, and with a few more whacks of the shovel, had an opening big enough to squeeze through.

"There it is, ma'am," he said. "Are we going in?"

"We are," she said, shining the airplane's large battery-operated trouble lantern down into the tunnel.

Krupp hesitated at the edge of the hole. Elizabeth turned and looked at him. "Colonel?" she asked, "Aren't you coming?"

He still hadn't said a word to her since the incident in the airplane.

"Problems, Colonel?"

He shook his head half-heartedly. "No," he finally managed to say.

The pilot was the first to slip through the limestone cover and into the tunnel. He helped Elizabeth down, leaving

Krupp to practically fall the eight feet into the tunnel beneath the limestone cap. Elizabeth got her footing and then played the big flashlight around.

The tunnel was very similar to the one that led to the gold chamber at Uxmaluna, the only difference being that this passageway was musty and oddly damp.

"Do you realize that we are the first people to come in here in fifteen hundred years?" Elizabeth said.

But neither the pilot nor Krupp was in the mood to celebrate the historic event.

They started walking, Elizabeth in the lead, the pilot beside her. Krupp bringing up the rear.

"What's your name?" she suddenly asked the pilot.

"Karlon," he answered.

"And how many people does it take to fly that airplane?"

"Just two," he said, after thinking for a moment. "One behind the controls, one to do a few simple things before take-off and landings."

"Really?" she asked. "Could you teach me how to do those simple things?"

The pilot didn't quite know what she was getting at, but he knew he'd be a fool not to play along.

"Yes, the procedures are very easy to learn," he said.

She instantly turned back to Krupp and held the flashlight under her chin for a moment to give her face an eerie look.

"Getting nervous, Colonel?" she asked.

She laughed and continued walking down the passageway, flashing the lantern from side to side in the neatly squared-off shaft.

Meanwhile, too far up for them to hear it, Hunter's AV-8B Harrier was passing high overhead.

Thirty minutes later, the trio reached a sealed-off entranceway sculpted exactly like the portal to the gold chamber at Uxmaluna.

"This is it," Elizabeth declared. "Look familiar, Colonel?"

Krupp was so jumpy he hardly heard her. Yes, it *did* look familiar — *too* familiar. Walking through the dark tunnel — so similar to the one at Uxmaluna—was like revisiting a nightmare. That, and the fact that he was trying to figure out just what she was up to, had him so taut, his muscles cramped when he moved.

Elizabeth turned to the pilot and told him to hammer in the slim piece of limestone. Using the shovel once again, he proceeded to bash at the soft stone.

"Excited, Colonel?" Elizabeth asked.

Krupp somehow got up the gumption to say, "If you are."

She laughed again, this time right in his face. Then she turned back to the business of knocking in the limestone barrier.

"Kick it in," she told the pilot, seeing that he had already put several large cracks in the barrier.

The pilot did as ordered. Three hard kicks of his boot and the pieces of limestone fell apart.

Elizabeth pushed her way past the pilot and entered the chamber first.

"I've done it!" they heard her cry out.

Both men burst onto the chamber—and stopped in their tracks.

"Jesus Christ!" the pilot said. Up until that moment he had had no idea exactly what they were digging for. Now, before him he saw more gold than he thought existed on the entire planet.

Even Krupp felt a jolt of excitement. The chamber was at least four times larger than the one up in the Yucatan—and it held that much more gold.

"There must have been a core of gold somewhere in the near Andes to the east," she said, explaining it more to herself than the two men. "The Nazca people found it, mined it and stored it here. When the Incas or the pre-Inca people started to move into the area, the Nazca people must have somehow made an alliance with the Mayans, and they agreed to hide some of their gold up in the Yucatan."

Her scenario may or may not have been accurate—closer examination might have shown her that the appropriate dates didn't match up. But this kind of scientific accuracy was irrelevant now—so bright was the shine of the tons of good before

327

her.

"How will we ever get all this out of here?" Krupp asked, continuing to take in row upon row of the same bowl-shaped ingots.

She suddenly turned and said: " *We?*' Just what do you mean by that?"

He began stumbling badly. "I thought . . . but you said . . . you asked what we'd do . . . *together* . . ."

She shook her head in pity. "I guess you just don't understand what's happening here, do you?" she asked.

Krupp immediately felt the tug of his instincts. One part of him wanted to break down and plead with her. Another part was slowly switching over to self-preservation. He was carrying a fully-loaded AK-47. She had the Colt automatic. In between them was the unarmed pilot.

"Well," she continued. "Let me show you *exactly* what's happening."

She turned and faced the pilot.

"Karlon? Come here."

The pilot did as told. She smiled and let her free hand roam all over his chest, stomach and, finally, his lower body. Her long fingers paused every few seconds between his legs.

"Can you and I fly that airplane out of here?" she asked in a stage whisper, her hand lingering around his crotch.

"Yes, ma'am," he said confidently. "Just say the word and we're out of here."

She turned back to Krupp. "See, Colonel?" she said. "Are you getting the pattern here? Like I said before, it's all about being a *real* man. Something you wouldn't know very much about . . ."

With that, she pulled the pilot's pants off, then slipped out of her own. She fondled the man erotically for several long moments. Then, before an astonished Krupp, they got down on the chamber floor and furiously engaged in every known sex act for the next five minutes.

The Nazi officer was on the verge of tears watching the display. He sank down into a corner and curled up like a kid about to be punished. He was shaking and having a hard time catching his breath. He tried to look away, but he found

328

it impossible. His eyes were glued on her face, her body. As before, she was moving like a crazy woman—hair incredibly savage, her rear end jiggling, her breasts bouncing up and down wildly.

Krupp felt a low whine start up in his eardrums. *Why was she doing this to him? Was she crazy? Or was he?*

As with the pilot before, she mounted the man and started pumping maniacally. Krupp was crying openly now. But after only a minute or so of this, the Nazi officer saw her hand move up behind the pilot's head. It was holding the .45 automatic. Time froze. Was she going to take out this pilot as she had the one in the airplane? In one instant, Krupp wanted her to do it—then there'd be no rival for him. But in the next he knew that if she did, how would they be able to fly out?

The buzz in his brain got louder as she brought the gun up to the unsuspecting man's head and pulled back the hammer. Climaxes approaching, Krupp saw her finger slowly pull the trigger.

"Do it!" he screamed.

She responded with a loud cry and a squeeze of the trigger . . .

Click!

Nothing happened.

She threw her head back and laughed wickedly at him as they finished their final orgasmic sex act. "Wishful thinking, Colonel," she said, out of breath and finally climbing off the exhausted, spent pilot.

"You're mad," the Nazi officer told her. *"Totally mad . . ."*

She stood and stared at him, not making any effort to rebutton her shirt or pull on her pants.

"Yes, I *am* quite mad, Colonel," she said, matter-of-factly. "But then again, so are you. Don't you hear voices in your head? I do. Those tiny voices just won't leave you alone, will they, Colonel? They just won't let you function, properly, like a *real* man . . ."

He put his hands up to his head. The buzzing got louder. He felt as if his brain was about to explode. How could this be happening to him?

"You're crazy!" he screamed at her. "You're like . . . an animal. A Black Widow!"

"Oh, don't be so dramatic," she said in a seductive whisper, taking a step closer to him. "Come on, Colonel. You know you've had this *weird* thing for me all along. I just wanted to make you jealous . . . Of course I'm not going to kill him — he has to fly us out of here! Don't you think I know that?"

She squeezed her breasts, her fingers lightly pinching her nipples.

"Come on, Colonel . . ." she repeated, now right up against him. "Make love to me. Screw me. *Rape me!* Right here, in the middle of all this *beautiful* gold."

Her hand went between his legs and to both their surprise, she found it wasn't as soft as usual.

"So that did the trick, eh?" she said, encouraging him with her fingers. "Now's your chance, Colonel. Come on . . ."

Now it was another part of Krupp's anatomy that felt as if it would burst.

"Do you want me to take your clothes off, Colonel?" she asked him, seductively squeezing her own body. "The cave air feels beautiful when you're naked. Believe me, I should know . . ."

She took the rifle from his shoulder and laid it on the ground next to him. Then she undid his shirt, his belt buckle and fly. He could hardly feel the clothes falling off him. He was so mixed up, emotionally and physically, that he was trembling violently. He *wanted* to make love to her — and for once, all parts of his body were in agreement.

But he was absolutely inexperienced in these matters. And despite the desperate situation, the strangest questions were running through his mind, ones he had last heard out in the schoolyard. What does one do first? What happens once a person is caught up in it all? Was it true that most people black out the first time? *To be or not to be?*

Suddenly it seemed like the glare from the gold was blinding him . . .

Just then, the pilot spoke up. "Yeah, come on, Colonel," he said sarcastically, at the same time slyly reaching for Krupp's discarded AK-47. "Give it to her. Can't you see she's begging for it? Let's see if you can do it . . ."

The buzzing in the Nazi's head became excruciating.

"Come on . . ." Elizabeth said, rubbing up against him.

"Come on!" the pilot egged him on.

"Now . . ." she said, digging her hands into his crotch.

"Give it to her!" the pilot yelled.

But Krupp couldn't hear any of it. The buzzing in his head was now too loud to bear.

He screamed and then he threw her roughly to the ground. In a second he was on top of her, exerting such a force that even she was surprised for a moment. Krupp clumsily started performing. In seconds Elizabeth was laughing madly. The pilot was screaming, "Do it! Give it to her! *Give it to her* . . ." all the while raising the rifle toward both of them.

Although he could clearly see the pilot aiming the gun at them, something in Krupp's brain wouldn't let him stop what he was doing. Not now . . . The Nazi pumped Elizabeth furiously, his eyes closed, his mouth drooling the strange white foam. He *was* blacking out. He couldn't stop. He cried out: *"Don't hurt me, Mommy!"* That's when Elizabeth put the gun up to Krupp's head and pulled the trigger, literally blowing his brains out.

Suddenly another shot rang out. Then another and another. The Afrikaner pilot was slammed up against the cavern wall by at least a dozen yellow-red tracer bullets. Someone standing in the doorway to the chamber had shot the pilot just as he was about to shoot Elizabeth.

It took a few moments for the smoke to clear and for the noise to stop echoing around the cavern. But once it did, Elizabeth looked up and saw a strange man wearing a pair of red, oversized goggles, standing in the doorway, a smoking M-16 in his hands . . .

Chapter 66

"Are you Elizabeth?" Hunter asked the woman, pushing his NightScope goggles back up on his forehead.

She was naked, covered with dirt and sticky. She also looked like she was about to go into a state of shock.

"Elizabeth Sandlake?" he asked her.

"Yes," she said. Then she started shaking uncontrollably. She looked at the shattered head of Krupp beside her and started screaming.

Hunter shouldered his rifle and immediately dragged her from the chamber, grabbing her clothes as they went.

"They . . . they were *raping* me!" she screamed. "They were going to kill me!"

Hunter hastily pulled her pants up and wrapped the shirt around her.

"I know," he said, turning her away from the carnage inside the gold chamber. "*I know*, but you won't have to worry about them anymore."

Then he held her so close to him he could feel her heart beating through his flight suit.

"I'm Major Hunter of the United American Air Force," he said. "I've been searching for you."

She was still sobbing uncontrollably.

"Listen," he said, picking her chin up. "I know who you are. I know your father. He's alive."

"What?" she asked through the torrent of tears. "That's impossible. They shot him. I saw them . . ."

"No," he said firmly. "They shot him but they didn't kill

332

him. He's safe, in Washington, right now. I saw him just a few days ago."

"I . . . I can't believe it," she said, still whimpering. "How did you ever find me? How did you even get here?"

Hunter shook his head. "Those are two very long stories that will have to wait."

She nearly collapsed in his arms. "My life has been like a nightmare for so long," she cried. "And it started when those horrible men landed at our ranch . . ."

He pulled her close to him again. "Well, you don't have to worry anymore," he said. "I'll protect you."

He didn't kiss her, although the thought crossed his mind. Instead he just held her close until she was able to compose herself.

When he thought she was ready, he said: "Okay, now let's get the hell out of here . . ."

She held back for a moment. "Did you see the treasure in there?"

He nodded. "Second one I've seen in as many days," he said. "But it's been here for more than a thousand years. It can wait here a little longer . . ."

With that, he wrapped the shirt around her again, and holding her up under her arms, led her back up the tunnel toward the surface.

It was slow going for a while, but Hunter could feel Elizabeth regaining her strength as they approached the entrance.

They walked up and around one long curve and finally, he saw it — a shaft of sunlight blazing through the hole in the limestone cap.

"At last," he said with relief, as they approached the daylight. He was getting real tired of tunnels and chambers and holes in the ground.

They reached the escape hole and Hunter was about to boost her up through when he heard a very disturbing sound.

"Let me go up first," he said instinctively. Then he leaped up and grabbed the outside rim of the hole in the limestone cover. With one great burst of energy and strength, he boosted himself up and halfway out of the hole.

333

Suddenly, he was face to face with a man who was about to jump in where he was coming out. The man raised his AK-47 and started to pull the trigger.

But Hunter was quicker. In less than an instant, he had his M-16 up in one hand, and holding on with the other, put a barrage into the man.

That done, he crawled halfway out of the hole and did a quick visual sweep. A big An-126 Soviet-built troop transport was just going right over his head. And to his dismay, the air seemed to be filled with heavily-equipped paratroopers.

But they weren't just any kind of paratroopers.

"Damn! *Skinheads!*" he yelled, confirming his suspicions by quickly examining the soldier crumpled beside him.

He immediately jumped back down into the tunnel.

"No . . ." she cried, not wanting to face the truth. "No! They can't be here . . . They're killers . . . How did they find us?"

"Same way I did," he said. He surmised that the surviving Nazis back at the Guatemala City refueling station got a message to The Twisted Cross HQ in Panama. They, in turn, must have dispatched the nearest force of Skinheads.

Grabbing hold of her hand, he started pulling her back down the tunnel. At the same time, he took a quick inventory of his resources. His M-16 was just about full, as usual, with his trademark tracer rounds. He also was carrying one flash grenade, one HE grenade, one "Super-Frag" grenade, and his NightScope goggles.

It wasn't much against at least two dozen airborne Skinheads . . .

Up on the surface, the Skinhead commander was soon standing beside the hole where one of his men had been shot.

He looked out onto the Nazca Plain and saw that most of his troop were now on the ground and retrieving the parachutes, their squad leaders screaming at them to hurry and get organized.

They had received the call for this particular mission only

a few hours before, and he knew it was one for which they weren't especially well-prepared. They weren't tunnel rats. They were actually a sapper unit — explosives and their detonation being their specialty. They had been training for an undercover terrorist campaign soon to be launched against the Kingdom of Brasilia in retaliation for non-payment of debts. But then the call came all the way down from the High Commander himself, so the next thing the 'Head commander knew, his unit was jumping with full packs onto some barren dust bowl in Peru with orders to track down a wacko Cross officer who murdered his commanding officer and a woman who may or may not be his accomplice. It was not exactly a situation best remedied by a bunch of explosives experts, so he could understand how the majority of his troops would be a little disorganized at first.

As soon as the entire two dozen of his troop were gathered around the hole, he ordered them in. "If you find the woman, take her alive," he told them. "Everyone else gets greased."

The Skinheads responded with a particularly rabid chorus of "Yes, sir!" then, one by one, they lined up to go through the hole and into the tunnel.

But their shortcomings in equipment and training soon became apparent. First, each was loaded down with a full pack of explosives and detonators, and a rifle and full ammunition supply. The load of bulging equipment made it very difficult for each soldier to fit down the narrow hole in the limestone cap, but it was a canon of military practice that every soldier goes into every situation with the equipment he was trained in.

The next problem, as it turned out, was that only one Skinhead in three had a flashlight. So they had to organize in the near-dark into groups of five and proceed slowly down the pitch-black cave.

It was time wasted by the Skinheads — time that would give Hunter the breathing space he needed . . .

Hunter and Elizabeth made it back down to the chamber's portal in barely 20 minutes, running full out the whole way.

She was close to going into shock at this point, so Hunter put her against the wall 50 feet beyond the entranceway to the chamber, and took her bootlaces.

He had a plan, but it was based on one important assumption: that was that even a repulsive Skinhead would stop and gawk at the immense gold chamber. Running back to the chamber entrance and using Elizabeth's already dimming flashlight, he took his HE grenade and tied it to the Super-Frag with half a piece of the bootlace. Then he placed the double-bomb just inside the chamber's portal, behind a cracked piece of limestone.

Next, he took his flash grenade, and using another bootlace, rigged it with a long pull cord and placed it just outside the entrance. Finally, he double-checked to make sure that his M-16 was properly loaded.

Then he hunkered down beside Elizabeth, pulled down his NightScope goggles and waited, hidden in the dark.

The first team of Skinheads arrived ten minutes later. One man holding a flashlight, four others huddled around him. Through his infra-red vision, Hunter could tell right away that these 'Heads were out of their element. The heavy packs, the lack of illuminating gear, their cautious means of approach.

He had no idea what they were carrying or even what their specialty was. But right away he knew someone had made a big mistake sending these guys into the tunnels.

The enemy soldiers found the chamber and, as Hunter knew they would, stepped blindly through the portal. He heard their shouted exclamations as they found the bodies of first Krupp, then the Afrikaner pilot, then the gold.

Another group of five materialized out of the inky darkness. They too moved as if they were stepping on glass with bare feet. And like their comrades, they were also sucked into the gold chamber like bugs flying into one of those strange meat-eating plants.

A third and fourth group appeared soon afterward, and they automatically joined the rest in examining the bullion.

Throughout it all he could hear the refrain of "oos" and "ahhs," as well an occasional "Damn!" One man called out: "Look at all this fucking gold!"

Hunter could also hear the senior man of the enemy soldiers bark out a couple of orders having to do with searching the bodies. It wasn't long before this officer was convinced that he had at least partly completed his mission: that was, finding the homicidal Colonel Krupp—dead or alive. In this case, very dead.

But if only he knew who popped the unit's advance scout back at the hole to the tunnel . . .

Suddenly there was a crash and an intense flash at the entrance to the chamber. It was so bright, it blinded most of his troops, their retinas already wide-open in the low light of the cavern.

"Down!" the officer yelled. "Everyone down!"

There was a collective thump as the 20 Skinhead troopers hit the floor of the gold chamber, extinguishing their lights in the process.

"Anyone buy it?" the officer called out in the darkness.

Several men answered back "no," then another called out: "It was only a flash grenade."

"Okay, maybe it was just a leftover booby trap or something," he said.

They lay there in silence for five long minutes.

Then the officer in charge spoke. "Everyone stay down," he ordered. "We're going to crawl out of here, nice and slow, back up the tunnel fifty paces, with no lights. Got it?"

There was a round of "Yeah," and slowly, the Skinheads started to back out of the pitch black chamber and into the even darker tunnel.

Hunter waited until half of them were out before he detonated the double-bomb . . .

Four Skinheads and their overall commander had stayed on the surface of the plain, guarding the entrance to the tunnel.

For them it seemed like an especially long wait—they had

337

no way of knowing that their comrades had found the gold chamber and the two bodies, because none of the troops carried radios. This was because, like all modern-day sappers, they knew that a wrong signal from a radio could set off an explosive's detonator.

So the five Skinheads on the surface were waiting nervously while their main force was roaming around in the unknown underground. Just 100 feet away sat the Fokker airplane — they had already checked out the body lying in its cabin. Another half mile beyond that was the unmarked AV-8B Harrier jumpjet. Just who that belonged to was unclear.

The sun was getting hotter on them and with each minute, the apprehension grew. The commander gave his four men permission to remove their packs as well as their standard-issue sleeveless black leather vests. The officer himself had just sat down and taken his jump helmet off when he thought he felt the ground rumbling. He stopped scratching his micro-inch hair cut and looked around.

"Does anyone feel that?" he asked.

But no sooner were the words out of his mouth when the whole ground started shaking for real. Then there was an enormous explosion, followed by a series of secondary bangs. Then, a whole section of the desert 100 feet from them suddenly blew up into the air in a tremendous burst of searing-hot red and orange fire.

Through the intense smoke they could see the Fokker suddenly disappear into the crater still being formed by the explosion. Two more blasts followed, opening up two smaller holes near the larger one. Then there was another. And another.

That's when it dawned on the commander.

"Jesus Christ!" he cried out. "It's a chain reaction. They're blowing themselves up down there!"

The explosions continued while the five Skinheads could only stand with their guns ready, feeling pathologically helpless.

Suddenly someone was firing on them, with tracer rounds yet! They took cover behind the mound of cleared-away dirt near the entrance to the tunnel, looking every which way for the source of the incoming tracer fire.

It didn't dawn on them until two of their number had been picked off that the shooting was coming from the still violently smoking crater.

"Charge him!" the Skinhead commander ordered his two remaining soldiers.

Without a moment's hesitation, the two Skinheads leapt up and ran full speed toward the crater, screaming wildly as they fired their weapons. They were cut down in three seconds by a withering barrage of tracer fire.

Now it was the 'Head commander who froze. He saw first one, then two figures emerge from the smoking crater and run toward the Harrier jumpjet. He didn't follow—he had only a sidearm, and he had to stay by the tunnel entrance just in case some of his men made it through the earthquaking series of explosions. Or so he told himself.

The Harrier was taking off before the commander was convinced that none of his troopers were coming back. His unit had failed miserably, thanks to the man piloting the jumpjet, he was sure. Just how the mysterious pilot with the tracer ammunition and the person with him survived the hell of blasts from below, the Skinhead officer never found out.

The Nazi commander could only watch as the Harrier gained altitude, and then, in a push of a button streaked off to the north, leaving him with no food, no water and no protection out in the fatal heat of the Peruvian sun.

Chapter 67

The 737 airliner and its five F-4 Phantom escorts entered Panamanian airspace just after 0900 hours.

As agreed, a strict radio silence had been maintained by the aircraft since it left Washington, DC seven hours before. Now that it was only one hundred miles away from its destination, the only contact between the aircraft and the control tower at the Panama City airport was a corresponding electronic acknowledgment of its IFF identification signal.

The mood at the airport itself was one of frenzied festivity. In a matter of 48 hours, the place had been transformed from a gray, dull military installation to one festooned with multicolored banners, posters, streamers and even a few balloons. A large wooden platform had been hastily erected at the end of the airport's central runway and seats for 80 people nailed down. An improvised sound system, complete with more than a dozen Marshall "stack" amplifiers bordered this reviewing stand on three sides. Two lecterns, each covered with a gaggle of microphones, were set up in front of the gallery and these were surrounded by no less than 20 video and film cameras, all of which would record the historic signing ceremony.

Off to the side, a helipad had been installed. This would serve as the landing area for the High Commander, who would chopper over from his skyscraper headquarters at the proper time. And in an effort to play down the militaristic aspect of the ceremony, the only soldiers present were dressed in formal starched white Twisted Cross uniforms.

Having little experience at these things, the staff of The Twisted Cross High Command had agreed to the suggestion that the protocol necessities be handled by the United Americans. To this end, there were telexed a schedule of events the day before, a timetable which was copied over and over and distributed to the 40 top Cross military dignitaries lucky enough to be tapped to attend the signing ceremony.

This schedule was as follows: Once the airliner landed, it would roll to the end of the central runway and wait until its escort completed a ceremonial flyby formation of the airport. At that point, another aircraft, this being a C-141 cargo ship carrying support personnel for the United American signing delegation, would land and take its place beside the 737. Then *its* accompanying escort, made up of 12 United American jet fighters, would perform a ceremonial flyby.

At this point, the 737 and the C-141 would taxi over to the reviewing stand area, officials of the United American delegation and their support people would disembark and be greeted by their counterparts in the Twisted Cross delegation. Simultaneously, the combined F-20 and F-4 escort flights would fly over in a "linked formation," an aerial symbol of the new-found cooperation between the United Americans and The Twisted Cross.

Then the signing ceremony would begin . . .

The 737 appeared over the airport 15 minutes later. It circled the airport twice, then came in for a routine landing. As planned, it followed two ground support trucks to the end of the central runway, where its pilots would cut back its engines to idle and wait.

This done, a low-level Twisted Cross functionary named Klapk climbed aboard the airplane for a strictly-meaningless landing rights documentation. Once aboard he quickly took in the scene inside the airliner's cabin. All of its 212 seats were filled with members of the United American delegation — some in military dress uniforms, most in simple suits and ties. There was much luggage about — Klapk knew that many in the UA delegates had accepted the High Commander's invitation to stay on in Panama for several days as part of a "working vacation."

Klapk then visited the flight deck where he was greeted by members of The Twisted Cross flight crew and a corresponding number of UA pilots. Klapk was struck by the fact that both sides were getting along very well with each other — almost like they were all longtime friends. It was at that moment that Klapk felt the Mutual Security Pact between the Twisted Cross and the United Americans would be a workable agreement.

Just as Klapk was leaving the airliner, the five Twisted Cross F-4 Phantom escorts flew over in formation, the first pass of their ceremonial flyby. Off in the distance he could see the smoky brown trails of the huge UA C-141 support craft descending for a landing. Somewhere a band started playing and a couple dozen balloons were released. Even a dullard like Klapk could appreciate the gaiety of it all.

A half mile from the reviewing stand, the dozen or so technicians working inside the "Snowball" — that was the airport's sophisticated South African-made flight traffic control radar station — picked up the 12-aircraft United American escort formation right on schedule. Their crew chief passed this information on to the airport control tower, and then he told his workers to relax — for them, the hard part of the day was over.

The UA F-20s streaked over the airport, flying in three, four-point diamond formations. The Twisted Cross dignitaries, already seated in the reviewing stand, craned their necks and shielded their eyes in an effort to watch the high-tech Tigersharks flyover.

At this point both the 737 and the just-landed C-141 rolled up to the designated area. More balloons were released, and the band played another rousing martial tune. The Cross welcoming committee, made up of ten senior members of the High Commander's Command staff, took their places at the end of the ceremonial red carpet and waited as the 737 taxied up to the movable stairway. At the same moment, the linked formation of F-20s and F-4s made the first of its scheduled four flybys.

The door to the 737 opened and a long procession of United American support personnel filed out, most of them carrying their own luggage. Then the first of the UA dignitaries appeared, descended the stairs and shook hands with the Twisted Cross welcoming delegation. The combined Tigershark-Phantom formation flew over once again, the band swung into its second martial tune and a collection of selected civilians, bussed in for the occasion to make noise, broke into a well-rehearsed ovation.

The handshakes over, a tall, burly man who had brought up the rear of the official UA delegation was directed to one of the microphones.

He was introduced as General David Jones.

The man stepped up to the microphone, adjusted it to his tall frame, and began to speak:

"Gentlemen of The Twisted Cross," he said. "I am *not* General David Jones. I am Major Shane of the Football City Special Forces and I am here to tell you that you will be shot immediately if you don't follow all my instructions. First of all, lay down any weapons you have and put your hands on your heads."

The initial reaction to the statement was a laugh from the gathered Twisted Cross officials. But then, as if in one swift motion, the suit-coated UA personnel lining both sides of the reviewing stand retrieved a wide variety of small but lethal weapons from under their jackets. Simultaneously, the rear ramp of the nearby C-141 opened and a long stream of heavily-armed Football City Special Forces troops began to pour out. At the same instant, four F-20s roared in low over the crowd, their screaming engines adding the right amount of intimidation to the situation.

In ten seconds, forty members of the uppermost command structure of The Twisted Cross realized that they were hopelessly surrounded . . .

At the same time, about 50 nautical miles west of Panama City, the crew of the *Veneto*-class heavy cruiser was preparing to sink an unarmed merchant ship that had attempted to gain entry to the Canal.

Deep in the ship's Combat Information Center, the attention was naturally surrounding the fire control officer, the man who would oversee the sinking of the hapless victim. But sitting a console at the other end of the CIC, one of the radar technicians saw a strange blip appear on his screen. He waited for the scope's arm to sweep around the field twice more before calling over his superior officer.

"Sir, can you see this?" he asked the officer, pointing to the blip which was getting closer to the ship.

The officer nodded and watched the screen for two more sweeps.

"Check its electronic profile," the officer ordered. He watched as the crewman punched a series of buttons. Then he heard the man swear under his breath.

"Well, what is it?" the officer asked.

The man was suddenly very nervous. "Sir, the computer says . . ."

"Says what?" the officer asked him in an agitated tone.

The man looked up at him. "It says it's an Exocet."

The officer's face immediately drained of all color.

"Re-check, quickly," he said to the man, leaning over the screen and watching as the blip drew even closer.

The crewman pushed the same buttons and found the computer came up with the same answer.

"It's definitely an Exocet profile, sir," he said, his voice trembling. "Impact in less than 40 seconds . . ."

"*Jesus Christ!*" the officer yelled out, leaping to hit the ship's attack alert button. Suddenly two dozen klaxons were blaring throughout the ship.

Those gathered around the fire control officer instantly turned around, stunned by the sudden chorus of warning sirens.

"What is it?" they called out in unison. "What's happening?"

The officer ran by them and out to the superstructure's railing, calling behind him: *"Exocet coming in!"*

Most of the officers also ran to the railing and looked out to the horizon, not wanting to believe what the defensive systems officer was telling them.

"There it is!" the officer cried out, pointing off to the north-east.

As one, they all spotted the telltale flare of light, flying just barely above the wavetops off in the distance.

In seconds it was upon them.

"Maybe it will miss!" someone cried out.

It didn't . . .

The sea-skimming missile slammed into the cruiser directly behind the CIC. Its warhead ignited on impact, and a tremendous explosion followed, instantly killing all inside the CIC as well as those officers standing on deck.

The ship, completely unprepared for such a strike, was rocked with a series of explosions as the flames quickly found its magazine and fuel supply. It started to go down in less than five minutes.

The crewmen on the nearby merchant ship were suddenly ecstatic. Many of the cruiser's sailors, upon abandoning ship, attempted to swim over to the steamer. But those who did found no lifeboats waiting for them, no ladders dropped over the side. Instead the merchant ship's captain immediately ordered his engines up to full speed and departed the area as quickly as possible.

The steamer was gone by the time the French-built *Aerospatiale* Super Frelon helicopter belonging to the Central American Tactical Service overflew the area and watched the cruiser, the victim of its perfectly-aimed Exocet missile, roll over and sink with the loss of all hands.

Chapter 68

At the opposite end of the Canal, Major "Catfish" Johnson, the commanding officer of the famous 7th Calvary, looked out of the C-130's window, crossed his fingers and breathed a sigh of relief.

All along the narrowing sides of Gatun Lake, the waterway which led from the Atlantic side to the canal, he saw at least a dozen separate fires burning. *Thank God,* he whispered to himself. He knew the fire represented Nazi AA and SAM sites that he been hit by the Chinook gunships of the CATS just minutes before.

"Okay, everyone up!" he called out. "The chopper jocks have done their job. Now let's do ours!"

As one, the 100 troopers inside the New York Herc C-130 stood up and hooked on their jump rings. A crewman opened a side door and within a minute a red light started flashing.

Johnson stood at the door, waiting. Trailing behind his lead aircraft were five more Hercs. Below he saw two more burning AA sites but also about a dozen Nazi surface craft speeding in the narrows of the lake.

One quick prayer later, the green light came on and the jump bell rang. Johnson braced himself and yelled: "Let's go boys!" With that, he dove out the door, instantly feeling the reassuring tug of his parachute opening.

"Red Zone, here we come . . ." he said.

* * *

For the Twisted Cross soldiers and officers based at San Valles it promised to be an easy day.

Only a minimum security force was on duty at the sprawling base which was located two miles from the main Atlantic-side Canal locks. Today was a time of celebration for the Nazi troops. They had been on 24-hour alert every day for the past three weeks and the troops were worn down as a result. So what better time to stand down than the day the Mutual Security Pact was to be signed with the United Americans? Besides, their top officers were at the signing ceremony, and the base, left to junior command, had taken on a relaxed atmosphere almost as soon as their commanders' choppers had departed for Panama City.

So very few people actually heard the high-pitched whine of the enormous C-5 gunship approaching.

One who did was a sergeant named Wyzenheimer. Caught drunk the night before by his squad lieutenant, he had been assigned a 14-hour shift, manning the base's fairly isolated north side tower.

Wyzenheimer was certain that he was hearing things when the strange whining noise first invaded his hungover and hurting eardrums. But when he turned his tired eyes to the northeast, he was stunned to see this huge airplane, roaring toward him no more than 500 feet off the ground.

Despite his post-inebriated condition, Wyzenheimer knew the airplane did not belong to the air inventory of The Twisted Cross. By the time he had reached for the tower telephone, the massive airplane was right above him, so close he could clearly see the United American markings on its wings and tail. He also saw a name written in fancy script lettering right below the airplane's cockpit windows.

It read: *Nozo.*

Though Wyzenheimer had no way of knowing it, the huge C-5 named *Nozo* (official designation: C-5B-23E/R No. 1), housed no less than 21 GE GAU8/A 30mm Avenger cannons, each capable of 4500 rounds per minute. The computer-controlled guns were lined up on the port side of the huge airplane, each muzzle housed in a three-by-three recessed porthole. The guns were loaded with shells made of depleted uranium—a projectile that spontaneously ignited upon hitting its target.

The Nazi sentry couldn't reach anyone on the phone. So all he could do was watch helplessly as the C-5 roared over the base, climbed and circled back. It dipped a little to the left and then, all 21 portholes automatically opened on the side of the airship. An instant later, he saw a tremendous wave of fire flash out of its left side. Inside of two seconds, the interior of the base was enveloped in a horrible yellow smoke.

The C-5 continued its murderous fire for 20 more seconds, then it climbed and flew away, like some huge prehistoric bird suddenly bored with what it was doing. Verging on a state of shock, Wyzenheimer watched in horror as the yellow smoke slowly lifted and blew away. When it did, he realized that there was nothing left of the base but half the mess hall and one of its three water tanks. In place of the three dozen elongated barracks buildings and the rows of tanks and troop transports there was now a huge, smoking, skeleton-filled crater.

It would be several more hours before Wyzenheimer would realize that of the 2000 men assigned to the base, he was the only survivor . . .

Even larger than the decimated base at San Valles, was the combined Twisted Cross Army & Naval Attack station located at Las Avitos on the mouth of the Pacific side of the Canal.

This facility, which housed 4300 regular army troops as well as three squadrons of naval attack craft, possessed the Canal Nazis' most sophisticated anti-aircraft fire control system. Rings of small Roland SAMs surrounded rings of Bofors 40-mm L/70 radar-guided anti-aircraft guns, which in turn protected a concentrated group of large SA-5 Soviet-built SAMs. Added to this were no less than three dozen smaller early warning radar sets scattered at various points up to ten miles from the base. These in turn were protected by small and mobile Matra R.440 Crotale SAM launchers.

So it was with complete and total surprise that shortly after nine that morning, the center of the Las Avitos base — including its all-important Combined Command Center — was obliterated by five, 7000-pound HE bombs.

Surviving Nazi radar operators who saw or heard the explosions stared at their radar screens in disbelief. Obviously the base was under air attack, yet their radar fields were all "clean" — meaning no enemy aircraft had been detected in the area.

For a while only two Canal Nazis knew exactly what had happened. Assigned to an observation post a full 60 miles away to the north, they spotted five white shapes passing high overhead minutes after hearing that the base at Las Avitos had been attacked.

The observers, well schooled in aircraft identification, knew right away the airplanes were United American B-1B swing-wing bombers. It would take them longer to figure out just how the B-1s had so successfully eluded the spider's web of Nazi radar stations around Las Avitos.

Chapter 69

Although by this time warning calls were flashing up and down the occupied Canal Zone, the highest officials in the Nazis' command structure weren't aware of the surprise attack situation.

Instead they were being rounded up from the airport reviewing stand and herded onto the 737 airliner.

Without a shot being fired, Major Shane's Football City Special Forces Rangers had captured all but the very top echelon of The Twisted Cross military command. Instantly surrounded by the suitcoat-and-tie clad commandos, the Nazi officials had little choice but to surrender and follow orders, which were to get on the 737 or get shot.

Only one man, the lowly functionary named Klapk, gave the Rangers any trouble. Perhaps because he was the one and only Twisted Cross official to board the 737 when it first came in, he felt the most duped that the United Americans had pulled off such a daring stunt.

"I refuse to go!" he screamed into the muzzle of one of the Rangers' M-16s. "This goes against all context of the Mutual Security Pact!"

"There ain't no Mutual Security Pact, pal," the Ranger told him gruffly. "Did you really think we'd make a deal with you Nazis?"

Klapk was astonished. "But . . . but you've gone back on your word," he said. "Your government made a promise to respect our sovereignty . . . This is absolutely reprehensible behavior . . ."

The Ranger hit Klapk with the butt of his rifle. "So is gassing six million people to death!" he hissed at him.

Although no shots had yet been fired at the airport, Shane and his officers knew the "peaceful" situation wouldn't last. The combined F-20/F-4 squadron — the Phantoms being flown by UA pilots — had been providing cover for the kidnap operation. Several pilots reported that security troops were already surrounding the airport and, worse yet, that a large enemy force was moving toward the airport from the interior of Panama City.

Shane's troops actually had two jobs to do. One was to neutralize the Nazi Command Staff, a mission which would be accomplished as soon as the 737 took off. The second assignment was much tougher; hold the Panama City Airport until reenforcements came.

Shane quickly walked up and down the 737's aisle, making sure each of the high level Twisted Cross officers was securely tied and gagged. Also loaded onto the airplane were the dozen or so honor guard soldiers, who now looked slightly ridiculous in their starched white uniforms. In the front row of the airplane were the two original 737 pilots, men who played along with the whole charade out of fear for their lives. They were wired — each had had explosives strapped to his chest. One wrong move and the UA men responsible had promised to flip a switch and blow the pilots to Kingdom Come.

Satisfied that the prisoners were secure, Shane spoke briefly with the UA pilots now at the controls of the 737. Then he gave them the okay to depart and suggested they do so quickly.

Already, the first mortar rounds from the alerted airport security forces were crashing down on the runway . . .

Chapter 70

For the first time in his life, Hunter was biting his fingernails.

"This is driving me crazy!" he said, not for the first time that day.

"Jesus, Hawk, will you settle down?" JT told him. "Have a belt if you're so jumpy."

They were sitting in a makeshift Ready Room at an airport called Terechecchi in the country of Big Banana, formerly Costa Rica. Just outside the building was the F-16XL, Sandlake's deactivator pod attached under its right wing. The airport and all its facilities were being rented by United Americans, initially for three days, but with an option to stay a whole month. The rundown but functioning airport would serve as the UA's advance base for the sneak attack on Panama.

Jones had been the first one to utter those words to Hunter. Although diplomats might prefer the term "pre-emptive," the UA attack on The Twisted Cross *was* a sneak attack—pure and simple. It was born of false promises and deception and more than a few intensive interrogations of the Nazi envoy, Colonel Frankel, in which nearly a gallon of sodium pentathol was used. (Frankel, like the kidnapped Nazi delegation, was on his way to a specially-built prison located near Kimball Mountain in Alaska.)

So it was a war fused by dirty tricks, all of them laid at the feet of the United Americans. Yet Jones felt no compunction at all in launching the attack. In fact, he had been its main architect—a fact that made it even more devious as the Nazis knew full well of Jones's straight-as-an-arrow reputation.

"No government—friend or foe—will ever trust me again," Jones had told Hunter earlier that day. "But it's a small price to pay to prevent the Nazis getting a chokehold in this hemisphere. A nuclear chokehold to boot."

Hunter couldn't have agreed with him more.

But now the Wingman was more antsy than at any time he could remember. In front of him and JT was an ice cold pot of coffee, a basket of half eaten biscuits and a worn-out VCR. They had been awake for six hours, five and a half of them spent continuously reviewing two videotapes.

The first one was made back in Washington one week ago to the day. It showed every aspect of the deactivator pod—how and why it worked, how it was powered, what to do if it got cranky. After watching it twice, Hunter knew the videotape by heart. The subsequent 20 showings were just what the UA pilots called "tired gravy."

It had taken him a little longer—actually four viewings—to commit the second videotape to memory. It was a high altitude sequence taken very early that morning by Captain "Crunch" O'Malley's RF-4 recon airplane of the entire length of the Canal. Special electronic "points" had then been edited into the video, each one corresponding with the location of one of the underwater nuclear mines, as indicated by a special radar imager that O'Malley had carried aloft with him.

It was over each one of these points that Hunter would have to crank up Sandlake's deactivator and bombard the underwater mines arming mechanism with signal-scrambling radio waves.

"Jesus, what time is it?" he asked Toomey.

JT took off his sunglasses—a rare occasion at any time—and looked Hunter right in the eye.

"What the hell is bugging you?" he asked. "You know

353

that you can't go in until the whole fucking Canal is softened up. We've got to wait for the word and it's still a half hour away at least. So why are you making me — and yourself — so fucking miserable?"

With that, he stormed out of the Ready Room, shaking his head.

Hunter knew his friend was right. Something *was* bugging him — it had been eating at him since he returned with Elizabeth.

What was it? He had fulfilled his promise. Elizabeth was back and safe. His timing couldn't have been any better — barely an hour after returning to Washington with her, the United American "sneak attack" plan went into effect. Jones, Fitz, JT, Ben and the others had worked around the clock to get all the ducks in a row while putting up a convincing front that they were actually intent on cutting a deal with the Canal Nazis.

And now they had just received word that the very critical initial operation — that being nothing less than the abduction of the Twisted Cross Command staff — had gone well.

So what was bugging him?

It was Elizabeth. Her return to Washington and to the arms of her hurting father was less than satisfying. Thinking back on it, it seemed like such a trivial thing. But all the feeling — the joyful tears, the endless embrace, the many, many thanks-yous — simply didn't happen.

When they were finally reunited in Jones's office, Elizabeth greeted her father with little more than a slight hug and barely a kiss on the cheek. Then she asked to be fed. The old man was visibly crushed.

So why should this bother Hunter? He had no pat answer. He told himself that he couldn't expect every one of his adventures to have a happy ending. He felt a little foolish now pining away over Elizabeth's photo, thinking that their first meeting would be right out of an old Hollywood movie and maybe, just maybe, end with them walking hand-in-hand into the sunset.

On the contrary, she barely had said a word to him on the way back — they had landed in Texas after two in-flight refuelings, then caught a quick flight to DC courtesy of a Texas Lear jet. At first, Hunter chalked it up to the residue of her harrowing experience. But now, he was beginning to suspect it was something more — or, more accurately, something *less*.

Suddenly, his thoughts were broken by the sound of JT's voice.

"Let's go, Hawk!" he yelled into the Ready Room. "You're up!"

The F-16XL was off and climbing in less than five minutes.

Hunter felt good being back in the saddle of a *real* jet fighter again. Despite the Harrier's many advantages, it was a specialty airplane — designed and flown primarily for ground attack. For the ability to take off and land vertically, it gave something away in speed and range. And flying the Kingfisher had been a kick in a way — it had served its purpose, getting him down on the Yucatan rare waterways. But its top speed was 170 mph and that was brand new.

His F-16XL could beat that speed by a factor of 10 . . .

So now with 40,000 pounds of pure thrust at his command, he climbed, straight up. Past 30,000 feet. Past 40,000 . . . 45,000 . . . 50,000 . . . 55,000 . . .

It was time to stop wondering about Elizabeth and what was and what he expected to be — they were rarely the same anyway.

It was time to go to work.

JT was on his right, Ben was on his left. They were both flying souped-up A-7E Strikefighters. All three of the aircraft were carrying four Sidewinders apiece, and Hunter was packing a Short Range Air Missile (SRAM) on his left side wing, which would help balance out the deactivator pod on the other.

All three were also packing fully-loaded cannons — one each on the A-7Es, no less than six in Hunter's highly-modified F-16XL Cranked Arrow.

They were 30 minutes from the Canal and all during the flight, they received immediate updates on the various actions along the waterway. The best news were the results from the air attacks on The Twisted Cross's main troop depots at San Valle and Las Avitos. The electronically radar-invisible B-1B *Ghost Riders* had flattened Las Avitos without a single shot being fired at them; the huge C-5 gunship *Nozo* had vaporized the base at San Valle.

There were also positive if sketchy reports on the 7th Cavalry's attempt to seize the main Atlantic side locks. Those aboard the CATS Chinooks returning from the action said that all of the key SAM and AA sites in the Red Area were destroyed, either by them or in the two subsequent air raids by Free Canadian CA-10 Thunderbolts. All reports said that the 7th got down on the ground in good shape and were moving on the locks. Meanwhile, offshore, a large seaborne force of United American soldiers were waiting to enter the Atlantic side of the waterway.

Ten minutes before, a squadron of Texan F-4X Super Phantoms ran right into a like number of Twisted Cross F-4s over the Pacific coast city of Balboa and a tremendous aerial battle was still in progress. The B-1Bs had returned to the Big Banana base, were refueled, bombed-up again and were ready to head out for their second mission in as many hours.

But the reports out of the Panama City Airport were less optimistic.

Some of the Texas Phantoms reported the airport was being shelled heavily from three sides by the Twisted Cross security force and a reinforced armored battalion called in from Panama City itself. The combined F-20/F-4 Diversion Squadron was carrying out ground attacks against the Twisted Cross troops, but already two F-4s and a precious F-20 had been downed in the action by enemy shoulder-launched SAMs.

And the bad news got worse: The Canal Nazis were bringing up heavy mobile artillery and would soon be raining down half-ton shells on Shane's Rangers. And should they decide to start hitting the runways, this would make it just about impossible for the ten troop- and equipment-filled C-141s reinforcement aircraft Shane was expecting to land.

The second phase of the "sneak attack" was beginning. More air strikes—by the Texan F-4s, the Canadian Thunderbolts and the CATS Chinooks—were in progress along the entire length of the Canal. A second wave of 7th Cavalry paratroopers were set to be inserted within the next ten minutes to reinforce their comrades on the ground in the so-called Red Zone. The B-1Bs were launching and would soon be back over the Pacific side battle zone, this time to loiter near the Pacific side of the Canal action and wait for a target of opportunity.

But the United American's big punch had yet to be thrown. Flying long-range from bases in Texas, a total of 15 B-52 Stratofortresses—each carrying 30 tons of explosives—would be over Panama City within 15 minutes.

Yet despite the massive show of military firepower, Hunter found it all very frustrating. His role was confined to one specific mission, deactivate the underwater nukes. An important mission, yes. By far the most important of the entire operation.

Important, but confining—and that just wasn't his style. And the waiting was killing him.

One of the secrets Sandlake had revealed to Jones and the others had to do with the arming procedure for the underwater nukes.

In a nutshell, it took a long time.

To arm the "Washbuckets" literally took just the flip of the switch—actually a computer switch. But the computer sequence, which drove a series of UHF arming commands, had to deal with each of the 53 nukes one at a time. And what's more, this had to be done on a "random" basis, because while the computer would arm the mines sequentially, the Canal Nazis hadn't deployed the mines that way.

But the beauty of Sandlake's invention was that it could scramble a mine's timing mechanism no matter what stage of arming it was up to. Just as long as the mine's arming procedure had commenced, the deactivator could fuck 'em up. The United Americans knew that this all-important mine-arming sequencer switch (MASS) was located in a virtually bomb-proof underground command center in the basement of The Twisted Cross skyscraper HQ in downtown Panama City. The thinking went that when the Canal Nazis realized they were in a desperate situation, a decision would be made and the MASS would be activated as a prelude to detonating one or all 53 of the underwater nukes. But the key was this: Once the MASS was flipped, the action would give off a burst of radio energy so intense that a detecting device attached to the F-16XL's deactivator pod would pick it up within a second of transmission. Then, and only then, could Hunter start his crucial deactivating run.

And until that time, he would be forced to be a mere spectator, endlessly circling Panama City, waiting for the UA to apply so much pressure on the Canal Nazis that they would finally crack and start down the road of nuclear destruction.

Chapter 71

Hunter, JT and Ben were still five minutes out from Panama City when they saw the B-52s approaching from the northeast.

Surrounding the 15 Stratofortresses were 18 F-105X Super Thunderchiefs of Fitzie's famed Shamrock Squadron. These venerable fighter-bombers were to perform two functions. First, half of them would protect the heavy eight-engine bombers. The others would engage in a tactic called "Wild Weasel." Simply put, these F-105s would break in three groups of three. Then one of the trio would act as a kind of decoy, being intentionally detected by, then jamming, the radar systems of any AA guns or SAMs in their assigned area. Once this was done, the other two would go in and blast the AA site with "smart bombs."

While Hunter and his friends climbed up to 30,000 feet, they watched half the F-105s break off and go into action. No sooner had they done this when a tremendous wall of long-range AA fire came up at the B-52s, still 20 miles from their target.

"Christ! They must have a SAM or an AA gun on the roof of every skyscraper!" JT quite accurately pointed out.

For the next five minutes they circled the city and watched the F-105s score hits just about every time the

Weasels went into action. But there were only so many smart bombs and Wild Weasels to go around.

One B-52 caught a SAM on its starboard wing. It went down in a ball of flames just minutes before it reached the target. Then another got clipped on its tail, the SAM destroying its rear stabilizer in a fiery *snap!* It too plunged into the suburbs below, still ten miles from the target.

When a third B-52 took a well-directed burst from a radar-guided AA gun, Hunter, Ben and JT had seen enough.

Actually assigned to escort Hunter's F-16XL, Ben and JT had agreed before taking off that they would not be shy in jumping into any situation where they felt the UA needed help. Hunter wholeheartedly endorsed the plan, although, technically, it was against orders.

So now they judged that the B-52s needed help. Leaving Hunter behind, both Strikefighters went into identical near-vertical dives. They passed through the B-52 formation, pulled up in front of it and within seconds were firing their nose cannons at a pair of AA guns situated on top of a seaside condo tower.

The two targets blew up just seconds before they overflew them. Climbing slightly to avoid colliding with the results of the explosions, they were immediately firing on another large AA site atop an office tower. A pair of close-in bursts later, the AA gun was a pile of burning metal.

The pair attacked three more targets and scored three more hits. That's when their radios suddenly crackled to life.

"Toomey! Ben! What on earth are you doing?" It was Jones's voice and, Hunter, eavesdropping on the conversation, could tell it sounded *very* angry.

The general was leading the B-52 strike, an extraordinary feat for the virtual leader of the democratic people of America. But Jones was never one to shy away from action.

Trouble was, neither were Ben and JT.

"Supressing AA fire, sir," JT answered as calmly as possible.

"Well, get the hell out of there, *now!*" Jones retorted. "And stick to your mission!"

Hunter knew the general was right. But he also knew that neither of his close friends were ashamed or sorry for what they had done. Still, they both rather sheepishly climbed back up to 30,000 feet and slipped back into the role of escorting the F-16XL.

A minute later, the B-52s started dropping their bombs.

It was over in 45 seconds. More than 350 tons of high explosives rained down on the city's all-important dock-side section, erasing a two-square mile area. The effects were devastating. The price was two more B-52s and a F-105X.

Shane and his men could not only see the massive B-52 raid—they could actually *feel* it.

This was even through the earth-quaking blasts from the Canal Nazis' big mobile guns. Still, even a B-52 strike couldn't help Shane's men at this point. Most of the F-4s and F-20s had departed by this time. Low on fuel and munitions, they had to head for the Big Banana base to replenish their stores and fill their tanks.

This meant the Football City Rangers would be without dedicated air support for 25 long minutes. Some of Fitz's F-105s were able to cover Shane for five minutes, but they too soon had to depart. Minutes later two Canadian CA-10s were diverted from an attack along the Canal to suppress a particularly large mobile gun plastering the Rangers' positions from the south. They disabled the big gun, but one of the Thunderbolts was hit in the process, forcing its pilot to crash land at the airport, and join the already encircled Football City Special Forces troops.

"Where the hell are those troop transports!" JT yelled out in frustration as he and Ben continued to circle the battle area. "Those guys down there are getting screwed!"

Not only did Shane's men need relief, the whole purpose of flying the UA troops into the Panama City airport was to have them break out and move as quickly as possible to capture the main Pacific side Canal locks.

But the way things were going, there wouldn't be much of an airport left by the time the transports arrived.

And things were quickly going from bad to worse.

Suddenly a half dozen Nazi F-4s showed up and started strafing the Rangers who were huddled in positions around the airport's terminal.

Suddenly Hunter's radio came alive. "Anyone up there?" he heard Shane's voice ask.

"Hang on, Shane," Hunter called back, quickly checking his radar scope and seeing that some of the F-20s were returning. "Your friends are just seven minutes away."

"We ain't got seven minutes, Hawk!" came the reply. "These F-4s are killing us. They must be being directed from somewhere."

Hunter knew that was something he *could* help with. He switched on his APG-56 radar and set it to ID Threat mode. This device would immediately identify any large source of radar emissions in the area.

"I'm getting a very hot reading right at the southern edge of the base," Hunter called back to Shane. "Could be their early warning radar hut doubling as a target spotter."

There was a long burst of crackle and static, then Shane came back on the line.

"There is a snowball hut way over there, Hawk," the man screamed over the noise of the continuous mortar and shell blasts. "But we ain't got anything long enough to grease it."

Hunter's first temptation was to quickly dive down to the deck and take out the radar station. But, just like Ben and JT's action minutes before, doing so would border on disobeying a direct order.

Anyway, that's what the SRAM was for . . .

Shane saw it coming.

It looked like a runaway car on a roller coaster, heading straight down until it was about 20 feet from the ground. Then it suddenly pulled and rocketed right over their heads.

"Jesus!" Shane himself yelled out as the missile went by at near supersonic speed.

With uncanny accuracy the SRAM did a slight left turn and smashed right into the white dome roof of the radar tracking building. A geyser of smoke and flame suddenly erupted from the building, followed by two secondary explosions.

Their electronic eyes and ears thus smashed, the Twisted Cross F-4s departed the area a few minutes later.

Hunter and the two Strikefighters had just completed their 45th circuit 30,000 feet above Panama City when his ears started buzzing.

It was the deactivator's warning sound, piped right into his helmet's intercom system. He punched a sequence of numbers into his flight control computer, seeking to get a confirmation on the message he was receiving from the pod. A few moments later everything came back "green" from his computer. That was all he needed. Somewhere deep in the Cross's bomb-proof basement HQ, someone flipped the MASS switch and started activating the underwater nukes. In doing so, that someone was sentencing the Canal and a large chunk of the entire Panamanian isthmus to death by atomic obliteration.

It was up to Hunter to make sure the sentence wasn't carried out.

"Go Hawk!" JT called over to him as he heard Hunter recite the pre-arranged numerical codes over his radio. For everyone in the know from Wa and JT, to Jones returning from the B-52 raid, the sequence 7-43-61-11-72 meant that Hunter was about to start his mission.

"Good luck, Hawk," Ben wished him. "Last one back buys the beer . . ."

Chapter 72

Major Frost was the first one to see him.

The Free Canadian pilot was behind the controls of a CA-10 Thunderbolt and leading an attack on a combined SAM-radar station just six miles in from Panama City. His two wingmen, also flying CA-10s and using Maverick missiles directed by PAVE PENNY laser seeker pods, had just delivered two direct hits on the enemy radar station when Frost's short-range radar system started beeping.

"Jesus, here he comes!" Frost cried out to his partners, recognizing the F-16XL's unmistakable radar signature.

Immediately, Frost pulled out of his planned strafing run and put the CA-10 into power climb, his two wingmen perfectly mimicking the maneuver.

"Still got a hot SAM down there, sir," one of his guys reported.

"I know," Frost answered. "But it's more important that we clear the area for Hawk."

All three of the squat, powerful attack jets leveled off at 5000 feet and turned west.

"There he is!" one of the wingmen called out.

Sure enough, Frost could see the distinctive red-white-and-blue Cranked Arrow design going full throttle around a bend in the waterway.

"God, he must be doing Mach and a half!" one of the

CA-10 pilots cried out. "I thought that was impossible at that altitude!"

"It is . . ." Frost told him. "But he's doing it anyway."

All three pilots watched in amazement at the F-16XL streaked underneath them doing at least 1000 mph, just barely above the surface of the water, all the while being shot at by enemy small arms fire from both sides of the waterway. The Free Canadians knew that at that speed and altitude, if a single bullet hit the airplane anywhere crucial, the F-16XL would hit the water and disintegrate in less than 1/100th of a second.

Frost punched into Hunter's radio frequency just as the pilot was counting down to his first underwater "target."

"I'm at ten . . ." he heard Hunter say, knowing that Jones, Ben, JT and many others were listening in. "Nine . . . eight . . . I'm starting frequency sequencer . . . six . . . five . . . main pod power on . . . three . . . two . . . one . . . *Zap!*"

Frost could hear a buzzer going off in Hunter's cockpit. Then he heard the F-16 pilot yell: "Got 'em! One down, fifty-two to go!"

Then he was gone — in a flash, twisting away from them and around another bend in the Canal.

"*In*credible . . ." was all Frost could say.

The next UA forces to see Hunter was a small Texan demolition team charged with blowing up a railroad bridge ten miles into the Canal. The span, which crossed the Canal at several locations, was the Canal Nazis main line of communications with the Atlantic side reaches of the waterway, and thus was covered with SAM sites. Already several Twisted Cross troop trains had been spotted crossing the bridge and heading for the Atlantic side. A United American air strike, carried out by two A-4 Skyhawks, was successful in disabling one locomotive. But intense ground fire made it impossible for the A-4s to take down the bridge itself.

So the Texans had been dropped in by helicopter twenty minutes before. Working quickly but under intense enemy fire, the sappers attached no less than 500 pounds of explosives to the main support beams of the RR bridge. Already two of their three helicopters that were covering them had been shot down by shoulder-launched SAMs, and a tight ring of Nazi troops was slowly closing in on the 20-man demo squad.

That's when their team leader heard a screeching sound coming from the west. His men even stopped working for a moment to look in that direction, fearing the worst. Instead, they saw the one and only F-16XL, traveling at close to 1200 mph no more than 25 feet above the water.

"It's Hunter!" the team leader yelled.

No sooner were the words out of his mouth when the delta-shaped high-tech fighter streaked by and *under* the span his troops were preparing to blow up. The jet left such a whirlwind in its path, it nearly knocked two of the sappers off the under pilings of the bridge.

As it would happen, the main concentration of fire being directed against the Texans was coming from three recoilless rifle sites located at a point a half mile down the waterway from the bridge. Somehow—and the Texans never really found out *just* how—Hunter knew this. As soon as he darted under the bridge, his airplane's nose exploded in a cough of fire and smoke. A quick but lethal burst of the F-16XL's six simultaneous-firing cannons completely destroyed the enemy's recoilless rifle nest in three seconds.

Then, as quick as that, the famous airplane was gone, and so was much of the enemy fire.

The Texans successfully blew the bridge five minutes later.

As Major Dantini of the Central American Tactical Service would later tell it, he was up to his neck in smelly water when he first heard the F-16XL coming.

He had just returned that morning from his trip to Washington to meet General Jones. It was during this meeting that Jones had revealed the whole "sneak attack" scenario for Dantini, the only such briefing given to an officer outside of the United American Army Command Staff.

At the time Jones had told him that Dantini and the CATS deserved an explanation of the United Americans' motives, especially in light of the fact that Washington had been using Radio CATS to broadcast its bogus news stories. It had taken awhile, but Dantini finally came around to an understanding of Jones's reasoning for the deception. From that point on he worked with the UA planners, detailing for them everything he knew about the Canal and the Nazi's defenses around it.

His only request had been that, seeing as the CATS would play a very major role during the first hours of the attack, he be allowed to be back with his unit before the fighting broke out. He was, courtesy of a balls-out chopper ride from Texas to a refueling/spyship off Mexico on to his island base off Panama.

He went in with the second wave of his choppers. Their assignment was to blow up a pump station 14 miles from Panama City. The target was high priority because it was one of several pumphouses that regulated the height of the water flow in the Canal. Should the Nazis get really desperate they could, with the turn of a few wheels, let millions of gallons of water flood into the Canal, thereby swamping and probably destroying a good part of both main lock systems.

The particular station Dantini and two of his Chinooks

368

were gunning for was built underground, deep in the woods, about a quarter mile from the bank of the waterway. Its location underground had been strictly an engineering decision by the original builders of the Canal. However, it made the critical target just about impervious to air attack.

So the CATS had taken on the job. Landing two Chinooks about a half mile downstream, Dantini and 15 of his men slogged through a drainage stream that ran parallel to the main waterway, hauling five big rocket-propelled grenade launchers. All they had to do was destroy the small gas turbine that was located on the exposed roof of the pumphouse, and thereby deprive it of the electricity it needed to operate.

It was a job that was a little out of their league—they being primarily chopper troops, but Dantini was sure his guys could handle it.

However, four Nazi fast attack boats showed up to prove them wrong.

No sooner had he and his men dropped into the smelly armpit-high drainage ditch when the Nazi boats appeared. Using .50 caliber machine guns, as well as small rocket launchers, the Nazi sailors were plastering Dantini's tiny strike force and succeeded in pinning it down just about 500 feet from its objective. Already five of his guys were severely wounded, the rancid water of the drainage stream making their critical wounds worse.

So it was under these circumstances, just as the Nazis were about to move in for the *coup de grace* on Dantini and his men, that he heard the strange screech of the approaching jet aircraft.

It was ear-splitting from ground level—a banshee-cry that was heard way before its source was seen. But when Dantini *did* first see it—despite the circumstances, he couldn't help but stare in awe at the airplane.

"So *that's* what it looks like," he thought as he spotted

369

the red-white-and-blue fighter coming toward him at close to Mach 2 barely 20 feet off the surface of the Canal.

Dantini knew that Hunter was concentrating on deactivating the mines — in fact he knew that Washbucket #18 was just a tenth of a mile down from his present, precarious position.

So it was with complete surprise when he saw the F-16XL's nose light up as it was still a mile from him. Suddenly the Canal water started erupting as if it were being hit by a giant rain of fiery boulders. In an instant there was a lot of confusion out on the Canal. Fire and water mixed and filled the air with a strange-colored smoky vapor. Pieces of metal and wood and bodies were flying everywhere. The F-16XL streaked through this maelstrom in a *nano*-second, so fast it was almost too quick to be seen by the human eye.

When the smoke cleared, all four enemy boats were simply gone.

Twenty minutes later, so was the pump station.

All along the Canal, United American troops and pilots reported seeing the F-16XL, dodging groundfire, AA guns, SAMs while blasting enemy gun positions, bridges, boat facilities, fuel barges, while at the same time deactivating the underwater nuclear mines.

That Hunter's Mach 2 run of the Canal only took barely two and a half minutes at the most was lost in all the tales that came from it. People swore they saw the F-16XL not only blasting sites down along the banks of the waterway, but also dogfighting enemy F-4s two or three miles up, blasting SAM sites as far as ten miles from the Canal Zone, blasting a column of enemy tanks that had tried to *retreat* into Big Banana which was nearly 100 miles from the action. Of these things folklore and leg-

370

ends are made.

The wildest story to come out of that incredible day of fighting was to be told over and over by 7th Cavalry commander Major "Catfish" Johnson.

And he, above all others, would swear his story was true.

Chapter 73

The 7th Cavalry, having parachuted in two waves near the Atlantic side Canal locks, had been fighting a two-pronged battle against a numerically superior force of Canal Nazis for nearly five hours. Aided by the CATS gunships and the Free Canadian CA-10 Thunderbolts, advance elements of the 7 Cav finally reached the first set of locks only to find that Nazi reenforcements had made it there before them.

Now, with his entire unit pinned down just 100 feet from their objective, Catfish was considering calling in the CATS troop copters to pull the Cav out. It wasn't that he was afraid for himself or his men. Like the original 7th Cavalry, he knew every one of them would fight to the last if necessary, especially against an enemy so repugnant as the Canal Nazis.

The reason he was considering the evacuation option was that they were fighting the area where Catfish knew the very last of the underwater nukes was located. He also knew that distance in war leads to desperation. And because they were battling the Nazis at the end of their communication line, so to speak, he knew that if anyone was going to get desperate, it would be the Cross officers charged with defending the locks. Taking the premise to its next logical conclusion, he knew if any of the nuclear bombs were to be detonated possibly by hand, it would be here, the furthest Nazi outpost from The Twisted Cross's HQ in Panama City.

So when planning for the mission, Catfish and Jones had agreed that, should things get very rough, the 7 Cav was to pull back.

And things had just gotten very rough.

The Nazis had brought up nine T-72 tanks and a dozen "Stalin Organ" multiple rocket launchers and with them were bombarding the 7th Cavalry, most of whom were pinned down along a highway which led to the locks.

One CA-10 was already down, crashed into the waterway, taking out a control station as it went in. Two of the CATS Chinooks were also hit and crashed landed. What was worse, scouts reported that several Nazi attack craft had moved up to the locks and that heavily-suited divers were preparing to go into the water. Catfish knew the only reason the Nazis would be going into the water was to do something nasty with the nuclear mines.

In the midst of all this, the F-16 appeared.

Looking down on the waterway from a slight rise, Catfish saw the jet fighter blazing down the Canal at 1200 mph. He watched as it neatly dodged two SAMs, all the while never diverting from its course, altitude or speed for more than a second.

But then, about a half mile from his position, the fighter ran into an incredible barrage of AA fire — a storm of AA shells that not even the Wingman could escape.

"Jesus, he's hit!" Catfish cried out, watching the action through his electronically-powered binoculars. A burst of smoke and flame had erupted under the fighter's left wing, probably from a 50-mm AA round. He instantly felt the pit of his stomach drop as he watched the F-16 pull up, smoke pouring from its underbelly.

Up it went — straight up, trailing flames and black vapor. Up until it was completely out of sight.

Catfish quickly checked his map and saw that the F-16 had been hit a quarter mile from the location of the very last underwater mine.

"*Damn!*" he cried out. "The crazy son of a bitch was able to get fifty-two of the bastards . . ."

Now through his own scope, Catfish could see the Nazi divers entering the water right over the last remaining active mine's location. He considered calling up his sharpshooters, but at the same time knew they would be too far away for a shot.

At that moment, the Nazis opened up with several larger guns they had brought up to complement their tanks. At the same moment, two Twisted Cross Phantoms arrived overhead and immediately peeled off and dropped napalm at the end of his column.

That was it. Catfish had seen enough. It killed him inside to do it, but he yelled back to his second-in-command to start getting the troops ready for a pullback and evacuation by air.

That's when he heard the strangest noise that had ever passed his eardrums.

At first it almost sounded like violins, oddly enough. Like an orchestra pit full of violins, all playing something different. Then the noise quickly changed pitch to something more electronic—almost like a blast of synthesized sound. And even quicker again, the noise took on another octave and it passed from a high piercing, oddly sweet sound to a full-throated roar . . .

And it was coming from straight overhead.

Catfish looked up. His men looked up. Even the Nazis on the Canal locks looked up.

Out from the sun it came. Fire. Smoke. Noise. Power. It was the F-16XL.

"Christ, is it crashing?" the 7 Cav second-in-command cried out. "How can he make that airplane do that?"

Catfish had no idea. He couldn't have put it into words if he wanted to.

The F-16 was coming straight down—and not nose first. It was level—like a Harrier—but dropping like a rocket. It was still smoking heavily and one wing was completely engulfed in flames. Yet it kept on coming. Right down nearly on top of the boat the Nazi divers were using. And then, almost impossibly, the F-16XL appeared to go into a hover.

Catfish was not an aerodynamics expert, but he knew what he was seeing appeared to defy the laws of gravity and flight. Only later would he learn that the maneuver was actually a combination of something called a "vertical translation" and "pitched-axis pointing"—seemingly impossible actions for any airplane other than Hunter's Control-Configured/Supersonic Cruise and Maneuvering prototype-adapted Cranked Arrow.

All the while, just about every gun in the Nazis arsenal had turned away from the 7th Cavalry and was now shooting at the F-16.

"He's bombarding the Goddamn thing!" Catfish yelled out, as the F-16XL just seemed to hang in mid-air for the longest time. The 7th Cavalry officer knew that the deactivator pod must have been burning red—not from the flames on the F-16's other wing but because Hunter was cranking the power up so high, intent—to the death, if necessary—on defusing the last nuke.

In the middle of all this, one of the Nazi F-4s pulled up and peeled off toward the strangely-configured F-16. It turned out to be a big mistake. No sooner had the enemy airplane turned in its direction did a Sidewinder flash out from *under* the flames of the F-16's wing and run a course straight and true right into the F-4's midsection. There was the usual huge explosion, and nothing left by a cloud of burning metal fibers.

A split-second later, the F-16 pulled up and roared away at an incredible rate of speed, still smoking heavily, its rear section almost entirely engulfed in flames.

Catfish had to shake his head to believe what he

thought he just witnessed. It had seemed like the fighter had just been able to freeze time itself. Yet, in reality, it had hung — or actually did a tight circle — over the crucial spot in the Canal for no more than one and a half seconds. But it had been long enough, he would learn later, to scramble the radio signals of the last nuke and thereby disarm it.

"Unbelievable . . ." he whispered.

Chapter 74

They found Hunter six miles away.

The pilot of a CATS Chinook, on his way to providing fire support for the 7th Cavalry, radioed back to his base that the F-16 was down, crashed in a swamp about a mile in from the shore of Gatun Lake.

A MedicVac chopper was quickly dispatched from a United American troopship just approaching the Atlantic end of the Canal. Upon landing in the swamp, the medics first reported that the pilot looked unconscious — or worse. But after slopping through the waist-deep water they found Hunter was simply sound asleep.

He refused to be evacuated. Instead he insisted on being dropped off at the CATS island base. From there he spent the rest of the daylight hours serving as a waist gunner on one of the Chinooks. He was there when troops waiting on the ships offshore finally landed and reenforced the 7th Cavalry. Two hours later, the United American flag was flying over the captured locks.

He was there when the C-141 transports finally came in for bumpy but successful landings at Panama City Airport, relieving Shane's brave troops and spearheading the breakout toward the Pacific side locks. His Chinook was instrumental in the successful battle for the locks that followed.

He climbed into an F-20 around dusk and joined Fitzgerald's Wild Weasel F-105X Super Thunderchiefs in another SAM suppressing mission over Panama City.

This action in turn cleared the way for a second massive B-52 strike on the center of the city which all but eliminated the last Nazi stronghold on the Pacific side of the Canal.

Midnight found him driving a Huey MedicVac chopper back and forth from the Panama City airport to the rented Big Banana air base. At 3 AM the next day, he was in the seat of a CA-10 Thunderbolt, flying alongside Major Frost on a nighttime mop up sweep of the Canal.

At dawn he was back in the swamp with his beloved airplane, supervising as one of the CATS mighty Sky Cranes lifted the damaged fighter out of the muck and onto one of the container ships offshore.

At noon, he was washed and dressed in a new flight suit and standing beside Jones during a brief ceremony at the Panama City Airport, during which Jones accepted the unconditional surrender of The Twisted Cross from a lowly officer in the Nazis' logistics section. As it turned out, he was the highest ranking officer left in the immediate area.

Everyone else, including the High Commander, had fled Panama City for parts unknown soon after the first bombs started falling on the capital city.

Epilogue

Hunter had just applied another coat of sun tan lotion to his face when he looked up and saw a young girl standing over him, handing him a package.

He stretched, flipped up his sunglasses and took the package from the kid.

"What's that?" Janine asked. She was lying on the beach beside him, soaking up the bright rays.

"I'm not sure," he said, wishing he had some money to tip the delivery girl.

"Go see Brother David," he said to the girl. "Tell him Hunter said to give you a gold piece."

The girl's eyes went wide with joy as she ran off the beach and back toward the huge pyramid-shaped Cancun resort hotel-turned-mission.

Lori, sunbathing topless on his other side, turned over and handed him a cold beer. Nearby, JT, Ben Wa and Fitz were playing poker with three of the other women "entertainers" who had taken sanctuary with the Fighting Brothers. Still further on, the commodore, Dantini, Burke and the entire four-man complement of the Cobra Brothers were setting up a large steel-grates-over-barrels barbecue stove in preparation for the shrimp and fish fry that was scheduled for noon.

Hunter popped his beer can—courtesy of Masoni and O'Gregg—and opened the package.

It was from Jones, a summary report of the war against The Twisted Cross which came to its successful conclusion exactly two weeks before that day.

He quickly glanced over the casualty reports. All things considered, they weren't too high—a total of 741 men killed, 3083 wounded. Estimates of Nazi dead were put at 6200, with twice as many wounded. A total of 23 UA aircraft were lost, including two F-20s and one C-141. Sixteen helicopters had been shot down or damaged beyond repair.

On the other hand, only seven Nazi F-4s had *survived* the battle. They had been dispatched to Texas where they would be broken down and used for parts.

The next page of the summary told the strange tale of what had happened at Uxmaluna.

The Nazis' gold recovery mission had proceeded for two days after the murder of Udet and the flight of Krupp. Not wanting to start a major action against the Nazis while they were still near the ancient site, Jones had decided to keep an aircap on the area to prevent anyone from escaping by chopper. Elements of the Football City Rangers dropped in and surrounded the site, ready to attack the Nazis as soon as they decided to make a break for it via the blasted-away jungle road.

But after two days on the ground, scouts for the Rangers reported that activity at the site had stopped—completely. Not only that, but it appeared that the site was completely deserted.

The Ranger officers in charge sent in two more advance parties who confirmed the report. The place was empty.

The Rangers moved in in force and their final report gave everyone who read it an advanced case of the creeps. All of the gold was still in the caves or in the tunnels. All of the Nazis' trucks were there, as were a few helicopters. There was even food on the tables of the mess areas, some of it still hot in the bowl.

But there weren't any Nazis, anywhere. A week of confounding land and air recon missions confirmed it. Just like the Mayans before them, all 280 Nazis of the Recovery Mission had simply disappeared.

* * *

Hunter fought off a shiver and took a long swig of his beer.

The rest of the report detailed the long range planning for occupation of the Canal. Major Dantini and his guys didn't know it yet, but they were about to be offered the job of administering protection over the waterway, using United American funds to hire local, trustworthy mercenaries. A large UA air base would also be established at Panama City, and UA naval units would regularly patrol both entrances to the Canal from now on.

As for the gold recovered by the Nazis from the other Maya sites, Jones and Brother David had held a meeting at Cancun a week before to discuss returning the bullion to the native tribes living near the sites, and basically letting them decide what to do with it. This meant that the enormous gold find at Uxmaluna — still a fairly well-kept secret — would now come under the control of the *Tulum* Indians.

The gold down under the Nazca Plain, now buried under tons of rubble, would stay right where it was for the time being.

The report finished up with a request from Jones that Hunter meet him in Dallas in two weeks time. Once there they would be able to pore over the large amount of Nazi documents captured when UA forces broke into the Twisted Cross HQ skyscraper. Dallas was selected as the meeting location because that's where Hunter's F-16XL was undergoing extensive damage repairs, the second time it had been in the GD shop in less than a year.

Hunter finished his beer and quickly opened another one. Also inside the package was a letter from Major Frost, postmarked Montreal. Hunter's fingers were trembling slightly as he ripped open the envelope and read the short note. It simply said that Frost had determined that Dominique was now part of an organization called Inner Light, a group which specialized in meditation, "openness" and "channeling." Frost promised to get an ex-

381

act location of their retreat in the Canadian Rockies and send it to Hunter as soon as possible.

He also reported that Hunter's letter to Dominique which he left in the care of mutual friends in Montreal had been hand-carried out to the Inner Light retreat. So for better or worse, Hunter had to assume she had received it.

He was making a mental note to buy Frost a case of Scotch when he noticed the package contained a third envelope, this one unmarked other than his name written across it.

He opened it and to his surprise, he found it contained a photograph of Elizabeth, with a note attached by tape. The note, which covered up all but her pretty face in the photo, simply said: "Surprise me as soon as you can. Love, Elizabeth."

He was anxious to look at the rest of the picture, but it took him a full minute to peel off the tape holding the note on. But when he did, he felt his jaw drop to his chin.

The photo showed her lying across a huge bed, absolutely naked . . .

As luck would have it, JT was walking by from getting a beer and caught a glimpse of the photo.

"All right, Hawker, my man!" he said after letting out a long wolf whistle. "Looks like your trip in that flying bucket of bolts wasn't a waste of time after all."

Hunter looked at the photo and then laid back down on the sand and covered his eyes.

"I'm not so sure," he said.

THE END